Illegal
Residents

By: Jose M. Ramirez Jr.

To my wife and two children who are my inspirations.
Thank you for pushing me to continue and convincing me not to give
up. This was only possible because of you.

~Chapter One~

Dorothy Cryan

"Hide!" says Mrs. Cryan, forcing Brianna to shuffle around, desperately trying to find somewhere she can hide with her three-month-old baby and hope he doesn't make a sound. "They're coming!" she urges her. "Hurry!"

Mrs. Cryan's a Caucasian lady who's never agreed with the government and helps anyone that needs assistance. She really believes in her heart, that everyone deserves a chance to live in the world God's created for us all. She rushes over and opens the door to a small room hidden under the steps, leading to the second floor of her house. "Hide in here!" she tells Brianna, as she puts a hand on her back to give her a shove and hurry the process. She closes the door and slides a wooden table to cover the entrance of the hidden space. Mrs. Cryan pauses for a second, she focuses on how fast her heart's beating, and raises her hands to see how bad they're shaking. She flinches when she hears a very loud bang on the door.

"Open up!" she hears. "Open up now, before we kick your door in!" She rushes toward it terribly nervous. No matter how many times she's put her life on the line to help people she doesn't have to help, she could never get used to it. "Open up!" she hears again.

"I'm coming!" she shouts, as she walks as quickly as possible toward the door. Mrs. Cryan's a widow who lost her husband ten years ago. She's a sixty-two-year-old woman with long, gray hair, who battles arthritis so she isn't very fast. She opens the door and is baffled at how quickly three of the four agents rush in, nearly knocking her down.

"What are you doing?" she asks. "You can't barge into my house."

"Why can't we come in?" asks the agent with the dark glasses and inane smile that stood outside. "It's not like we need a search warrant," he says as he steps in.

Mrs. Cryan's shocked when she notices half the neighborhood residents standing outside, nosily gawking at her house.

"Kill her also!" one shouts.

"Yeah! I heard a baby in there!" shouts another.

Mrs. Cryan closes the door and leaves the palm of her hand resting on it with her head bowed, and deeply inhales. She turns around and flinches, the agent is standing not one foot away. Mrs. Cryan takes a step back and is pinned with her back against the door. "What do you want?" she asks.

"Hi. I'm Agent Rodney Phillips and I work with the F.F.A.. All I want from you, Dorothy, is for you to be honest with me, OK? That is your name, right? Dorothy Cryan?"

She nervously nods her head in agreement and looks up toward the stairs as if she could see through walls. "Are they breaking my stuff? What are they looking for?" she asks, as the sound seems a bit violent and she's afraid it might startle the baby, causing him to cry and putting them all at risk.

Agent Phillips is a tall, slim, clean cut man who's hair is jet-black and very slick. He dresses in fine suits and never wears the same tie twice. The creases on his pants are razor sharp, and his shoes are very shiny. His skin is extremely pallid, he looks bloodless. "Where is it!?" he demands to know.

"Where's what? What are you talking about?" she replies, while still looking up.

"Why are you so nervous? Huh?"

"I am not nervous. I just don't see the need to toss my stuff around, looking for something that isn't here. What are you looking for anyway?"

"You see, Dorothy," he says. "I've been doing this for quite some time, and have learned a thing or two over the years. Like noticing when someone's nervous and hiding something. You know what I've also learned, Dorothy?" he sarcastically asks. "I've also learned to get answers to questions without the one being asked telling me. The body language speaks a thousand words. For example, you keep looking up those stairs, which only suggests that what we're looking for is up there," he says, while pointing a thumb to the staircase behind him.

Dorothy can't believe it, the plan to keep looking worked. She figured he would think they're upstairs if she kept looking up. She's hoping she'll get a chance to sneak them out the back without neighbors noticing.

Agent Phillips takes his shades off and looks at her with a smile. "This is the part where I go upstairs to find what I'm looking for, Ms. Cryan," he says with a wicked smirk.

"OK," she replies. "It's Mrs. by the way!" Dorothy doesn't like to be referred to as *'Ms.,'* she feels it's a form of disrespect.

Agent Phillips immediately turned to go up the stairs right after telling her he would, but quickly turns back after she makes that comment. He gets very close to her, so close she could feel his breath. He pins her against the door and stares into her eyes. "It's Ms.," he says. "Your husband's dead, and who knows, maybe a handsome fella like me will want to take you on one day, so stop calling yourself Mrs., it makes you sound old."

He provocatively moves a strand of hair that hangs over her face to the back of an ear with one finger.

Dorothy's terrified, and regrets making the comment.

He looks at her and slowly walks backward. "I'll be going upstairs now," he tells her, then bites his bottom lip. He turns and begins to go up, and while climbing, reaches into his back pocket and pulls out a pair of medical gloves.

Dorothy's very anxious, her heart is racing and her hands are sweating. She cannot wait until he makes it to the top and knows she has to swiftly react. He gets to the last step, when the other agents start rushing down.

"There's nothing up there!" says Agent Brown, obviously very angry. He rushes toward Dorothy and slams both hands against the door, with each hand to one side of her face. He bangs so hard, the vibration makes her head jolt a bit.

Dorothy's terrified. She flinches violently and thinks he'll kill her. "What do you want!?" she asks as she sobs. Dorothy's helped many people in the past, but cannot remember a time she's been more petrified.

"Where is it!?" he shouts, while banging his hands against the door again.

Agent Phillips is right behind him now, so grabs him by the arm.

"Let me go!" shouts Brown, while shoving it away. Agent Brown grunts as he moves away from Dorothy, the look Phillips gives him gave him no choice. Brown's a thirty-eight-year-old agent who's envious of Agent Phillips. He doesn't appreciate the fact he's four years his senior and been on the job longer, yet has to answer to him. He's a very tall, heavyset, ginger man who wears a long, beige trench jacket over his suit. His hair is a distinguishable red and freckles cover his entire body. He goes berserk, grabs the table Dorothy used to shield the opening to the room Brianna's in, and slams it down, causing it to shatter into pieces as it hits the floor. Agent Phillips rushes toward him, grabs him by the shirt, and slams him into the wall.

Dorothy's ready to give in, she's sure they'll discover them inside. *"No way the baby will sleep through this,"* she thinks to herself.

"You will control yourself!" shouts Phillips, with his hands clamped to Agent Brown's shirt. "Do you understand me!? Are you out of your God damned mind!?"

Agent Brown calms down, he knows he must follow orders. He feels Agent Phillips's saliva spraying his face as he yells. The two other agents look at each other and don't know how to respond, until Agent Mitchell suggest they move to the job they were on their way to when they were stopped.

"OK, fellas. Let's go," says Agent Phillips. "We'll take this one as a loss, even though I know there was someone upstairs."

Brianna's terrified, through the whole ordeal she's been trying her best to keep the baby quiet. Luckily, she has the baby with his head on a pillow and wrapped with the sides up to keep his ears covered. She's surprised he's still asleep, then notices he begins to wake up. She realizes she left his bottle in the refrigerator when she rushed to hide, so prepares her breasts.

Brianna hears the front door to the house open and is relieved to hear they're leaving, when the baby Suddenly starts to mewl. She quickly muffles his mouth and presses down, but it's too late, Agent Brown heard the low whimper.

"Did you hear that!?"

Agent Phillips turns and reminds him he's told him to calm down. It seems only Agent Brown heard the cry.

"I'm telling you!" he enthusiastically says. "There's a baby in here!" He demands Dorothy to show him the way to the basement.

"There's no basement," she replies. "My house is on stilts."

"Didn't you notice that when we entered, Brown?" asks Agent Phillips, getting a chuckle from Agent Moore. "Better yet, don't you think I would've asked to search it by now?" Agent Phillips is annoyed and demands him to go wait in the car.

"How about the backyard, boss. Tell her to show us the backyard!"

"I'll check the backyard!" Phillips responds. He commands Agent Moore to escort Agent Brown to the car, and demands they wait there. "Whoever was here was upstairs and somehow escaped," he says while looking at Dorothy.

"That's why you should let me kill her!" says Agent Brown.

Dorothy's shocked.

"We are not killing her, but I promise you, if I find it in the backyard I will personally get you from the car so you could put a couple of bullets in her head."

Satisfied, Agent Brown exits the house. As he does, he looks at Dorothy and mumbles, "I'll be back, bitch."

As they walk outside, the curious onlookers cheer them on. They are sure they found the baby. "Did you kill it!?" one loudly asks. They continue to cheer even though they're ignored by the agents.

Brianna's still muffling the baby's mouth. She knows it's dangerous and could hurt him, but if she doesn't, and they get discovered, not only will they get murdered but they will also kill Dorothy. Brianna cannot allow that to happen, she's very appreciative of Dorothy and all she's done. She first met Dorothy while out grocery shopping. Dorothy paid when she saw Brianna didn't have enough DD's. She noticed she kept trying to scan the chip implanted in her wrist, but didn't have enough. She offered to pay after noticing she was buying baby formula and diapers along with her groceries. Dorothy couldn't help but notice Brianna was about to pop, as big as her belly was.

"How far along are you, honey?"

"I'm eight months now," she responds.

"Oh, that's wonderful," she says, as she helps pack her bags. "Does anyone know you're pregnant?" she loudly whispers.

Brianna's confused. "Of course."

"I don't mean anyone," she continues. "Does anyone in the government know?"

"Well, I can't afford to get the care I need but my friend is a paternal nurse and keeps tabs on me."

"OK, good," says Dorothy, completely confusing Brianna.

"Where will you have your baby?"

"I'm going to have him at the Community hospital, it's all I can afford."

"Don't. Go here when you're ready," she tells her as she gives her a piece of paper. "Ask for Dr. Gus. You tell him I sent you, my name is Dorothy. It'll be free of charge so don't worry about the cost. I've got to go now," she hurriedly says.

"But wait...!" Brianna tries. But it was too late, Dorothy rushed away.

"You know the consequences if I find something in the back, right, Dorothy?" asks Agent Phillips. "I hope you've learned from what happened to your husband what occurs when you aide an Illegal Resident," he starts explaining. He tells Agent Mitchell to stay behind and keep a lookout.

Brianna hears everything, but misses when Phillips tells Agent Mitchell to stay behind, and thinks they all went to the back. She uses this as an opportunity to release her grip and somehow sneak out. She releases it, but notices the baby's limp. He had stopped crying but it seems he isn't breathing. She screams hysterically, causing Agent Mitchell to hear her cries. He immediately pulls his gun and starts feeling on the wall to find the opening. At this point, Brianna doesn't care, she continues sobbing as Agent Mitchell finds a way to get it open. As he opens it, he sees Brianna kneeling with the baby in her arms. Agent Mitchell points the gun at her face. He sees tears streaming down her cheeks while her eyes fill with tears that have not yet fallen. Brianna stares into the barrel, waiting for him to pull the trigger, but is nonplus-sed when he raises a finger over his mouth instead.

"Shhhh...," he says. "Is he alive?"

"I think he's dead!" she replies, sobbing uncontrollably.

"Shhhh...!"

Agent Mitchell's an average sized man with dark brown, shoulder length hair, who looks much younger than his actual age. It's hard to distinguish his shirt from his tie because he wears all black. He gets down on his knees and puts the gun on the floor by his side. He asks her to pass the baby, but she's a little hesitant. She thinks he just wants to make sure he's dead before he kills her. She knows the order is to kill the baby first, then kill the parents. She passes him with no other choice. Mitchell puts an ear against his little chest, then lays him on the floor and starts pumping on it lightly. After a few pumps, he puts his lips over the baby's mouth to blow air in carefully. After pumping his chest again, they're both relieved to hear him cry. Agent Mitchell looks down at the baby with a sense of satisfaction. "You better shut him up," he tells Brianna, while looking toward the back. "Go upstairs and keep him quiet." She bolts toward the stairs. "Don't forget his milk that's in the fridge!" he says, convincing her that he must have known all along there was a baby in the house.

Out in the back, Agent Phillips is scoping the place out. He keeps looking up at the windows trying to figure out how the person he was convinced was there escaped. "Your husband was a pretty decorated agent in our organization but had to be termed for failing to carry out a term. Can't have a bleeding heart doing this type of work," he tells Dorothy.

"How can you live with yourself!? How can you kill innocent people and be convinced it's justified!?" she angrily snaps back, while ignoring the comment about her husband. She doesn't want him to think she's picked up on it, she knows he's dangerous.

"See, it's simple, Ms. Cryan. It's either my life or theirs. You have to understand why it needs to be done. We as a people, we're running out of food, water, we're running out of our own natural resources. We're the owners of this country and everyone else just don't matter. Hate to be blunt about it but it's sincerely how I feel. They were given the opportunity to leave and decided to stay, so it's on us to get rid of them. It could be easy, all they have to do is register their babies, get the vaccination, and let them live a healthy, normal life. Instead, they risk having guys like me chasing them around, killing them and their entire families. And for what? Just to have the opportunity to call themselves grandparents later on in life. If you ask me, it isn't worth it. If I was given that choice I'd gladly take the vaccine. They should look at the bright side," he arrogantly says. "At least they won't have to pay child support."

"That's bullshit!" Dorothy angrily states. "You deprive them of having kids, having their own families!"

"It is necessary!" he snaps back.

"It is not necessary. You're killing off races that God has created. You will have to stand before him to be judged one day, and you will not be forgiven!"

"He won't judge me!" he rudely interrupts. "He doesn't even exist. Tell me, if your God is real, why does he allow this to happen!?"

Dorothy rolls her eyes in disgust. She figures she'll just be quiet and hopefully he'll leave. She's always thought the organization was responsible for her husband's death, hearing what Phillips just said only confirms her suspicions. She looks at him as he speaks and thinks of a million ways she'd kill him given the slim chance.

"Are you done?" she asks.

While looking around, he nods his head to confirm he is, but looks up to the house before going inside and notices a light that was pre-viously lit, is suddenly off. He rushes in to meet Mitchell. Seems Brianna might have turned it off.

"What's up, boss?" says Mitchell, reacting to how Phillips runs in.

Dorothy's oblivious. She doesn't think Brianna's moved from the spot with the agent guarding it.

"There's someone upstairs. I'm sure there was a light on, now it's off!"

"No, boss, that was me. I turned it off just two minutes ago. I had to take a leak."

Confused, Dorothy wonders why he wouldn't use the bathroom that's less than ten feet away from him. She secretly hopes Brianna used this as an opportunity to escape.

"Whew... I almost had the pleasure of killing me an Illegal Resident," he says, purposely making the comment to get under Dorothy's skin.

Dorothy walks them to the front door and is greeted by the curious crowd when she opens it. A burst of cheers erupts as the agents walk out. A reporter rushes over with her cameraman, hoping to get updates and see if a term has been executed. The public is supposed to report Escaped Illegal Residents, but there are some like Mrs. Dorothy Cryan, who would risk their lives for the sake of the human race.

As Agent Phillips starts talking to the reporter with the bright lights shining on his face, Dorothy closes the door and breaks down. The tears are from all kinds of emotions. She's relieved that they're gone, but worried about Brianna. She rushes to the hiding spot but to her surprise, she isn't there. She doesn't think she's in the house, and figures she must have escaped when Mitchell went upstairs. She worries and hopes she isn't caught with an infant out of danger he might be scanned. She doesn't know if it's safe yet. Dorothy fears for her life. She might have to pack up and leave town with the angry mob outside that will most likely retaliate against her.

"Why...?" she hears a voice say.

Startled, she looks to the top of the stairs and sees Brianna standing there, quietly crying. "Why did you have me go to Dr. Gus? I had accepted our fate and knew I would never be a grandma. I thought he would vaccinate him. I should have known when you asked if anyone in the government knew of my pregnancy. I didn't think...!'"

"There's a reason I did it," Dorothy softly says as she looks toward the floor.

"No. The only thing you've done is kill my son!" she interrupts, as she walks down. "He'll be hunted like an animal for the rest of his life. You've killed every single person that'll be around him when his day comes!"

"I did it for the same reason I've done it for countless people. I did it so he can live a normal life. Your son should be able to have a wife and family."

"Have a family with who? Another Escaped Illegal Resident? I've accepted our fates, it's time you do the same. I would not have risked my son's life for him to be a father!"

Dorothy cannot disagree more, but figures she'd let her vent. She refuses to tell her he's been vaccinated. "One day, you'll realize why I did what I did. Only then, will you come to the realization that I did it out of the kindness of my heart, and to make the world a better place. The night it all comes together, you'll remember me."

Brianna doesn't know what to make of that statement and watches as Mrs. Cryan walks away. She heads upstairs but is stopped in her tracks by a really loud boom. She runs back down and into the kitchen, and begins to hectically scream.

Dorothy grabbed her Husband's double barrel shotgun and sat on the kitchen chair. She placed the handle on the floor and the barrel under her chin before pulling the trigger. Brianna's never witnessed anything like this before, her whole head is gone. Brain matter drips from the ceiling and she's horrified.

There's a note on the table that reads:

"I hope God forgives me for this, so I can finally be with my Dear Fred."

Brianna's heartbroken and doesn't know what to do. She's trapped in the house and will most likely be targeted if seen. Brianna's a really pretty, twenty-three-year-old black girl who escaped out the back door when agents stormed her house to term her little brother. A term is performed on a child that hasn't been vaccinated. What the vaccination does, is kill any chance of a person being able to reproduce. You have a zero-percent probability of having or making a child after you're injected. The purpose of it is population control. After the great war as many called it, vegetation's been unable to blossom like they once had, the water is highly contaminated and cannot be drank. The government was forced to build a wall around the entire country during the war. They made it crystal clear when they announced that only white Americans will be able to live in the country. They gave everyone else the option to leave, even though they knew there was no way out. Many people protested the vaccine when it was first enforced, but after years of rallying to deaf ears, they eventually gave up. Most *Illegal Residents*, which is what they call all minorities, have faced the fact they'll rather live a normal life instead of being hunted down and dying gruesome deaths.

The F.F.A. agents, (Federally Funded Army), are the ones that track down *Escaped Illegal Residents*, which is what they call Illegal Residents who aren't injected. Their job is to execute them, and they're demanded to make it as gruesome as possible while one of the agents record it. They want to show the country, to provide them with entertainment and convince other Illegal Residents to refrain from avoiding the injection.

They're also commanded to kill everyone around the Escaped Illegal Resident, they do not tolerate anyone who associates with them.

~*Chapter Two*~

The Senao Family

"Someone's at the door!" yells Carlito, the youngest son of Carlos Senao, a descendant from the island of Puerto Rico with a rather large family of six kids and a sister who lives with them.

"Who can it be," he wonders, as he makes his way toward the door. He opens it and is confronted by Agent Phillips and his men.

"Hello, Carlos Senoa."

"Hello, sir," Carlos responds. "It's Senao. How can I help you?" He extends his hand for a shake but Phillips only looks at it.

"Excuse me," he says as he pushes his way inside, while asking him what he had said.

"It's Carlos Senao. You said Senoa," he says, as his words die down at the sight of the four agents walking into his home.

As an intimidation tactic, the agents walk in but don't say a word for five minutes. Instead, they walk around grabbing little figurines Carlos's deceased mother had collected to look at them. There's one of a nice crystal crucifix, which was her favorite, and Agent Phillips spots it. He grabs it, throws it in the air, and catches it. He puts it back onto the shelf in its original spot, takes the pinkie of his right hand and places it behind the figurine. He slowly pushes it toward the edge, until it tumbles down and shatters on the hard wooden floor.

Carlos knows who they are, and knows he can't do anything about it. But not Sofia. Sofia's Carlos's youngest daughter, she's twelve. She's very little for her age and wears a denim jumpsuit with a white t-shirt underneath. Her hair is unkempt with a crooked part in the middle that separates her pigtails, and looks to have not been combed in days. She has big chinky eyes and has always been the spoiled and spunky one. She rushes toward Agent Phillips and pushes him against the stand, causing more figurines to fall and shatter.

"Why did you break it!?" she tries to demand to know.

"Listen here, miss!" he says, as he grabs her by one of her pigtails. "You ever touch me again, I'll make you watch as I kill your entire family!"

"GET OFF OF ME...!" she shouts.

Carlos is livid, but uses every muscle in his body to restrain himself from attacking Phillips. He knows they'll kill them all if he even thinks about it. Carlos is a thirty-eight-year-old man who's worked odd jobs for the better part of his life and lives on a tree-lined block in a run-down neighborhood. His wife Sonia's a self taught nurse, and only attends to Illegal Residents. It's often difficult for her to find work with most not being able to afford the care.

Agent Phillips shoves Sofia so hard she tumbles onto the floor, causing her to injure an elbow. Carlos rushes to her aid and is fuming. Sofia cries and complains of her arm as he tries to comfort her.

"Now we can get down to business!" says Agent Phillips. He adjusts the front of his suit and wags his arms to get comfortable in it. "I need everyone that lives in this house down here, right now!"

"Go get your brothers and sister, Carlito!" demands Carlos.

Carlito runs half way up the stairs with his brother Roberto close behind, and nervously yells for them to come down.

"Where's your wife?"

"My wife's at work."

"I need your wife here, right now."

"She should be home any minute."

Carlos's kids start making their way down. His two oldest sons, which are sixteen and fifteen, stare at the agents as they walk by.

Celine, who is Carlos's eldest daughter and twin to his fifteen-year-old son is the last one to enter.

Phillips takes a seat.

"OK now. Let's get started. Carlos? Why are you still here?"

"What do you mean?"

"Why are you still in my country? Why didn't you get out when given a chance!?"

"There was no way, sir."

"What do you mean there was no way?"

"There were no flights out, it was impossible!"

"Why didn't you walk out then!? Or swim, I know you must know how to swim," he says, then stares at him for around five seconds.

Carlos fumbles his words and decides to just be quiet. He knows these guys are bad news.

"I need everyone to state their names, and age, starting with you," says Phillips, as he points toward Carlos's sixteen-year-old son.

Felipe doesn't answer. He doesn't know they're F.F.A. agents. Had he known, he would've started speaking as soon as he was pointed at.

"Let me try this again. I need everyone to state their names, and age, starting with you!" he says, while again pointing at Felipe. Felipe ignores his father's loud whispers demanding him to answer.

"His name is Felipe!" shouts Carlos. "It's Felipe Senao!"

"Let him answer," says Phillips. "He's a big boy, isn't he?"

Annoyed he can't get Felipe to answer, he gets up and grabs Sophia by the same arm she just injured.

"Ouch!" she screams. "Help me, Daddy!"

Phillips grabs his gun that seems to be twice the size of Sophia's face and puts the tip of the barrel against her right temple.

"My name is Felipe Senao, sir!" yells Felipe. "I'm sixteen!"

Felipe realizes who the gentlemen are now. He thought they were court appointed child service agents that come around every once in a while, trying to extort DD's from his parents in exchange for letting them keep their children. The Senao's are very poor, and many nights they cannot eat. Felipe tries his hardest to provide while going to school. He often gets into fights either for protecting a sibling, or to teach someone that he will not be bullied for his appearance. He's a very strong, wide-shouldered kid who has strength beyond his years.

"See, that wasn't so hard, was it?" Phillips says. "I don't like you!" he tells Sophia as he pushes her away. He then points at Carlito and demands the information.

Without hesitating, Carlito answers. "My name is Carlito, and I'm eight!"

"Good boy. Your brother's got a lot to learn from you," he says, causing Carlito to nervously smile. "And you?" he says, this time pointing at Oscar.

"My name is Oscar," he responds. "I'm fifteen years old."

"Oscar what!?" shouts Phillips, taking a firm grip of the handle to the gun that's now on his lap.

"Oscar Senao," he nervously responds.

"OK, Oscar Senoa," says Phillips, purposely mispronouncing the name again. He turns his attention to Sophia and stares at her for five seconds. "How about you, you little brat!?"

"My name is Sophia Senao. I'm twelve years old," she says, while trying to control her emotional sniffling.

"What a sweet little name for such an evil little child," he says, while staring at her, causing her to shield her face with her little hands. "How about you?" he asks Roberto.

"My name is Roberto Senao. I'm seven years old."

"Do I look like an idiot to you!?"

Roberto has a very flummoxed look on his face.

"Do you not think I'd know your last name is Senoa by now?" again mispronouncing it. "Answer me! Do I look like an idiot to you!?" he asks, this time with a higher tone.

"N... no!" says Roberto, obviously very nervous.

Phillips starts to chuckle, which makes Agents Brown and Moore do the same. They see tiny droplets of sweat developing on Roberto's forehead. He turns his attention to Celine, who's sitting there secretly hoping this is all a dream. She once missed a party she was supposed to attend because Carlos's car broke down. They raided the party and found two Escaped Illegal Residents. Everyone inside was slaughtered, it was a bloodbath, a bunch of kids murdered in cold blood. They hung the bodies of the Escaped Illegal Residents outside of the venue and didn't allow anyone to take them down for six months. By the time they were lowered, there was nothing left but bones.

"My name is Celine. I'm fifteen years old."

Phillips immediately lifts his gun and with one shot, puts a bullet right between the eyes of Oscar.

"Oh my God!" screams Carlos.

The kids start screaming and scrambling around, trying to find cover.

"Oh my Lord!" he screams. He rushes over and cradles his son in his arms sobbing. He tries to cover the hole in the back of his head, but it's so big his hand goes into his skull. "Oh my God! Why did you kill my son!?" he screams at the top of his lungs.

Mitchell comes over to inspect the wound and gives Phillips a look of disbelief.

"You watch your tone with me!" Phillips says to Carlos, as he points the gun at him.

"Why did you kill my son?" he asks again, this time in a much-lowered voice.

"Your son lied to me, Mr. Senoa. He said he's fifteen years old, and Celine here also said she's fifteen, which means one was lying so I spared the cuter one. No-one lies to me and gets away with it!"

Mitchell's bewildered. Phillips knew there were two fifteen year old's in the house, it's clearly on the list.

"They're twins!" he responds, while sobbing uncontrollably. "You killed my son! Oh my God! You killed my son!" he cries.

"Why didn't one of them specify they were twins. They don't look alike!" he arrogantly says.

Everyone's hysterical, they cannot believe what they've just witnessed. Sophia's traumatized, she's huddled on a couch with Carlito and Roberto. Felipe's rocking back and forth on a chair he moved to after his brother was executed. He's covered in the blood that ricocheted off the wall behind the couch they both sat on. Celine's sitting on the opposite couch with her face buried in her hands sobbing.

"Someone's coming, boss!" says Mitchell, who went back to standing guard at the window.

Sonia walks in to an eerie silence. No-one wants to be the first to witness the reaction she's going to have when she sees what's happened. This will destroy her. "What are you guys up to!?" she yells, as she takes her jacket off by the door.

She walks into the living room and the first person she sees is Phillips. She looks toward her husband and collapses onto her knees, frantically screaming and demanding to know what happened.

Agent Brown has his right hand into the opening of his suit, ready to pull out and fire if he has to in an instant. They're all ruthless criminals with the exception of Agent Mitchell. Not to say he wouldn't kill, because he does, and he does so gruesomely, but he would much rather be the agent that records it most times.

Sonia notices the gun on Phillips's lap and can only assume he's the one responsible for killing her child. She doesn't want to go next to his body, which is spawned on her husband's lap as he lays in a state of shock. He hasn't said one word. He hasn't even looked at his wife.

"OK, I'm going to have to scan your three youngest children, and if all goes well, we'll be out of here," says Mitchell, as if nothing had just happened.

Sonia stands, but cannot take the stress and faints, making her body look like it folds up as she goes limp and hits the floor.

Mitchell goes to Sophia and asks for her arm. After scanning it, he determines she's been vaccinated. He repeats the process with Roberto, and Carlito, who also prove to have been vaccinated. "OK, boss, there is no Escaped Illegal Resident here and everyone on the list is account-ed for."

Felipe's busy trying to wake his mother up and Phillips walks by. He looks up at him, but knows he'll be killed in a heartbeat if he tries anything. He gets his mom up but she looked to be hoping it was all a dream, because she gets hysterical again after looking at his body.

As they're getting ready to leave, Carlos comes back to his senses and gently moves his son's body off of him. All the while, he stares at Phillips who stares back with the gun in his hand.

"We got a tip that you were harboring an Escaped Illegal Resident here," he tells Carlos. "Looks like one of your neighbors don't like you too much," he says with a smirk.

Carlos hasn't said a word and only stares at him. Phillips raises his pistol and points it right at his face. Carlos doesn't react at all, he just sits there, his eyes piercing right through Phillips.

"OK, let's get moving, gentlemen," he tells the other agents as he lowers the gun. "Consider this your lucky day, buddy. In spite of what just happened here," Phillips says, as he looks at Oscar's body. "You're extremely lucky."

Moore stops Phillips as they're walking out. "Don't you think we should check the rest of the house just in case?"

Phillips looks at Moore and tells him he didn't get an inkling, no sign at all there's anyone else in the house. "Besides," he tells him. "Everyone on the list is accounted for." Phillips believes he's trained himself so well he can feel the presence of people around him. He's almost certain there's no-one else in the house but decides to listen to Moore, just to prove to himself that his skill is as accurate as he believes. As soon as Carlos finds out they're considering checking the rest of the house, he becomes talkative.

"You guys enjoy the rest of your night!" he says, drawing suspicion from Phillips.

As soon as he says it, Phillips runs back inside and grabs Sonia around her neck. While grabbing her in a choke hold, he presses his gun so hard into her temple, Carlos could see it indenting into her skin.

Brown draws his pistol while Mitchell and Moore run up the stairs to check the other rooms. With his hands up, Carlos pleads for Phillips not to hurt his wife. Felipe knows they'll find his aunt upstairs and contemplates running for his life, but doesn't want to leave his family behind. With no other choice and one swift movement, he bolts toward a window and dives out, causing the glass to shatter as he plows through it head first. Both Phillips and Brown get a few shots off in his direction, but they're not sure if he's been hit. Phillips orders Brown to give chase while still holding onto Sonia. He hears a commotion upstairs and is certain they found someone.

"Get off of me!" he hears a voice say.

Phillips loves to kill and gets the ultimate gratification every time he takes a life.

Sophia sees her mother struggling, so grabs a vase and tosses it toward Phillips's head. She throws it with all her might but misses. Phillips turns and gives her the meanest look, then turns back and extends his gun toward Carlos. He shoots him three times in the chest, killing him instantly. He then throws a kick back connecting it to Sophia's stomach, making her drop to her hands and knees. She hears the frantic screams from her siblings and figures she'll stay down.

Agent Brown storms back in the front door declaring that Felipe had gotten away. He's staggered down breathing heavily with his hands on his knees. He displays a little excitement as Moore and Mitchell come down the stairs with a lady and a child. Moore leads with a fistful of Angie's hair, and is pretty much dragging her down. When they make it to the bottom he shoves her to the floor and points his gun at her face. Mitchell follows with what appears to be a one-year-old toddler. He holds him by his left ankle. The baby hangs upside down and his cries fill the room. Sophia looks up and realizes this is it, she, as well as her entire family is about to die.

"Tie her up!" demands Phillips, as he points towards Sophia with his gun as if it were a finger. With one swoop, he swings the gun to the back of Sonia's head, knocking her out cold.

Agent Brown grabs Sophia by the back of her shirt and sits her on the chair Felipe had previously sat on. Celine's on the couch with Roberto and Carlito, they're terrified. Angie seems to not care, she keeps getting up trying to rush toward her baby that's still hanging, but Moore keeps knocking her down. Agent Brown wraps duct tape around Sophia's tiny torso and chair, then proceeds to wrap her legs to the wood. Phillips takes his blazer off, revealing his white shirt and uniquely designed tie. He's wearing a holster of a pretty significant size which he just put his huge gun into. He puts his foot on the couch and grabs a knife he has holstered to his ankle.

"Proceed with the term, Agent Mitchell!" he says.

Agent Moore rushes to activate the camera on his lenses.

With the baby still hanging and faintly crying, Mitchell grabs his gun and points it at his head. Angie has to be held down by Phillips. Mitchell intentionally shoots a single shot through his cranium and in her direction. He wants to make sure she knows her kid's blood is on her. She and Phillips are splattered with it. Phillips loves it, he licks some off his lips before knocking Angie out with the handle of the knife.

He stands back up and notices he didn't hear a flinch from anyone. He notices that Celine, Roberto, and Carlito were huddled all along and completely missed it. He looks at Sophia and her eyes are so tightly shut, you couldn't pry them open if you tried. He doesn't appreciate it, it makes him angry. He walks over to Sonia who's squirming on the floor, beginning to wake up, and puts two bullets through the back of her head. The kids go crazy and Carlito tries to run. As he reaches the front door, Brown puts him down with four shots to the back.

Phillips looks at Sophia and sees she still has her eyes closed, so goes to his briefcase and pulls out a needle that had already been threaded. He walks over and while facing her, sits atop her, pinning her down even more. He grabs her top eyelid and starts sewing it to her eyebrow, but she cannot take the pain and passes out.

When she awakes, she sees they patiently waited for her. She sees that Roberto, Celine, and Angie are all tied to chairs across from hers. She cannot blink, her top eyelids have been tightly sewn onto the skin right below her eyebrows.

"Remember what I said to you earlier today, Sophie?"

"Don't call me that! Only my dad can call me Sophie!" she snottily responds.

"Your dad can't call you anything!" Phillips angrily says. "Right, Carlos!?" he asks, looking at his body as if it could answer back. "Tape her mouth shut!" he demands from Brown. "I told you earlier today, that if you ever put your hands on me again, I would make you watch as I killed your entire family. And frankly, you closing your eyes while I do so is kind of disrespectful!"

He walks over to Angie and forces her to look at him by pulling her hair. He peels the tape off of her mouth, puts the tip of the knife on her neck, and gently sticks it in as he looks into her eyes. Angie starts gargling blood and choking, and her body violently shakes.

Celine's sitting right next to her. She tries to scream, but can't with the duct tape covering her mouth. Angie's body continues to shake and jerk, until it goes completely motionless. Phillips closes his eyes while gripping her hair and deeply inhales, as if he's sucking up her soul.

Sophia tries hard to wiggle free, but can't, she's too tightly tied.

Phillips turns his attention to Celine. One by one, he'll gladly kill them all.

"Let me get one of these kills," says Agent Moore. Phillips is having too good of a time but agrees to give him one.

"You can have him," he says as he points toward Roberto.

Sophia starts making loud mumbling sounds as if she's carrying a conversation and it catches Phillips's attention.

"Oh, you're trying to say something." He walks over and peels the tape off of her mouth. As soon as he does, she spits at him. It misses his face which she was aiming for but lands on his tie. Although it's already stained with Angie's blood, he gets really upset that she'd try to damage it. "You little bitch!" he shouts. He smacks her across the face with the back of his hand.

Sophia's unfazed and begins to laugh. "Go ahead and kill us!" she says. "We will be with our parents again while you stay stuck in this brutal world!"

"It's only brutal for your kind of people, so I'll be alright!" he arrogantly answers. He then walks over to Celine, and without warning, starts stabbing her in her chest. He stabs her so many times even his fellow agents look at each other in disbelief. He must have stabbed her chest and torso at least fifty times, although it seemed she was dead after the second stab with the way her body went limp. This is an intimate kill for him, Sophia has him to his boiling point. He finishes and stands there breathing heavily. It looks like he's in another world, he looks deranged. He just stands there staring into nothing while clutching the knife by his side. The place is very quiet, all you could hear are the drops of blood dripping off the tip of the blade and hitting the wooden floor. Moore, Brown, and Mitchell are uncharacteristically very quiet. Moore's focused on making sure the camera on the custom made glasses is still recording. He doesn't want to screw this up and disappoint Phillips in any way, shape, or form. Mitchell's squatting down on his toes with his elbows on his knees, watching it all unfold. He's still gripping the pistol he used to execute the term. Brown's pacing back and forth with his trench coat open and his tie swinging loose.

Roberto breathes heavily. His nose is stuffed from so much weeping and he's struggling to get air.

Sophia looks at him. "Don't worry, Robbie!" she says. "We'll soon be with Mami and Papi!" This makes him convulse, which rapidly increases his breathing that he's already struggling with.

"You won't!" Phillips screams to her. He's still standing in the same position, but turned his head toward Sophia when she spoke.

Agent Moore thinks about reminding Phillips that the next kill is his when he sees him snap out of his trance, but decides not to.

"YES...! I...! WILL...!" Sophia shouts back. "And I can't wait, so get it over with already!"

It isn't obvious to the other agents as to who's losing their minds more, Phillips, or Sophia. She slowly moves her head from shoulder to shoulder, while calmly saying, "Kill him. Kill him. Kill him."

This makes Phillips snap, and with one swing he nearly decapitates Roberto. He swings his knife so hard, he feels the trajectory change when the blade rubs against his spine. Roberto's head falls back, and to Sophia, it looks like he has none. All she sees is blood that resembles a water fountain as it gushes out of his neck area. She squints and desperately tries to close her eyes but it's impossible.

"Is that all you got!?" she aggressively asks.

Mitchell and Brown look at each other. They cannot believe such a young girl could be so brave. They'd of thought she was just being stupid under other circumstances, but know she realizes she will die regardless of what happens.

Phillips walks to his briefcase, pulls out a hand towel and wipes the blade of the knife.

"Let's get out of here!" he demands.

The agents are confused. They know that under no circumstances are they to allow anyone to live.

"What about her!?" asks Mitchell, as he stands up.

Phillips looks at Sophia. "I want her to live with what she's seen here tonight for the rest of her life."

"Are you kidding me!?" asks Brown.

"We can't let her live, boss!" says Moore. He removes the glasses and walks toward him. "What are you doing?" he whispers.

"No. What are 'YOU' doing?" Phillips responds.

"Do you not remember the consequences of not killing her?"

"I do. I just hope you remember the consequences of questioning me."

Mitchell was going to interrupt but stops himself. He knows it's a bluff, Phillips would be the last person to ever spare anyone. He bets he'll blow her head off right before walking out.

Moore backs off. He looks back at the other agents and wonders why they're not trying to talk some sense into him.

"He doesn't dare!" says Sophia.

Phillips softly laughs to himself while putting his items into the briefcase.

Mitchell's sure Phillips is going to kill her. It has been recorded and there's no way to hide the fact that they left someone alive. Moore keeps looking at Mitchell but cannot say anything for fear of Phillips hearing him.

"Wait for me in the car," he instructs. Moore's hesitant but knows he has to comply.

Mitchell escorts them out and is sure Phillips will use this as a chance to finish the job. He looks back as he steps out and sees him pull out the gun that had already been holstered.

Phillips hears the door close and outstretches his arm, until the barrel of the gun is inches away from Sophia's forehead.

Sophia anticipates the shot. Her life flashes before her eyes. She sees her parents faces, and remembers all the good times in life with them. She thinks of her siblings, especially Oscar, he was her favorite brother. She remembers how hard her father worked to provide a decent life. She thinks of many things in a fraction of a second.

"You will not see your parents again," Phillips says.

Sophia sees the gun lowering. "Kill me!" she shouts. At this point, she has nothing to lose. She's lost her family and basically has nothing, nowhere to go, or no-one to turn to.

"I will not give you the pleasure," he loudly whispers.

"You have to kill me!" she desperately says. "Those are the rules!" Again she spits at him, hoping it'll make him do it, but is too small to reach high enough to get the pleasure of landing it on his face.

Phillips looks at her and pulls the knife out. Sophia sees the blood that wasn't properly wiped, drying on the blade, making it look rusty.

"I have never, in all the years I've been doing this, come across someone that's pushed me to the limit you've pushed me to tonight," he tells her. "I'm a man of my word, and when I told you earlier tonight that you weren't going to your mommy and poppy, I meant it. I would love nothing more than to see you grow up to be a young lady that has connected herself to other people. It would be a pleasure to have the opportunity to do this to you again."

He leans over and slits the duct tape that ties her torso to the back of the chair. "You let your legs loose," he says right before walking out.

Sophia sits there and doesn't want to move. She feels helpless but knows she has to get the stitches off of her eyes.

As Phillips approaches the car with its engine running, he notices they're all staring at him. Moore's too terrified to say anything and hopes Mitchell starts the conversation.

"Is she dead?" asks Mitchell.

Phillips looks back after climbing into the passenger seat. "Of course she is," he responds.

"Are you sure?" Moore questions. "We didn't hear a gunshot."

As Brown steps on it to pull off, Phillips steadily stares at him through the rearview mirror. "Sometimes, I feel the need to wrap my hands around someone's neck and squeeze," he mysteriously says.

With the blaring look he gives him as he says it, Moore has no choice but to look away. He knows he's describing what he's done to Sophia, but says it in a way that makes him feel as if it's what he wants to do to him...

~Chapter Three~

Fred and Dorothy Cryan

"It all started on the 12th day, of the 9th month, in the year 1999, that's when the world changed for us as we once knew it. A nuclear bomb was detonated in New York City that killed the majority of the population in the five boroughs, and hundreds of thousands in New Jersey and surrounding areas. The blast was so powerful, until the present year of '2036,' a fifty-mile radius around the city is still un-inhabitable. The impact of the bomb was so forceful, it damaged power grids across the country, forcing the entire nation to stay in darkness for nearly a decade. Our current President, Ronald Thump, stopped the voting process and declared he will be President until the day he dies. While many speculated that it was done by our own government, he declares war."

"The United States stunned the world when they unveiled the missile defense system they'd worked on for decades before the war began. It was so unique, it made it impossible for a missile to enter our air space, preventing other countries from being able to attack *us."*

"Food rapidly ran out and the general public started rioting. Criminals roamed the streets, sometimes committing unspeakable acts. Neighborhoods were destroyed by the same residents that called them home. President Thump declared Marshall Law. He gave full control to the US Military, while he, his family, and anyone who was important to him made their way to unknown underground bunkers. With a curfew in place, the Army was deployed to try and restore peace. Soldiers arrested anyone who didn't obey laws and put them in heavily guarded camps, where many starved to death."

"After years of trying, the Army eventually gave up, and would only focus on the high-class areas of the country. Religious hysteria made matters worse, with many claiming it was the end of times. There were priests who at your behest, would kill your child, claiming you'd give them a sure passage to heaven by getting them out of this cruel world."

"After ten years of chaos and our population being eliminated to about half the amount, the government starts restoring power, while all along having energy at all major government institutions powered by giant generators that got its energy from the little sunlight that shined. They built filtration systems throughout the entire country to keep the air from becoming radioactive. The systems were capable of cleaning the airs up to five-hundred feet high, but the smog that blocks the sun's brightness still linger until this day."

"The war lasted twenty-two years and didn't end until 2021, yet we're still behind as it set us back at least half a century. The United States showed its might and toppled most countries, leaving the rest of the world mostly in ruins. In some cases, they gave who they thought should rule a nation the opportunity to do so, but in most, they used laser-firing satellites to wipe them off the face of the earth."

"While the war was raging, the United States built a wall surrounding the entire country excluding our waters, and grounded all

flights entering or leaving the country. The border with Canada was walled, the one with Mexico was walled, the United States was determined to isolate itself from the rest of the world."

"Our missile defense system consisted of three satellites that were placed right above our atmosphere. They shot laser beams that were so accurate and advanced, they could disintegrate any square inch of land in a fraction of a second. The government claims the blasts were so powerful, they could penetrate the earth, causing them to emerge out the opposite side of our planet if they raised the frequencies high enough. They were designed to shoot down anything traveling within a one-hundred-mile radius around the country. The walls shoot one-hundred million volts of electricity to anything that touches them on the other side, and are magnetic. They stand at fifty-feet high and are impenetrable. If a missile miraculously passed the defense system, it'd be sucked down by the magnetic force, causing it to drop on the other side."

"Our Military were like Gods on the battlefields. They didn't have to step foot on foreign soil, but could destroy it in seconds. Our three satellites were able to cover the entire planet, we could destroy cities instantly. The world dropped to their knees to us. The United States wanted the people to know this. During Marshall Law, soldiers on jeeps would ride around, with one blaring through a bullhorn all that the country was doing overseas."

"When the war broke out it was like hell on earth, the people went crazy. Kids were being snatched from their parents, fathers were being killed in front of their families, and women were being raped in the streets. There were cities reduced to half its size because of violent acts being committed by its own citizens. There was no trust in our fellow humans. People were hungry, stores got looted, the old were terrified, it was as if it turned into a civil war."

"The local authorities weren't effective, life was chaos for them also. Little by little they dwindled down, until there were none left. The

majority barricaded themselves in their homes and decided it was time to protect their loved ones."

"In 2003, the government came up with the Impla-chip, a chip every single American must have implanted in their wrist. It's used for everything. It's how you sign your name, it's how you buy, it's how you sell. The government introduced it as a way to track anyone at any time, but rarely used it for that purpose. The government puts DD's on every American's impla-chip on the first day of each month, with Illegal Residents getting much less. Dollars are no longer used, gold is no longer valuable, the only thing that matters are your DD's. DD's are Digital-Dollars. The sum of DD's on the general public's wrist is reset on the first of each month, meaning that if you don't use them, you lose them, it doesn't matter how they were earned."

"In 2023, they enforced the HNC vaccine. Every Illegal Resident born after November 28th, 2023, must receive this vaccine on the day they're born. The Doctor has thirty minutes to vaccinate the child, it is very dangerous to inject a child after that time frame."

"The government decided to start the Federally Funded Army to get the population under control, as food was rapidly running out. It consists of hardened criminals. They went into prisons and gave inmates an opportunity they couldn't refuse. They offered the most vicious criminals a chance to work for them in exchange for their freedom. The agents are all former inmates that were either facing execution or the rest of their lives in prison. But it came at an expense, they were implanted with a special Impla-chip that would disperse a very potent poison, killing them instantly, if they didn't follow procedure or decided to try and escape. After making their selections, the government released a gas at all prisons that killed the remaining inmates," says the man on television, with millions of viewers nationwide. He televises the same mini-documentary every week, with millions tuning in every time it's broadcasted.

"Run, honey. Run!" says Fred to his wife, on September 14th, 1999. It's been two days since our soil has been attacked and a city is still on fire. The news goes around and people all over the country are panicking. The way the entire country went into darkness at the same time has everyone thinking the worse.

Fred and Dorothy are a happily married young couple who one day eloped. She found out she was pregnant and hurried to get married to avoid shaming her family. She's a twenty-five-year-old free spirited young lady who loves nothing more in life than her husband Fred. They've both had a crush on each other since childhood, but it wasn't until about two years ago that Fred's built up enough courage to let her know how he feels. They now have an adorable seven-month-old child that they both cherish.

"Faster!" he says as he runs for his life, while trying to lug the baby seat with one hand and tug Dorothy with the other. On their trails are two biker gang members, who seem to get a thrill out of watching them run away. Their intentions aren't to catch them, they just want to scare them. As they run, the men chuckle and move not nearly as fast as they look capable of. Fred starts to slow down, he's exhausted. Out of nowhere, a car swerves and makes a loud screeching sound caused by the tires skidding on the asphalt.

"Get in!" says the driver, as she pushes the door open.

Fred and Dorothy jump into the back seat and don't consider she opened the front door. They're both breathing heavily and desperately trying to catch their breaths.

The young lady behind the wheel is Aughra, she takes off while the passenger door's still open. The motion of the car forces it closed when she pulls off at top speeds. She looks back at them as their sur-roundings blur by. "Are you guys OK?" she asks, while chewing gum and looking excited at the heroism she's just displayed.

Dorothy notices how disheveled the young lady looks. Her hair is a mess and the liner on her eyes are smudgy, causing them to look as if they're bruised. "We're fine. Thank you very much," she says.

Fred's sitting back with his eyes tightly closed and his face facing the ceiling of the car. "Thank you thank you thank you..." he loudly whispers.

"What the hell are you two doing out there?" asks Aughra. "Did y'all not see what happened in the city? Someone nuked us!" she says, with a sense of excitement in her tone. Aughra's a wild child who's into drinking and partying. She's a very petite nine-teen-year-old who must weigh ninety pounds soaking wet. Her parents were drug addicts who kicked her out into the streets when she was just fifteen. She then spent the next two years of her life with a man twice her age, who'd slap her around every so often. Aughra's an only child who struggled in school and seemed to always gravitate toward the wrong crowd. She has long, blond hair that seems to be knotted, almost as if she's trying to grow dreadlocks.

"That wasn't a nuclear bomb," says Fred, while Dorothy attends to the baby who won't stop crying.

"I'm not a scientist, sir, but there's no way a bomb could be so strong we'd feel the vibration way over here. It felt like we had an earthquake."

"Yea. I know." he says. "But it's impossible, this country will never let its guard down to that extent."

"OK then. Maybe it wasn't," she says, without hiding her doubts. "That's what everyone's saying happened."

"It just can't be," says Fred, while looking out the window, astounded by the scenes they're passing.

"Everyone's going crazy," she says, while making a sharp right turn.

"You want to slow down?" asks Fred, as Dorothy seemed to lose her balance, which caused the baby to lose grip of her nipple.

"What are you doing out?" she asks. "It's very dangerous out in these streets."

"We had to rush out of our building," responds Dorothy. "Someone set it on fire." Dorothy notices through the rear view mirror from the back seat that Aughra seems to be enjoying this. She can't wipe the silly smile off of her face.

"Do you think this is the end of the world, guys?"

"This isn't the end of the world," fusses Fred. He looks at Dorothy who's buttoning her shirt after finally getting the baby to sleep.

"What an angel. What's his name? How old is he?" asks Aughra. She's forced to step on the brakes, making the Cryan's jerk. "Watch out, asshole!" she screams out the window as she speeds back off.

"His name is Gregory, he's seven months now," says Dorothy.

"Aww. I have a cousin named Gregory. Haven't seen him in years. Everyone calls him Greggy," she says with a low chuckle. "Cute, right?"

"Yea, but I wouldn't call my son Greggy," responds Dorothy with half a smile. "We'll call him Greg."

"Too predictable," she says, finally drawing a smile from her. "I almost had a kid once," says Aughra, her expression now somber.

Fred looks away, he wants no part of this conversation. He figures he'd let the ladies discuss this and sits back on his seat. He lays his head back and closes his eyes. There is no way he could possibly fall asleep with the amount of adrenaline that's rushed through his body just minutes ago, but nothing stops him from trying to give the impression he is. Dorothy also considers trying to dodge the conversation but figures it'd be rude.

"What do you mean, almost?" she hesitantly asks.

"When I was seventeen," she says, while looking at Dorothy through the mirror. "I got pregnant by the man I loved and he killed the baby."

This shocks Dorothy, hitting her like a ton of bricks. She never expected that response from Aughra. How does she continue this discussion.

"He was a jealous man, I couldn't do anything. I couldn't even have friends," she says. "He was convinced the baby I was carrying wasn't his. One night, when I was eight months pregnant, he came home after many hours out drinking with friends and woke me. He called me a whore and claimed someone must have jumped out the window when they saw him coming because I had it open to get breeze while I slept. I'm now trying again. My boyfriend and I have been trying for a year now, but it's just not happening."

Dorothy's teary eyed. She gets very emotional at the slightest sob story. Although free spirited, she's one of the purest, kindest people you could ever meet. Her parents were very religious and she attended church three times a week with them. She often dreamt of becoming a nun when she grew up and is as pure as they come. She remembers thinking as a teen, that the only man in the world she would ever marry is Fred Cryan. They've been friends their entire lives and she's always had a secret crush on him. She figured if she couldn't have him, she'd dedicate herself to God.

"Oh Lord," Dorothy mumbles, while looking down at her hands, her eyes filling with tears. "I'm so sorry."

"What the hell!" says Aughra. "Are you crying?" She starts to laugh. "Honey, I've stopped crying long ago. The one lesson my loser dad ever taught me was to not dwell on anything," she says, while stopping the vehicle in a not so subtle neighborhood. "Always told me not to stress anything I couldn't control. This is my home," she says, while pointing to a house that looks like it barely stands and is in desperate need of a paint job. "You guys are welcome to come in, up to you." Aughra opens the door to climb out. "Or you can camp out in my car for the night, but I must warn you, it is very dangerous around here."

"We couldn't," says Dorothy.

"Don't be silly," she responds. "There's no way I'll let you keep that baby out in the streets tonight anyway."

Fred wants to get into some shelter so convinces her to go in.

They approach the house, and walk through a waist high metal fence that makes a sound as it rubs against concrete slabs that lay uneven on the ground. Ahead of them, is an aisle leading to the steps. On each side, are unkempt bushes that seem to have not been trimmed in years. Aughra opens her front door and out rushes a cat. Fred flinches at the sudden movement, causing both ladies to giggle.

They walk inside and are both surprised at the appearance. Although dark, it seems to be very clean.

"You like it, huh?" gloats Aughra.

"I love it," says Dorothy.

"Very nice place you have here," says Fred, while looking up at the tall ceilings that the darkness swallows up.

"My boyfriend fixed it up. Looked horrible when we first bought it, almost as bad as the outside.

"Where's your boyfriend?" asks Dorothy.

"He'll be here any minute. Let me show you your room."

Navigating easily through the dark house, Aughra rushes toward the stairs.

"Hold on. We can't see," says Dorothy.

That night, being unable to sleep, Fred gets off of the bed. He paces back and forth, occasionally looking at his wife as she lays sound asleep. He notices the baby begin to wiggle and move, so grabs the baby formula his wife had prepared and watches as his son suckles on the baby bottle. The child is his pride, his world, his everything.

Fred must have fallen asleep with the baby in his arms and panics when he awakes the next morning and doesn't find him. He jumps up and sees his wife's not in the bed. While trying to rush toward the door, he trips over his own feet, causing him to tumble and hit the floor. He rapidly gets back up, runs toward the door and heads down the stairs. He hurries to the sound of voices and slides due to a sudden stop, as the shiny wooden floor is too smooth for the socks on his feet.

"Good morning, honey," says Dorothy, while having a freshly cooked breakfast ready for him.

"How did you...?"

"Gas is still on, Fred," says Aughra. "Who knows how long it'll last."

Fred wished for nothing more than a hot breakfast that night. "Good morning, my little man," he says to Gregory, who's sits in his seat which is on the table. Gregory has his eyes wide open and gives his father a smile with each movement he makes.

Aughra walks over to Gregory. She pokes his hand with a finger, knowing the baby will grip it. "He's so cute," she says as he grabs a hold of it. "You're going to have to be careful, Dorothy. He'll have women fighting over him."

The room's filled with smiles, until it suddenly becomes filled with the sound of motorcycles approaching. The sound seems to get closer, then comes to a sudden halt. Fred could tell it's two of them when he hears one engine shut off slightly before the other, and notices Aughra becomes very tense.

"Who's that?" he asks.

"That's my boyfriend," she says.

Fred feels a sense of relief. He grabs a glass Dorothy had given him full of warm water and starts to drink, then the front door opens. He spits the water back into the cup when he sees who it is. At this point, he doesn't know what to think. Looks like Dorothy also recognizes them, because Fred looks at her and she's shaking.

"Hi there," says the gentleman that walks in. "My name is Roy, and this here," he says, while pointing to the man that's with him, "Is Jay."

Aughra walks across the room and for some odd reason doesn't introduce anyone. Fred senses something's not right, they're the ones who chased them into her car.

"Are you OK?" asks Roy, as his buddy goes over and sits on the couch in the living room. Roy's a big guy who dresses in dirty jeans and a leather vest with a logo on the back. At six-foot-four, and almost two-hundred-seventy pounds, he's bullied his way through life. He first met Aughra two years ago. He had to rush his sister to the hospital and offered her a ride when he saw her waiting on a bus that wasn't coming until the next morning. She was heading home after being beaten so bad she miscarried. Aughra was by his side when he lost his sister three weeks later due to the sickness that hospitalized her. Since then, he's turned to drugs and partying. He's abandoned his other siblings and wants nothing to do with them. He turned to crime, which is the only thing he's ever been good at. He knows how to intimidate, and strike fear in others hearts.

"I need to use the restroom," Dorothy nervously says. She needs time to settle herself down. Although soft spoken, Roy's a very big man. He stops Dorothy in her tracks by standing in front of her when she begins to walk toward the bathroom by the kitchen.

"You can't use that one," he says, while raising his hand over her head to point up the stairs. "Use the one up there."

Fred's mind is racing, he has no clue what's going on. "*Why would he send her all the way upstairs,*" he wonders. He watches as Dorothy disappears down the hallway toward the bathroom after climbing to the top.

Jay jumps off the couch and runs toward the window. Aughra's desperately trying to turn the stove back on, but is unable to. "There's someone out there!" Jay shouts to Roy, who pulls out a long revolver that's tucked in his waistband and lunges toward the door. He takes two shots at a man who looks to be contemplating stealing his bike, making him run away.

"Stay away from my house!" he shouts as the man flees. "Is the tank full?" he asks Aughra, referring to the car she brought the Cryan's in.

"There's enough gas in the car," she aggressively says. "Wish there was some damn gas in this stove!"

He puts the gun on the table and starts walking toward the bathroom he stopped Dorothy from entering. Fred hears the stream of urine hitting the toilet bowl water as he urinates with the door open.

Dorothy rushes down, the sound of gunfire has her hoping they didn't hurt Fred, and is filled with relief when she sees he's unharmed. "What was that?" she asks.

"I was trying to swat a fly," says Roy, while walking out of the bathroom, still zipping his pants.

Fred gives Dorothy a nervous stare. He also feels the need to use the restroom but is afraid to leave her alone with them.

"What a handsome little fella you have here," Roy tells Fred. The baby looks at him and kicks his little legs, then grins, and makes a little sound. "He likes me!" he says to Aughra. "Did you see the smile he gave me!?"

Fred relaxes a little. He feels a sense of safety and announces he has to go. He starts going toward the stairs, but is stopped by Roy.

"Where are you going?" he asks.

"I have to go to the bathroom," replies Fred, feeling a bit more at ease.

"Use this one." Fred's confused. He wonders why he'd stop Dorothy from using it but is allowing him. Roy grabs the gun from the table and tucks it back into his waist. Aughra looks at him as if she wonders why he'd let him use that bathroom.

Fred's greeted by a weird odor when he enters. After urinating, he places his hands on the sink and stares himself in the mirror. He can't believe what the world has come to and figures it'll go back to normal really soon. He turns the water on and notices his reflection on the faucet. The water flows, and he sees it's yellowish, so puts one hand under the stream until it clears up.

Jay's gotten off the couch and has joined Roy in making silly faces to make Gregory smile, while Dorothy, and Aughra hold a conversation about what must be going on in the city.

Fred places both hands under the water to form a cup. He then lifts them and wets his face, allowing himself to see the water drops roll off of his chin and back into the sink in his reflection. He opens the medicine cabinet and can't help but notice medication that's usually prescribed to patients with Alzheimer's, so grabs the bottle to look at the label. According to it, it's prescribed to someone named *'Carol Brooks.'* Fred slides the shower curtain aside and is nauseated by the sight he encounters. He turns to his left and vomits in the sink, then falls to his knees while holding on to it. There's an elderly lady laying in her own blood. She lays with a hole in her forehead and her eyes wide open as if she's in shock. It almost looks as if her head is stuck to the porcelain. He see chunks of brain scattered all over the bathtub.

Roy and Aughra look at each other when they hear the commotion inside.

Fred's still over the sink and doesn't know what to do. Dorothy runs and tries to open the door, but it's locked. She bangs on it with her palm, while yelling for him to open up. As he does, he quickly steps out to spare her from having to see that sight.

"What's wrong, Fred," says Roy. "You look like you've just seen a ghost. Wait a minute, wait a minute," he says. "You didn't really think this was our house, did you? It's Carol's house!"

He pulls out his gun and steps toward Fred.

Fred freezes. With the barrel in his face he hears Aughra demand Roy to stop.

"Don't kill them!" she says. "They're good people. Please, babe!"

Roy lowers the gun then swiftly swings it, striking Fred in the left temple and knocking him out. Jay grabs Dorothy who tries to rush to her husband's side and also knocks her out with the butt of his weapon.

"Wouldn't it be easier to just kill them?" asks Roy.

Aughra walks over to Gregory and makes a funny face, causing him to smile. "It's time to go now, my dear Greggy!" she says, while tapping his little nose with a finger.

She grabs the baby seat and off she goes with Roy and Jay...

~Chapter Four~

The Agents

"Pull over!" Phillips tells Agent Brown two blocks from the head-quarters. The car comes to a screech and he demands them to follow him. Though suspicious, they all comply, and not because they want to, but because they have to. They stop and huddle in a small circle. "Give me the glasses," Phillips tells Moore.

He fumbles a bit but manages to pull them out of the inside pocket of his blazer. Agent Moore's a very clumsy guy, he makes many mis-takes and is viewed as a wimp by his fellow agents. He's a very short man who wears thick framed glasses and uses the assistance of shoes with really thick soles to make himself look a few inches taller. Al-though his kills are gruesome, he's considered the weakest link among them. After passing him the glasses, Phillips throws them not four feet from the circle, pulls out his gun and shoots them. Moore's very con-cerned, he thinks Phillips exacerbated the problem. *"How will we explain this,"* he wonders.

"OK, here's the story," Phillips says to their attention. "We found the Escaped Illegal Resident and executed him. In all, it was him and nine Illegal Residents. We'll say Moore was recording and Felipe shot at him, but the bullet struck the glasses and he killed the little bastard. This is nice DD's we're getting, gentlemen. Good job, everyone."

"With all due respect!" says Agent Brown. "Do you not think they'll send someone over to inspect the scene and confirm the kills?"

Phillips is a step ahead though. "Yes. I've thought of that," he responds. "That's why I've decided to plant a body there on my way home tonight. They won't go out this late to inspect it, they'll do it in the morning."

As much as Brown hates to agree with Phillips he realizes he's right, and they all head back to the car.

Upon arriving at the headquarters, they're seen by a member of another team. "We executed three terms today!" the man tells Phillips as he walks by. He seems to be very proud of himself when he brags about it.

"We only had one," Phillips responds, while trying to brush him off.

"Wow. Sorry, man," he sarcastically states as Phillips gets further away. "Maybe next time, my friend!" he says, this time shouting and getting stares from passerby.

Phillips raises his hand from afar and sticks his middle finger up, while nonchalantly continuing to walk toward the entrance of the building. The agent sees this and chuckles before walking away. They are very competitive, sometimes different groups make wagers for DD's to see who could get more terms in a month, some agents make off really well when they win. Phillips isn't into the fun and games, he goes in, does his job then goes home. He hardly associates with anyone other than his fellow agents.

The government created one-thousand teams of four men. These teams enter states and take out as many Escaped Illegal Residents as possible. They sometimes jump from state to state, almost as if the government is declaring war on its own people.

They enter Mr. Goodman's office which reeks of smelly socks and cigarette smoke. "Good evening," says Phillips, trying to catch his attention.

Mr. Goodman sits there with his legs up and his eyes closed. He's a fat older gentleman who runs this section of the building and is portrayed as a very mean individual. He shuffles to get his legs off the desk and immediately lights a cigarette when he hears Phillips's voice.

"I wanted to see you gentlemen," he says. He takes a pull of the cigarette that looks to be poorly rolled. "What happened tonight?"

"We executed a term, sir," Phillips responds posthaste. He doesn't want Moore to have a chance to open his mouth.

"Nine Illegal Residents also, sir," says Moore, getting a tap in the arm by Mitchell and a stare by Phillips that insinuates for him to shut up.

"We'll talk about that later. I want to know what happened with Mrs. Cryan."

Phillips is relieved that he gets more time before he has to explain the recording and assures him everything went well.

"Why would you even enter that woman's home? That's Fred's wife for God's sake!" he angrily says.

Phillips gulps. He feels toward Mr. Goodman the way most feel toward him, he doesn't want to upset him. Mr. Goodman will get you torn to bits and pieces in a second. He has men that'll do unimaginable things to you. As mean and crude as Phillips is, he's a saint compared to some of them.

"How the hell you end up in her house!? Do you not know better!?"

"W... we," Phillips tries.

"We were on our way to the Senao residence when a lady wildly stopped us by jumping in front of the car," interrupts Mitchell. "She was screaming and saying there's an Escaped Illegal Resident in the house. We didn't realize it was her residence until she opened her door," he says, even though they knew that was her home.

This calms Mr. Goodman a little. He nods his head and puts the cigarette out in an ashtray that's overflowing with half smoked cigarettes. He knows he can confide in Mitchell. "She was a lovely lady," he says, and lights another cigarette.

The agents look at each other.

"Yes, she's a lovely lady," Phillips agrees.

"You don't know, do you?"

They're all curious and listening, none want to be the one to ask what he's talking about.

"Know what?" ask Moore.

"Dorothy's dead," he sadly says.

"Wha... what? We didn't!" starts Agent Brown. They all get an uneasy feeling and don't want him to think they had anything to do with it. Fred was one of his favorite agents, and the only one that wasn't recruited from prison. He simply got the job because he was a really good friend of his.

"Relax!" he says. "It was a self-inflicted gunshot wound."

The agents can't believe it.

"No Way!" thinks Agent Phillips.

"We were there a few hours ago," says Mitchell. "There's no way!"

"Neighbors say they heard a loud bang, which was also heard by a news crew right after you guys pulled off," he explains. "Let's have a moment of silence for Mrs. Cryan." They close their eyes and bow their heads, then cross their hands with the right one over the left, as they do when one of their men go down, and remain silent for approximately fifteen seconds.

"OK now, back to work. What did you guys accomplish today?" asks Mr. Goodman.

"Nine Illegal Resident and one Escapee," Moore swiftly responds, drawing glances from his men.

"You should let your leader speak, son," Goodman tells him.

Moore's new to the crew. He came from another district to replace the agent that replaced Fred ten years prior, who had to be poisoned. Mr. Goodman personally hit the button that released the venom into his system when he decided all of a sudden, that he wanted out. Some believe he went mad as a result of the job.

"No. Let him speak," says Phillips, with a huge smirk on his face. He will use this as an opportunity to mention the recording. "He's a hero!" he exuberantly says, making Mr. Goodman raise his eyebrows and show interest in wanting to hear about it. "An Illegal Resident shot at him, and you should have seen him, he drew his weapon really quick and put him down in an instant," he says, while hoping beyond hope that Goodman buys this bull. Phillips has never been in this predicament, he's always done everything by the book. "We almost lost him today. The bullet went through the glasses and damaged the recorder, but at least he's still here. You should have seen him, boss, he filled that fool with lead! I'm glad you're still with us, brother," he says as he hugs Moore with a sentimental look on his face.

"What a load of bologna," thinks Moore.

Goodman seems to believe it. At first he had a sense of doubt, but then thought to himself and realized Phillips of all people, wouldn't be stupid enough to come up with such a bogus story. He's one of his top agents and doubts he'd be such a fool.

"Let me see the glasses," he says, making Phillips pass them to him. "Yep, they're damaged. You gentlemen know I can't pay you until this is confirmed, right?" At this point Phillips doesn't care about the pay, he just wants out of there. He has to plant two bodies to make it look like Felipe and Sophia were among those killed.

Mitchell intends to go home to his son, he's been trying to make up for a lot of lost time. His son resents the fact his father went to jail when he was only two years old, and didn't get to meet him until he was released for the work program. Mitchell was seven years into his life sentence, which was thirteen years ago, when they came up with the F.F.A.. Jacob was excited as a nine-year-old boy to finally meet his father. Mitchell's sister cared for the boy while he was incarcerated and never took him at his behest, he didn't want his son to see him caged up like an animal. Mitchell then had to tell his son he had to be away for an additional four years to train to be an F.F.A. agent. He hated the fact he had to disappoint him.

For the last nine years, Mitchell's been trying to make it up to him. He desperately wants to make everything right but it's difficult when he's occasionally sent to other states for weeks at a time. He tries to take Jacob along, but he rarely wants to go. Jacob was already thirteen when Mitchell finally came home, and had a group of friends he rather spend time with. He often made plans to spend time with his dad, only to blow him off and take off with friends. Jacob's twenty-two now, and they seem to have a decent relationship. That doesn't stop him from reminding his father every once in a while how his absence made him feel. This has taken a toll on Mitchell, and he needs help.

Mitchell stays as the other agents walk out of Goodman's office. He stares at him as if he has something to tell him and waits until they're alone.

"Did you get me the information?" he asks him.

"Yes, I have," responds Goodman, as he passes him a business card. "She's here every Tuesday. I'll introduce you."

Mitchell turns around to excuse himself from his office while realizing he has the opportunity to meet her the next day.

"Don't lose your mind on me, Mitchell," says Mr. Goodman, stopping him half way out the door.

"OK, I'll try not to," he responds, while waving the business card.

"Good. I'd hate to have to push that button," says Goodman, while pointing at a metal box. The Box is a P1-simulator, it has a numerical keypad and a small red button. Each agent has a code embedded into their Impla-chip. If their code is entered, and the button is pushed, they're dead. It releases a toxic poison strong enough to put an elephant down in less than three minutes.

Mitchell approaches his house which is elevated on a hill in a town specifically built for agents. It's barricaded and very safe, they even have their own market where they can buy food. It's filled with fresh fruits and vegetables along with dairy products and freshly cut meats. Mitchell often wonders how it's possible to have so much there, but so little elsewhere. Most Illegal Residents struggle to eat with the amount off DD's they receive, yet they have plenty. He figures it's the agency's way of keeping the agents well fed, so doesn't think much of it.

He makes it to his house and notices the living room light is dimly lit, suggesting his son is home. Before he enters, he takes a slight pause at the door. Something's killing Mitchell, he senses a strong guilt but knows he has to go in. He enters and encounters a very nice aroma. His son has prepared a home cooked meal of mashed potatoes with steamed vegetables and steak.

"Good evening, Son."

"Hi, Pops. How was your day?"

"It was a tough one, but hey, I'm still alive." He looks at the plate that's prepared for him on the table.

"Sit and eat," Jacob tells him.

Being an F.F.A. agent is a very dangerous job, they deal with a lot of desperate people who are capable of doing anything. Although having a rocky relationship with him, Jacob worries for his father every day.

"Goodnight, Dad," he says as he walks away.

"Aren't you going to eat?"

"I already ate," he replies. "I have to get up early for work. Enjoy the food."

Jacob has a really good job as an inspector of large projects being done in their city. Mitchell's extremely proud of him. Considering the life he's had, he's turned out to be a very responsible young man.

Mitchell wakes up bright and early, the fact he'll finally have a chance to get a lot off of his chest has him anxious. He washes up, gets dressed and is ready to go. As soon as he parks his vehicle outside the headquarters, he spots Mr. Goodman wobbling across the lot.

"Good morning, sir!" he shouts.

"Hey there!" yells Mr. Goodman. "Meet me after work, I've already scheduled your appointment with Dr. Murphy."

After work that night he reports to Goodman's office.

"I guess you guys got nothing today," Goodman tells him, as it's required for them to report to his office to get paid for any kills. "I'm surprised they haven't passed by to get paid for last night's job. Give me your hand," he demands.

Mitchell stretches his arm to get his DD's scanned.

"Very good job yesterday," Goodman tells him. "I hear it was a mess."

Mitchell isn't surprised. Phillips told him earlier he was able to plant the body, which assured him he killed Sophia. *"He would have slipped up by now and said 'bodies' if he had to replace her also,"* he wonders.

"Yes," he responds. "Thank You." Mitchell almost sticks his finger, '*as he always does when nervous*,' into his ear to caress a little ball of meat that blocks his hearing but catches himself. Everyone knows of this weird little habit and he doesn't want to display nervousness.

"Good evening, gentlemen," says a woman that's walked through the door.

"Hi, Doctor Murphy," Goodman says with a huge grin on his face. "This is Bradley Mitchell."

"How are you, sir," she says, while extending her hand for a shake.

'She's hot,' is the first thing Mitchell thinks. Dr. Murphy is a very attractive twenty-eight-year-old woman with long legs that are draped in nylon. She wears a skirt that hangs to right above her knees, and a very crisp, white, button down shirt so tight, it reveals her shape which is bottle-like. Long strands of her golden blond hair hang over her face and reflect off the lens of her glasses.

"I'm OK, ma'am. Thank you for asking. And you?"

Mitchell grabs her hand and the firmness makes him shiver. He hasn't been with another woman since Jacob's mom passed away. He's been lonely for a very long time, but isn't going to start looking for romance now, he wants to talk.

"If you'll follow me to my office," she says while beginning to walk out.

Mr. Goodman gives Mitchell an instigating wink as he begins to follow. "Dr. Murphy!?" he shouts, making her stop and look back. "There's one thing you should know about this fella. He sticks a finger in his ear when he's nervous or lying," he says with a chuckle.

They walk into her office and Mitchell's impressed at the fanciness. The leather couches are so shiny you could almost see your reflection on them. The rugs are priceless, he feels guilty walking over them. The lights shine perfectly and the paintings on the walls are elegant.

"Sit down, sir," she says. She sits across from him with a clipboard in her hands, and crosses one leg over the other.

"Let's start," she says. "What's your occupation?"

"I'm an F.F.A. agent," he answers.

"And what do you do?"

Mitchell pauses.

"Listen to me, Agent..." she opens the paper to remind herself of his name. "Mitchell... the point of you talking to me is for you to tell me everything. If I ask what you do for a living your answer must be that you kill people, no sugar coating it, you have to be blunt. I'm going to help you relieve some of the stress you carry. Sometimes people just need someone to talk to, helps to just let it out."

Mitchell knows this is routine but always struggles to answer that question.

"What qualifies you..." he thinks out loud.

"My qualifications are my two Masters degrees in psychology. Look, anything said in this room is strictly confidential. You must be able to confide in me."

"Yes. I also know you must report it to Mr. Goodman which means you will tell someone."

"You weren't mandated to have this talk, so no-one knows what is said in here," she snaps back.

Mitchell wanted to be sure and unwinds a bit. He takes his blazer off to get comfortable.

"Feel free to lay down if you want," says Dr. Murphy.

Mitchell considers it but decides to stay sitting upright, he's feeling a bit more relaxed.

"Where do I start?" he asks, while rotating his shoulders as if he's getting prepared to fight.

"What bothers you?"

"Everything bothers me."

"What made you become an agent?"

"I was in prison and there was no food. You literally had to kill to eat. They came in and offered a bunch of us the opportunity. It was either stay in there and starve to death, or take the job, so I took it."

"How long have you been doing this?"

"Nine years now. Thirteen if you count the training."

"What were you in jail for?"

Mitchell pauses. He's never told anyone what he was incarcerated for.

"Mitchell!? You must talk. You have fifty-three minutes left."

"Is this timed?" he asks, drawing a smile from her. "I thought only the yearly ones are timed."

"Yes, each session is usually sixty minutes."

"I can't say everything in an hour," he says, this time drawing a chuckle.

"You can see me again next Tuesday if you wish. This takes time."

"OK. Where do you want me to start?"

"Start from the beginning. Tell me about life growing up."

Mitchell's feeling the pressure and feels his perspiration rising. "I, I really don't know where to begin."

"Begin with your life. Tell me about your parents."

"My mom," he says while bowing his head. "She was a sweetheart. She was very protective of me, always told me not to go with anyone. Said people will come to me claiming I was theirs, as many did after the war with kidnappings running rampant. She just wanted me to know they were lying. She would hold me close everywhere we went. When I was two years old my sister was born. She was my only friend growing up. We often went nights without eating with the food shortages, but we had each other."

"Tell me about your fa..."

"I don't know my dad," he answers before she could even finish the question. "I grew up with my mother's boyfriend and he was very mean, he'd always beat me. Sometimes I'd act like I was sleeping when I saw him coming home, only for him to wake me up and beat me anyway."

"Why did he beat you?"

"Sometimes for no reason, it all depended on the mood he was in that day. He was never able to find work which made him take his frustrations out on us. He even considered going to New York City to find work with the clean up and restoration. He was willing to drive seven hours to get there and come home on weekends. I wanted him to go, I didn't want my mother harmed anymore. I would hear her weeping at night when she thought we were asleep."

"Where is he now?"

"I don't know. One day he went out to look for work and never came back. Mom cried for days but I was secretly glad. I didn't tell her how I felt because I didn't want to hurt her, but I was glad he never came home. I remember laying on my bed after the third day, hoping someone killed him."

"How old were you when he left?"

"I was eleven at the time, my sister was nine. She was also glad he left for Mom's sake, but she loved her father. She was his pride and joy, he never hurt her..."

"He never hit your sister?"

"No, just me and Mom. One time, he grabbed me over his knees and turned a lit cigarette off in my ear, just because she and I had an argument over a toy of mine she wouldn't give me. After he did it, he shoved me in the basement and locked me in there for three days. He fried my eardrum. Why would he...?"

"Sometimes people do things no-one can understand," she says. "That no-one can explain."

Mitchell lifts his right hand and sticks a finger in his ear.

"Are you being truthful, Brad?" she asks, as she remembers what Goodman said about his habit.

"I don't know why it happens, I guess it's a way for my body to remind me."

"Remind you of what?"

He turns his face to the left, revealing his ear that she hadn't noticed. There's a ball of meat in the entrance to his ear canal.

"This is what he did," he says.

"Where's your mom now?"

"I don't know. She took off a year after he disappeared and left us with Maggie," he sadly says.

"Who's Maggie? Why did she leave?"

"Maggie was my lover."

"Wait... wait... wait. Let's back this up, I'm confused."

"OK, let me explain," he quickly says. "My Mom is Bette, Bette Mitchell. When she left us she was thirty-one." Murphy's writing it down to keep up. "Her best friend was Maggie. Maggie would do anything for her, they were very close. Maggie would urge my mom to leave Roger and was happy when he disappeared."

"Yes. But you were twelve! How old was she?" she interrupts.

"She was twenty-nine. Shortly after my mother left, I started having sexual relations with her, well, shall I say, she started having sexual relations with me. At first it made me nervous and only happened on nights she came home drunk, but then we fell in love. My sister hated me for it. She tolerated it because I'm her brother but hardly ever said a word to Maggie. Right before I turned fourteen, Maggie became pregnant."

Murphy moves around uncomfortably in her chair, listening intently. "You have a child?"

"Yes. Jacob. Fine young man," he proudly says.

"Where's your son now?"

"Should be working. He lives with me, he's twenty-two."

Murphy looks at the paper to confirm his age and sees he's only thirty-six. "What exactly happened? How did you end up in jail?"

"My sister told me my mom had a conversation with her the night before she left," he says, again dodging the question as to why he went to prison. "She told me Mom told her I wasn't hers, that I was adopted. I know she was frustrated seeing me with Maggie but those words really hurt. She'd go off until the wee hours of the night with friends just to be spiteful and I always worried. She was forced to tend to my son when I was jailed and did a great job with him, probably better than I would have. She was only fourteen and cared for him until I came out. Haven't seen her since a year after I came home.

Murphy sees he keeps dodging the question and asks again.

"She didn't make it," he says, again ignoring the question.

"Who didn't make what?"

"She died while giving birth to Jacob. We had a hard time getting proper care for her with the way things were."

"How does your son feel about it?"

"He doesn't know she died giving birth to him. He thinks she died of cancer," he says with a look of regret.

"Do you think lying to him is in his best interest?"

"No," he responds. "It kills me every day. I've been good at keeping things from him lately."

"What do you mean lately?"

"Nothing," he says. "I must have thought out loud again. I lost my mind when she died and couldn't take it. I became violent, and was jailed for minor offenses twice before the final time."

Murphy's heard a lot of different stories in the past, some are horrifying but this one's different. Most agents go to her office and show no feelings, but Mitchell is disparate. She senses he has a good heart and might be in the wrong line of work. She almost feels sorry for him, and struggles to imagine him hurting anyone. She figures she'll let the question go and hopes he makes it in for another sit-down so she can try and get it out of him.

"Tell me, Mitchell. Do you like what you do?"

"No, I don't like it. Most of our victims are children. It hurts to see their parents crying and begging for us to spare them. I used to have nightmares every night, but they went away. I Guess I'm used to it now. Can you do me a favor?"

"Depends."

"Do you know anyone who might be able to prove that Bette is my mom? My sister says she told her I was adopted, but that's impossible, I was born the year of the war and there haven't been adoptions since then. It's been eating at me through the years and I really need to know she's my mother."

"Sure, I know someone right here in this building. If you give me a second, I'll grab a kit then stop by his office and drop it off, should have the results by next week. Look, from the sounds of it, I'm sure she's your mom and I'm sure she loved you as much as you've told me you loved her. I will try and track her down for you, but can't promise any results."

"That would be great," says Mitchell, while shaking his leg in anxiousness...

After pricking him with a small needle, she announces the time is up and gives him her business card. "Hope to see you again, Mitchell," she says with a smile.

"You will, and I can't wait. I might be able to put this all behind me. I really feel in my heart she's my mother."

"I'm sure she is," she says as he walks out...

~Chapter Five~

Brianna

Brianna's been rummaging through the streets for two days now. She managed to escape out the back when locals rushed into Dorothy's house to see what the loud bang was. She has the baby bundled up and hanging off of her chest on a harness, with a jacket over him, causing her to appear impregnated. The only people she has to worry about are F.F.A. agents, there are no local authorities. F.F.A. agents tend to pull over and scan any Illegal Resident they happen to see, so she's being careful, but doesn't know where to go. She cannot turn to the child's dad, because he told her that if she ever became pregnant she had to stay away. He doesn't even know he has a son, she took off before she informed him of the pregnancy.

She sees Doctor Gus's Office from across the street but con-templates going there. She remembers how he reacted when an Illegal Resident showed up unexpectedly while she was giving birth. The baby has taken a toll on her back, he's very heavy and unusually big to be four months old. She decides to cross the street, but notices a car slowly driving by. She ducks between parked cars and it seems they didn't notice her, because they continue driving. As a precaution, she stays there for a couple of minutes. She stands and slowly jogs across the street while clutching the baby's back and pulling him closer against her chest. She lightly taps on his door and sees her reflection in the glass. *"Maybe the soft tap will give him a different reaction when he opens,"* she thinks.

"Who is it?" he asks. He peels the blinds hanging inside to peek out. She hears the key turn and is relieved he hasn't started yelling. "It's you," he mysteriously whispers when he opens the door. He looks over her shoulder to make sure no-one sees her enter. "Come inside," he says. He grabs her by the shoulder and pulls her in. "Follow me."

He takes her to the lower level, which is the same place he took her when she gave birth. "How's the child?" he asks.

"He's fine," she responds. She begins to remove the jacket and release the straps that tie her child on.

As they enter his laboratory, Brianna notices two Illegal Residents who look like they're ready to give birth. "Why are you doing this to us!?" she shouts. She places the baby in a bassinet, then rushes over to his patients and tries to convince them that getting the vaccine is the best decision. She wants them to know that it's not worth running by repeatedly shouting it.

"What are you talking about?" asks Gus. "I inject all of my babies. These here," he says while pointing to the patients. "Are young women that don't have the luxury of giving birth in a government hospital. Do you think they'd let me operate here if I wasn't injecting the babies? These young women can't afford it, so I do it for free."

"Wha... what!? Why didn't you inject mine?"

"I did," he says.

This confuses Brianna, and makes her wonder why Mrs. Cryan would tell her to hide. "It can't be. I know you didn't."

Gus opens a drawer on his desk and pulls out a scanner, then walks to the baby and grabs his little arm. He scans his chip and shows Brianna the indication he's been vaccinated. She sits in a chair nearby and cups her face with her hands.

"This doesn't make sense," she says. "Why did Mrs. Cryan?"

"Blow her head off?"

Brianna feels offended by the remark and doesn't hide it. "That is not what I meant!" she shouts. "Why did she make me hide? How dare you! Can you be a bit more sensitive, please!"

"I'm sorry, but it had to happen. Mrs. Cryan said she would when she found him. I didn't know until about a week ago, that a baby that survives the thirty-minute mark would show to be vaccinated, so I'm guessing that's why she told you to hide."

"Found who? What thirty-minute mark? What are you talking about?"

"You need some sleep, hun. There's a room right over there," he says while pointing to a door on the side of his lab. "Take a shower, get comfortable, and let me finish my work here. We'll talk first thing in the morning. I swear to tell you everything and believe me, you want to know."

Brianna's shocked when she wakes up the next morning and looks toward the bassinet. She sees the baby sitting up with a thumb in his mouth. *"How?"* she wonders. *"He's only four months, there's no way he could have the strength to sit up yet."* She walks over to him, slowly and in amazement. He steadily follows her every step with his big hazel eyes. Brianna rushes out of the room and shouts for Dr. Gus, but her voice only echos through the lab.

"What is it?" he yells, while coming half way down the stairs.

"Hurry! Come here!" she shouts.

Dr. Gus tries to hurry, but struggles with each step. He's a heavy-set older gentleman that uses the assistance of a cane to navigate around.

Upon entering, Dr. Gus is surprised. *"No way,"* he thinks to himself.

"How is this possible?" asks Brianna.

"How did she...?"

"How did she what!?" she yells. "What are you not telling me?"

"I have to run some test on him," he exuberantly says while grabbing the baby.

"Tests for what?" she demands to know.

After sedating him, Dr. Gus grabs a small glass slab and puts a drop of the baby's blood on it. He hobbles over with Brianna close behind, following his every step, while anxious for answers. There's a baby on a bassinet nearby that appears to be sleeping. Brianna figures one of the patients had given birth overnight, and the baby's down there to get the chip implanted and injected with the HNC vaccine. She's too anxious to ask questions and watches as Dr. Gus looks through the microscope. He jolts back after taking a peep, and almost falls off of the stool that looks way too little to hold him up.

"What is it?" she impatiently asks.

"Your baby is special," he says with a huge grin on his face.

Brianna looks at him and thinks he's lost it.

"We need to talk."

"Yea, I know," she hurriedly responds.

"OK. I'm going to talk and you're going to listen," he says, wanting verification that she understood. "OK?"

"OK," she agrees.

"Dorothy was a very nice lady. She's done a lot to help a lot of people throughout the years but has never been the same since her husband died. Your child was the eleventh kid she'd sent me with specific instructions. She was somehow convinced there will be a child born that'll change the world as we know it. She's been sending me them with the promise that I'll wait at least thirty-four minutes on the one's she handpicks before I inject them, and unfortunately, yours was the only one who made it. Well, he was the second one, but the first one was termed a couple of days ago, and she didn't send me that one, it was years ago. I tried to tell her about that child but she didn't think it was possible for the child to have been born yet.

Brianna's puzzled. "Why would she...?"

"Shhhh," he says. "She read a lot into a Prophet from the 1600's. He's predicted everything that's happened, except, he predicted it really didn't happen. According to him, the force of the world would pull this off to distract the people. I'm not sure what he meant by that, because the world is real and it's all really occurred. She was a very spiritual woman who didn't give up, she sent me countless kids. Most were to be given the vaccine the normal way, but the ones that were hand pick- ed by her, with them, I had to wait thirty-four minutes. It took a toll on her, having the blood of all those children on her hands really messed her up. She told me this was her calling in the world, and that once she finds him, she'd take her own life as payment to God. She was con- vinced this was his work and she'll be let into his kingdom for doing so. The prophet said in a dialogue, that there will be a baby born that'll reject the mark of the beast after the time has expired. No-one ever knew what he meant and many skeptics tried to debunk the theory. She figured that's what he implied when Fred told her about the time limit on the vaccine.

"I don't understand. Why thirty-four minutes?"

"A baby is not supposed to survive if you inject them thirty mi- nutes after they're born. The only way the vaccine is effective, is if it's done within thirty minutes of time of birth. If not, they'd go around injecting all Illegal Residents."

It makes sense to her. "So why use my baby as a test subject?"

"You don't understand. She felt a weird connection to your child, told me the Lord himself told her it was him. She knew it. She some- how felt it and it looks like she was right. It's unheard of for a child to survive it, let me show you." Dr. Gus goes over to the bassinet. He wakes the sleeping baby up, then sticks him with a needle.

"This baby was born an hour ago," he says as the needle enters.

"NO...!" tries Brianna. But it's too late, she watches as the baby takes his final breath which happens almost immediately.

"You killed him...! What...!?"

"Don't worry, child," he says. He adjusts his glasses by pushing the middle of them back with a finger.

"Oh my God! What is wrong with you!?"

"His mother didn't make it," he says. "Her blood pressure rose too high and she fell into cardiac arrest while giving birth. She had no-one I could take him to, said her entire family was termed."

"Did you have to kill him!?"

"I really didn't have to," he says, and shrugs his shoulders. "I suppose I could have let him survive to be hunted down."

Phillips, Mitchell, Brown, and Moore, are commanded by Mr. Goodman to make their rounds and go check up on Dr. Gus. He sends agents every month to check on him and make sure he's not into any funny business.

"What now?" asks Brianna, while biting her nails in nervousness.

"I'm going to run more test on him, and if it's what I think, you must try your best to make it to the Fort immediately.

"What's the Fort?"

"It's about eighty miles southeast from here. It'll be a rough and dangerous journey, but you have to try your best to make it there."

He draws more blood and takes a look at a new drop. "Unbelievable," he says. "He's growing at rapid speeds, two to three times faster than an average human."

"What?"

"This is amazing. You have to make it there, they'll know what to do."

The Fort is a small town on the foot of a mountain that's really well protected and not even the F.F.A. attempt to enter anymore. Their leader is Leon Wang, he's an Illegal Resident of Chinese descent that watched as his parents and little brother were slaughtered. He claims an F.F.A. agent spared him and let him run out of a back door. He's never speculated on who it was, but says he owes him his life. Since the attack, he's dedicated himself to protecting all Illegal Residents of all nationalities. He started countless protest movements against the government, but like all others, stopped after years of trying. He's set up this Fort and allows any Illegal Resident to enter, granted they follow rules. Wang has a cool and collected demeanor, but gets really riled up when it comes to politics. He's dared the government to strike his Fort down with their satellite beams or bomb loaded warplanes, but they've not obliged. Wang has also read the words of the infamous Prophet, and he also believes.

"Right now he has the strength of a one-year-old, and it doesn't make sense. I have to scan his brain if you don't mind." Dr. Gus grabs an instrument that sorta looks like a blow dryer, puts it aimed at the baby's forehead, and holds it there for about ten seconds. It prints out a tiny paper that he struggles to read. Seems the baby has a pea sized growth on the left side of his brain but Dr. Gus doesn't have the medical equipment needed to look more into it. This stuns him. *"What can it be,"* he wonders. He looks at the baby in disbelief, the child looks almost too big for the bassinet.

Dr. Gus hears someone at the door and dreads having to walk all the way upstairs. With no choice, he makes his way up. Brianna takes a peek into the microscope when he finally makes it to the top. She sees her son's blood has little specs of semen like cells that eat each other up repeatedly, until they become big, they then break up and re-peat the process. *"Is this normal?"* she wonders. She hears a com-motion and is surprised at the men rushing into the lab. She recognizes their voices and knows this is bad, but feels the comfort of knowing her son's been vaccinated. The last one to enter is Mitchell, he takes it slow as he walks behind Dr. Gus.

"Hello, cutie," says Agent Brown as he approaches Brianna. He grabs her hand and kisses it.

"Enough, you pig," Phillips meanly says.

"What are y'all doing here?" Gus demands to know. "Agents were here just four days ago."

Mitchell freezes when he sees Brianna, but she hasn't seen him yet. Brown has her nerves racking, she recognizes his voice and remembers how mean he is. Brianna looks across the room and finally sees Mitchell. He hopes she stays calm and doesn't give in to Phillips once he starts his charades. The baby has sat up and has turned around in the sitting position, his big hazel eyes making contact with that of Mitchell's.

"Weird looking baby. Isn't he too big for this crib?" says Phillips, while walking toward the bassinet and pulling the scanner out his blazer's right pocket.

Mitchell's concerned. He's sure beyond a doubt that the baby isn't vaccinated and a term is about to take place. He thinks about stopping Phillips, but knows he can't.

Phillips has a weird feeling as he approaches the baby. He feels very lightheaded and struggles to keep his balance.

"Are you alright?" asks Mitchell. He goes over to give him a hand.

Gus and Brianna look at each other and Mitchell notices. Phillips scans the baby and verifies he's been vaccinated. Mitchell is shocked, and wonders why Brianna was hiding that night.

Agent Brown turns his attention to the dead baby in the other bassinet. "What's happened here?" he asks, while looking in Gus's direction.

"The poor thing didn't make it," he replies, hoping he doesn't ask for details.

"What do you mean he didn't make it?"

"I didn't inject him in time."

Mitchell's feeling quite uncomfortable. The baby stares at him as if he's the only one in the room, and doesn't take his eyes off of him.

"Sounds to me like you're following that wonton eating fool's words," says Phillips. All agents hate Wang, many have tried to penetrate the Fort and have all failed. The border to the place is heavily guarded, no-one has ever even made it to the entrance.

"You really believe a child will be born that stops this?"

"No. I didn't intentionally do it," replies Gus.

Brianna and Mitchell notice the baby has fallen back, almost as if he has fainted. Brianna runs toward him, making Phillips flinch and reach for his gun. He watches as Brianna tends to the baby and has a weird thought.

"Maybe that baby has survived it," he says, while looking toward Brianna who's tending to him.

"Come on, boss, you've scanned him," says Mitchell, hoping Phillips doesn't do what he thinks he's about to do.

Phillips pulls out his gun and walks toward the bassinet.

Agent Moore is busy walking around and happens to look into the microscope. *"That's weird,"* he wonders. He opens drawers, hoping to find something interesting.

"Why shouldn't I kill them?" Phillips demands, while pointing the gun at the baby. Brianna's hysterically crying, pleading for Phillips to leave them alone, then sees the baby open his eyes.

Dr. Gus's a few steps away and is shaking. He's heard stories of terms but never thought he'd be part of one.

"It'll be a waste, boss," replies Mitchell, knowing there's no hope. He's seen this look in Phillips's eyes and it never goes well.

Brianna weirdly walks away from the bassinet and stands next to Gus. She's in a trance-like form but smells the stench produced by

Gus's defecation, he's so afraid he's excreted on himself.

Mitchell doesn't know if he should forcefully stop Phillips, but would never dare to anyway. Phillips looks at Brianna and can't believe how calm she's become. He looks back into the bassinet and sees the baby laying on his back, wide eyed, steadily staring at him. Phillips tries to pull the trigger but can't, it hurts every time he attempts to pull it. He oddly puts the gun down and stares at the child. After around thirty seconds, he declares it's time to go. Brown's already waiting by the steps with two fingers pinching his nose.

Mitchell passes by the bassinet to peek inside on his way out, and notices the baby is sound asleep. He can't believe what's just happened. He has never seen Phillips spare anyone.

As soon as they exit the front door, Phillips becomes irate. He grabs Mitchell by the front of his blazer and slams him into the brick wall. "Don't you ever question me again!" he shouts. He pulls him a bit, only to slam him into it again.

Mitchell swipes his arms down to break his hold and grabs him with the same technique. He spins him around and slams him into the same wall. "Let me tell you something!" he yells in his face. "Don't you ever cross this line with me again!" he angrily shouts. "Show me the same respect I show you. Don't you ever put your hands on me again!"

Moore and Brown are shocked. No-one has ever roughed Phillips up like this.

"ENOUGH!" shouts Brown. Mitchell releases his grip, only to get a left hook landed by Phillips across the face. The force buckles him but he's able to stay on his feet. Brown and Moore immediately get in between them, each holds one back.

"I will kill you!" shouts Phillips, while wildly swinging his arms to get out of Moore's grasp, trying to get at Mitchell.

Inside, Dr. Gus excuses himself to go clean up.

Brianna's tending to the baby. She's crouched over the bassinet doing everything possible to ensure he's as comfortable as can be.

"Did you see that?" she hears, with Gus's voice getting louder the closer he comes. "That was incredible!"

"What? What are you talking about?"

"Come on now, you can't turn a blind eye to that. Your son's powers protected us from being savagely murdered. *'Excuse me by the way for my accident.'* I believe it was the baby who made that agent unable to shoot."

"You're crazy. How can it be possible for him to make him unable to shoot? Maybe he just grew a heart."

"No, they don't spare anyone, especially those four. Something weird happened here today and I hope by the grace of God that the little man here had something to do with it. You need to get him to the Fort and you need to do it now. In fact, give me a couple of days and I'll get you there myself. You can stay here in the meantime, they won't be back."

Brown jumps in the driver's seat and they head back to the agency. Phillips is still bothered by the lack of respect he feels Mitchell has shown. Mitchell's cool, he doesn't seem to be stressing it too much.

"Jesus Christ," says Moore. "You guys are worse than two broads on their rags."

Phillips gives him the usual look through the mirror.

"Come on, man, I'm joking. I'm just trying to get the spirit up in here."

"Do not say that name again," Phillips demands.

"What name? Jesus Christ? Oh yeah, I forgot. You don't believe in him."

"I don't!" he aggressively states. "And you shouldn't either."

"OK, so explain. You don't believe in God, but you so call claim you feel people's souls pass through you?"

Mitchell's never heard it put that way before and agrees that he has a point. Brown's attentively listening while driving and can't believe Moore is questioning Phillips. Moore is only doing it because he senses Phillips's vulnerability after getting roughed up by Mitchell.

"I just do," he says, while looking at the back of the car that's ahead of them. "I just do..."

~*Chapter Six*~

Sophia

Sophia's hungry and dehydrated. She took off from her house the day after her family was slaughtered. She hurried to cut the thread that prevented her eyes from closing as soon as Phillips left the house. She sat there staring at her family members bodies, until she fell asleep and awoke the next morning only to realize the nightmare she wished she dreamt, was real. She didn't want to live anymore, she wanted to be with her family. She remembers looking down in pure horror and sobbing at the sight of them dead on the floor. On the way out the back, she almost tripped over two bodies that were sprawled right outside the back door, but couldn't recognize them.

She purposelessly walks around the streets that are littered with debris and has nowhere to go. She walks along a block of houses that have all been burned down, and never rebuilt. The wind blows litter into her feet as she slowly walks. She has no strength, she has no determination, she wishes they had killed her. She hasn't eaten for three days and feels very woozy. All of a sudden, she catches a headache so bad it drops her to her knees and she passes out.

She awakes to the smell of something cooking and realizes it's daylight when she looks toward a window. The last thing she remembers, is staring straight ahead into a dark street that seemed to stretch into nowhere. She looks down and sees there's a needle in her arm, with a tube connected to it that snakes all the way up to a bag full of fluid that hangs above her. She snatches the needle out, rolls off of the bed and onto the floor. As she gets closer to the door, she hears voices that come from the other room. She gently opens it to peek out, and out of nowhere, a small boy appears in the crack from the other side.

"BOO!" she hears the boy say, making her flinch so hard she takes a step back and falls onto her butt. "She's awake, Mommy!" she hears the boy yell.

A lady walks into the room who appears to be around her mom's age. "How are you, honey?" asks the lady. She outstretches her arm to help her up.

Sophia denies her hand and gets up on her own. She notices the house is very neat, and the child that scared her is standing behind the woman, shyly shielding himself with her leg. "Where am I?" she asks.

"We found you passed out in the middle of the road on our way home last night," responds the lady. "You must be careful, we could have run you over. Come on," she urges her. "You need something to eat."

Sophia's hesitant but her hunger makes her agree. She walks out behind the lady and kid who keeps looking back at her. She approaches the table, and notices six plates have been prepared.

"Sit down, honey," says the lady. She pulls out a seat that Sophia climbs on.

Sophia looks at the food and can barely resist the temptation of grabbing the big chicken leg that's still steaming.

"Dinner's ready!" the lady shouts.

Sophia hears people coming down the stairs. The first to enter is Amanda, who's around Sophia's age. She looks at Sophia and rolls her eyes, then sits at the table and completely ignores the fact a strange face sits across from her. Sophia feels awkward and doesn't know if she should introduce herself.

Gabriel follows, he's around fifteen years old. He immediately sits in the seat next to Sophia's and starts a conversation with her.

"My name is Gabriel," he tells her, and stretches out his hand.

Sophia looks at it but doesn't shake it. She's starving and just wants them to hurry up so she could eat.

"I'm Robbie," says the little boy, as he sits at his tiny table on a chair that's perfectly sized for him.

She looks at him and thinks of her brother Roberto. They all sit and wait. She's sure there are two people remaining considering the amount of plates.

"Dinner's ready!" shouts the lady again, this time with a much-aggravated tone. She slams a spatula down against the table, making Sophia flinch. "I'm Sorry, Hun," she says, which causes Amanda to smirk.

Amanda's the thirteen-year-old daughter who's at the age where she thinks the world revolves around her, she has a really snobby attitude that really irks Gabriel.

Finally, Sophia hears someone coming down. She counts the number of steps the person takes in her mind with the anticipation of finally being able to eat. It's the woman's husband Richard. He walks in with a smile and immediately turns his attention toward Sophia.

"How are you, honey?" he asks. "My name is Richard. I'm sure you've met my wife Lucy, my daughter Amanda," he says, while pointing toward her. "And my son Gabriel. The little fella over there is Robbie."

Sophia looks at the woman who doesn't seem to be happy.

"Where is she?" asks Lucy.

"She'll be down," he responds. "Give her a minute."

He focuses his attention back to Sophia. She watches as Amanda gets up, lifts her chair a little before plopping it down, after moving a couple of inches away from Richard. Sophia hears someone else coming down the stairs and is finally ready to eat. She looks at the girl that's walking toward the table and sees she's an Illegal Resident. Here she is, sitting at a table with a family of white Americans, and there enters a girl that doesn't seem to belong there. The girl is clutching a teddy bear close to her chest and has a look of concern on her face. Sophia feels a little more comfortable, she realizes she isn't the only Illegal Resident. The girl sits on the only empty chair which is between Amanda, and Lucy. Amanda cuts her eyes, and gets up to move her chair away from her, but back closer to her father.

"You're such a little brat," Gabriel says over the table, causing Amanda to stick her middle finger up.

"Have manners, young lady!" shouts Lucy.

"Tell him to leave me alone!" she responds with a disrespectful attitude.

Lucy outstretches her hands to grab both Gabriel's, and the little girl's. Gabriel outstretches his to grab Sophia's, but she's hesitant. She looks across the table and sees Amanda's also not offering her hands. The girl usually sits in the seat Sophia's in, and Amanda doesn't want to touch her.

"Must we go through this every single night," Amanda snottily says. She extends her hands and grabs Richard's, and the girl's. "Any day now!" she shouts at Sophia with a look of disgust.

Sophia grabs Gabriel's, and Richard's hands. She watches them all bow their heads, then bows her own.

"Thank you, Lord, for the food you provided my family here today. May the world become a better place for everyone, and may you guide us in finding this child's family. Amen," says Lucy.

"Amen," they all say at once.

They all stop and look at Sophia.

She immediately grabs the chicken leg and starts chomping on it. With the chicken juices coating her fingers, she continues to eat until she hits the bone. She notices the tranquility in the room and turns her eyes up when she feels them looking at her.

"Slow down," says Amanda. "It's not going to fly away."

"Let her be," says Richard. "The poor thing is hungry."

"So what's your name, and where are you from?" asks Lucy.

Sophia's hesitant to answer. She continues to eat while thinking of what to say.

"My name is So... Sonia. I roamed away from my family at the market and lost them."

"Are you Mexican?" asks Amanda from across the table, while smirking from ear to ear. "Do you speak Spanish?"

"No! I'm American, but my family is from Puerto Rico," Sophia snaps back. "And yes, I speak Spanish."

"We'll help you find your parents," Lucy sincerely says.

"We sure will," says Richard.

Richard's finished eating and declares he'll go upstairs to shower and hit the bed. He stands and pauses a second to look at the little girl until she gives him eye contact. He then walks off. Amanda looks at Lucy to see if she'd seen the look Richard just gave the girl. She feels a sense of alleviation when she notices her mom noticed the look. Lucy looks down at her plate and slowly chews the food in her mouth. She wipes her lips with the rag on her lap and announces she's done, and takes off after Richard. Sophia misses it all, she's too busy eating her food. Robbie's on his table playing with the noodles that were served with the chicken. He gets up and runs across the kitchen, headed toward the stairs.

"What time is it?" Sophia asks Gabriel.

"It's seven," he says. "Why?"

"Why does your dad go to bed so early?"

"Because of his dirty perversions!" yells Amanda. She aggressively gets up and stomps her way up the stairs.

Sophia looks at the girl who sits across the table.

"Don't listen to her," says Gabriel, referring to Amanda. "She's a snot-nose."

Amanda doesn't like her father. She's claimed to her mother in the past that he's said inappropriate things to her, but her mother has brushed her off. She cannot believe the man she married would be capable of such a thing. Although he's never touched her in a sexual way, she's always felt uncomfortable around him. It's a feeling she has, he's looked at her in ways that have made her feel very uncomfortable. The comments and looks stopped about a year ago, but Amanda still remembers and doesn't trust him. She has slept with her bedroom door locked for as long as she could remember, and could swear on a few separate occasions, she's seen her doorknob slowly turn only for the person on the other side to realize it was locked.

"You got somewhere to go?" Gabriel asks Sophia.

Sophia doesn't know how to answer. She must have forgotten she asked for the time and cannot think of anywhere else she could go.

"You just asked me the time," he says and chuckles. "So I asked if you got somewhere to go. It's a joke."

Sophia doesn't find it humorous and continues to stare at the girl. "What's your name?" she asks. The girl stares into her plate.

"Her name is Patrice," answers Gabriel. "She doesn't speak much."

"Can I see your teddy bear?"

Patrice hesitantly passes it.

"I had one just like this," Sophia tells her.

"I'm going to hang out in the living room," Gabriel tells the girls as he begins to walk away. "Y'all are welcome to join me."

Patrice looks back at him. She always navigates to him when he's around, he's the only one she feels a sense of comfort with. She looks at Sophia and sees she has her teddy bear sitting on the table with its back leaned against a cup of water.

"You want him back?" Sophia asks.

Patrice nods her head to notify Sophia she does.

"OK then, tell me how old you are."

"I'm eight," Patrice cheerily replies with a big smile on her face. Patrice's an eight-year-old tanned skinned child. She's the product of a gang rape inflicted on her mom who's of Haitian descent. Her house was raided by F.F.A. agents a little under nine years ago. They entered the house looking for an Escaped Illegal Resident, but didn't find any. Her mom was a full figured, sexy Haitian woman who caught the attention of the agents. They repeatedly raped and beat her over the course of a six-hour period while her son and husband were bound and forced to watch. They ravaged her over and over, causing her to get pregnant with Patrice. After the assault, her husband fled, he could not get himself to touch her again. Their son was murdered as a warning for them to keep their mouths shut. The agency eventually found out, and each agent was poisoned. Not for the brutal nature of the attack, but because their commander was disgusted that they'd even touch an Illegal Resident in a sexual manner. Patrice was a constant reminder to her mom every time she looked at her. She's the cause of her life being torn apart and couldn't handle it. She drove her to a far away market around one year ago, left her there and took off. Patrice was picked up by Richard, who searched the entire market looking for her parents.

"Do you like it here?"

"A little. They cut my hair," she says, and looks to get sad. Patrice has really short hair, it's fluffy and resembles a little Afro. "It was so long," she mumbles.

"It'll grow back," says Sophia, while passing her the teddy bear.

Sophia notices from the kitchen that Gabriel's struggling with the television in the living room. He keeps tapping the sides of it as if that would make it work.

All of a sudden, Lucy comes back down. "Did you introduce yourself, honey?" she asks Patrice.

"Yes. I showed her my teddy bear."

"That's good. Why don't you ladies go sit in the living room with Gabriel so I can clean up in here."

Patrice slides off of the chair and lands on the floor. Sophia gets up, starts stacking the used dishes and sorting the utensils. Lucy sees this and feels appreciated. She's a really kind woman who tries with all of her might to keep her family intact. She's recently had her oldest daughter run off. Her daughter could not tolerate her father's ways, he's overly protective and doesn't let his kids have a social life. Her daughter left with no trace, and Lucy suffers every single day with the thought of not knowing her whereabouts.

"You don't have to," says Lucy, as she grabs the stack of plates. "Thank you, though. Go play."

At about 9 pm, Lucy comes back down, and notices Patrice had fallen asleep on the couch. She looks across and sees Gabriel and Sophia with their faces buried in books.

"Bedtime!" she states, making them break out of the trance they seemed to be in. Gabriel's always reading very sophisticated books. "Grab her," she tells him, referring to Patrice. Gabriel usually has to carry her to bed because she's always around him.

Lucy shows Sophia to her room.

She enters and notices a well-dressed bed with very clean sheets. The pillows look fluffy and the bed's positioned so you get the breeze from a window nearby. The walls are pink and there are stuffed animals everywhere. There's a closet with mirrored doors, and Sophia walks toward it to see her reflection.

"This is your room," says Lucy, as she begins to walk out. "Hope you like it."

Sophia sees Gabriel leave a room that's across from hers, meaning that's Patrice's, and slowly closes her door. She has a really weird feeling but goes over and sits on the bed. She lays back with her legs hanging off of it and falls into a deep sleep.

On the second day there, Sophia feels a lot less tense. All she's done is read books with Gabriel while cuddling with Patrice who's always nearby. Gabriel has her reading all sorts of weird stuff that are way beyond their years. Sophia doesn't have much interest, but it's the only thing she could do with Amanda only coming out of her room when it's time to eat.

"How do you like that book? Does it sound familiar?"

Sophia looks at him and doesn't know how to respond. She hasn't begun to read it.

"Whats going on in the world now," he says. "He's predicted all of this."

Sophia was apathetic and mostly attending to Patrice. "Predicted this...?"

"Yes. Some say the Fort is the place he refers to in one of his dialogues. Personally I think it's nonsense."

Sophia opens the book and begins to read.

"That was amazing," she says, after about two hours. Gabriel looks over and sees her shake her head as if she were trying to shake water off.

"You should read it entirely," he says.

Sophia looks over and sees Patrice has fallen asleep with her head resting on her leg. "I did," she responds, while trying to gently move without waking her. "The part about the child is interesting."

Gabriel's baffled. He's sure there's no way she could have read a five thousand page tome in two hours. He asks her every specific question he could think of regarding the book, and she answers every one in detail. He's sure she must have read it before. To him, it seemed she was sitting there shuffling through the pages as if they had pictures.

"You think the child has been born?" she asks.

"Don't be silly. I don't believe it."

"Even if he's been born, most likely he's the one that's born twelve years prior," Sophia states.

"What are you talking about?"

"According to him, there will be a child born twelve years before the baby he speaks of in the book, right? That child will only develop specific abilities and be very fastidious."

Confused, Gabriel begins to explain he's never heard of that, and tries to persuade her that the Prophet never said it.

"It's there, on page 2,482."

Gabriel quickly grabs the book and shuffles through the pages.

She's right, how could he have missed that, he had convinced himself he read the entire book.

"How could you? How did you read the book that quick? Say the truth, you've read it before, right?"

"No. I've read sixty-two books since I've been here," she says. "I don't know how I do it, I was never able to. I've always hated reading but can't get enough now. I can imagine the whole thing in my head, it feels like I'm inside the book. It's weird."

All along, Gabriel thought she grabbed different books because the previous one didn't interest her. He cannot believe she's able to read so fast. He asks her numerous questions about the books he's seen her with, and she answers every one precisely.

"You read it in two hours."

"Two hours? Seemed way longer than that," she says. "I have a headache. I'm going to lay down."

Sophia has a pounding headache that drops her to her knees when she enters her room. It's the worse headache she's ever had and it feels like her head will explode. She kneels in the middle of the room in agony, grabs her temples with her palms and feels like her head is being jack-hammered. She falls forward and lands face down, sprawled across the floor.

She awakes at three in the morning to the sound of footsteps in the hallway. She makes her way to the door, gently opens it to take a peek, and sees Richard coming up the hallway while looking over his shoulders. She watches as he gets very close to Patrice's door and grabs the knob. He stands there for five seconds before he finally twists. Sofia's petrified, *"What's going on?"* she asks herself. Richard opens Patrice's door just enough for him to fit through. He's being careful not to make a sound and closes it behind him. She contemplates barging out, to at least cause a distraction, when she hears a little scream followed by a muffing sound. She's not sure if it came from the room but figures she'll go for it. As she's about to jostle out, she notices Lucy rapidly walking up the hallway. She walks to Patrice's door and does the same exact thing Richard did. After pausing, she twists the knob but doesn't walk in. She stays there with the door cracked and peeks through it. That eases Sophia's mind, she was thinking the worse. For a second, she thought that maybe Richard was doing something to Patrice, but there's no way Lucy would stand there and let something like that happen.

"What an embarrassment that would've been," she says to herself.

Sophia opens her door again after thirty minutes. She sees that Lucy is still there peeking through the crack. All she could see is Lucy's back, all she discerns is her long, silk nightgown that was tied in the front when she passed by.

Richard finally leaves the room and is greeted by Lucy. He grabs her around the waist and gives her a long, deep kiss, before he turns her around. Sophia notices Lucy's gown is now open and her breasts are exposed.

"Maybe he read her a story," she says to herself.

Sophia doesn't want to take the chance. She sticks her head out and looks down the hallway. When she's sure they're gone, she creeps across the tiled floor, gets to Patrice's door and lets herself in. She enters and sees Patrice move then stay still. She approaches her bed, but it seems she's sound asleep. She shakes her and tells her she knows she's awake, so she can stop acting.

"What are you doing here," she asks.

"What just happened? Did he touch you?"

"Who?" she responds.

"You know who. Richard!" she says, while grabbing her by the arms. "Did he touch you?"

"No. He read me a bedtime story."

Sophia has doubts because Patrice's acting unusually tense, but there seems to be nothing physically wrong with her. "Why at this time?" she asks.

"I Couldn't sleep."

The next morning, Sophia awakes to Richard standing in front of her bed. She pops up and shuffles her legs, trying to move backward in the sitting position until the headboard stops her. "What do you want?" she asks as her heart rapidly beats.

"I don't allow this," he says, while pointing to Patrice who's laying next to her. "Everyone has their own room for a reason. Time to get up, breakfast is ready."

Sofia had convinced Patrice to come lay with her for the rest of the night, despite Patrice telling her it could get her into trouble. If that was allowed, she'd sleep in Gabriel's room, even if it meant she had to sleep on the floor.

Before going down for breakfast, Sophia grabs Patrice and stands her to face eye to eye. She knows Patrice is hiding something, she could feel it. She assures her she could feel comfortable in confiding in her and begs to know what happened. "Did he touch you?"

Patrice bows her head, and Sophia's heart is pumping.

"No," she replies, with tears filling her eyes.

"What's wrong? What did he do? He touched you, didn't he?"

With her head bowed, she nods to assure her he didn't. "He touches himself and makes me watch," she says.

Sophia's flabbergasted. "But, but." She wants to know the details, but doesn't want her to have to relive it. "But Lucy was there!" she blurts out.

"She always stands there when he comes into my room," she says with her head still bowed. "He makes me smile at her, says it makes her happy."

"Has he ever touched you!?" Sophia asks, while intently waiting for an answer.

"Only when he's drunk. He'll cover my mouth and tell me to make noises while he touches himself."

"Oh my God," Sophia thinks to herself. She has to get her out of there and knows it.

"Do you know where the Fort is?" Sophia asks Gabriel later that evening.

"It's southeast from here," he says. "Around eighty or ninety miles. You're not thinking of going, are you? It's a trap. Don't do it, Sonia. The place doesn't exist."

"My father always said the same thing, *'It's fake, it doesn't exist,'* I personally believe it's worth going."

"You're crazy," he replies. "You'll never make it. You have to pass those high-end neighborhoods where residents are far from friendly. They actually agree with what the government has done and don't rely on F.F.A. Agents. They take matters into their own hands."

Sophia looks intent.

"Don't do it, Sonia," says Gabriel.

"It's Sophia..." she says. "I'm going to the Fort and I'm taking Patrice with me..."

~*Chapter Seven*~

President Thump

"We have to get out of here!" says Agent Scott, as he barges into the oval office, on November 28th, 2023. President Thump's sitting at his desk having a chat with someone Scott has never seen. "We have to go!" he shouts. Thump looks at the gentleman sitting on the other side of his desk. "Guess it's time to go," he tells him. The gentleman gets up and heads toward the door.

Scott looks as Thump takes his time. After getting up, he slowly starts adjusting his tie. "We have to go," he stresses.

"It's not that big a deal, son, we're secure," he says. Thump's bothered about something and doesn't want to leave the white house. He's just passed the harshest law in the history of mankind, yet doesn't fear for his safety. Thump's three years removed from coming out of an underground bunker. He'd given the military full control when he declared Marshall law, but took it back only four years into the war. The military was to only deal with the general public.

There's a special department of Soldiers that handle matters such as a nuclear bomb. This department is the N.A.A. (National Atomic Agency). They're the ones who operate the satellites we have that rain fire.

"Sir, we have to go!" Scott says again, while looking back at his men who are waiting to escort the President to the helicopter. "They're making their way through the gates and we can no longer hold them back."

Large crowds of protesters have gathered at the white house gates. They came out in droves when he passed the law for all Illegal Residents to be injected with the HNC vaccine.

"They've just penetrated the gates!" one agent shouts. Scott grabs Thump by the arm and forcefully drags him out. They head up to the top level where a helicopter waits with the propeller buzzing, ready to go.

As the chopper hovers before taking off, Thump looks down. He had no idea of the severity of the matter until he sees how many people are running across the front lawn. The white house has been taken over by citizens and Thump has to be flown to an undisclosed location.

Thump is a sixty-two-year-old man who grew up around politics. He watched as his father became vice President of the country and have always dreamt of making it all the way to the top. He often ran his father's campaigns and was determined to become President of this country. He's developed the attitude to do so throughout his life, and has made a lot of enemies along the way. He's a very aggressive man with a balding head that has hair only on its sides.

Government facilities are up to date with everything, they've even developed gadgets that only government personnel, and anyone that's wealthy know exist. They've made strides in manufacturing everything they need for a future with no Illegal Residents. Thump enters his office and is satisfied. It's no white house, but he could make it work until they can figure things out. He knows he has a challenge ahead but will not give in when it comes to the vaccine.

"Where are we?" he asks Scott.

"We're at the N.A.A. headquarters, sir."

"Good. I need you to hurry and get Lieutenant Weinberg up here, immediately!"

"Yes, sir," says Scott, as he hurries toward the door.

Thump enters an adjacent room that'll serve as his sleeping quarters and is delighted when he walks in. He loves the king size bed they've prepared and the lighting's perfect. He walks over and enters another room. It's a bathroom with a sink bigger than most people's bathtub. *"I'm going to love this,"* he says to himself. He rubs the tips of his fingers against the shiny tiled wall, making it screech. *"This place is spotless,"* he thinks.

He walks back out and realizes the Lieutenant has arrived.

Weinberg stands in salute while he walks in, and Scott is given a look by Thump that suggests he needs to leave the room.

"Sit down," says Thump. He lights a cigar.

Weinberg lifts his pants around the thigh area and has a seat.

"Is this under control?" he asks, referring to the countless people that have gathered at all government facilities to protest the vaccine.

Weinberg looks at him as if he has something to say but instead nods his head in agreement. Thump notices, but doesn't want him to elaborate. He doesn't care what he has to say.

"It better be," he says, then blows smoke into the air.

Weinberg can't hold back. "How can you do this!? You cannot.!"

"I can do anything I want," Thump interrupts. "You know what these people did when the bomb went off, you seen. You were the ones patrolling the streets and they beat you!" he angrily says. "They destroyed this country. You think I want someone fighting for me that got beat by ordinary people?"

"In war we use guns," Weinberg snaps back. "How could we win, when we were outnumbered one thousand to one and couldn't use firearms?"

"I gave you permission to use guns," says Thump, while slamming a finger onto the table to get his point across.

"No. You gave permission to use guns on Illegal Residents. You specifically told me that we are not to shoot at our own people, but could shoot at Illegal Residents at will. Let me reiterate. You told me we could shoot at minorities at will, you have not come up with the term *'Illegal Residents'* yet! This is bad, Ronald, you better not do this. Things will get out of line."

"I said no such thing," says Thump.

Weinberg's shocked. He cannot believe Thump just denied saying it. *"With the world the way it is, why would he deny it. Why would he even care?"* he wonders.

Weinberg's a tall older gentleman with a thick white mustache. He was the military commander when all hell broke loose. He was given full control when it was determined it'd be best for Thump to go into hiding. Although Thump had everything he needed in the bunker to lead the war, they thought it'd be best for Weinberg to take control. With strict rules, and authority only on our land, Weinberg did the best he could. Most of his soldiers decided they'd take the chance of being deemed deserters and went off to be with their families.

"SCOTT!" shouts Thump.

Scott comes barging in, the way Thump yells makes him think something's wrong.

"Disarm this gentleman and escort him out of the building," he says. "I relieve you of your duties, Lieutenant Weinberg. You are no longer needed."

Thump has alienated everyone. He was questionably elected President in 1998, and the first thing he attempted was to stop the voting process. His team consists of very few people. He relieved all branches of the government and has formed an oligarchy with the few he associates with.

"You can't... Get off of me!" Weinberg tells Scott while shoving his arm away. "You will not get away with this," he says as he places his gun and badge on the desk. "I will make sure of it."

As they exit the room, Scott looks back at Thump and gets eye contact. Thump bows his head while looking him in the eyes, silently commanding something.

Weinberg stares at the glowing numbers on the elevator as it gets lower and lower. They end up in the parking garage that's hidden under the building and only accessible to government employees. Weinberg slowly walks to his car with Scott right behind him. He's expecting to get his head shot off from behind. He figures Scott will wait until he gets in his car so decides to strike first. He swings an elbow, striking Scott between the nose and mouth. Scott takes a few steps back, feeling dazed, while holding his nose that's profusely bleeding. Weinberg charges him and unholsters his gun.

"Wait, wait," says Scott, as he lifts both hands that glimmer red with the blood that gushes out of his nose and covers them.

Weinberg pulls the trigger. The bullet strikes Scott right above his left eye, causing his lifeless body to drop on its back. He turns around, runs toward his car, and takes off with tires screeching.

Back at the office, Thump gets unwanted company.

Krystle Morris walks in demanding answers. "What the hell are you doing?" she aggressively asks.

Thump knows what she's asking but acts as if he has no idea what she's talking about. "What do you mean? What are you talking about?" he asks, and ignites the same cigar that had gone out.

"Why would you do this? Why would you...?"

"Why would I what!?" he shouts. "Get to the point!"

Krystle's a thirty-year-old black woman who was taken along when everyone scattered and went into hiding in bunkers. She's the daughter of the US justice at the time, who was a really good friend of Thump. He assisted in setting up several campaigns for Thump's father and has since died of natural causes.

"Why would you do this to our people?"

"I didn't do this to your people," he responds. "Your people did this to your people. When the war broke out, what did you all do? Instead of coming together, you decide to kill each other. This country didn't have to suffer the way it did."

Krystle's sadness turns into rage. She was given a position with the N.A.A. and have done very well while there. She overlooks the six men who control the satellites and keeps them in line. Thump had given her the job because of the bond he had with her father. He was one of a very few in the circle of people Thump associated with while rising in the political ranks.

"Are you insinuating that it was only our people? With all due respect, sir, there were all kinds of people out there," she says, while pointing with her hand toward nothing. "Including your kind."

She has a point and Thump knows it. When the bomb went off in New York City, it had a ripple effect throughout the entire country.

People in all walks of life lost their minds, everyone thought the worse. Everyone thought it was the end.

"When I say your people, I mean all immigrants," he says. "You all destroyed this country."

"You can't do this, sir," she says, with tears welling in her eyes. "Please," she pleads. "Do it for my father. He wouldn't want this."

"I'm going to tell you what I've told everyone that's begged me not to do it. It's done, there's no changing my mind. This is something that needs to happen. The people are hungry and will only get hungrier. I cannot take food out of the mouths of my fellow Americans to feed immigrants who don't belong in this country. I gave you all a chance to leave when this started, and I warned this would eventually happen. I even told your dad, I wish he was still alive so he could tell you. This is America, honey. I'm sorry."

Thump took control of the war after four years in the bunker. He was informed of everything that had happened on our streets and announced he wants everyone out. In his mind, he wants this country to be rich. He wants only one race to exist on our soil but plans to eventually get rid of anyone who is not wealthy.

"So you mean to tell me you're going to inject us all? How will you manage? Our people will fight back."

"No no no," he interrupts. "See, that's what's wrong with you people, you don't listen. Anyone who was born before today could have all the babies they want. Unfortunately though, your babies won't be having babies."

Krystle doesn't know whether she should be relieved, or ashamed of herself. Relieved because she can have the baby she and her husband have been trying to have, or ashamed for even thinking that. She's not happy with Thump and shows it as she stomps her way out of his office. There is only a handful of Illegal Residents that work for Thump, and they were all referred to him by Krystle's dad. They too have the luxury of saving their DD's like all government employees.

"Congratulations," everyone says to Thump as he walks down the hall. Word is, the first injection has been administered and he's proud. He's strolling by and wants to be seen, he loves the attention. As he's getting back to his office, he hears the elevator ring and something tells him to look back. He gets ecstatic when he sees his brother step out of it. They were both placed in different bunkers where neither knew where the other was. At the time of the attack, all politicians had to make it to the white house where there was a cabinet full of sealed envelopes. If an emergency were to occur, they had to select one and take off. In the envelope were their destinations, which mean that not two people knew the whereabouts of the other unless they were in the same bunker and only realized it when they got there. The politicians were allowed to take anyone along with them. The bunkers were so big, they could each easily house one thousand families and had everything they might need inside. They were built in case of a catastrophic event, and were meant to save only wealthy people.

"How the hell are you, bro?" says his brother. His brother was always the problem child, and although Thump got him into politics, it was a job he was neither good at nor qualified for.

"I'm good. When did you get out?" he asks, while giving him a handshake and hug. Thump's referring to the bunker he was in. "Let's go to my office, we have a lot of catching up to do."

They enter and Randy sits on Thump's seat. He starts spinning the chair half way around from side to side. "This is nothing like the white house," he says.

"Yea. I know. I miss it."

"OK, I need to know everything that went on," says Randy, as he gets up and helps himself to a drink. Randy had no idea what went on while he was in the bunker and didn't care. He lived a stress-free life and didn't want to be bothered with it.

"Sit down, it's a long story. The force of the bomb that went off in New York sent underground shock waves that crippled power grids throughout the country. It was so intense, it activated the San Andreas fault, causing an earthquake that forced a huge chunk of California to hit the water."

Randy wonders how the hell that could be possible but continues listening.

"I declared War on the world because no-one would claim responsibility and it really pissed me off. I have a team that has developed a satellite system that shoot beams, making it rain fire. These things are extraordinary. We could raise the frequency so high, the impact could have the force of ten nuclear bombs. We're practically the only ones left and I'm going to do what's right for the American people. I've developed a vaccine that can secure a better future."

"I've heard," says Randy, as he bows his head and stares at the whiskey in his cup. "I understand what you're trying to do, I really do. But don't you think it's time we break the cycle?"

"What cycle?"

"You're acting just like Dad. Listen, I can't tell you what to do, you're the better brother," he says, and takes a sip. "Look at you, my little brother is the leader of the world. I just want you to do what's right for the people. I hear we've lost a lot already."

"Yes, half our population's perished."

"Do you think that should happen in the greatest nation in the world?"

Thump thinks for a second. "No," he says. "I'm going to do what's right. I'm going to give the people of this country their home back by getting rid of all Illegal Residents."

"If that's what you think is right, brother, go for it," says Randy, while lifting his glass to toast, before taking another sip.

Thump hears someone lightly tapping on the door and shouts for them to enter.

It's Jordan, he's another F.F.A. agent. "I'm sorry to bother you this lovely evening, sir, but I've got some horrible news," he says, then stops.

"Go on then," Thump snaps.

"Agent Brian Scott was found dead a couple of hours ago in the parking lot."

"What!? A couple of hours ago!?" Thump grunts as he stands, slams both fists on the table and is obviously aggravated. "Why was I not informed of this?"

"I'm very sorry, sir," says Jordan. "Agency policy is that we investigate it thoroughly before we say anything."

"And who wrote that policy?" he dominantly asks.

Jordan's froze, and doesn't know what to say. "My, my boss, sir."

"Do you know who I am, young man?"

"Yes," he nervously replies.

"You tell your boss I need a word with him. Now get out of my sight!"

90

Thump drops his body onto the chair with his arms hanging on the sides. He can't believe Scott's dead. Thump recruited him, as well as eight other agents to replace the secret service. He wasn't your meanest, toughest killer, but he was smart, a quality Thump likes.

"What's wrong, bro?" asks Randy, who notices Thump's body language. Randy's never known Thump to be an emotional guy, so his reaction has him a bit confused. He didn't even shed a single tear when their dad passed away, and Thump was very fond of him.

"I just lost my best guy," he regretfully says.

"Don't worry. You have me now," he responds, then gulps down the rest of his drink.

Until this day, Krystle still works for Thump, and after many years of trying to conceive, she has finally given up. By thirty-five, she started to realize it might never happen, now at forty-three, she's learned to live with it.

Thump is still in the N.A.A. headquarters. The white house was taken back, but they think it's best for him to stay there.

Krystle's job is to make sure the soldiers are vigilant at all times, even though the war ended many years ago. She is called over by one of them while sitting at her post. She goes over and leans downward, until her head is shielded by his partition.

"What's up, Larry. Everything alright?"

"Yea, everything's fine, but I need a private moment with you, if you don't mind. I need to show you something."

"Sure, Larry. Follow me, we'll go to an interrogation room."

Larry grabs his laptop, puts it under his arm and follows Krystle. Larry's the jokester of the group. He tries to liven the place up from time to time as they've gone fifteen years without orchestrating an attack, but it doesn't work, because the other soldiers don't entertain his actions. They enter the room and he quickly puts the laptop on the desk. He immediately looks at the double sided mirror, walks toward it and cups his hands as if he could look through.

"Is there anyone in there?" he nervously asks.

"No," she responds with a grin. Krystle thinks this is another one of his silly games.

"Are you sure? Can you check, please?"

Krystle senses this is a little serious. Larry looks way too tense. She exits the room and he listens as she quickly opens another door. He hears it close, right before Krystle walks back in.

"No-one's in there," she says, while looking past him to focus on the laptop. "What do you need to show me?"

"OK. Before I do, I just want you to know something. What I've observed could be a weird coincidence and I'm not implying it's going on." He's being cautious, he knows the close relationship her dad and Thump had. He opens the laptop, which is already on, and she sees the grid targets for the satellites.

"You're not supposed to have that information on your personal computer," she quickly says. "Are you crazy!?"

"Let me show you then I'll delete it." He points out a coordinate on one of the grids that was fired upon sixteen years ago, and plays it.

Krystle doesn't see much.

"You saw that, right?" he asks.

Krystle's confused and doesn't understand. All she sees is an aerial shot of earth that looks to have had a giant sand storm.

"This is an attack we executed sixteen years ago."

"Uh. OK," she says, still not understanding.

"Now look at this," he says, while skipping to another frame. He shows her what appears to be the same exact attack.

"That's the same video," she insinuates.

"It isn't," he anxiously says. "This is an attack that happened twenty years ago. How can that be a coincidence? Same exact coordinates. Why would we attack the same place twice?" He shuffles to another video.

"Look at this one," he says, while showing her the attack that was performed before the one he originally showed her. He proceeds to show the attack that was performed before that one. It's identical.

Krystle sits down and is dumbfounded. "What are you implying here?"

"It's like a pattern, just think about it. The human mind cannot detect patterns so far apart, so we weren't supposed to notice."

"How did you notice it then?"

"I have a photographic memory. I had to go back and look at every single frame. There are over three-hundred of them, it took me hours."

"So what do you think this is? And what made you look into it after so many years?"

"I don't know," he replies. "I don't think we've committed as many attacks as they're leading us to believe. I think this war was over long before we think it ended, who knows. I don't want you to think I'd believe we never attacked in the first place."

"What? Why would you say that?"

"Just don't want you to think that that's what I think."

While packing up the equipment to get ready to go, Krystle stops Larry. "Who can we tell about this?" she loudly whispers to him, while standing very close.

"Tell them what?" he responds. "The whole world is gone. There's no-one to tell."

"I'm going to ask him."

"No," urges Larry. "Don't do it, he's dangerous." Larry looks toward the entrance and sees a clean shaven, well dressed, handsome black man looking at them.

"Who's that?" he asks. "Don't look, there's someone watching us. Are you sure there wasn't anyone in that room?"

"Who is it?" she asks.

"I don't know. He's staring at us."

"Kiss me," she says to his surprise.

"What? I will not..."

"Do it," she says.

Larry grabs Krystle and gives her a deep kiss, causing the gentleman to turn around and leave. "It worked," he says. "He left."

Krystle makes her way home that night and is furious. Her husband left and didn't notify her, causing her to struggle to find a ride. She approaches the house and notices his car lights are still on, meaning he just made it there. She walks in and sees him barge down the stairs with a suitcase stuffed so poorly, it has clothes sticking out of it. She can tell there's something wrong because he hasn't even looked at her.

"You going somewhere?" she asks as he passes by her to go into a drawer that has his little personal effects. He's disheveled. His shirt hangs out of his pants and his tie is loose, revealing the top button of his shirt unfastened.

"What are you doing?"

He keeps pacing around, thinking of what else to take, then stops and faces her. "You know, I've spent the better part of my adult life trying to make you happy," he says. He lifts the suitcase by the handle.

Krystle and her husband have a troubled marriage. Her being unable to conceive has put a strain on their relationship, because he often blamed her.

"What are you talking about, Dwayne!?" she yells. "Where are you going!?"

Without saying another word, he walks out of the door and enters his car.

"What is wrong with you," she cries.

"There is nothing wrong with me," he says. "I loved you."

Krystle lets the car door go to put her hands over her face.

"Seeing you kiss that man today only assured me that we don't belong together," he says as he peels off.

Krystle falls to her knees after realizing the person Larry spoke about was her husband. She could think of no possible way to explain it, and can only watch as he drives off...

~Chapter Eight~

The Fort

The Fort is a town that sits at the foot of a mountain. It grew bigger, and bigger each day as more, and more Illegal Residents entered with the promise of a better future. They were forced to stop when Thump had Communities intentionally built around it for the wealthy to stop them from entering. It is heavily wooded and overlooks the Communities. These Communities are filled with ruthless folks who try and kill as many Illegal Residents as possible. To enter the Fort, Illegal Residents have no choice but to try and sidle through without being seen. The few that attempt it are often captured and killed. The residents hang their bodies from trees and off of rooftops to make a statement to the next Illegal Resident who dared pass by.

It's a thirty-mile trek from the entrance of the fifth community, to the entrance of the Fort. You have to travel twenty-nine miles by foot before getting to the one-mile stretch that separates it from the first Community. Every once in a while, the folks at the Communities send groups of armed members to the Fort, only to have most of them never return. The Fort is highly secure and has a mix of all people. While the majority are Illegal Residents, there is a large number of Caucasians who support and have joined them. Thump's idea of the vaccine is not supported by most Americans.

When they try and cross that one mile stretch they're often met with fury. Members of the Fort guard the wooded area and try their best to bring them in alive. They often shoot to injure, so they can drag them in, but many times there are too many so they're forced to kill. F.F.A. agents for years have tried to enter, but have been forced to halt their missions. Seems like no-one's capable of entering unless they're allowed in.

The Communities are each governed by one leader, the highest in rank is General Eric Reid. He's been personally hand picked by Thump to be his successor if anything were to happen to him. He rules the 3rd Community which is where they hold their monthly meetings. Reid's ruthless, he was charged with thirty war crimes and was in Leavenworth prison facing twenty life sentences. He was pardoned by Thump shortly after the war began. He's a tall, heavyset white man with a huge beer belly. He dresses in jeans with plaid shirts, and always has a cowboy hat on. You could hear Eric coming from a mile away by the sounds his boots make every time he takes a step. He wears alligator skin cowboy boots with two inch heels and very pointy tips. Since his Community is in the middle, it's where they keep the massive antenna that receives radio waves from a satellite above, allowing only the wealthy access to the internet.

General Reid's a very mean and arrogant individual who's hated by some of his own people. He's enforced a law, where only colored-eyed white folks could reside in his Community. He believes that those with dark eyes are mixed in some way. Other leaders tried to fight the law, but it was enforced, and with Thump's backing he made it a law at all Communities when they complained. Thump considered it for the entire country but figured he'd have to get rid of way too many people.

Reid didn't care. When he enforced it, he personally executed and ordered the execution of anyone with dark eyes. With some being family members and friends of other leaders, it made matters very tense. Everyone was to inform him when they saw someone with dark eyes or pay the consequences. His most ruthless men were ordered to go door to door, and execute anyone who didn't have colored eyes. There were mothers who personally took their children to him, hoping he'd spare them, but had to watch as Reid put a bullet through their heads instead. It's been two years since that attack, and since then, no-one with dark eyes can enter, and if a child is born with dark eyes now, they're allowed to live. They're certain they were made by two people with colored eyes.

At the Fort, they love when they're able to bring a community member in alive. It's a pleasure to Leon. They tie them to wooden trolleys and pull them around so the people could hit them with any-thing they could get their hands on. After riding them around, they tie them in a barn specifically designed for torture. They're forced to kneel with their arms outstretched with each chained to one side. Leon then gets the pleasure of forcefully getting information while slowly killing them.

Leon loves it, he remembers the day they killed his family every time he kills one of them. He often thinks of the agent who spared him, the one who died to save his life. Leon's a fairly short, twenty-one-year-old Asian who was only ten when his parents and two-year-old brother were butchered. He watched as his little brother was termed even before they scanned him to see if he'd been vaccinated. The Doctor that delivered him informed his parents they forgot to inject the child, and refused to take the risk of injecting him after the thirty-minute mark. His parents kept moving around, trying to avoid him being scanned, until Phillips got the list with their names on it.

"We've got to go, boys," says Phillips. "We have a list."

Phillips, Brown, McLean, and Cryan pile into the car. Cryan sits on the passenger seat and Phillips drives. Cryan's rage has died down. He used the job as a way to let his frustrations out, losing his son filled him with rage. He was brutal in the beginning. He had some of the most ruthless kills although he was the only non-criminal of the group. He now tries his best to derail the team as much as possible and has decided he'd let Goodman know he's done. He no longer wants to kill, this will be his last job. Phillips is suspicious and notices his little antics, but doesn't want to tell Goodman. Cryan wasn't given the same Impla-chip as the others. His doesn't contain the poison.

They make their way to the Wang house. Cryan asks Phillips if he'd do him the favor and drive by his house so he could check on Dorothy who was ill when he left for work.

"NO," he says. "Must you always try to stall us?"

Phillips continues to drive, and as always, there's an awkward silence in the car. They approach the house and Cryan sees someone in the window of the second floor. The person quickly closes the curtain.

"Did you see what I saw?" asks Phillips.

"What did you see?"

Phillips knows he seen them, it's because of him that he looked up. He stops the car in the driveway and nods his head in disappointment.

Before they could knock, Leon's dad opens the door and acts as if he's surprised to see them. "Hello there. I was just going to the market, how can I help you gentlemen?" he says, and closes the door behind him.

With no warning, McLean kicks the door with so much force the frame collapses inward.

"You're not going anywhere," says Phillips.

Leon's upstairs hiding under a bed with his little brother.

His mom is shaking like a leaf. She's prayed for years for this day to never come.

"I need everyone in this household down here, now," Phillips announces.

Leon's father is being pinned against the wall by McLean.

Phillips walks toward Leon's mom and looks her in the face. "Go get them!" he shouts.

Brown's already upstairs and in the bedroom the kids are hiding in. He looks around before flipping the mattress over and sees them cowering under the bed. They're cuddled up, with Leon holding his little brother tight. As he drags them out, their mother comes running up.

"Please," she pleads. She falls to her knees and puts her hands together as if she's praying. "It was the hospital's fault," she cries. She leans forward and puts her forehead on the floor, then gets back up and puts her hands back together.

Brown grabs Leon's little brother by the back of his shirt while tightly holding on to Leon's wrist.

Leon's dad is being pinned to the wall with McLean's elbow on his throat and sees the kids were found. He reaches for a screwdriver that lays on a table nearby, and swiftly swings it, making it enter into McLean's neck.

The blood immediately starts spraying onto Leon's dad. McLean's in shock, and takes a few steps back while holding on to the wound.

Phillips pulls out his gun and empties it into Leon's father's chest.

The kids start screaming on the way down. Leon tries with all of his might to release himself from Brown's grip to rush to his dad.

His mom is close behind and pushes Brown down the remaining steps, causing them all to tumble.

While falling, Brown spins his body to land on his back.

McLean's collapsed, and Cryan is trying to put as much pressure as possible on the wound. With his hands soaked in blood, he watches as McLean perishes.

100

As Brown lands, he pulls out his gun and shoots Leon's mom in the forehead, causing her to fall back and land in the middle of the staircase. He gets up and immediately grabs Leon's brother again.

"This is over!" shouts Cryan. "We broke protocol. We were supposed to kill the little fella first. We can get in trouble for this, let's go." He's hoping Phillips calls it off.

"Not a chance," says Phillips. "They've killed one of my men and they will pay."

Leon's on the floor pretending to be unconscious. He watches as Phillips walks over to Brown and snatches his brother away like a rag doll. Phillips forces the child to lay on the floor and grabs him by both ankles. The boy tries to kick his legs around to avoid the grip, while screaming. With one swoop, Phillips lifts. He swings him all the way up over his shoulders and slams the boy into a glass coffee table in the middle of the room. The impact of his body slamming into the table causes the glass to shatter into thousands of tiny pieces. Cryan looks away. Brown's standing over McLean's body but is looking at what Phillips is doing. Phillips does it again. The sound of the kid's limp body hitting the glass covered floor makes Cryan sick. He repeatedly does it, until he no longer has the strength to continue. Leon jumps up and bolts toward the kitchen when he sees Phillips is no longer physically able to do it again.

"Get him!" Phillips demands. Cryan runs after him while pulling out his gun. He enters the kitchen and notices Leon had gotten the door open, but froze and closed it before leaning with his back against the wall. Cryan points his gun at him. Something tells him to do it one last time, but he can't.

"Get out!" he tells him. "Go!"

Leon opens the door and sprints out. Cryan starts to turn to report he's gotten away, but as he turns completely around, he sees Brown and Phillips standing there. Brown is still clutching the gun he killed Leon's mom with.

"So you let him go, huh?" Phillips says.

Cryan drops his gun.

"Give me your gun," Phillips tells Brown, drawing a weird look from him. "Give me it, mine is empty!"

Phillips grabs the gun and with no hesitation, shoots Cryan in the face. His brain splatters on the little panes of glass framed on the door Leon just ran out of. They both watch as his body drops and the back of his head slams into the bottom of the door with its eyes open.

Leon wishes he had an opportunity to thank him. He runs the Fort with his best friend Ahmed who's family was also slaughtered. He also claims Cryan found him in a hiding spot but acted as if he didn't see him. Their third partner's William, everyone calls him Willie. William is a blue-eyed, blond-haired, white American who was really good friends with Ahmed until his family was slaughtered. They separated when Ahmed went on the run and found themselves at the Fort a few years later. Willie goes on runs for the Fort once a month. He doesn't draw suspicion when he goes and buys ton loads of food from one of the Communities.

Between the three, they've come up with many unique fighting styles. They've been practicing for years and have become lethal with their hands, knives, and guns. They practice every single morning from 4 am, to 7 am, and are now flawless.

Since the government puts DD's on everyone's chip on the first of each month, the people at the Fort form a line, and one by one, they put their DD's into Willie's chip. They have to hold theirs over his for five seconds in order to transfer them. Willie has stacked so much food in the pantry they could go at least a year without having to risk going out.

"I say we take a break for a couple of month's, Lee," Willie tells Leon. "We have enough food to last us a while. We can keep the same routine, I'll hold the DD's." Being that Willie's white and from a wealthy family, he got the chip that only people that will remain have. He can keep the DD's, they'll never reset.

Leon agrees as he watches Ahmed walking toward them. Ahmed's a twenty-seven-year-old who's family is from Iran. They thought they could get away with having his mom give birth at home and paid the ultimate price. They were also brutally murdered by Phillips and his men. Ahmed says Cryan found him hiding in a closet and closed the door. Even Ahmed himself was convinced he didn't see him, as savvy as he did it. Seven members of his family were murdered. He had nowhere to go and roamed around for years before learning of the Fort.

The Fort has a population of just under one thousand people. With most being women and children, Leon doesn't have the manpower to overtake the Community closest to him. He'd love nothing more than to be able to march in there and do to them what they've done to his family. Leon understands they personally had nothing to do with it, but the way they keep trying to invade only assures him that they have bad intentions.

General Reid enters his house which is in the middle of Community-*three*.

"Welcome home, honey," says his cheery wife. Reid has not one drop of humor in him. He never smiles and is always cranky.

"Bring me a cup of coffee," he demands. He sits on his couch and turns the TV on. With nothing on the only channel, he decides to grab his laptop. They have full internet access and state of the art computers in the Communities, but can only watch old videos.

He starts to play solitaire and notices he has a message. It seems to be written in Chinese. *"This is weird,"* he wonders. He clicks on a link to translate it.

"Hi. My name is Moshi," the message reads. "I'm in japan. Where are you from?"

Reid's suspicious and doesn't want to answer. *"No way he's in Japan,"* he thinks to himself.

"My name is Nicholas, and I'm in Russia," he responds.

"Cool," says Moshi. "What do you think about what's going on in the states?" Moshi knows exactly where Reid is but is playing along.

"What's going on in the states?" Reid types.

"You know. How they alienated the world. How they grounded all flights and secretly deal with only the Chinese now."

Reid's convinced someone's messing with him. Then suddenly, the connection is lost.

Moshi's a computer hacker from Japan who has gone into American files and has figured the whole thing out. He's the one who gave Larry the evidence he's taking credit for. Larry was confused, because according to the attacks, Japan should have been wiped out. He also thought someone in the department was testing him, but Moshi proved himself when he started showing him the grids. Moshi's arguably the best hacker in the world, and with the US blocking access, it's amazing he was able to penetrate the security.

"Take me to the N.A.A.," Reid tells his driver the next day.

"Sir, that's like eight hours away."

"Look at me, son. Look at my face closely," he says while pointing at his own face. "Does it look like I don't know that!?"

Reid wants an explanation and wants it face to face. This Moshi guy has him on edge and he wants the truth.

They make it there in seven hours and seventeen minutes.

"That's a record," the driver proudly says.

"Of course it is. It's the only thing you're good at," Reid arrogantly snaps back.

He walks into the building with the intentions of getting an explanation from Thump on this Moshi guy, and runs into Krystle, who gives him directions to his office. She looks stressed out and feels worthless.

Reid walks into Thump's office and excuses a gentleman sitting there.

"What's going on?" he asks Thump.

Thump ignores him, stands up, and turns to make himself a drink. "You want one?"

"Sure," says Reid. He sits on the chair the gentleman got off of.

"Let me guess," says Thump as he passes him the drink. "Moshi's messaged you."

"You know about him!?" Reid stresses. "I thought no-one could cross the lines. Do you realize what could happen?"

"We have this under control," says Thump. "It has to be someone here doing it, there is no way possible. We have our best guys trying to track their IP address. We'll find whoever is responsible for this and we'll deal with him. He's messaging everybody, sometimes just those stupid little faces. The person doing this will have a face to face meeting with Buchanan," he says as he stares ahead in a daze for a second.

"This could end very bad," says Reid. "Very bad..."

~Chapter Nine~

Agent Kenneth Brown

Mr. Goodman enters the lobby of the agency and stumbles into Phillips and his men.

"Good morning," says Phillips. Goodman's overweight, and it looks like he struggles to walk. Phillips stares at his shirt which is not properly tucked in, and notice that his glasses sit crookedly on his nose. Half of his shirt is sticking out and his suspenders are too tight, making his pants rise and revealing the tube socks he wears with dress shoes. His untied tie lays around his neck with each tip hanging over his big belly.

"Good morning," he replies. He looks at Phillips and proclaims they have the day off. Phillips doesn't like it, it's the last thing he wanted to hear. He's in a very bad mood this particular morning. He had an argument with his wife because he didn't think his coffee was hot enough. Phillips has a very dysfunctional family. He and his wife have never really gotten along and he only married her because she became pregnant.

Although Phillips was fortunate to grow up with a wealthy family, he was always in trouble. He'd always get into situations his parents had to buy him out of. He's now a family man with two daughters and two sons, the oldest being his son Pete. They often clash as Phillips thinks his son is too weak. He's tried to toughen him up throughout the years with tough love, but Pete was always reading a book or studying. His youngest is his daughter Cathy, she's his pride and joy.

"What do you mean we're off?" Phillips responds, obviously annoyed.

Mr. Goodman walks up to him and gets too close for comfort, making Phillips take a step back. "You might want to watch your tone with me, Rodney," he says. "I'm not having the best day of my life today. I caught a flat on the way here, then realized I didn't have a spare." He looks back at the other agents. "You men have your yearly evaluations today, so report to Dr. Murphy."

All agents are required to report once a year to get their stress levels evaluated, Phillips hates these meetings.

Mitchell interrupts. "But, sir, I have a sit down with Murphy tomorrow."

"Who's Murphy?" Phillips asks.

"The new head Doctor," answers Goodman. He turns his attention back to Mitchell. "Up to you," he tells him. "You can get it over with today or take the day off, it doesn't matter to me."

Mitchell figures he'll see Dr. Murphy the next day. Besides, his son has told him he has the day off so he'll spend time with him. He's been wanting to tell him something and could use this as an opportunity. Goodman's walked away and is headed up to his office, while Brown, Moore, and Phillips huddle up, wondering who Dr. Murphy is.

Dr. Murphy started the job last year, right after Phillips's team got evaluated. She took over for Dr. Unger who suddenly died of a heart attack.

"Mitch, wait," says Phillips. "Who's Dr. Murphy? How come I've never heard of him?"

"It's a her. She took over for Unger. I'm going home," he says as he walks away.

Phillips feels disrespected and thinks Mitchell is re-lieved that he didn't have to kill anyone. He's beginning to remind him of Fred.

As Mitchell drives home, he's trying to determine whether he should have the discussion he's been wanting to have with his son to-day, or wait until he speaks to Murphy again. He gets closer and sees Jacob sitting on the steps leading to the front door of the house.

"Hey, Dad! What are you doing home so early?" says Jacob, as Mitchell steps out of the car.

"I took the day off."

"Cool. Want to see something?" Jacob reaches for a backpack that lays nearby.

"Where have the years gone?" Mitchell wonders. He goes over and sits next to him. Mitchell's full of guilt and misery that haunts him every day. He cannot comprehend why his life took the turn it did.

"Sure," he responds, giving Jacob his undivided attention.

Jacob pulls out a laptop. "I've been saving my DD's for this," he says.

This has driven Mitchell crazy for years now. He does what he does because he has to, but can't figure out why they're entitled to all these luxuries while people struggle to live day to day. He doesn't give Jacob his honest opinion and acts as if it doesn't bother him. Mitchell's a simple man who doesn't get satisfaction on taking advantage of things that aren't provided to all people. He cannot believe the govern-ment has gotten away with what they've been doing for the last thir-teen years. He grabs the laptop from Jacob and stares at the glowing screen.

"What good is it if you really can't do much. What, you just stare at it?"

"No, Dad, you could do plenty. You can log on to sites that have videos from years ago, and you can pretty much listen to any song made before the war."

The laptop makes a little bell sound and a box pops up.

"I don't know what that is," Jacob says. "It's been happening since I got it. At first it was Chinese lettering, but now it's a little yellow face with its tongue sticking out."

"It's a message," says Mitchell. "I've seen this before."

Mitchell doesn't know how to use it but has seen it in government buildings. "People use it to communicate with one another," he tells him. Mitchell doesn't know how to read or write and is ashamed to admit it to his son. "Why don't you write something back?" he asks as he passes it back to him.

"It's in Chinese, I don't understand it. Oh, it says translate right here," Jacob points out. "Why didn't you tell me?"

He responds to the text and little face and says "Hi," but there's no response.

"Are you alright, Son?"

"I'm fine. Why?"

"I don't know. You've looked really sad lately and I know there's something bothering you. You know you can speak to me about anything, right?"

"I know, Dad. It's just..."

"Tell me, Son."

"OK. I was seeing a girl for quite some time, and all of a sudden, she left, just disappeared. I don't know what happened to her, I just hope she's OK."

"Was she your girlfriend? Were you two sexually active?" he anxiously asks.

"Yes, and yes," Jacob responds, not believing he's having this conversation with his dad.

Mitchell puts his head down and nervously twiddles his fingers. "We have to find her then," he says.

Jacob agrees.

Back at the Headquarters, the agents are making their way to Dr. Murphy's office. Phillips thinks about stopping by Goodman's to get some insight on her, but the element of surprise is too intriguing so he decides to just go for it.

As they get closer, Agent Brown decides he'll be the first to enter. He walks to her door, twists the knob and makes his way in.

Dr. Murphy flinches at the sound of the door. No-one has ever entered her office without knocking first.

"Excuse me," she says.

Brown goes directly to the chair and sits on it. "Let's get this over with. I know how it goes, I have an hour."

"What's your name?" she asks, looking quite annoyed, while shuffling through a pile of papers.

"I'm Agent Brown. Kenneth Brown."

"OK, Agent Brown, let's get this over with," she snottily replies. She can tell this is going to be a rough one. "According to our records, you're thirty-eight years old. Correct?"

"Correct," he responds.

"What's your occupation, Agent Brown?"

"I'm an F.F.A. agent," he quickly responds.

He knows how it is, they ask stupid little questions and think they're helping you.

"And what do you do?"

"I kill people, Ma'am."

"Do you like what you do?"

Brown pauses for a second and looks at her. "Would you like it?"

"Doesn't matter what I'd like, this is about you. Do you like your job?"

"Yes," he sarcastically answers. "I love it. I just love to kill kids."

Murphy backs off a little, the frustration of him barging in has her acting unprofessional and she realizes it. "Do you remember life before the war?" she sincerely asks.

"No, I don't. I was just one. My parents told me stories though. I grew up through the worse of the postwar, everyone went crazy, it was unbelievable. You had no choice but to get yourself in some kind of trouble."

"Tell me about your family growing up."

"We were very tight knit, and did good considering what was happening. My father had a lot of money so we didn't have it as bad as some people. My dad had stockpiled on many canned foods throughout the years, he knew this would someday happen. He stored it in a refrigerated underground compartment he built. Everyone thought he was crazy when he built it, but it paid off."

"Do you feel bad for Illegal Residents?"

This catches Brown by surprise and he doesn't know how to respond.

"Sometimes," he says. "It's like, I know I have this job and I know what it entails, on the other hand, I have this chip that'll kill me if I get out of line. That idiot Phillips is hoping I slip up, but I won't. I will not give him the satisfaction. Anyway, it's kind of messed up what the government is doing, and again, I'll continue to do my job, but it's inhumane. They make us kill babies for god's sake. When everything went crazy after the war, I thought it couldn't get any worse but it has. Don't you watch when they televise a term?"

"No I don't," she quickly answers. "Tell me, why'd you go to prison?"

"Since I've been a kid, I've had a really bad temper and always struggled to control it. I mean, can you blame me with what I grew up around? It was never really bad for us because we had money. The government isolated us and only policed our streets when they couldn't maintain the public. Illegal Residents could kill each other and the army would do nothing. One night, my father was in the yard getting canned goods and was gunned down in cold blood and robbed for the food. I wondered how it was possible for them to penetrate the security provided for us. I went out and shot the first Illegal Resident I laid my eyes on. It happened to be a single mother of three who was out desperately trying to find water to give her children. The military arrested me. Two years into my sentence, I found out the man that murdered my father was our next door neighbor's son, one of our own."

"How old were you?"

"I was seventeen when they locked me up, twenty-five when they released me into this program."

"But as I understand, they only recruited stone cold killers. What you committed was a crime of passion, it wasn't malicious."

"When they recruited me they said they respected the fact I went out and killed one without thinking twice. They loved the fact that I left a secure perimeter to go out there."

"How was the training?"

"What training?" he asks.

Murphy's referring to the training Mitchell mentioned.

"I didn't do any training."

Murphy's perplexed. She's sure Mitchell told her he had to go to training for four years after being released from prison.

"Is there any kind of training for agents?"

"Not that I'm aware of. There's the psych ward you have to admit yourself into if you've committed a domestic crime, I believe it's three or four years," he answers.

Murphy's dumbfounded. *"No wonder he kept dodging the question,"* she thinks to herself.

"Do you have a family?"

"Yes, two daughters."

"Do you love them?"

"Of course I do, with all of my heart."

"How was life in jail?"

"It was rough, there was very little food and guards, that mixture was deadly. Earlier you said I wasn't malicious, but you should have seen me in there. I was stuck in there with a bunch of killers, a sheep surrounded by hungry wolves. I had to fight for my life. It got to the point that no-one would mess with me, I learned very quick. I got so vicious they respected me. I stabbed so many people I lost count. The last number I remember is thirty-two."

"You killed thirty-two people?"

"No! I stabbed thirty-two people. If they died they died because there was no infirmary. No-one wanted to work there, not even the guards. The few that remained would not break up scuffles. They'd let us fight until we were tired or someone got killed."

Agent Brown's feeling very comfortable with Dr. Murphy, a lot more comfortable than he'd ever felt with Unger.

"How old are your daughters?"

"Eight-year-old twins. I'd kill or die for them in a second."

"I'm sure you would," says Murphy, with a huge grin on her face. "How about your wife, tell me about her."

"My wife is a sick lady. She's developed a very bad case of asthma. She says it started shortly after the war began, and with so many people dying of cancer it has me kind of nervous. I wouldn't know what to do without her. If I could take off now, I would."

That surprises Murphy. She didn't expect for him to blatantly blurt that out. "Have you ever considered it?"

"No," he quickly says. Brown would have never said that around Unger. He was a mean old man who would've stormed out of there and into Goodman's office to report it in a second. Brown's feeling too relaxed and has let his guard down. He knows she's required to report that to Goodman and it'll result in a tongue lashing or worse, because exhibiting negativity toward the agency, wanting to kill a fellow agent, or mentioning you want to flee are three of the department's strictest rules.

"I'll keep that off the record," she says to his relief.

"How about your team, tell me about them. Do you get along with them?"

"I hate Phillips, he's an arrogant prick who thinks his shit don't stink!" he angrily says with no hesitation. "I'm sorry, I didn't mean to overreact but I really hate him. He always looks down on us. I've been on the team a week longer than he has, and he ends up commanding me. He doesn't have the integrity to lead himself, yet he leads a team."

Murphy listens, she can see the problem's more than just a workplace issue. She senses envy.

"I don't want you to think I'm jealous because I'm not. The guy doesn't even talk to us and gets upset when anyone says anything in the car. He invokes a hostile work environment. I've even thought about transferring just to get away from him. Now Mitchell, that's a cool man right there. He's down to earth and never looks down on anyone, not even on Moore. He'll actually hold a conversation with you and seems very smart. He speaks a lot about his son, he loves him dearly. That's a man I would work under with no hesitation, but Phillips, he's an idiot."

"You got there before Phillips?"

"Yes. Practically the same time but he was a twenty-one-year-old punk. They even had him commanding Cryan. Too bad!"

"Too bad what?"

"I can't say. Damn, why did I mention it. I could truly destroy him if I wanted to and he knows it."

"Not from in here," she says. "This is confidential."

She's hoping he says what he wants to say. *"How could he destroy Phillips,"* she wonders.

"You'd think he'd treat me better. He drove Mrs. Cryan to kill herself."

Murphy's eyes grow big.

"That poor lady," he says. He hopes she thinks the Cryan remark was about Dorothy.

"No-one drives anyone to kill themselves. Your reference was about Fred Cryan, not Dorothy."

"I can't. He'll kill me."

"Who? Who'll kill you?"

He's referring to Goodman but figures he'd have her believe it's Phillips he's worried about.

"How would he kill you? How would he even know you told me?"

"He will get it out of you. Phillips is a lot smarter than he looks."

"No-one gets anything out of me," she replies. "This is what I do, it's my job."

"Phillips killed...!" He can't believe he's saying it. He figures she kept him wanting to leave off of the record so trusts her. "Goodman knows exactly what happened that day, but stressed that I should never say a word to another soul. Phillips used Goodman as a shield from being disciplined for killing a team member."

"Did Phillips kill Fred?" She's hoping for an answer.

Brown looks at her and nods his head.

Murphy's shocked. She's never encountered an agent who's spilled the beans on another so quickly. She sees how much hate this man has for Phillips and knows that's a bad combination for the F.F.A.. Her job is to evaluate these guys and report to Mr. Goodman. So far, he's said two things that are frowned upon in the agency.

"Tell me about your previous partner, the one who took Fred's spot."

Brown's feeling relaxed and he's talking. "That poor fella, I forgot about him. He was set up. Phillips told Mr. Goodman he wanted to run but that was a lie. What he said was that if the chip didn't have the poison, he would. Randolph loved his job. Lasted nine years with us. He was a good guy with an insane temper. Not even Phillips could compare to him which made him feel threatened."

As he speaks she writes everything down.

"How about Moore?" She looks at the time and sees she has only seven minutes left with him.

"Moore's Moore, he's a clumsy fella who always tends to piss Phillips off. I tell him all the time to be careful because Phillips is dangerous, but he has a stupid little sense of humor and thinks everything's funny. He's gotten me to the point where I just want to pull out my gun and shoot him myself."

Brown notices that Murphy immediately writes that down. "You said this is confidential, right?"

"Oh, yeah," she says while looking down at the paper. "I just write the information so I could remember for our next session.

"This one's over. I'm here every Tuesday if you require additional counseling. Next time, knock please." She extends her hand to pass him her business card and walks him to the door where Phillips, and Moore are patiently waiting. They watch as Brown walks out and notice her in the doorway. Phillips walks toward Brown, while Moore stares at Murphy.

"I need thirty minutes, gentlemen," she says as she steps out of her office and closes the door behind her. Brown notices she has the paper she wrote her notes on in her hand. He thinks about following her, and dragging her into the first empty room he sees before strangling her to death.

Moore's infatuated, he follows her every movement with his eyes. He even follows her down the corridor.

Brown has hell to pay if she tells Mr. Goodman what was said in that room...

~Chapter Ten~

Agents Rodney Phillips and Jack Moore

Phillips declares he's next to go in, which disappoints Moore who is anxious to get in there with Murphy.

Brown decides to stick around, the lack of knowledge of where Murphy has gone is driving him crazy.

"She is so hot," Moore tells them. "Mr. Goodman is a lucky man."

"What do you mean?" asks Brown.

"Well, I followed her, she went straight into his office and hasn't come back."

Brown's concerned, he hadn't asked him because he didn't want them to think he's hiding something. It's been fifteen minutes and she's still in there. Brown is losing it. In his mind, she's in Goodman's office telling him everything he'd said.

"Her legs, they're so long and look so smooth," says Moore, while looking mesmerized.

Phillips looks at him and rolls his eyes. *"You're looking desperate,"* he says.

Moore doesn't care, he feels like a teenager in love.

You could see the look of concern on Brown's face. He regrets saying what he's said and panics when he sees her walk back up the hallway. He's hoping she doesn't tell him Goodman needs to see him, even though he knows Goodman would've shouted his name by now.

Mr. Goodman doesn't hold back, he loves nothing more than a chance to verbally discipline one of his agents in front of everyone.

"Give me five minutes, gentlemen," says Murphy. She walks by and goes into her office.

"She needs to hurry," says Phillips. "I got somewhere to go."

Brown exhales. He's held his breath since the second he saw her turn and head up the hallway. He's relieved she didn't tell him what he was expecting.

"Who's next?" she asks.

Moore tries to make eye contact with her but it doesn't work. She noticed how he looked at her when she walked by and it gave her a creepy feeling. Phillips walks through her door and turns around to look at the men before shutting it. When he turns, he notices Murphy had already sat down with a pen in her hand and a clipboard on her lap.

"Good day, Agent."

He doesn't answer. Instead, he makes his way to the chair while looking around.

"You've fixed this place up," he says as he removes his dark glasses. "It almost looks as good as you." Although Phillips is a ruthless killer, he could be very charming when he wants to be.

Murphy ignores the comment. "Let's get started. I'm Doctor Murphy. I'm the permanent Doctor here now and been assigned by Mr. Goodman to give your yearly evaluation. I require for you to be truthful while answering a question or making a statement. My job is to provide feedback to Goodman on whether I think you're mentally capable of performing your job. Understood?"

"Yes, Ma'am."

"Can you please state your name and age."

Phillips knows she has the answers in her face, but also knows this is routine. "My name is Rodney Phillips and I'm thirty-four years young." It reminds him of when he used the same routine with the Senao family.

"You're quite young to be an agent. How old were you when you started?"

"I was twenty-one when I was recruited. Still wet behind the ears," he jokingly says.

"Do you like your job?"

Immediately Phillips answers. "I love it," he says with passion. "I'd rather do nothing else." In Phillips's case it's true, but all agents know you must answer that question and convince the Doctor that you mean it. Most of them hate their jobs and only do it because they have to, but none will dare admit to a Doctor that they dislike it.

"What's today's date?"

"Today is April 17th, 2036," he answers.

"Tell me about your family."

"I live with my wife and four kids. Pete's my oldest, he's fifteen. I was forced to marry my wife when she was six months pregnant with him. Her father threatened my life if I didn't, said he'd hunt me down and kill me. We got a local priest to marry us. It was nothing big with the world the way it was, only a few members of her family attended."

"Why didn't your family attend?"

"My family members are a bunch of lames. They don't get along with me, but I can't blame them with what I put them through. As if life wasn't bad enough, I put them through many hardships. My dad disowned me when I got married and my sister disappeared, haven't seen her in ages."

"If I could find her for you, would you like that?"

Deep down inside Phillips would love it, but he will show no weakness. "No, I wouldn't. To hell with all of them!"

120

"So your father disowned you because you got married?"

"Yes, he thought I was too good for her. He didn't take too kindly that she was from a poor family. One time he kicked her out of the house, it was so embarrassing. That bastard made me as strong as I am though."

"How about your mom?"

Phillips had a real close bond with his mother. He regrets everything he's done through the years for her sake. She had no problem with his marriage and wished she could be there when he said his vows, but couldn't shame her husband by attending.

"My mom is a bimbo," he says. Murphy lifts her brows. "She always did as my dad said. She was his puppet."

Murphy can't believe the lack of emotion with this one. He doesn't blink faster, doesn't play with his fingers, all signs indicate he tells the truth.

"My wife and I don't get along. My son doesn't get along with me either, I been hated my entire life. I've tried to toughen him up but he always has his face buried in a book. I pretty much have to force them all to watch the terms when they're televised. Except for my youngest, I'd never allow her to watch. That's something everyone else should experience, and if they don't, they get punished. My son would turn his face but has learned that he must look."

"How do you punish them?"

"Twenty belt lashes to the back, and I swing hard."

Murphy realizes how heartless Phillips is. "Tell me about your time in prison. Why were you in there?"

"I was in jail for only a year and it was horrible. The dangers you encountered were diabolic. There was no order. The inmates did as they pleased because the cells were never closed. It was horrific, you had to fight for survival. I was glad I was picked for this program, they told me my actions in there only assured them I'd fit right in. I was jailed for killing my wife's father. He pushed me a little too far, and when I was twenty, I bashed his brains in with a brick. There's only so much one could take. You know what happens to a rock with a constant drip of water hitting it, right?"

"What happens to it?"

"Eventually, the drops make a hole through it."

It takes a second for Murphy to be sure of what he's trying to imply.

"My wife didn't take me back until three years after my release. She couldn't resist, I knew she'd eventually give in. My three other kids are nine, seven, and five."

"Tell me about them."

"My son Sam is the nine-year-old, he's going to be a tough one and is very smart. He gets on a laptop and figures things out. He has a friend on it that he keeps messaging, some Asian kid. I don't like it, and don't ask me how an Asian got his hands on a laptop, but I let him be. My daughter Amy is seven, she's the little sassy one who struggles to get along with Sam, they're always fighting about something. My youngest is Cathy. I know parents shouldn't have a favorite, but she is mine. She's the apple of my eye and everyone knows it."

"Sounds like you really love her."

"I do. I love all my children but she's special."

"Tell me, did you require any training after being released? I hear you have to go to a psych ward for a domestic crime and you killed your wife's father, which signifies one."

"No training. The ward is for people who kill a loved one, like a brother, or a sister, a mother, or a father," he says.

Murphy's still trying to figure out exactly what Mitchell did to land him in prison. "How about your fellow agents, how do you get along with them?"

"I sorta get along with them all except for Brown. The guy is a knucklehead, he concerns me. Every once in a while he looks at me as if he's contemplating something, but I know he knows better. The one I mostly respect is Mitchell, the man does his job and does it well. I cannot say anything negative about him, I'd be lying if I did. He's a decent fella."

"What's the issue with Brown, why the animosity? Would you like for him to be transferred?"

"No, no, it's fine. I will not be the one to request for someone to be transferred because I'm concerned about them. I'm not worried, he can dream all he wants. He knows he's no match so why bother. Besides, I prefer to keep him close. The issue is that he questions me about everything. Sometimes I think he's just jealous."

"To my knowledge, you worked with an agent named Randolph."

For the first time tonight, Murphy senses some discomfort from Phillips. He moves in his chair, suggesting he feels bothered by the sound of Randolph's name.

Phillips is no fool, he immediately feels suspicious as to why she would ask about him. He remembers Brown was in there and thinks he might have said something.

"Randolph was a good man, as ruthless as they come. After nine years the job seemed to catch up to him, and he started jabbering about wanting to run. Me being the leader, I had to report it. It hurt Goodman to have to enter that code and hit the switch but he had no choice."

"Do you think it's catching up to you?"

"Me? No, never. I want to do this until the day I die."

"Did you work with Fred Cryan?"

This convinces Phillips that Brown said something. "I have, he was another good one. I looked up to him as a father. I gave him his due respect, he was the only one of us that didn't have to be there, he could walk away at any time. Poor guy got gunned down by an Illegal Resident when we executed a term." Phillips wants to see how she reacts, but gets no indication she knows anything. Still, he's suspicious.

"And Agent Moore?" Murphy purposely leaves him for last. She wants some input on the creep before he enters her office.

"Moore is just brainless, he doesn't belong in the F.F.A. but that's my opinion. He trembles at the sight of an attractive woman and seems to fall into a daze. He's kind of a creep," he says. "I'd be careful if I were you." Phillips sees the time has expired and announces he'd excuse himself.

Murphy stands and extends her hand. She passes him a business card and assures him she'll be available every Tuesday if he wants additional counseling.

Phillips rushes out of her office and immediately heads to Mr. Goodman's. He passes by Brown and gives him a threatening look.

Moore begins to walk toward the door and has a look of delight on his face.

Phillips didn't get an indication from Murphy that she knew anything, but found it strange she'd ask about both Randolph, and Cryan. He wants assurance from Goodman that nothing is going on.

"My name is Dr. Murphy, and I'm the new psychiatrist for this agency," she says.

Moore has entered and is walking around with his hands tucked into his pants pockets, making his blazer swing behind.

"You want to sit?"

Moore's too busy looking around. He looks at the paintings on the walls in awe. "You paint this?" he asks, while looking back at her. All of his attention suddenly shifted from her beauty to his surroundings.

"No, I didn't. I need you to sit."

He turns and walks toward the chair, but takes his time. He stares at Murphy, forcing her to change the direction of her vision. Moore sits, crosses his legs and places his hands on them. "Are you alright?" he asks. "We can start whenever you're ready."

"I'm fine," she says. "Can you please state your name and age?"

"My name is Jack Moore. I'm thirty-five years old."

"What's today's date?"

Without hesitation, he answers. "It's April 17th, 2036."

"Tell me about your family. Do you have a wife, kids?"

"No wife, no kids, which means I'm available."

Murphy quickly brushes it off. "Tell me about your parents."

"My parents are both dead. They died in a car wreck when I was really young and I don't remember them. I was raised by my Grandma who cared for me my entire life. I considered her more than my mom, she was my queen," he says, sounding very sophisticated.

Phillips knocks on Goodman's door and lets himself in.

"We need to talk," Goodman tells him. "Close the door."

Phillips anxiously closes it.

"Where's Agent Brown?"

"He's waiting on Moore. Why, what did he say to Murphy?"

"Nothing," Goodman snaps. "She says he has a strong shell. She tried but he wouldn't bite."

"Can you trust her, boss?"

"Who, Murphy? Absolutely!" he stresses.

"Do you have any friends?" Murphy asks.

"No. I have no-one. Just how I like it."

"Tell me about life in prison."

"I was locked up for three years before they gave me this wonderful opportunity. It was exciting in there, it was like a free for all. I killed around forty prisoners and seven guards. They called me the devil, I was forced to do some pretty crazy stuff. One time, a Mexican inmate thought I had to be dealt with because in his opinion, I've killed too many prisoners. He entered my cell but didn't live to regret it. I threw him over the railing that guards the third level one piece at a time, until there were nothing but innards left in my cell. I didn't want to get out until they assured me the job required me to kill."

Murphy's horrified. Her hands are sweating, causing her fingers to slip on the pen as she writes details. Moore's manner of speaking is very calm and collected, the slowness of his speech freaks her out.

"Another time, a guard had the audacity to try and break up a fight I was in because he thought I'd stabbed the guy too many times. I turned the knife on him and cut his head off with a shank while the other guards cowered." He notices Murphy's terrified by the way she's acting and continues. "I had them horrified. I was basically the only one on the third level. They'd sleep piled on one another before they dared close their eyes anywhere near me. I was the king in there. The little bit of food provided came to me first, and I'd eat until I was full before I gave them my leftovers. The guards wanted no part of me either. I had them fearing for their lives."

"Do you like your job?" Murphy interrupts. She cannot hear any more of that. *"This is going to be a long hour,"* she thinks to herself.

Brown watches as Phillips makes his way back. He doesn't know where he went but is sure it had to be to Goodman's office. This brings back his concerns, he knows Goodman would tell him if he had said anything because they're in it together. Phillips sits on the row of chairs that are opposite to the one he sits in and spreads his arms across the backs of the others.

"You think Mitchell's alright?" he asks.

Brown's blindsided. *"What is he talking about?"* he wonders. "I think Mitchell is fine. Why, is there something wrong?"

"Nah, he's just acting a little weird lately."

"Yea, I spoke to him about it. Says he has some terrible news for his son but doesn't know how to tell him. He's alright though, it's personal."

"Wow. I didn't know. Hope he figures it out, because things like that can eat at a man, trust me. How did your meeting with Murphy go?"

"It went fine. Almost as fine as she is," says Brown as they both chuckle.

"I love my job," Moore responds. "There's nothing better than killing, the feeling is amazing. I must say, Phillips kills the bulk of the people though. The adrenaline's the same when you watch so I don't mind. Especially watching him kill, the guy is a beast. He's nothing compared to the group I was with in the other district but he kills well. We were complete monsters back then," he proudly says. "Especially Buchanan. He's done so well he personally works for Thump now. If there's a guy that would cause you nightmares, it's him. We had to be separated, the terms were so gruesome they weren't allowed to televise them. Buchanan would chop Illegal Resident's fingers off and keep them in his pocket. One by one, he'd put them in his mouth to suckle and chew on until he'd spit out tiny bones."

Murphy cannot believe she just heard that. *"This cannot be true,"* she thinks to herself.

"He was once accused of baking a three-month-old Illegal Resident and forcing his family to eat it. His daughter once mentioned it, but recanted her story at his behest. No-one knows if it's true, but I can confirm one thing, he did take the baby's body. I don't know whether he did what he was accused of doing and I don't care, all I know is that he split the baby's chest open and pulled out whatever he could from its torso. He then put the body in his backpack."

Murphy spits a bit of the water she just sipped.

Moore notices the fluids in the cup make tiny waves because of her shivering hands as she puts it down on a table.

"Buchanan's a gentle giant."

She can no longer take it. "OK, enough of Buchanan. This is a-bout you. Why were you arrested?"

Without hesitating he starts to explain. "When I was a kid, I was infatuated with barbie dolls. Don't know if you've heard of them, but my grandma used to collect them until the war. She had many of them.

I loved how you could detach the entire doll and put her body back together. I loved the blond hair, and always told myself I'd marry a girl that looks just like them. I tried my hardest to find this girl, but they all shewed me away. Girls don't like five-foot-two guys that wear glasses with tape holding them together for some reason. I got sick and tired of being rejected, but knew I needed her. By the time I was nineteen, I was known as the body piece serial killer."

This catches Murphy off guard. She would've never thought in a million years she'd be sitting in the same room with this creep. He's one of the nation's most notorious serial killers and there she is, sitting with him.

"I took a piece of each one to build my dream woman. I'd drug them up, then drag them into my grandma's basement. I detached them just like I did the dolls before I decided what piece to take. Sometimes a foot, other times a hand," he slowly says. "I'd strangle them to death before I cut them up, it'd be cruel to cut into them while they're still alive. Plus, I loved the look on their faces as they expired. I was caught before I got my final piece. I had her whole body sewn together and was only missing her head."

Murphy cringes her teeth, she sees she still has twenty-three minutes with this creep and wishes she could run out of there. She realizes the perspiration on her forehead is noticeable when he grabs a tissue and tells her to wipe it. Everyone knows of the body piece serial killer and they actually televised it one time through the channel. All along, she thought maybe Phillips was the worse of these criminals but Moore has proved her wrong.

"Have you ever had someone you've loved romantically?"

"No," he answers. "I've never been with a woman. I'm a virgin."

Murphy's stumped. She's never met a man that'd admit to that so quickly and figures he's fibbing.

"So you never sexually did anything with the women you killed?"

She knows he didn't, because that's what stumped investigators.

They've always wondered why'd he go through such extremes if those weren't his intentions.

"No. That would give me a direct path to hell."

"And what you've done doesn't?"

"It might," he says. "Unless God understands why I did it."

"And why is that?"

"Because I needed a soul mate and couldn't find her. I know it's highly doubtful, and I've accepted the fact that I'll most likely go to hell when I die, but there's nothing wrong with a little wishful thinking."

"You seem like a devout man."

"Not really. Always went to church as a child with my grandma but I no longer go. I am convinced there's a heaven though."

"Why's that? Why are you convinced that it exists?"

"Because If there's a hell, there has to be a heaven."

"Why are you convinced there's a hell?"

"Because we're in it," he says.

Murphy pauses for a second, then continues. "Tell me about your fellow agents. Do you get along with them? Do they know why you went to prison?"

"I get along with everyone," he says. "I rarely run into someone who rubs me the wrong way. Even the people I kill, I get along with. It is nothing personal, I'm just doing my job. These agents don't know me personally and I'd like to keep it that way. Sometimes they say I'm weak, and they may all think I'm gormless, but I don't bother explaining who I am. If they knew they wouldn't say such hurtful things," he sarcastically says with a low chuckle. "They have no idea what ruthless is. I'll make them all look like saints. My favorite is Mitchell, he's a decent fella who doesn't deserve to be doing this type of work. Brown's weird, he has some sort of fascination to Phillips and it's disturbing. He tails him around like a lost puppy and gets upset with every decision Phillips makes. Phillips is Phillips, he gets off by telling you what to do and how to do it. He'll easily get under your skin if it's not thick enough."

"Have you ever thought about killing one of them?"

"Absolutely not! As long as I work with them, they're my brothers."

Murphy sees she has eight minutes left and it can't be over fast enough. She intends on rushing to Goodman's office. She needs verification on his story about who he is. She also needs to know who Buchanan is, and wants to be assured she'd never have to sit with him.

"We might all have our differences here and there, but I'll kill in an instant for any one of those gentlemen. Not much bothers me, I can handle myself. I think my time is up," he says as he looks at the clock on the wall.

"We technically have four minutes left," she replies. Deep down inside, she wants it to be over.

"OK then. I'll use this time to sit here and stare at your beauty."

Murphy moves around uncomfortably in her chair. She can't think of anything else to say and it feels like his eyes will burn a hole right through her.

"You look just like a barbie doll," he says, while looking as if he's in a trance, then gets up to leave.

She passes him a business card that shakes as he grabs it. "I'm here every Tuesday if you require additional counseling," she fights with herself to say.

"You wouldn't want that," he says as he turns to leave. "I can tell."

She slumps herself down in her chair when he's finally gone. She's still shaking and needs a minute before she goes to Goodman's office. She wants to be certain they're gone before she walks out. After taking a peep and seeing they've left, she makes her way to his office, pushes her way inside and demands answers.

"Is that the body piece serial killer!? And who's Buchanan!?" she frantically asks while pointing toward the door.

"Who? What are you talking about? How do you know about Buchanan?"

"Agent Moore! Is he the body piece serial killer!?"

"Don't be silly. The body piece serial killer works with Buchanan and they're in another district. I'd never allow those animals to work for me, they're horrible."

"He just told me in detail what he did to those girls."

"It can't possibly be, but now that I remember, they were split up and Buchanan works for Thump now."

"That's what he told me," says Murphy.

Goodman, now confused, checks Moore's code in the database and realizes it's him.

"Why would Thump send him here," he wonders.

Murphy rushes back to her office to call it a day. She desperately needs to get home and clear her head. As she gets closer, she sees an envelope was left outside of her office. It's from forensics and it must be Mitchell's results. She enters and gently opens the envelope to pull out a folded piece of paper.

Just when she thought it wasn't possible for her day to get any worse, she reads it.

"Oh, no...!" she says. She throws herself onto the seat. "This just can't be...!"

~Chapter Eleven~

Leon's Session

At daytime, the Fort's bustling, people of all kinds interact and help each other in every way possible. Leon has educated his people on the importance of knowing that everyone's equal. With little vegetation growing, you have old folks who try their best to grow fruits and vegetables. They often pray for them to blossom, but it's just not enough sunlight. There are teachers who've joined the Fort, just to teach the children. They teach them how to read, write, and basic math. They struggle when it comes to history and can only teach them how days were right before the war.

At night, it is very dark. The Fort doesn't have electricity so they have to depend on candles and fires to provide light. Leon's tried to build a home for himself, but every time he has, he's always found a family that can use it more. He sleeps in a six by six foot shed he's built that's about six-feet high, and not far from the entrance. He wants to be the first one there when his men announce that they found someone in the woods.

"We're going to need some firewood and cloth," Leon tells Ahmed. They're sitting on a huge boulder that sits on the edge of one of the trails that snake into the Fort. The trails are covered in gravel that makes crunching sounds with each step you take.

"Do we need it now?"

"For tonight. I'm going to hold a session."

Ahmed's bummed. That requires a lot of tree limbs that have to be poked into the earth to provide light.

"We haven't had a session in a while," says Ahmed.

"It's time I tell everyone."

"Tell everyone what?"

Leon looks at Ahmed and thinks of how the years have gone, and how far they've come. Leon was a young boy when he was approached by a lady who told him he was destined to build the Fort. In the beginning, it was just him and a few other kids. They gathered as many adults as possible and asked if they'd join. They practiced everything from shooting long distances, to being able to disarm someone without the use of a weapon and have mastered their techniques.

"What is it you want to tell everyone?"

"That's classified," he says with a grin. "You'll be there. You'll know. Where's Willie?"

"I don't know," Ahmed responds, while looking toward the sky.

Leon looks up and stares at the sky that many say was once blue. "Just imagine how hot it would be if the air wasn't polluted," he tells Ahmed. "Some say the sun used to shine so bright you couldn't look at it, but that can't be. How would it be possible to avoid it?"

"Mrs. Kent says you just couldn't look directly at it," says Ahmed.

"I don't know, it's just weird to me."

Mrs. Kent's a sixty-five-year-old white woman who left her family to join the Fort. Her husband supported the government's decision and it disgusted her. She left behind two sons and a pet dog. They all turned their backs on her when she expressed her opinion on the matter.

They would call her un-American and would barely speak to her. She's been in the Fort for four years now and it's where she calls home. She loves it there, regardless of the conditions she wouldn't want to be anywhere else. She left a multi-million dollar home to live as if she's in the stone ages but doesn't regret it one bit. She often huddles as many kids as possible and tells them bible stories while sitting around a campfire. Everyone there loves her, she's who everyone turns to when they need advice.

"What's the session going to be about?" asks Ahmed.

"About everything," he says as he gets off of the boulder. "I have a really bad feeling."

"What's going on?"

"I don't know, just a really weird feeling. Something is not right."

Ahmed worries. He has no idea what's wrong or what the session will be about, and watches as Leon walks away. "I'll start getting the wood ready," he shouts to him.

Leon continues to walk. He wants to check up on Willie. He's missed today's practice and it has him concerned. Willie's missed a couple the past few weeks and always comes with a different excuse as to why he couldn't participate. This has only recently started happening, and Leon needs to know what's going on. He walks into Willie's tent-like hut but he isn't inside. As he steps out, he sees Ahmed running in his direction.

"Leon," he says as he approaches. "I just saw Willie. He just entered the gate and for some reason looked as if he was trying to avoid being seen."

"Where is he now?"

"I don't know. What is going on, why is he hiding?"

"Beats me," says Leon. He looks in the distance, hoping to spot him. "You sure he was outside of the gate?"

"Yes, ask Joe. He let him in."

They both look and see Willie walking toward them. He slows

down as soon as he sees them. He looks unraveled and his shirt is soaking wet from the sweat pouring out of him.

"Where were you?" asks Leon, well before Willie gets close enough to answer without shouting.

"I was over by Mrs. Kent."

Both Ahmed and Leon look at each other. Leon kept telling him about Willie's excuses but could never really prove it to him. Ahmed and Willie are really close, so Leon's hoping Ahmed deals with it. Ahmed grabs him by the shirt and shoves him into a tree.

Willie's bright blue eyes stare at him in disbelief. "What are you doing!? Get off of me!"

"Where were you!?" he angrily demands.

"I was with Mrs. Kent, you can ask her," he says, while looking at Leon to see his reaction.

Leon wouldn't do that, he's sure he passed by and told her to say he was there. He knows Mrs. Kent would be truthful anyway, but will not put her in a position where she has to make that decision. Leon loves Willie and Ahmed, they're like three brothers.

Still clutching his shirt, Ahmed swings Willie to the left and turns, causing him to fall on his back.

"Tell me!" he shouts.

"OK, OK. Let me get up and I'll tell you."

Ahmed releases his grip at Leon's signal and watches as Willie makes it back onto his feet.

"OK. You might kill me for this," he tells Leon. "I just want you to know that if you want me out, I'll go, just don't hurt me. The reason I been staying out is because I have a girlfriend."

Ahmed and Leon look at each other.

"I been seeing her for three weeks now and I really like her. Remember the day I told you those men were staking us out when they saw us buying all the food?" Leon nods. "She's the one I told helped us by distracting them long enough for us to get out of there. I really like her and I'm sorry."

Leon sympathizes. He won't be the cause of anyone losing out on a chance to find love. A thought comes to his mind. *"Why not let Willie go live his days in the Community while reporting to us every week."*

"Do you want to live there?"

Willie looks confused. He said that hoping Leon wouldn't beat his brains in for lying but he's quick to shew him away.

"Uh. No! This is my home. I want to live here!"

"OK. I wouldn't mind having one of us living with them, checking everything out."

They hear a commotion and become aware of what it is when a little kid runs toward them.

"They got an intruder!" the kid shouts.

Leon needs this, he could release some stress and demands them to skip the trolley ride and take him directly to the barn.

"I'll be there in a minute," he tells them. Ahmed and Willie go off to escort the intruder.

Later that day, on the way to the barn, Leon sees Ahmed has gathered a crew to help him get the giant torches ready. He greets Mrs. Kent as he walks by.

"Can I have a word with you?" she asks.

"Sure," says Leon. Like everyone else, he feels a close bond with her. She's the closest he'll ever come to having a mom again.

Mrs. Kent grabs him by the arm and they begin to slowly walk. "I don't mean to be nosy or malicious in any way, and you know I wouldn't do, or say anything to come in between you boys, but I think you might need to have a talk with Willie," she says. "He came to me today, and was very concerned. Said he's come from the other side and might regret something he's done."

With Willie explaining to him earlier that day, he assures her there is nothing to worry about. "I had a talk with him about it already."

"You don't understand," she tries.

Leon does understand. He understands Willie's in love and he will not come in between that. He doesn't care who it is, he'll support him.

Mrs. Kent has a concerned look on her face and appears to have something else to say.

"I have to go now," he says. He releases himself from her clutch and starts to walk away.

Leon pushes the barn doors open and sees the man on his knees with his arms tied to each side. Seems the guy is still knocked out, but Leon will wait until he wakes up. He goes over to a chest-high wooden table that was built to hold certain instruments they want to keep out of the reach of children. Leon takes his shirt off, revealing his ripped physique. He patiently waits, then notices the man is coming to. He slowly approaches him and sees his left eye swollen shut. He sees blood coming out of his mouth and notices he's missing a few of his front teeth.

"Who are you, and where are you from?" Leon demands.

The man looks confused, it seems the head trauma still has him dazed. "Where am I?" he asks. He struggles to look through his one good eye that's covered in dried blood.

"Who are you!" screams Leon. "Where are you from!?" he savagely asks. He grabs him by the hair, pulls his head back and gets really close to his face. "You're going to tell me who you are and where you're from," he says, before shoving his head forward and walking toward the table.

"Where am I?" he asks. "I can't see!" The man struggles to talk, he has a really bad lisp.

Leon grabs what appears to be an ice cream scoop with the front tip filed, making it pointy. He also grabs a tiny pair of scissors and puts it into the back pocket of his jeans. The man looks to be around forty, with dark brown hair and green eyes. He keeps asking where he's at, and ignores Leon every time he asks who he is. This has Leon beyond angry, he's furious. Leon's an easy going guy who turns animalistic when he gets riled up. He walks toward him, and again grabs his hair.

"Who are you!?" he demands.

The man has finally had enough. He sees the scoop in Leon's hand and isn't sure what he'd do with it.

"My name is Andy. Andy Logan. Please don't hurt me!?"

"Where are you from, Andy?"

"I'm from Community-*three*. I didn't mean to walk on your land, I promise. I didn't know where I was."

Leon knows he's lying, you don't accidentally walk into the woods. Only those who come with bad intentions attempt to cross the border of the first Community. Especially if you're from Community-*three*, there's no way you accidentally wandered into the woods. The first Community is the one closest to the Fort, it was the first one built and they call it Community-*one*.

"What do you want here?"

"I don't want anything. I told you, it was a mistake. If you let me go, I promise, you'll never see my face again. Please, I have a family."

"I had a family too!" shouts Leon. "But they were savagely slaughtered by men just like you. I stood there and watched as my father was gunned down. I screamed when my mom was shot through her forehead and until this day, I can still hear the sound of my two-year-old brother's body being slammed through a table and onto the floor, over, and over again. You want me to have mercy on you!? There is no mercy in this world."

He walks toward him with the scoop in his hand. He again grabs him by the hair, puts the pointy part over his right eye and pushes it in. The man screams and tries to wiggle free, but the chains are too tight. He feels his eye being scooped out, then feels it hanging out of the socket and leaning into his cheek. Leon pulls out the scissors and begins to cut the tiny veins, causing the man to faint. Leon grabs his eye and drops it into a rusty bucket that has some kind of fluid inside. He then grabs a pair of pliers and sits on the ground in front of him. He will wait.

Ahmed explains to Willie about the session and they both try to figure out what'd be said. They hope Leon doesn't make them take the podium and talk in front of everyone, they hate it.

The man is beginning to wake up, so Leon starts to stand. His intention is to inflict as much pain as possible before stopping as he gets to the edge of death. He walks to the man and grabs his fingers in his hand. With his four fingers scrunched up in his grip, he takes the pliers and starts pulling his fingernails off. The man is screaming in pain, it's excruciating and he can't take it.

"Please stop!" he screams. "I'll tell you anything."

"I don't need to know anything from you," says Leon. He looks to be demented. He grabs his other hand and does the same. When he's done, he puts the eight fingernails into the bucket he dropped his eye in.

"I give up!" the man shouts.

"There is no giving up! You will not leave this barn alive!"

"So kill me already!" the man screams.

Leon grabs a saw that's on the table and rushes toward him. He puts it on the man's neck and watches the little teeth on the blade cut through his skin. He repeatedly pushes it back and forth and the blood splatters all over the place. He keeps sawing at it, until he feels the teeth get to the other side of his spinal bones. He then suddenly stops. The man's head is almost off. It falls to the side and seems to be barely holding on by its skin.

Leon lays on his back in the middle of the barn floor. He's soaked in blood and needs a minute to catch his breath. When he finally does, he unlocks the barn and sees Willie and Ahmed out there waiting on him. They expect nothing less than for him to come out drenched in blood, so they aren't surprised.

"You got to get ready, man," says Ahmed. "The session starts soon."

"What is it about?" asks Willie.

"Will you guys clean this up for me?"

"Of course," says Ahmed. "Go get ready."

As they enter, Willie goes straight to the table and grabs a knife. He walks to the man and holds his head up by its hair. With no hesitation, he cuts the remaining skin to free the head from the body.

Ahmed stares at him.

"What?" asks Willie. "Easier to carry the body now. What do you think the session will be about?"

"I have no idea."

A session's done once in a while, it's when the entire Fort come together for Leon to inform them of something. No-one likes sessions because it's usually to inform them of something bad, and the last thing they want to hear is more negative news.

Leon steps out of his hut. He sees the fires glowing and everyone settled under, and around a little cliff he stands on every time he makes an announcement. He walks and can't stand the silence, not one person has made a sound. He remembers the first sessions, they were full of life and everyone was pumped. Now it's different and he senses guilt, he's the leader and the fault is on him.

Ahmed is in the crowd and has lost track of Willie.

"I will like to start by taking a second to thank you all for coming out," he begins to announce. *"I know you all dread it considering how boring I am,"* he says, trying to get at least one chuckle.

Nothing. Everyone stands there and no-one has made a sound.

140

Leon's having second thoughts and wonders if he should bring it up. He looks down at the crowd and sees Mrs. Kent clutching a bible in her hands. Just when he was about to call it off and apologize to everyone for wasting their time, she nods at him.

"We don't have much here," he says. *"But we have each other and we have life. Every day we wake up, we should thank the Lord for giving us another day to wait on him."* The crowd is still silent. *"I know a lady, she was the one who financed this all,"* he says, as he waves his hand to show what he's talking about, referring to the Fort. *"According to her, she spent her entire life's savings on this place. It pains me to see you all sad and down, when we should be filled with the spirit God gave us. We should rejoice every day. We should pray that when he arrives, he shows mercy on everyone responsible for this. The rich man is trying to take over this country and he will, but only over my dead body. We have love here. We have people of all kinds that have come together to support one another. This assures me that we still have hope, and we might have a brighter future."*

The crowd is beginning to loosen up and Leon sees movement within them.

"I started this when I was only thirteen years old. This lady came along and told me I was destined to. As crazy as I sound to you, she sounded to me. 'Can't be me,' I thought to myself. She spent all of her money and sent most of you here. You all remember her," he says, while pointing to the section where the teachers and Doctors are, getting nods from them.

The crowd is buzzing. They all turn to the person next to them, wondering who he's talking about.

"She sent us teachers for our children, Doctors for our ill, and she didn't do it because she had to, she did it because she cared. Many of you wonder who I'm talking about and many of you know who she is. She's the one who introduced me to this," he says, while raising a book he carried under his arm when he entered. *"It disappoints me to know that I left this book available for anyone to read, and not one single person did. In this book you'll learn our fate. Since not one of you read it, I will educate you a little about it. There was a man in the 1600's who predicted all of this. He predicted there will one day come a phantom war, the same war I also thought never happened for many years. As you're all aware, it did happen. He was wrong and so was I,"* he says, while poking his finger into the book. *"But I believe he's coming. I believe our savior will one day arrive."*

Everyone in the crowd is wondering what he's talking about. They don't think there's any help coming, they're despondent.

"He predicted this Fort. In his inscriptions he called it 'The Land.' He called it the land that will be ruled by the man of the country of the red dragon until the chosen one arrives. I know he speaks of this place, I can feel it. I'm the man from the country of the red dragon."

Most in the crowd look at him as if they think he's lost his mind.

"In this book, it says that a baby will be born that'll survive the mark of the beast. Does anyone know what that mark is?"

"The chip!" someone shouts.

"No," he says. *"The mark is the vaccine. Think about it, if you're not injected within thirty minutes of time of birth, you die. If you do, you cannot have any children, thus killing your population. He says in*

this book that a child will survive the mark after the time has expired. He says there will be another child born twelve years before the one he speaks of in this book, and together they will form one. Together, they will be powerful, and together, they will uncover everything. I know this means we'll have to wait at least twelve years and many more before the child becomes of age, but I want you all to know he's coming. When? No-one knows, but I'd love for it to be in my lifetime. I'd love to see the look on their faces when they realize this insanity is over. From this day on, it's mandatory for every child nine years of age and older to join in our practices," he says, drawing cheers from the kids. *"We'll get ready and we'll be strong. Our children will learn to use the arms this government once allowed us to carry, and will also learn to kill someone with their bare hands so they won't have to depend on them. We will not sit here and wait to be invaded then lose when we finally are. We will train and surprise them when they feel brave enough to enter."*

The crowd goes wild and Leon is shocked. He hasn't seen this much spirit in a long time. They're so loud, they're heard in Community-*one*, where General Reid's preparing troops to look for Andy. They all look toward the woods when they hear the crowd's roar.

"I want everyone to grab the hand of the person next to them and join me in a prayer," Leon says.

Everyone grabs the hand of the person nearest.

"We want to thank our Lord, for the biggest blessing of all. The gift of life," he says.

Everyone's gone silent and have bowed their heads.

"We'll patiently wait for you to send us our savior, and we will pray in your name until our time has come to enter your paradise. Amen."

"Amen," everyone says, then burst out in a louder roar.

"What's that all about?" Reid asks the young man next to him.

"I don't know," he answers. "I hope it's not over. We have to go. Now...!"

~Chapter Twelve~

Sophia's Journey

Sophia and Patrice are about a mile into their journey, but Sophia feels as if they're almost there. She knows she has to be extremely careful walking with an eight-year-old child in the middle of the night. She waited until everyone was asleep before she grabbed Patrice and escaped out the back door. She's heartbroken with what she's told her and knew she had to get her out of there as soon as possible. Her father's always said the Fort's a made up place, and would call it a fairy tale. She doesn't even know if it really exists.

Suddenly, she hears a sound behind them, but when she turns, she sees no-one. Sophia grabs Patrice's arm and speeds up the velocity of her walk. She keeps looking back and focuses on a parked car that's charred, that's the only place anyone could hide without being seen. She turns the corner where there's a fence with its wires ripped off. Patrice's struggling to keep up, with one hand holding on to Sophia's and the other hugging her teddy bear into her ribs. They cross a street and hide beside a building. Sophia peeks and sees no-one. They stand there for five minutes with her having to hush Patrice every once in a while. Still, she doesn't see anyone, so figures it's safe to proceed.

Patrice is tired and has been telling Sophia she needs a rest for the last mile, but Sophia thinks they're close and doesn't want to stop. Her speed causes Patrice to fall when her legs give in, and she barely has enough strength to get back on her feet. Sophia walks her to a bus stop shelter so she could sit on the bench and rest. She looks in the direction they came from and sees someone cower behind an overloaded dump container.

"Who's there!?" she shouts. Patrice is amused by the echo. Sophia can't see much and gets no response. "I know you're there. Come out!"

She could hardly see, but definitely just seen someone pop their head out. "You ready?" she loudly whispers to Patrice, who nods her head to say she isn't. Sophia has no choice but to walk toward the dumpster. She slowly walks toward it, and can feel her heart beating. She crouches down and picks up a stick that appears to belong to the burnt house that's across the street.

"Don't go," says Patrice, as Sophia slowly walks.

Sophia knows she has to, she cannot risk getting cornered. She bangs on the dumpster with the stick, making it snap in half, and demands for whoever is there to come out. The person comes out with their hands up. They have a baseball cap on that cover their eyes, making it difficult to see who it is.

"Slow down," the person says and begins to laugh.

"Gabriel!?"

He continues to laugh while walking toward her.

"You idiot, you nearly scared the life out of me," she says while holding her chest. Patrice runs toward them when she sees it's him.

Sophia's knees are trembling and her heart is rapidly beating, but feels a tremendous sense of relief knowing it's him.

"What are you doing out here?" she asks.

"I've been following you since you left the house."

"Why were you hiding?"

"I figured I'd wait until we're far enough, this way you won't be able to tell me to go back."

"You'll get in trouble when your parents find out."

"They'll get over it, just like they did with my sister. We need a car."

"No we don't, we're almost there," says Sophia.

"Almost there? I told you it's like eighty miles away."

Sophia's ignorant when it comes to distance and has no idea how long a mile is.

"We have around seventy-six miles to go. Well, you do. I'm going to get you to the entrance of the Community, from there you have to trek it thirty miles and hope no-one catches you."

Sophia doesn't pay attention. She's focused on the distance, and can't believe that after all the walking they've done, they've only gone four miles.

Gabriel has a friend that lives not far away who might be able to lend them a car.

"Why are you so nice? Why help us make it there?" Sophia asks Gabriel as they begin to walk. "I mean..." she pauses.

"You can say it. Why help you if I'm white...?"

Sophia doesn't admit that's what she insinuated but her silence assures him it is.

"Let me ask you something. How many white people have been cruel to you? Because I'm white, and have yet to meet another white person who agrees with what's going on. We don't want this, it's cruel and I haven't met one person that condones it. We'll rather risk our lives saving an Illegal Resident than believe in what they're doing."

Sophia thinks about it and realizes he's right. Besides Richard, all other white people she's run into have been pleasant. She can't think of one bad moment and remembers what her father's always told her.

"You cannot judge all people by the actions of a few."

"Now the rich people you want to look out for, and unfortunately, the Communities you have to cross to get to the Fort are full of them. They're ruthless, Sophia, you have to be very careful. You know the prediction of the Prophet about the kid?" he asks. "You think it's true? Do you think it'll really happen?"

"Look at this," she says while looking around. "There was a war he claimed wouldn't happen. How would they even know he survived the mark of the beast if no-one knows what the mark of the beast is. It can't be the chip, we all survived it, and it can't be the vaccine because we survived that also. I don't know about his predictions, I just want to go somewhere safe."

Dr. Gus wants Brianna to get to the Fort so bad he takes the chance and tries sneaking her in himself, three days after she got to him. A mile before they make it to the entrance of Community-*five,* he stops the car to hide her and the baby in the back. Dr. Gus has a four-by-four truck that looks very old but runs really good. He lays her in the back and throws a carpet over them. He figures they won't check his car once he shows identification proving his sister lives in Community-*two.* As he approaches the front gate, he's stopped by a fence that guards the entrance. There's a man in a booth that looks as if he doesn't want to be bothered and staggers out. Dr. Gus has his ID out, hoping he'll just push a button and open the gate. Instead, the man walks toward the back of the car and peeks through the windows. He claims to see something move and demands Gus to open the back. This makes Gus's heart drop. He steps out of the vehicle and gives the man a funny face, then motions his head as if he's trying to tell him something. The man pulls out his gun and smashes through the back window.

"I have a gift for General Reid in there," Dr. Gus says. "I brought him a very pretty Illegal Resident."

The man shoves the carpet over and grabs Brianna by the arm, forcibly dragging her out, causing her to hit the stoned driveway.

"You better have a good explanation for this." He hasn't noticed the baby. Gus had to say what he said to protect himself, and is debating on whether he should mention the baby for some leniency from Reid. A car comes to a skid on the gravel and two men rush out of it. They grab Brianna, shove her into the car and pull off.

"You get in your car and follow them," the man tells Gus while pointing at his face. They make him follow them to a two-story building in Community-*three*. Reid's Inside, and infuriated. The building's used to hold monthly meetings and operate everyday issues in the Communities, it's like the white house to them. With Reid being the leader, he's always there, but never this late. He's huddled inside with the four other Governors. They've just learned they've lost half the team of men they sent out to look for Andy. Reid's already been notified of Brianna and Gus. He walks out as soon as they arrive and goes directly to them. He stares at Gus for a while, then asks for his identification.

"Gustoff? Annie Gustoff?" asks Reid, as he reads the card Gus passes him, which indicates what relative resides there.

"That's my sister. My name is Robert Gustoff. I was coming to see her and ran into this really pretty lady on the way, so I knocked her out and dragged her in here for you, sir," he says.

"And why'd you do that?" he asks as he looks toward Brianna, who's wiggling around, trying to loosen herself from his man's grip. She cannot speak with the tape over her mouth but keeps attempting to scream something.

"I thought you'd like her, sir."

Brianna's movements and sounds are annoying Reid. "Take the tape off," he tells his man.

Gus looks at Brianna. He winks at her when she gives him eye contact, convincing her to go along with it. When the man peels the tape, she says nothing.

Reid looks at her, then back at his man."Put it back on!" he demands.

"That was very kind of you," he tells Gus, and shakes his hand. "Your sister is a fine lady. Don't mess that up," he softly whispers to him while tightly holding his hand and pulling him closer.

Gus's concerned for the baby, and knows he has to get him to the Fort. He feels bad for Brianna because there's no way she'll get out of this. He heads to his car while Reid instructs his men to take her to the pit.

"We're here," says Gabriel. They approach a very nice house, but instead of going in, he walks to the side of it and heads toward the back with Sophia and Patrice following.

"Where are we?" Sophia asks.

"This is my friend's house," he responds.

They enter the backyard and see Jose. He's laid back on a beach chair with only a flood light shining and appears to be sleeping.

Gabriel tries to wake him without making a sound. "Wake up," he loudly whispers, and shakes his leg.

Jose wakes up and is surprised to see him. "What's up, man! How are you!?" he tells Gabriel.

They both swing a hand, causing them to make a loud clapping sound when they clash against each other.

"I need a favor from you, man. I need a car," Gabriel says with a look of concern. He knows that if he convinces Jose it's an emergency he'd lend him one.

Jose's only seventeen, but a very skilled mechanic. His dad would force him as a child to help him fix cars and he's mastered it. He can take a car completely apart and put it back together, something even his father can't do.

"It's like two in the morning. What the hell do you need a car for?"

Gabriel and Jose are really good friends. Jose often fought for him when they were growing up. Kids in the neighborhood would pick on him because he wouldn't fight back. One day Jose asked him why. He said he'd get grounded if he got into any kind of trouble, and since that day, Jose has stuck up for him every single time. He knew the reason he didn't defend himself was because it wasn't in him to fight. They now live far apart and have not seen each other in years.

"I'm going to be honest with you. I need a car to get to the Communities."

"Are you crazy!? With them? You must have a death wish. You know you can't be seen with an Illegal Resident around there."

Patrice hides behind Sophia with a really concerned look on her face.

"I'm not going in, they are. They need to get to the Fort."

"They'll never make it and you know it."

"I've been telling them, but they really want to go."

"I'll go in if you do," Jose tells Gabriel with a smile.

"Go in where?"

"To the Fort. Let's do it."

"You crazy? Hell no!"

"This could be a mission, like the ones we used to play when we were younger. It'll be fun. You're not going to let these girls go alone, are you?"

Sophia's hoping Gabriel agrees, and so is Patrice. Her little eyes go back and forth to Jose and Gabriel, she looks at each one every time they speak.

Gabriel looks at Patrice and notices the sad face she gives him every time she wants something. As much as he doesn't want to, he agrees.

"Let's go," says Jose. He slowly runs toward the front of the house with them all chasing.

Brianna's been shoved into a room that has concrete walls, and there's nowhere to sit besides a flimsy mattress on the floor that's filthy. There's a little ray of light that shines through the window that's too high to look out of. She's sure Dr. Gus will be back for her any minute now, but she's really scared. The men that pushed her in told her to get ready. She doesn't know what they meant, but kinda figures it isn't anything good. She feels around the walls and rubs her hands on something slimy every once in a while, but can't see what it is.

General Reid arrives at his house and is told his daughter came over with her husband and their child. He's naturally rude, and doesn't like the fact that they came unannounced. No-one in the Communities has ever met his son-in-law. He didn't want him for her and seems to be embarrassed, so never takes them out when they visit.

He fusses with his wife when she tells him they're upstairs sleeping, then leaves. General Reid and his wife Suzy are complete different individuals, while he has a stone cold heart, hers is very warm. She's a well-respected, very nice lady who tends to help anyone when needed. She's one of the few in the Communities who's scared to voice their opinions about what's going on. She comes from a poor family and was fortunate when she met Reid. She left her home at an early age, and doesn't even know if her parents are still alive. Seeing her husband bothered about something has her really concerned. She noticed he was upset before he knew they were there, which means it has to be something else.

The next morning she awakes and realizes her husband's returned when she hears him telling their grandson how tough he wants him to be. As she begins to get breakfast prepared, her daughter comes down and asks if she's seen her son.

"He's out front with his grandpa." Her daughter goes to wash up, but instead lays back down.

"Come here, kid," Reid tells a boy that appears to be around sixteen years old, and is well known in the Community as being a bully. "You want to make fifty DD's?" The boy of course says yes.

"I want you to fight him," he says as he points at his grandson.

The boy looks confused and doesn't want to get on Reid's bad side. His grandson panics and has a horrified look on his face.

"I want you to beat him to a pulp," he tells him.

Reid's grandson is an eleven-year-old boy who's really chubby for his age. The boy rushes toward him, knocks him to the ground and repeatedly punches him while pinning him down, forcing blood to squirt out of his nose.

"Hit him! Hit him! Hit him!" screams Reid.

The commotion forces Suzy, her daughter, and son-in-law to run out of the house to see what's going on. The boy gets off of him and takes off as soon as he sees them come out. Reid's son-in-law jumps down the stairs to come to the aid of his son.

"What the hell is wrong with you!?" his daughter shouts at him. "That's your grandchild! Why would you...!"

"He has to learn," Reid meanly interrupts. "How you expect him to be tough if you treat him like a little girl?"

Reid's daughter announces she's going home. Her husband walks their son inside with a rag over his face to stop the bleeding.

Suzy looks at Reid with a sad expression. Without uttering a word, she climbs the steps and makes her way back into the house.

Brianna's still trapped and is petrified. She can now see that the walls are stained with what appears to be blood and it has her on edge.

Sophia, Patrice, Gabriel, and Jose are trying to find a way to get through the gate. The only way would be to climb it, but it has barbed wire. Jose runs back to the car which is about a block away, and comes back with a thick blanket he uses when fixing a vehicle. It's heavily stained with oil but still helpful. He tosses it over the gate and it lands right over the barbed wire.

"I'll go first," he says. He makes it over but drops a gun when he lands on the other side.

"What is that!?" asks Sophia. She sees him quickly tuck it back into his waist.

"An extra level of security," he says as he looks at her through the fence. Sophia's having second thoughts. When they kept saying this could be dangerous, she never listened. *"How dangerous could it be,"* she would ask herself.

General Reid's prepared to have a sit down with his men, when all of a sudden, Gus walks in.

"What are you doing here?" he asks.

"I, I came to see if you enjoyed my gift, sir."

The building's opened to the public so Reid isn't surprised he made it in so easily.

Dr. Gus keeps staring at a young man sitting next to Reid who has really blue eyes. They almost look fake.

"I haven't tasted it yet."

Gus is relieved. He needs Brianna and he needs her now. The baby will not stop crying and seems to need his mom, and he's sure she's downstairs in the pits. The pits are used to torture Illegal Residents and prep them to be hung somewhere, but with fewer daring to pass, they hardly get the opportunity anymore.

"She looks like she'll be good," says Reid. "I'm going to tear her up and hang her in five different places."

This doesn't surprise Gus, everyone knows how ruthless Reid is.

"OK. I'll get going now. Tell me how she tastes." Gus waits until the rest of the gentlemen go in. As soon as everyone enters, and they close the door, he rushes down the hallway and enters a door that has steps leading downstairs. There are corridors with different dungeon-like rooms and he has to find the one Brianna's in. He opens a door and is rushed by a Hispanic kid who quickly runs out and up the stairs. Gus gets so startled he almost takes off, but knows he has to find her.

"Brianna," he loudly whispers. "Gus?" he hears. He hobbles over and opens the door. Brianna insists on staying with him when he tells her to run ahead because he can't move fast enough. Just as they're about to leave the building, they notice two gentlemen entering.

"Get behind me," he tells her. Brianna quickly moves behind him and goes around as they pass.

"Good thing I'm big, right?" he tells her with a nervous smile. They exit the building and hurry into his car.

Sophia and the rest have almost crossed Community-*five*. It isn't filled yet, so it was easy to get through. They need water, so they contemplate going into a house. Jose walks around it, peeking through windows to make sure there's no-one inside. When he's sure there isn't, they break in and immediately make their way to the kitchen. They were hoping there would be water but there isn't any. Patrice is coughing and needs to rest. After a few minutes, they hear what sounds like the front door opening and all shuffle around. There's someone walking in and they have nowhere to hide.

"In here," says Jose. He guides them into a closet that's built for mops and brooms. It isn't big enough for them all, but they manage to squeeze in. Jose's the last one in and grabs his gun before closing the door. They stay silent while listening to the sounds of footsteps walking around the house, then hold their breaths when they realize they've entered the kitchen.

"It'll only cost you one million dollars," they hear a voice say.

They then hear the voice of a woman.

"We'll take it. When can we move in?"

"You can move in now if you want."

"Great," says the woman. She walks toward the sink, turns the faucet on, but nothing comes out. "Can you do me a favor?" she asks. "I turned the faucet on because I want the water to run for a little while. Can you turn it on tonight? I'll start moving in tomorrow."

"Absolutely," he says. "I'll turn it on as soon as you sign."

The woman lifts her sleeve and gets her chip scanned to complete the transaction.

"SOLD!" they hear.

They spring out of the closet when they leave and can't believe the close call.

"The water will soon be on, then we have to keep moving," says Jose. Patrice sits on the floor with her back against the wall, so Sophia goes to comfort her.

"You OK?" she asks. Patrice nods her head and confirms that she is.

"Did you hear that?" Sophia asks out loud. "He said a million dollars. Why say a million dollars if we've been using DD's for years now?"

She makes Jose and Gabriel wonder. They didn't pick it up, but agree that that's what he said. They wait for hours then hear a sound and notice the water's beginning to flow.

Jose rushes toward the sink when it starts streaming out.

"NO!" says Sophia. "The water's contaminated!"

Jose and Gabriel begin to laugh.

"We would've been dead by now." He cups his hands under the stream and slurps away.

The water's been contaminated for years now and isn't safe to drink, but most Illegal Residents had no other choice. With the military providing bottled water to only the rich, they had to risk their lives to get hydrated. For years they've been drinking it, and have yet to hear of anyone dying. In Sophia's case, her dad struggled every day to make sure he provided clean water for his family, even if it's all he brought home after a hard day's work.

It's Sophia's turn to drink, and without hesitating, and barely able to reach the faucet, she also cups her hands and fills herself with Fluids.

156

The meeting's concluded and one of the gentlemen turns to Reid on his way out. "When was the last time you got the pleasure of killing an Illegal Resident?" he asks.

"I have two of them now," replies Reid. "It's going to be a show when I get my paws on them."

The man chuckles and walks out.

"Go give them water," Reid says to the blue-eyed kid.

"OK. Then I must go, sir. They're expecting me."

Gus is speeding and the ride is bumpy.

"I need to get to my son," says Brianna. "Hurry up!"

"Listen, honey," he says. He occasionally looks at her while concentrating on the road. "I cannot go all the way with you, but I'll point you in the direction."

"But, but, what if...?"

"You'll be fine," he says. "Your son is destined to live."

"They're gone, sir!" says the blue-eyed kid as he rushes back in.

"What!? What do you mean they're gone!? How can it be!?" he meanly asks. *"Dr. Gus,"* he thinks to himself.

Sophia prepares Patrice to keep moving and they hear the sound of glass breaking in one of the rooms. Jose grabs his gun, leans his back on the wall, and slowly walks toward the door. He positions himself to shoot and goes for it. As he turns toward the doorway to the room they heard the sound come from, someone punches him in the face, causing him to drop the gun. The person grabs him in a choke hold and drags him into the room. Gabriel runs toward the door, grabs the gun and points inside.

"Drop the knife!" he shouts. Sophia can see the gun shaking in his hand and is huddled with Patrice who's covering her ears, just in case he shoots. Gabriel demands him to drop the knife again. The person

157

has a knife to Jose's throat and Gabriel doesn't know what to do. The guy looks possessed, he isn't saying anything and just stares at Gabriel. He takes the chance and pulls the trigger, but nothing comes out. Jose's gun was empty all along.

The man begins to laugh. "Give me everything you have!" he demands.

Sophia stands when she hears the voice. "No," she says. "It can't be." She starts to walk toward the door Gabriel's facing.

"Get back!" Gabriel yells. "He has a knife!"

She continues, then falls to her knees sobbing when she makes it there and looks inside. The guy lets Jose go, drops the knife and leans his back against a wall while his eyes fill with tears.

"Felipe!" she says. He rushes toward her and throws himself onto his knees to hold her tight.

"Oh my God! My little sister," he cries as they both loudly sob. "I thought I'd never see you again."

"They killed Mami, and Papi," she cries. "They killed everybody...!"

Gabriel and Jose have to look away, they get teary eyed and don't want anyone to notice. Patrice's standing in the doorway with her arms by her sides, holding the teddy bear that's hanging by an arm.

"We will make it to the Fort," says Jose. "I can just feel it...!"

~Chapter Thirteen~

Agent Bradley Mitchell

"Look, Dad, he replied," Jacob tells his father first thing in the morning. Mitchell could hardly sleep that night, he tossed and turned but couldn't get comfortable. He's looking forward to speaking to Dr. Murphy again and the thought of what he'd say prevented him from falling asleep.

"What did he say?"

"He says he's in Japan. His name is Moshi."

"He says he's where?"

"In Japan, but how could that be, Dad. I thought Japan was destroyed?"

"It was. Don't listen to him, Son." Mitchell puts on his tie and takes a sip of the coffee Jacob's made.

"He's pretty convinced. He keeps putting that stupid little yellow face with its tongue sticking out every time I ask him a question."

"It's someone messing with you, Son. I have to go now, don't let this guy get into your head. There is no way he's in japan, it's probably one of those spoiled rich kids playing games."

Mitchell meets his fellow agents at the headquarters. There hasn't been any lists and Phillips is itching to go to work.

They spot Goodman coming with a paper in his hand, and as he approaches, he passes Phillips a list.

"You have to be careful with this one, they're said to be a family of criminals. Let one of your men enter first, make it Brown, he's fast," Goodman secretly whispers to him.

Phillips wonders why he'd suggest for him to let brown enter first. He doesn't know whether to feel disrespected, or honored that Mr. Goodman cared that much to warn him. They hop in the vehicle, and when Phillips sees there are thirteen people on the list he pumps his fist and comes alive. "We have a big one here, fellas. Let's go do what we do best."

They approach the house that has a chest high fence around it. They exit the car and Phillips tries to open it, but instead, they're startled when two muscular pit bulls race toward the fence viciously barking. Brown flinches so hard he almost falls. Moore is closest, but doesn't react at all.

"You're one weird puppy," Phillips tells him. Mitchell pulls out his gun and signals for Phillips to do the same.

"At the same time," he says.

Moore's impressed at how they simultaneously shoot without counting it down, but make it sound like a single shot. One dog dies immediately and the other runs toward the back but collapses midway there. All four have their guns drawn now, they're sure someone would run out at the sound of gunfire.

Moore enters the fence, runs to the side of the house and tries to catch a glimpse inside but is unable to with curtains hanging in the way. He tries to lift a window, but it's locked. Phillips remembers what Goodman told him and explains that Brown will kick the door in while they stand cover.

With no hesitation, Brown gets into position, and with one lunge forward, he plants the sole of his foot to the door with as much force as possible. As soon as the door opens, there's a shotgun blast that tears through his chin and neck area. Mitchell rushes in thinking someone did it but the house is empty. The shotgun is hanging from the ceiling with a thin rope attached that pulled the trigger as soon as the door was opened.

"It was a setup," says Mitchell as Phillips enters with his gun drawn. Moore approaches Brown, half of his chin is missing and his neck looks like mangled meat. He holds his head up, silently telling him to let go. Brown is choking on his blood and Moore knows he's suffering. He considers shooting him in the head to end it, then sees him take his final breath. Phillips crouches down and Mitchell bows his head. Although they have their differences, they all feel it when a fellow agent dies. As much animosity they have toward each other is as much respect. Phillips looks at the gun that's hanging as he rises up. *"Who could have done this,"* he wonders. He sees the gun is new, and knows there's no way an Illegal Resident could have a gun in such good condition.

"We have to make it back to Goodman," he says as he leaves the house, still gripping his gun. He passes the dog's corpse, shoots it a-gain and continues walking. "What are y'all waiting for!?" he shouts.

They hurry out of the car to demand an explanation from Mr. Goodman and run into the agent that keeps bragging to Phillips.

"I got an Escaped Illegal..."

Phillips doesn't let him finish the statement. He swings his fist and connects it to the agent's cheek bone, knocking him down. Mitchell has to stop Phillips from continuing the assault by grabbing and hold-ing him back.

"What the hell is wrong with you!?" says the agent who's now sitting on the ground holding his face.

Phillips barges into Goodman's office with Mitchell, and Moore right behind him. He demands answers and doesn't care about the consequences. Mitchell looks at Phillips and wonders if he should risk it all for a guy he didn't even like. The way he's speaking will surely result in disciplinary action being taken.

"You watch how you talk to me, young man!"

"Mr. Goodman?" interrupts Mitchell. "We were set up. There was a shotgun that went off when the door was opened. The house was empty but there were curtains in the windows, so whoever did this was trying to avoid us looking inside!"

"I! Want! Answers!" yells Phillips.

Mitchell's taken aback and Moore has a huge smirk on his face.

"I need you gentleman to give Phillips and I a minute."

Mitchell believes he's crossed the line and is concerned for him.

"It had to be done," says Goodman.

Phillips has both fist on his desk and his head bowed. He thought Goodman would send him home to say his goodbyes to his family before releasing the poison with the way he spoke to him.

"What do you mean?"

"He spoke too much, but that was hardly my concern. What concerned me the most is how fast I heard he spoke. He told her everything, even about Fred."

"But you told me...?"

"I had to think on it before I reacted. He could have brought us both down."

"Why not just poison him? What if someone else had opened the door? What if it were me!?"

"I have faith in you Phillips, I knew I could trust you'd do as I say."

"Why not poison him?"

"And explain it how to the other men?"

Phillips knows he has a point, but thinks of what to say to Mitchell and Moore.

"Rodney? When your boys ask, tell them I said I'll take care of it. Then tell them how you dropped to your knees and begged for your life," he says. "If it weren't for these circumstances you'd be dead by now. Don't you ever come in here with that nonsense again. Now get out of my office!" he tells him while turning his back.

Phillips leaves the office and the announcement of Brown's death is made through the intercom. Everyone in the building simultaneously bow their heads, cross their hands and remain silent.

Phillips sees the agent he just punched in the face after they've paid their respects.

"I'm sorry, sir," the agent tells him and extends his hand. "I had no idea."

Phillips silently walks away and leaves him standing there. The thought of punching him in the face again crosses his mind but he decides to keep the peace.

Mitchell goes and sits in the row of chairs outside of Dr. Murphy's office. She will not be there for another four hours but he decides to stick it out. He's having memories of Brown and thinks of his daughters. With his head bowed, he notices someone sits on the row of chairs across from his. It's Moore, he comes over to see how Mitchell's doing. Moore didn't have such a close relationship with Brown so it didn't impact him as much.

"That was a setup," Moore calmly states. Mitchell thinks the same thing, but the way he says it makes it sound as if he's sure it was. Moore rests his elbows on his knees and leans forward. "Brown knew this was coming, he told me it would happen. He mentioned he'd said something to Dr. Murphy that he shouldn't have. He told her that Phillips killed Cryan," he blatantly says.

Mitchell's surprised. "*Even if he did tell him that, why would he be telling me. Why tell anyone,"* he thinks. Mitchell's always thought there was more to the Cryan story than Phillips had him believe, but doesn't care at this point.

"I'm only telling you this because he told me to tell you. He stressed for me to tell you that Phillips killed Fred, but only if he was killed."

Mitchell's speechless. *"Why would he want him to tell me?"* he wonders.

"Told me to tell you this was done by our own men, and wanted me to warn you about them. Especially Phillips. He must have liked you, because he also told me to tell you to try and get out. We both know that's impossible but I admire his wishful thinking."

Mitchell doesn't want to get into it. Even if it was his men, what could he do, and how could he get out of it. He has no choice but to live the rest of his days as a killer while trying his best to avoid messing up along the way. *"If Brown said something to cause this, then he should have known better,"* he thinks.

"I'll be going now," Moore says as he gets up. He goes over and puts a hand on Mitchell's shoulder. "You take care now, I'll see you tomorrow."

Mitchell sits there and stares at Murphy's door for the next two hours. He thinks of Brown and wonders why he'd tell Moore to tell him Phillips killed Fred.

"Agent Mitchell!?" he hears, with the sounds of heels increasing their speed and getting louder. He looks and sees Murphy approaching. "I am so sorry for your loss," she tells him. "You don't have to do this to yourself today, you should go home and get some rest."

"No. I'm ready to say it all," he sadly says. He follows her into her office, removes his blazer and sits on the chair. She looks at his holster which looks really old and notices something very weird.

"Where did you get that holster?" she asks him.

"Oh, it was in a pile back when I started. It screamed for me to grab it. It was by far the worse looking one."

Murphy's amused. *"What a coincidence,"* she thinks.

"OK. Being that I interviewed you last week, we're going to skip the basic part and jump right into it. Tell me your thoughts on what happened to Agent Brown today."

Mitchell knows she's fishing for information for Goodman so doesn't play into it. "Illegal Residents must have booby-trapped the house before taking off."

That's the answer she wanted to hear, it's the same one Goodman gave her when she asked what had happened. She kind of feels sorry for Mitchell and doesn't want to have to report something that might get him killed. She has no idea Goodman's in any way responsible for his death.

"I didn't come here to discuss Brown today," he says. "I have things that are bothering me and I wasn't completely honest with you the last time. I want you to speak to me as a person, not on the record."

For some reason Mitchell feels he could trust her. He doesn't sense she had anything to do with Brown's murder and was only doing her job when she reported to Goodman.

"OK." She gets up and drops the clipboard on her desk. "Not here. Let's go sit outside."

They sit on a bench and Mitchell looks around before beginning to speak. "My son," he says. "I haven't been completely honest with him. He has a girlfriend he's never introduced me to and has no idea I know who it is. I followed him one night and seen him with the young lady. I didn't think at the time it was his girlfriend, and still don't know for sure, but he'd be risking his life being with her and I don't know what to do."

"What are you talking about?" she asks.

"She left about a year ago and he doesn't know why."

"What exactly are you saying?"

"She has a baby he doesn't know about."

Murphy's stunned. It bewilders her as to why he'd keep his son in the dark about something so important. She's worried about the test, and hopes he doesn't ask about it. It'll kill her to give him such horrible news at this time.

"Let me get this straight. Your son has a girlfriend who has a child that he doesn't know about? What is wrong with you?" she asks. She's trying to revert negativity, hoping he doesn't remember he asked her to check on his mom. "How do you know it's his?"

"I don't," he says. "But he looks exactly like him. Maybe I'm just jumping to conclusions."

"And you have the audacity to say he'd be risking his life being with her..."

"She's an Illegal Resident."

"I've figured that out," she responds. "You need to go home and tell him."

Murphy knows she has to give him the results. The reason she dragged him outside is because she's concerned there might be a recording device in her office. She knows Goodman's antics and doesn't trust him. He'd told her he knew the results when she reported them to him and stressed she must not tell him, or else. It kind of scared her and made her contemplate going to work for the N.A.A., but remembered about Buchanan.

"Promise me you'll tell him."

Mitchell thinks about it. "I promise," he pledges.

"Are you ready to tell me why you were imprisoned?"

Mitchell bows his head. He was hoping she didn't ask as much as she's hoping he doesn't ask about the results.

"It's time to come clean," she states.

"Why can't you just ask Goodman?" he asks. "I'm sure he knows."

"Actually he doesn't. Thump doesn't disclose those details."

"OK. I'll tell you. I wasn't honest with you last week, so it's the least I could do. I just want you to know that I'm not the same man I was back then."

Murphy turns to face him while still on the bench. *"This can't be that bad,"* she thinks.

"When I told you my mom left, I lied," he says, then takes a pause. "She told me they had stopped the relationship. When I was twelve, she, her boyfriend, and Maggie were heavily drinking. When they were drunk my mom told Maggie to take me in the room and have her way with me. It made my mom's boyfriend happy because my mom messed around with Maggie and he didn't like it. He'd often beat her over it, it's the reason he left. After that night, it's like I fell in love. I'd tell my mom how I felt about her but she'd laugh it off."

Murphy's interestingly listening.

"She gave birth to my child when I was fourteen and I loved her to death. I thought they'd stopped messing around long ago, until they informed me they never had when I caught them in bed together with my son laying nearby. I lost it," he says. "I bashed them to death with an iron after the elephant statue I used broke as I beat my mom's head in with it. The memories haunt me until this day. I can still feel myself plucking chunks of brain off of my face," he says as he cringes.

"But you went to jail at the age of sixteen."

"It took them two years to find the bodies. My sister helped me bury them in our backyard, but never forgave me for killing Mom. We were young and didn't dig the hole deep enough. A neighbor reported seeing skeletal remains sticking out of the ground after a bad rainstorm. My sister escaped out the back and took Jacob with her when they came to arrest me."

Murphy looks at Mitchell and can't believe he was ever capable of such savagery.

"A mom is supposed to love her children, she's supposed to be there and support them. She didn't think I was serious about Maggie but I really loved her. The part that haunts me the most, is that it happened when my son was just ten months old, and when I was done, I looked at him. He was holding on to the railing and standing up in his crib. It's the first time he ever stood up, and he was smiling at me. I thank God every single day that Jacob doesn't remember it. The reason I asked you to check and see if she's my mom, is because in some sense I was hoping she wasn't. It kills me every day knowing I killed my own mother," he says with a tear rolling down his cheek. "I'm not sure I even want to know anymore, I know she was. I can feel it and that's what kills me."

Murphy figures she'll probably be doing him a favor by giving him the news, and doesn't know whether to blurt it out or wait until he asks.

"Do you know where your daughter-in-law is now?"

"Not sure. Last time I saw her she was at a Doctor's office. Phillips almost blew my grandson's brains out right in front of me and I couldn't do anything." Mitchell fails to mention he also encountered them in Mrs. Cryan's house.

"What? Why? Hasn't he been vaccinated?"

"He thought somehow the baby survived being injected after the thirty-minute mark."

"That's impossible," she says.

"Not according to the folks at the Fort. They believe in an ancient Prophet that says a child will be born that'll survive the mark of the beast, and they're convinced the vaccine is the mark. The kid is supposed to save them all, don't ask me how."

"Yea, but they all survive the vaccine. What do you mean he almost shot his brains out?"

"It was weird. I've never seen Phillips spare someone he said he'd kill. I was relieved he didn't, but it sorta looked like he couldn't."

"He couldn't?"

"Yea, it was weird, it looked as if the trigger was stuck. His facial expressions looked as if he was straining to pull it until he finally gave up."

"Does she know who you are?"

"No. Jacob's never introduced us. He was probably afraid of my reaction. To me it doesn't matter, but it's not me he has to worry about. If the government became aware he has a child with an Illegal Resident they'd hunt us all down. Well, them. Mr. Goodman would poison me to get me out of the way.

"How do you feel about what's being done, especially now that you know your grandson's interracial?"

"Since you're asking me off the record, I've always hated it. How can a government do this to its own people. The only reason they took the rest of the world out is because they knew they wouldn't ignore these atrocities. It's inhumane what we do to them just because they didn't get a vaccine. How about you, how do you feel about it?" he asks.

"Pretty much the same way you feel. I'm sure most agents hate their jobs but do it because they have no choice. We all act as if we love what we do, when in reality, we're dying slowly inside. There will be no Illegal Residents in about fifty years from now. They cannot grow old like us with the insufficient amount of food and medication they're provided. Us humans, we're the most vicious animals on this planet," she says. "I've interviewed every kind of agent there is, and the viciousness of their stories don't seem to surprise me anymore. With each agent that walks into my office, I lose more and more faith in humanity. I hope the people at the Fort are right, I hope someone does come along and stops this before it's too late. Everyone deserves a chance to live."

Mitchell's surprised to hear this, and is convinced she didn't maliciously tell Goodman what Brown said. He wonders if she'd know the real circumstances of his death.

"Did they tell you how he died?"

"Who, Brown? Same thing you said, Illegal Residents booby-trapped the house."

"That is not what happened. Brown told Moore yesterday after work that if he was killed, for him to tell me that our men did it. Told him to tell me that Phillips killed Cryan, said he told you the same thing."

"I was doing my job when I reported it to Goodman. You think he ordered this?"

Murphy becomes concerned. *"If he did this to one of his men, what would he do to me,"* she wonders. "Doesn't make sense. Why not just poison him?"

"He wouldn't be able to justify it," Mitchell responds.

Seems like Mitchell's forgotten about the results, because he starts to get up, but Murphy has to tell him. He'd be very upset if he found out and she didn't mention it.

"Sit down," she says.

"It's been an hour," he responds.

She grabs his hand and puts a tiny glass vial in it. He looks at it and notices it has a red fluid inside.

"Drink this, but don't drink it until you get home. I need to tell you something, Mitchell, it's something you really need to know."

Mitchell still looks at the vial. "What is this?" he asks.

"It's something that will help you. Listen to me..."

"I don't know about this," he says as he sits. "I'm not one to take medication."

"Just take it as soon as you get home, I'll pass by to check on you in the morning. Since I'm going there, I'll help you have that discussion with your son but I'll only help if you drink it. We'll make something up."

Mitchell likes the idea, it'd be fun to have someone over. She grabs both his hands and turns him to face her while still sitting. Her mind is racing and she hopes this doesn't turn out as bad as she thinks it will.

"Remember when you asked me to check on Bette?"

"No, no, I don't want to know. You don't have to confirm it, it'll just make me feel worse."

"Mitchell!?" she says while giving him a demanding look. "I have to tell you this for God's sake, just listen. It's something you ought to know..!"

Mitchell senses something's not right. "What is it?" He looks at Murphy and notices she gets teary eyed. "What is it?" he asks again.

She sucks her lips in as if she were rubbing them together to smear lipstick, and has an extremely sad expression on her face.

Mitchell thinks the worse. *"What can it be,"* he thinks.

"Bette is not your mother," she says, then bows her head.

Mitchell is shocked. There's no way he'd have thought what his sister told him years ago would be true. "What the hell are you talking about!?" he loudly asks as he stands, causing a couple passing by to look at him.

"It can't be." Mitchell paces back and forth, rubbing his hands over his face. "What now. How could this happen...?"

Mitchell's devastated. Through the years he's kept the memory of his mom in his head. The memories turn to dark ugly ones when he re-members what he'd done to her.

"Sit down." She tries to comfort him by grabbing him in her arms when he sits. As the tears roll onto her shoulder, she pushes him away but holds on to his hands.

"I have something else to tell you."

Mitchell's had enough bad news, the entire session's been a roller coaster ride. "No!" he says. "Enough!"

"When I struggled to give you this news, it wasn't about Bette not being your mom. As soon as I seen that holster, and you told me how you got it, I knew I had to tell you. Your parents were incredible peo-ple, Bradley. That's your father's holster."

"What do you mean? Goodman told me it's a former agent's holster and this program is only thirteen years old."

"He didn't lie when he told you that. Your father was an Agent. Your name is not Bradley Mitchell," she tells him. Your real name is Gregory Cryan..."

"What!? Are you telling me that...?"

"Yes. Fred and Dorothy Cryan are your parents. You were taken away from them as an infant, and they looked for you for over two decades."

Mitchell loses his strength and falls on the floor. He forces himself onto his knees and leans his head back with his arms outstretched to the sides, and his fists clenched...

"PHILLIPS!!!" he screams...

He steps out of his vehicle in front of his house and again falls to his knees. Jacob runs out and helps him up by lifting him by the armpit.

"You OK, Dad?" Mitchell looks like a mess and his son is concerned. "What happened?"

Mitchell pulls the vial out as he enters the house and takes the little cap off. He believes Murphy's trying to poison him for Goodman, but the guilt he lives with and the news he's just gotten makes him want to give up anyway. Jacob watches as he begins to lift it to his mouth.

"No!" he shouts. "What is that?" but it's too late, Mitchell gulps it down and is hoping she's poisoned him. As soon as the fluid enters his stomach, he screams in agony. He holds his abdomen and balls himself up on a couch in excruciating pain.

"She poisoned me," he thinks...

~Chapter Fourteen~

Buchanan

Krystle's been a mess for the last couple of days and hasn't heard a word from her husband. She's sitting in the lobby to the N.A.A. building and wishes she'd see him walk in. The lobby of the building is an open area full of stands where you can purchase pretty much anything, it's where most employees go on their lunch breaks. All of a sudden, she sees Larry. He hasn't noticed her and she hopes he doesn't. The last thing she needs is for her husband to see her talking to him if he happens to come back. She acts as if she doesn't see him but he spots her. He hesitates to go over. The rumor of what's happened has been going around and he feels very guilty, but decides to approach her and apologize anyway.

"How are you?" he asks.

Krystle acts as if she's surprised to see him. "I'm well," she responds.

"I've been wanting to tell you," he starts. "I'm so very sorry about what's happened."

"It's no problem," she replies. "My husband and I have been having problems for quite some time and I've worried this day might come, so don't blame yourself. If you remember correctly, I was the one who told you to kiss me." Krystle only told him to kiss her because she knew how anyone would react to seeing a white man kiss an Illegal Resident. She knew the person would leave to go tell Thump, forcing her to have to explain it later. She figured if the person stayed after the kiss, then they were being watched for what was said in that room.

Larry's always had a crush on Krystle, but knew she was married and it's why he's never told her how he feels. He didn't know who her husband was because relationships are not to be disclosed in the N.A.A.. He also knows it'd be impossible to be with her because of her skin color. The government frowns upon interracial relationships and look down on white people who dare to be intimate with an Illegal Resident. Larry doesn't know what else to say, so decides he'll go upstairs.

"Wait," she says. "Remember what you told me. What exactly do you think happened?"

"I don't know." Larry's concerned she'll mention it to Thump with the way she's feeling. He senses her sadness and doesn't want to risk her saying anything to anyone.

"I got more to show you," he tells her. "You're going to love it. Come by my office later."

Krystle's curious and can't wait to see what he's talking about.

"What time?"

"Meet me there at three," he says as he walks off.

Krystle's beginning to believe something's going on. The evidence Larry showed her wasn't enough to convince her to approach Thump about it just yet. Depending on what else he shows her, she'll make that determination. She looks toward the entrance and sees a huge figure enter, the man is so tall he has to duck his head to enter the building.

He walks closer and she's appalled at his size, he must be well over seven feet tall and easily weigh over four-hundred pounds. She looks at his shoes that look to be at least four times the size of hers. He's dressed in plaid overalls that are filthy, and has a checkered jacket on with suede patches at the elbows that's open. Under it, he wears what should be a white t-shirt that's yellowish in color, and he carries a very mucky backpack. When he gets close enough for her to see his facial features, she becomes frightened. He has no neck, and his head is completely bald, it looks to be connected to his body. She looks at his hands and gulps, the size of his fingers make her tremble. She sees a mist of saliva spraying out of his mouth as he talks while walking by. *"The sound of his voice doesn't match his appearance,"* she thinks to herself. She waits until he enters the elevator and goes toward it to focus on the lights above. She wants to know what floor he stops on so she could avoid it. Her heart drops when she sees it stops on the eighth floor, which is the floor she works on. *"What is that smell,"* she wonders.

Although Thump has some really mean men, he decides to make his brother his right-hand man after news of Scott's demise.

Randy opens the door for Mr. Walker. Walker's the man who oversees all operations in the building.

"You wanted to see me, sir?" he asks.

"One of my men was killed the other night and I wasn't informed for hours. Why is that? I let it slide thirteen years ago when Scott was killed, and warned it should never happen again so this is unacceptable." Thump's referring to an agent that was killed by an unknown culprit.

"I'm sorry, sir, but the procedure's for us to investigate every possible scenario before we say anything to anyone. This way there's no conflict of interest."

"Well, I need to know when anyone that's associated with me is hurt in any way. Do you understand me!?"

Mr. Walker knows he has to comply and agrees. "I'm sorry, sir, I should have known better."

"Don't you ever let it happen again! Now get out of here!"

Mr. Walker leaves his office and is mystified by the gentleman walking toward him. He wants to get out of the way and notices how everyone stops what they're doing to look at this individual. The man's accompanied by three men that are of normal size, but look small next to him. Walker leans against the wall to give him space to pass and panics when the man gives him a glimpse as he walks by.

The door shakes when the man knocks and Walker can't help but notice his humongous hands.

"Who is it knocking this way!" Randy aggressively shouts as he yanks the door open. He's shocked at the sight of the man and immediately regrets asking in the manner he did.

"You wanted to see me, sir?" the man asks while looking over Randy's head.

"Buchanan!" says Thump. "Come in!"

Buchanan's Thump's most ruthless killer, he was the only one recruited from the prison he was in. Many accused him of cannibalism and no other inmate took the chance of joining when they found out he accepted the job.

Buchanan ducks his head and enters the office.

Randy looks at him in disbelief.

"You got a problem?" he asks, when he notices the stare.

"Uh, no. Not at all," Randy nervously responds.

"Buchanan, this is my brother Randy.

Buchanan extends his hand but Randy doesn't know how to grab it, he thinks that maybe he's supposed to grab a finger.

"Nice to meet you," he says, and extends his hand. He feels the sliminess of Buchanan's palm and immediately pulls his hand away.

"I would sit but I don't want to break your furniture," Buchanan tells Thump.

Randy raises his hand, sniffs it and almost pukes. He blows his cheeks out at the smell and rushes out of the office to wash it.

Buchanan looks back at him as he barges out. "Your brother is weird," he tells Thump.

"I've got a bit of bad news for you, Buchanan," Thump regretfully tells him. "You must have a sit-down with the department's Doctor. I was able to avoid it when you were with the F.F.A., but at the N.A.A. it's mandatory. There's no way to avoid it."

Thump's hoping this goes quick, he cannot bare the smell on Buchanan. He hopes it's caused by something stuffed in the backpack and not body odor. It smells like rotten meat, and for as long as Thump has known him, he's worn the same exact outfit so it's possible it could be him. The agents Buchanan work with have grown accustomed to the smell and hardly notice it anymore.

"But I can't!" he responds. "I've got to be out there killing people and that's a waste of time!"

"It's only an hour. Look, I'll give you a gift if you sit down with him. I'll give you the man that killed Agent Scott, and I've built a special room just for you."

"Weinberg," Buchanan loudly whispers. He grins while rolling his eyes up to stare at the ceiling. "You have Weinberg," he says as he rapidly blinks. "Set up the meeting!"

Thump can tell he's very satisfied. Buchanan seems to be in a trance at the thought of getting his hands on Weinberg. After thirteen years, Thump's men have finally found him. He wanted to personally kill him but figures he'll give him to Buchanan, which is far worse.

"When do I get him?" he asks.

"After the meeting, which will be held at eight o'clock tonight."

Thump expected for Buchanan to leave his office once he gave him the specifics, but he stays. He moves toward the door and extends an arm, signaling that he must leave. Buchanan ducks to leave the room with Thump close behind. His head is right above Buchanan's waist and the backpack inches in front of his face. The noisome vapors get really intense. Thump covers his nose and mouth with one hand while closing the door with the other. He walks toward his desk waving a hand inches away from his nose when he's finally gone.

It's two-thirty and Krystle's anxious to meet with Larry. She's told Randy to notify Thump she'll take the rest of the day off when she saw him buying an air freshener for his office. She doesn't want to come close to the man that's just passed by. The anticipation of what Larry will tell her has her going crazy, so she decides to go to the thirteenth floor to wait the next half hour. On the way up, the elevator stops on the eighth floor. Krystle's horrified when the doors open and sees Buchanan and his men getting ready to enter.

"Going up!" she quickly says. The men look at her and step in. Buchanan has to bend his knees to avoid the elevator ceiling. The smell hits Krystle, so she immediately grabs her nose, but quickly releases the grip when Buchanan looks at her. She looks as the elevator lights shine to reveal the floor they're on. It's the longest five story elevator ride she's ever taken. She noticed one of the men press the button to the fifteenth floor when they entered, and dreads having to walk past them to get off on the thirteenth. As the elevator comes to a stop and the doors open, she stays as if she's glued to the wall. The doors begin to close, so Buchanan puts an arm out to stop them.

"This is your floor," he tells her. She slowly walks in between them, steps off and turns around. With her heart rapidly beating, she stares as the doors close and they all stare back. Right before the door completely closes, Buchanan winks.

"Hey, you," she hears. "I didn't think you'd come."

"Did you see that big man?" she asks.

"Must be Buchanan, everyone keeps telling me how big he is," he says with a chuckle. "I have a session with him tonight."

"You? You're a psychiatrist?"

"Yes. This will be my first sit-down though. Thump says he'll let me make the decision on being the permanent Doctor here after I see this gentleman. He tried to intimidate me by telling me he's big. How big can he really be?"

"He's big," she says. "He's really scary, you shouldn't have the sit-down with him. He smells like he's dead. Well, one of them do."

"Don't be silly," he responds. "I've studied many years for this. Look at the simple questions I have to ask him," he tells her while passing her a clipboard.

Krystle doesn't bother to look at it, his appearance alone is reason enough for her not to come close. She realizes she hasn't seen anyone, which is odd.

"Where is everyone?" she asks, as they approach his office's door.

"Come in. All four people that work on this floor are on their breaks," he says as she enters.

Larry's a forty-two-year-old man who's beginning to go bald, you could see his scalp through the little bit of hair on the top of his head. He grew up having to adjust to life after the war. He was a harmless kid who would cower behind his father at the thought of any trouble and wears really thick glasses. He was always into his books and took his studies very seriously. After realizing his job with the satellites was over, he decided to go for this one, which is what he's studied for.

"Did you tell anyone what we spoke about?" he asks as she takes a seat.

"No," she replies. "I came close to telling Thump but decided not to."

Larry becomes concerned. *"How can I convince her not to tell him anything,"* he wonders. "OK then, there's nothing to show you."

"What!? What do you mean there's nothing to show me? I just took the worse elevator ride of my life to get here, you're showing me something!"

179

"I cannot risk you telling Thump anything I tell you."

"He won't know it was you. What stops me from going to his office right now and telling him what you've already shown me?"

"Thump's smarter than you think, I bet he knows you're up here right now."

"I doubt that," she responds. "He doesn't even know I'm in the building. I told his brother to inform him that I'd go home for the rest of the day."

Larry's delighted to hear that. He's stuck in a very desperate situation and there's only one way to shut her up.

"There's a man named Moshi who claims he's in Japan," he starts. "He somehow believes the United States government made this all up, says the war never happened and assured me the rest of the world is fine. According to him, there's an international law that makes it legal for countries to shut their borders. Says we grounded all flights and didn't let anyone in or out. Since no-one could penetrate our internet security, no-one knows what's going on. If the world found out that this government slaughters its own people they would invade. Moshi claims he could get us a news feed that will stream in countries all over the world. He says it takes time and asked me to be patient. I do not want to be the one to expose such conspiracy, I want no part of it. You can if you want to, but you can't say anything to Thump."

"I don't know who's crazier, the one that came up with this nonsense or the one who believes it," she says. "There is no way this was all made up. Don't you remember the sky being blue, how do you explain that?"

"He...!" Larry stops himself. "I agree with you, it's bogus. That's why we shouldn't bring it up to Thump either way. You know how offended he'd be?"

"What else did this Moshi guy tell you?"

"Not much," he replies. Larry keeps the part of the filtration systems to himself. Moshi's proved that they do the complete opposite of what the government claims. They were actually designed to provide a clear gas that remains transparent until it rises to about five-hundred feet high. The fumes then turn into a yellowish color that makes the air look polluted. They were built all over the country, with only four needed to produce the effect of pollution to a state as big as Texas.

"Look, he's sent me pictures of himself," he says as he opens his laptop. Larry wishes he knew she wouldn't say anything to Thump, but deep down inside, he knows she will. Larry, like many others, don't agree with what's being done, but has no choice but to do his job. He isn't a hardened criminal or fierce killer, but isn't one to betray his country either.

"So what he says must be true?" She moves her head forward to get a closer look.

"You scroll through them by clicking this," he shows her. Larry stands as she looks through the pictures and grabs a coffee mug that's on top of a file cabinet. He raises it over her head and swings it down, causing it to shatter as it hits the top of her skull. Krystle collapses sideways and falls with the chair. He gets on top of her as she wiggles around semi-knocked out, and sits over her torso. He wraps his hands around her neck and squeezes with all of his might. Larry's never kill-ed anyone. He thought it'd be easier but it takes a surprisingly long time before she stops kicking and clawing at his hands. Krystle des-perately attempted to scratch his face but couldn't reach. She dies that day, right there on his office floor. With his hands severely scratched he rises, and can't believe what he's just done.

After driving to a desolate neighborhood to dispose of her corpse, he rushes back to prepare for the sit-down with Buchanan. He gets back at 7 pm and has an hour to get ready.

After washing up and changing his clothes, he makes it to his potential future office with thirteen minutes to spare. He walks in and is taken aback by the luxurious look. He sits on a chair to the table and

181

rubs his wounded hands all over the shiny wood. Larry feels little vibrations that seem to be getting more, and more forceful. It's Buchanan and his men making their way down the carpeted hallway, leading to the office. Larry wonders what the rumbles are and hears a knock on the door. He looks at the clock that hangs on the wall and sees he's ten minutes early. He walks toward the door and pulls it open, his intention is to make him wait until eight o'clock sharp.

"Can I come in?"

"Sure," says Larry. He looks at Buchanan in disbelief. When Thump, and everyone else told him he was big, he never thought he'd be monstrous.

"Sit down," says Larry. Then it hits him, the odor is horrible. *"No way he can possibly smell like this,"* he thinks to himself.

Buchanan sits on the three seated sofa and looks like an adult sitting on kids furniture. He stares as Larry makes his way to a chair that's across from the couch. The smell is really distracting. Larry unknowingly keeps pinching his nostrils closed.

"What's in the backpack?" he asks.

Buchanan takes it off of his shoulders and places it on the floor between his feet.

"I'm not obligated to disclose my personal possessions, sir. I'd rather not answer that."

The smell has Larry convinced that he will not last an hour.

"OK. Let's get this started. What is your name and how old are you?"

"My name is Steve Buchanan, sir, and I'm fifty years old."

Buchanan has a high-pitched vocal that isn't deep at all. It's weird to everyone that comes across him and hears him speak.

"Do you remember life before the war?" Larry starts.

"I do," he says. "I was thirteen when it broke out. Some pretty sick stuff happened out there."

"Tell me about your parents. How was life growing up?" Larry's trying to rush, somehow thinking it'd make the hour go quicker.

"Life was hard for me. My mom had eight children and I was the youngest. I was diagnosed with schizophrenia as a child and suffered from a rare condition called Gigantism. My siblings always neglected me. They wouldn't admit in school that I was their brother and would deny it when someone asked. They must have really been embarrassed, because they knew that if they said I'm their brother, they'd be safe. Everyone in school was afraid of me, even the teachers. When my father had a family day at work, he'd take everyone and leave me home. He'd try to make me feel good about myself by telling me he needed me to guard the house since I'm so big, and strong, but I knew better. My brothers wouldn't get physical with me. I was the youngest, but I was also the biggest, and strongest," he proudly says. "My mom loved me to death, she would call me her little monster, it was the pet name she gave me. She didn't tolerate my siblings making fun of me and I got tired of complaining when they did it behind her back," he says, and rapidly blinks. Buchanan also suffers from blepharospasm, which causes him to involuntarily blink multiple times.

"Did you have any friends growing up?"

"I had a friend but he died."

Larry coughs, the smell is gut wrenching. "How did he die?"

Larry looks at Buchanan's hands which are resting on his lap and cannot believe the size of them.

"I had to kill him. He was trying to mess around with my sister, and no-one messes around with Steve Buchanan's sister," he says.

Larry notices Buchanan glow after making that statement, almost as if it made him proud. "Where's your family now?"

"They're all dead. I killed them on my 20th birthday."

Larry writes it down to check on it later. He's skeptical about someone blatantly confessing to something of such nature so quickly.

"Except for my favorite sister Sara. I spared her, but only because she promised she'd keep her mouth shut. We took off together, and with everything going on, no-one bothered investigating. They wrote it off as if an Illegal Resident did it."

"Isn't that why you went to prison? How did you kill them?" Larry rapidly asks. The smell is still there but no longer seems to bother him. He's interestingly listening.

"I shot them all while they slept. I had a silencer on the gun so no-one heard it. I'll never forget that night," he says with a grin. "It was as if someone was taking pictures and the flash went off in each room, causing it to light up every time I squeezed the trigger. I started with my oldest brother, he made my life miserable every single day and deserved it more than anyone. He's the only one I awoke before letting him have it. I shot him point blank right in his forehead as soon as he sat up. I swear, his head emptied out on the wall behind him, everything came out," he says as he makes a mini explosion signal with his huge hands. "My mom was the last one. It hurt me to pull the trigger but I had to see the flash effect one more time. I ended up shooting her until the gun was empty just to see it flash over and over. I reloaded my weapon three times that night. Ninety-six bullets wasted just because I wanted to see a flash."

"I didn't go to jail until I was thirty. Some idiot thought I wouldn't find out he was mocking me, but when I did, I paid him a visit. I killed him, his wife, their two daughters and pet dog. That's why I went to prison."

Larry's extremely disturbed. "Tell me about your family. Do you have a wife, kids?"

"I've got three kids and a dull wife. She only started giving birth after I came out of prison. I figured it's time to start making little ones and stopped pulling out."

Larry looks a bit uncomfortable. "How long have you been married?"

"We've never been married, that would be illegal. I've been with her since I was twenty.

"You've been with her since you killed your family? What do you mean it'd be illegal?"

Larry's extremely confused, but eager for details.

"In the beginning she wanted nothing to do with me, so I kept her tied in the basement. The only time she'd show me love was when I forced her to. I practically had to rape her every time I needed sex. You would think she'd be a little more grateful, right?"

Larry's lost. "Where is she now?"

"Home."

"You're still together?"

"Yes. We have three wonderful kids. She's learned to except me over the years, but still suffers from what happened all those years ago and cannot get herself to move on."

"What happened all those years ago? And what did you mean when you said you saved her life?".

"What I did to my family still affects her. Even now, she still refuses to have sex with me, but doesn't try to stop me when I force myself onto her anymore. She doesn't even move."

"How did you save her life?"

"I didn't kill her, I told you that."

Larry's just realized he's talking about the sister he spared. He didn't think someone could be this mentally gone.

"What's her name?" Larry wants to confirm his suspicions.

"Her name is Sara. She's given me three beautiful kids and I love them. "What was *'her'* name?" asks Buchanan, confusing Larry. "The woman you killed today. What was her name?"

Larry's shaken. *"What the hell,"* he thinks to himself. "I haven't killed anyone," he nervously replies.

"You did! I smelled it as soon as I walked in, and you have a look in your eyes that I've seen quite often. I can tell it was a female by the scratches on your hands, and I can tell it was today because they're fresh. So what was her name?"

"I am not obligated to answer that. This is about you, not me. Tell me, according to our records, you've been accused of cannibalism a few times, even while in prison. Can you confirm this isn't true."

Buchanan was accused of eating body pieces when in prison, he picked up a craving for it when they almost starved to death. There wasn't enough food to feed such a huge man and it kept other prisoners from trying to harm him.

"It's true," he blatantly says. "Have you ever eaten human meat? It's the only meat you can eat raw and not shit your brains out the next day. Do you eat pork? It's the same thing, only human meat is much more tender when cooked the proper way."

Larry's astounded. Just when he thought he couldn't hear anything worse come out of his mouth, he speaks again.

"The younger the body, the tenderer it is. Babies are the best."

Larry's heard rumors about Buchanan and just like everyone else, dismissed them as something someone wouldn't do. Hearing it makes his stomach turn.

"So you really ate the baby people claimed you did?"

"Yes. Who cares, it was an Illegal Resident and it fed my entire family. Fingertips are the best, I'm going to bring you a couple of them tomorrow. You put them in your mouth and suck on them. After a while, the skin starts falling off. They taste just like beets and are obviously very good for you. They've kept me strong," he says, while clumsily flexing himself.

"That will not be necessary, I don't want fingertips." Larry doesn't know if he wants to keep the job at this point. He'll go mad with a few more of these stories and doesn't think he's cut out for it.

"You'll love them, I promise," he says as he rapidly blinks.

"Do your kids know you and their mom are related?"

"No. They have no idea. We will tell them when the time is right."

"Why would you tell them? Don't you think that's something that should be kept secret?"

"They deserve to know. They should know there's nothing wrong with it. I see how one of my twelve-year-old boys look at his sister and I want him to go for it, I want him to know it's fine."

"What!? How can you possibly condone that? How old is your daughter? What do you mean one of your twelve-year-old sons!?"

"My daughter's eleven, and I see the look in my son's eyes when he looks at her. It's the same look I had when I looked at Sara as a boy. My boys are twelve-year-old twins, and they look just like me. They're almost as big as I am already. They're identical, they even have the same exact birthmark."

Larry sees the time has expired so gives Buchanan a business card. Buchanan tells him he had fun and asks if he's sure he doesn't want him to bring a finger or two. Larry assures him it's not necessary and doesn't think he'll keep the job. Somehow he thinks Thump purposely sent him in there for that reason and it worked, he will not sit for another hour with this lunatic. Buchanan struggles to get up and extends his hand when he finally does. Larry grabs it, but quickly pulls away when he feels the moisture.

"See you next time," says Buchanan. He grabs his bag and exits the room.

"There will be no next time...!" Larry thinks to himself...

~Chapter Fifteen~

The Suicidal

Jacob's panicking and doesn't know what to do. As his father balls himself on the couch, moaning in agony, he scrambles around, looking for a way to comfort him. He grabs a pillow and stuffs it under his head. Mitchell's in intense pain and signals he has to regurgitate. Jacob rushes to the kitchen, grabs a garbage pail and places it on the floor next to him. Jacob has no-one, he was alienated by his friends when he started seeing Brianna. None of them wanted to risk the chance of being caught associating with them for fear of retribution.

"What's wrong, Dad? What was that you drank!?"

Jacob thinks of Brianna and wishes she was there with him. For over a year now, he's wondered what's happened to her. He knows how dangerous it is for Illegal Residents and has faced the fact that he might never see her again. He carefully tried not to impregnate her, and made her promise that if it happened, she is to make sure the child is vaccinated and they would have to live separately. The thought of her leaving because she became pregnant has repeatedly passed his mind.

Mitchell squirms his upper body off of the couch and pukes in the pail. It's three in the morning and Jacob fears the worse, he thinks his father will die. He goes to him and starts rubbing his back with tears streaming down his face.

"What happened, Pops? Did they do this?" He's referring to the F.F.A., but Mitchell assures him it wasn't by nodding his head before going down and puking some more. Jacob figures it can't be the poison but asked anyway. His father's told him it kills you in less than a minute, so he'd be dead by now.

Mitchell struggles to breathe. He lays his head back to stare at the ceiling and closes his eyes. To Jacob, it looks like he's asleep. He could hear him breathe so tries to wake him up. He shakes him softly, but Mitchell doesn't move. Jacob desperately starts shaking him and begins to sob.

"Wake up, Dad! Don't do this to me! Wake up...!" he yells. He lowers his head onto Mitchell's stomach. "Don't do this to me!"

Mitchell hasn't moved. Jacob can tell he's alive because he's breathing, but it seems he's in a comatose state. It's too late to take him to the village infirmary so he decides to wait it out the night. He figures as long as he's breathing, he'll be OK.

Jacob sits on the other couch and tells himself he'll stay up all night to watch him, but nods off.

He awakes the next morning to the smell of bacon cooking and the sound of it sizzling. He looks toward the couch his father slept on, but he isn't there. He takes a blanket off of himself that wasn't on him the night before and slowly walks toward the kitchen. He's surprised to see Mitchell fully dressed for work with an apron on, cooking breakfast.

"What? What's going on!?"

Mitchell turns. "Good morning, Son."

"How are you feeling?" asks Jacob.

Mitchell remembers the conversation he had with Murphy and is satisfied that she failed on the attempt of his life, he can only assume she made it all up.

"I'm fine, Son. I ate a steak sandwich for lunch and it made me sick," he says. "I feel great now, I've never felt better. We need to talk, come on."

Mitchell intends to tell his son everything. He also intends to take a few days off to help him find Brianna. He'll send them away as far as possible, because Murphy poisoning him is the first of many attacks that might be attempted. Mitchell puts the fixed plates with fried eggs and bacon on the table and tells Jacob to sit. Before he could say anything, they hear a knock on the door. *"Who could it be,"* they both wonder. Mitchell or Jacob never get any visitors so Mitchell pulls his gun out of the holster. He tells Jacob to stay in the kitchen while he goes to check who it is. Jacob peeks as Mitchell slowly walks to the front door, and sees him pull the curtain hanging to the side.

"You've got to be kidding me," thinks Mitchell. He puts the gun back into the holster, then pauses for a second and thinks of what Murphy had told him about the Cryan's. He's sure it was her way of gaining his trust but wishes he knew it was true.

"What are you doing here!?" he asks as he yanks the door open. "You've got some nerve!"

Jacob walks closer. When he sees her, he's amazed his dad even associates with someone with her looks.

"How are you feeling?" she asks.

Mitchell's wondering what this is all about. He wonders why she'd be there after trying to assassinate him.

"Can I come in?" Murphy carries a briefcase with her.

"Sure," says Jacob. He has no idea the danger Mitchell thinks he's in, but is excited that his father has a visitor. He immediately grabs the pail his father used the night before and runs toward the kitchen with it.

"Sorry for the mess," says Mitchell, as she looks around.

"Definitely a bachelor's pad," she says with a grin.

"Sit down," he says, and guides her to the couch. "Want something to drink? Would you like a cup of coffee?"

"Sure," she says.

Jacob shouts he'll bring it, then immediately walks in with two mugs and hands one to each of them. Murphy puts hers on the table and Mitchell takes a sip of his.

"How are you feeling?" she asks.

"I'm feeling fine. What was that...?" Before he could continue she interrupts.

"We have to talk, Mitchell. In private."

Jacob gets up to excuse himself, but Mitchell sticks an arm in his way.

"I'm sorry, but whatever you have to tell me can be said in front of him, so if you don't mind, I'd like for him to stay here."

Jacob's never felt prouder in his life. He sits back down with a huge grin on his face.

"You sure?"

"I am. I will never keep anything from him again. I thought I'd die last night, and he was the only thing I could think of."

Murphy blushes and doesn't know how to hide it.

Jacob notices and keeps looking at his dad for a reaction but Mitchell doesn't look at him.

"OK. The findings I told you about last night."

Mitchell's prepared for her to tell him they're inaccurate.

"Goodman knows, so you have to be careful."

"You mean to tell me it's true!?" Mitchell thinks of how close he was to his mom and didn't even know it. He thinks of how easily they would have killed her had they found his son's girlfriend in her house that day. He really can't comprehend why she was hiding, especially knowing the baby's been vaccinated.

"What do you mean?" she replies.

"What you told me! Is it true!?"

"About your parents? Of course it's true. Look, Mitchell, I'm a professional but I'm also human. I know what happened to Agent Brown isn't a coincidence. I'm going to resign today. I cannot be part of an organization that kills its members. Everything I've told you is true, I don't lie."

"What about your parents, Dad, where are my grandparents?" asks Jacob.

"Unfortunately for me, they're dead, Son," Mitchell sadly replies. "How can it be?" he asks her.

Murphy pulls a piece of paper out of the briefcase and passes it to him. "According to the tests, Fred, and Dorothy Cryan show a 99.9% chance of being your parents. You ever hear the name Aughra?"

Mitchell doesn't recognize the name.

"How about Roy?"

Mitchell stops her. "Roy? I've heard that name before. Roger had a friend that would always call him Roy, it made him angry every time he did. I think his name was Jay."

"I ran additional tests and it seems there's no record of Bette Mitchell. The code on your registered mom's chip suggests her name is Aughra, not Bette. Aughra's accomplice in crime was Roy. Roy Berger. And guess what?"

"What?" he asks.

"I looked into Aughra's background and she has a cousin named Jason. Also known as Jay."

This is all Mitchell needed to hear. He's never run into anyone that's had anything negative to say about his father and it fills him with pride to know he's his son. He remembers seeing his mom a week ago, and had no idea she was the woman that suffered through so much pain to bring him into the world. He noticed one family member in the house, but didn't notice the one he wishes he had. His life would have been so much different had he grown up with them.

Jacob feels bad for his father. "How do you know they're dead, Dad?"

"I know, Son."

Murphy gives Mitchell a tiny piece of paper and asks him to put saliva on it. At first he's a little weary, but eventually obliges. She puts it on the coffee table and stares at it.

Mitchell and Jacob look at each other, they have no idea what she's doing. They watch as the piece of paper turns blue, relieving her. She sticks it into the briefcase and closes it, grabs her mug and takes a sip.

Mitchell looks at her, expecting answers. "What was that?" he asks.

She just smiles, then takes another sip. "When you first walked into my office, I thought you were just another agent who was going to sit there and brag about his nefarious deeds, but you proved me wrong. I can tell you have a good heart, and I can tell you two really love each other," she says. "I've never met an agent like you, Mitchell."

"Call me Greg," he says, drawing a chuckle from her.

"You shouldn't be doing this," she tells him. "This job isn't for you, you should run and never come back. That's what I'm about to do, and hopefully I'll end up in the Fort where everyone's equal."

Jacob looks extremely interested. He's heard of the Fort and wouldn't mind going himself.

Mitchell's staggered. *"How does she expect me to run when she knows they could kill me with the push of a button,"* he thinks. "You and I both know I can't go anywhere.

"That's not true, Brad. I mean, Greg.

Jacob's sitting on the edge of his seat and begins to bite his nails.

"I intentionally poisoned you last night, but it was an antidote to control the one you have in your chip. What it does is make you immune to it. The pain is unbearable but it works. The venom will not affect you when it's dispersed, they cannot kill you."

Mitchell drops his mug. *"No Way!"* he wonders.

"You can no longer be poisoned which means you could do whatever you want now."

Mitchell doesn't believe it and there's no way for her to prove the antidote worked. He figures he'll go in and request time off to help his son find Brianna anyway.

"Did you speak to your son yet?" she asks him.

Jacob wonders what she's talking about.

"I was about to when you came."

"You want me to tell him?" she asks.

"No. I got this."

"Do you need privacy?" Mitchell doesn't know how Jacob will react and figures her presence would soften the blow.

"No," he says, then turns to his son.

Jacob looks really confused then gets an excited persona.

"My grandparents are alive, aren't they!?"

"No, Son. It's kind of bad news." Mitchell looks at Murphy and gets a nod.

"How do I start? When I asked you what was going on, it's because I know there's something bothering you. I followed you one day and seen you with your girlfriend."

Jacob's never told Mitchell about his girlfriend because he knows the dangers of it. He fell madly in love with her and it got to the point that he didn't care. He'd sneak to go see her and once thought of risking it all to stay there. Most of all, he didn't want to disappoint his father. He didn't know how he'd feel about him being with an Illegal resident.

"I saw her the other day and...!"

This shocks Jacob. "Is she OK? Where is she!?" he anxiously interrupts. "I'm sorry I didn't tell you about her, Dad. It's just... She's an Illegal Resident."

"It doesn't matter to me, Son. I'll support you no matter who you're with. I seen her at a Doctor's office, but I passed by on the way home last night and she's no longer there. The doors were wide open and everything's gone. Looks like Dr. Gus took off also. But..."

"But what!?" he quickly replies.

"When I was sick last night..."

Murphy's listening while sipping her coffee.

"You might call me crazy, but I had a vision. No, it was a dream. I don't know what it was. I had a dream while awake and seen Mrs. Cryan," he says as he looks toward Murphy. "She told me we could find them at the Fort."

"Them!? Find who!? Who was she talking about!?" Jacob asks.

"Your Girlfriend and your son."

Deep down inside, Jacob knew that's why she left. She didn't appreciate the fact that he'd tell her she had to move away and always told him that if it happened, she would disappear and he would never see her again.

"I have a son?" Jacob doesn't seem surprised.

"We will find them. You've got to see him, he looks just like you."

Jacob smiles. "I want to find them. You care to join us?" he asks while looking at Murphy.

"If it means going to the Fort I'm in, but only after I give Mr. Goodman my resignation papers which I intend to do today."

"I'll tell Goodman I need the rest of the week off, he should have no problem with it, I've never requested a leave," says Mitchell. "You go ahead, I'll wait an hour before I go in. I don't want him to suspect anything. You can meet us back here, we'll leave tonight," he tells Murphy.

"See you later," she says as she stands to go. "Before I go, remember. Goodman knows I know of your parents and demanded for me not to say anything, so I didn't. OK?"

"Of course," he responds. "I have no idea who my parents are."

"Yes you do. Your mom is Bette!"

"Right," he says with a smirk.

Jacob looks at them and hopes something comes out of it. He's never seen his father even speak to a woman and knows this would make him happy.

Mitchell gets to the F.F.A. and runs into Agent Moore.

"We just got a list," Moore tells him. "And another partner."

Mitchell was hoping that of all days, this would be the one with no list. Moore just told him of another partner so he'll try to convince Goodman he isn't needed for this one.

"He's a suicidal," he whispers to Mitchell.

"Who?"

"The new guy."

A suicidal is an agent who knows he's about to be poisoned but is given an ultimatum. He can go out doing something to help the Agency, which buys him a few more days to be with his family. They are used to take out a member on a team, but it can only be done with one of the agents having knowledge of it.

The suicidal's job is to kill Mitchell, forcing Phillips to take him down. It's Goodman's way of killing one of his men without having to justify it. He cannot risk booby trapping another job and drawing suspicions. He also doesn't want to face the same firestorm that fell upon him when he poisoned Randolph without definite proof. Mitchell figures it's most likely for him and thanks Moore for the information.

"No problem. Watch Phillips. It might not happen today, but it's going to happen," Moore tells him.

Mitchell wants to take off but doesn't trust that the poison won't kill him. He wants to give himself at least three days to help his son find Brianna and send them away.

He walks into Goodman's office which is filled with cigarette smoke.

"Hey, Mitch. How are you?"

Goodman seems a little happy, and it draws his suspicions.

"Hey, boss, I was hoping to speak with you. I need the rest of the week off. You think it's possible? I'm having issues with my son and need some personal time."

"You're taking off? I never thought I'd see that happen. Work this last list for me, then you could take the time to fix your family," he arrogantly says.

"I was hoping I could go now. My son is waiting on me."

"Not going to happen!" he says and lights a cigarette. "I need you for this one."

Mitchell knows there's no way out and has to risk it. He wishes he knew for sure Murphy was right about the poison, he'd just run. As he begins to leave the office, Goodman stops him.

"Hope you don't think I'm stupid enough to not see what's going on here. It's not a coincidence that Murphy resigned today and now all of a sudden, you need time off. You lucky son of a gun," he tells him with a chuckle.

As he leaves the office, Phillips, and the new agent begin to enter. He gets nothing but a glance from Phillips and a long stare from the agent. He turns as the door is closing and notices all three of them looking at him.

They approach a house after a long ride of silence and park in the driveway.

"OK, fellas," says Phillips. "We have four people on the list. It's two forty year old's, a sixteen-year-old, and a ten-year-old. We have to make sure the boy's been vaccinated. Mitchell doesn't like this. A suicidal will help you with at least three lists to feel you out before they kill you, but with him asking for time off, he's afraid Goodman gave the order. They knock on the door and get a reply from a woman who jumps back as if she contemplates fleeing when she sees them.

"I'm Agent Phillips and I need to come in!" he aggressively says as he pushes his way inside. "I need everyone in the house down here, right now!"

The lady calls for everyone to come down and is obviously shaken.

Mitchell notices a wheelchair by the steps leading to the second floor of the house. They watch a man carry a grown child down the steps and put him on the wheelchair.

"How are you?" asks the man. He turns around and gives his hand.

As always, Phillips denies it and walks past him, toward the child.

"What's his name?" he asks .

"His name is Javier," answers the woman.

Mitchell spots another grown child coming down the stairs. She has a two piece, long sleeve pajama set on and looks as if she's just seen a ghost.

"What's wrong with him?"

"He has cerebra..." the woman tries, but struggles to pronounce it with her heavy Spanish accent.

"He has Cerebral Palsy," says the young girl.

Phillips scans the boy and sees he wasn't vaccinated.

Mitchell doesn't think he'd consider doing anything under the circumstances, the kid can't move. Before Phillips could react, the father begins to speak.

"Hi. I'm Javier. We know our boy wasn't vaccinated, the Doctor said it'd be a major risk injecting him in his condition."

"No. You know what the risk is? The risk is him growing up and producing a child," Phillips says, and grabs his gun.

Mitchell's devastated. He's hoping Phillips is bluffing but he's seen this look before.

"Where the hell are you from, Javier!? Why are you still in this country!?" shouts Phillips.

Moore's leaning against a wall. He occasionally looks at Mitchell

198

to see how he's holding up and could care less what Phillips does.

"I'm from Venezuela, sir. Please, the Doctor..."

Phillips raises the gun at him.

The suicidal agent looks at Phillips in astonishment. "Can't we let this one go?" he asks.

Phillips looks back at him with the gun steadily aimed at Javier Sr.. "You of all people should know this has to happen!" he shouts to the agent, then turns the gun on Javier Jr.. His dad rushes toward Phillips but is quickly subdued by the agent. This assures Mitchell what Moore told him is true, especially after getting an '*I told you so,*' grin from him.

"Ave Maria por favor no me lo mate," shouts the mom. She pleads for them to spare him. While holding his father, Agent Stewart nods for Phillips not to do it, but loses the strength in his knees when he pulls the trigger. Agent Phillips misses. The bullet goes through the kid's shoulder and disappears into the wall behind him.

Javier's father struggles to get out of Stewart's grip to rush at Phillips, but Stewart puts his gun facing upward under his chin. He pulls the trigger, causing blood to spray on the ceiling. He leans down and puts his hands on his knees to hold himself up. The young girl and her mom stand together, clutching one another as they wail. Phillips walks toward Javier, who's still expressionless, and puts the barrel of the gun to his forehead. The mom attempts to rush but is stopped by two bullets to the chest that come out of Moore's gun. Phillips stares at the kid and gives the impression that he might not do it. Just when they thought he wouldn't, he pulls the trigger. None of the agents look.

Phillips oddly walks away and doesn't act as if he's sucking his soul up, *as he always does,* and it surprises them.

Agent Stewart is, and has always been a family man. He was wrongfully accused of killing three soldiers when they patrolled the streets and went to prison. He proved he was at work when the assault occurred, but they didn't take it into consideration. They locked him up and sentenced him to the rest of his natural life in Jail. While in there, he was forced to become fierce. He's recently refused to term an infant and it's how he ended up here.

Moore walks toward the girl who's kneeling down uncontrollably sobbing and shuts her up with a shot to the head. Mitchell watches and feels he's done, he's convinced he doesn't want to do this anymore. The only regret he'll have if he's killed, is that he wasn't able to help Jacob find Brianna and his son, but as far as the job is concerned, he's ready for it to happen.

Stewart loses it. "Drop it!" he shouts to Phillips, and aims the gun at him. Phillips is shocked and tightly grips his pistol's handle. Moore's behind Stewart and puts his gun on the floor as if he was the one demanded to put it down, but doesn't look concerned at all.

Mitchell raises his hands while focusing back and forth to Phillips and Stewart. He's relieved he isn't on the other side of the weapon. *"Could it be that the suicidal's here for Phillips and Moore's the agent that takes him out?"* he thinks.

"DROP IT!" he yells.

"Are you crazy? What are you doing...?" responds Phillips, while slowly raising his gun.

"Don't be stupid! You better drop it!" Stewart demands.

Phillips complies and bends to place the gun on the floor while looking at him. "Do you know what you're doing here? This will piss Goodman off," he says.

"Do you know what YOU'RE doing!? Are you proud of what you've just done!?" he asks, with the gun still pointed at him. "Tell your partner what we're doing here! TELL HIM!" he shouts.

Phillips looks at Mitchell with a dumbfounded expression. He's never had anything against him but was ordered to execute this mission, so he had no choice.

Agent Stewart looks toward Mitchell. "Get out!" he yells. "GET OUT NOW!" he stresses, this time pointing the gun at him. Phillips takes the opportunity to reach for his weapon, making Stewart rapidly turn and repeatedly shoot. He empties his gun in Phillips's direction and Mitchell bolts.

Phillips freezes in shock. He feels himself for bullet holes and realizes he isn't wounded. Stewart seems confused and looks at his gun. Moore calmly walks up behind him and sticks a knife into his neck. He plunges it in so deep, only the handle is exposed. He then pushes the knife forward with so much force it tears Stewart's Adam's apple out, exposing his larynx to Phillips. Stewart drops to the floor and Moore holds the knife at his side.

"I put blanks in his gun," he tells Phillips. "The only live bullet was in the chamber and he wasted it on him," he says as he points to Javier Sr.'s body.

Phillips isn't dumb. He grabs his gun and raises it at Moore. He knows he must have put blanks in for no other reason than to save Mitchell. Phillips doesn't know how, but he assumes Moore got information and must have known Stewart was a suicidal.

"Why did you put blanks in his gun?" he asks, while walking closer, with his pistol pointed at his face.

Moore follows Phillips's every step with his eyes until he gets close enough to touch. He slowly raises a hand, and puts a finger on the tip of the barrel.

"You don't want to do that," he says with the tip of his finger over the muzzle of the gun.

Phillips is in awe. *"What the hell,"* he thinks.

"You have no idea what I could do to you with these hands."

Phillips is muddled. Surely, Moore has seen what he's capable of and is surprised he'd even think that.

"My father would end you. If I were you, I'd put that gun down and get in the car with me to tell Goodman what's happened here. We have to inform him that Mitchell's escaped." He turns his back to him and the gun is aimed at the back of his head.

Phillips has the perfect opportunity to put him down, but doesn't. "Who are you?" he asks as Moore reaches the door.

"It doesn't matter. Let's go."

They arrive at the F.F.A. around the same time Mitchell makes it home.

"Let's go!" yells Mitchell. He exits his car and runs toward the house. Jacob runs out with Murphy close behind. "We have to go!" he stresses. Mitchell believes he has no time and thinks he'll die any second, so wants to get as far as possible before it happens. He's sure Phillips is dead, and knows it's only a matter of time before it's figured out.

"What happened?" asks Murphy. She sees how anxious he is.

"We don't have a lot of time! Let's go! We've got to get out of here!"

Jacob's panicking and his adrenaline's pumping. He jumps in the car, looks out the back window and can't help but notice how Mitchell is sweating.

Murphy grabs Mitchell by the arms and demands for him to tell her the issue.

"Phillips is dead," he tells her, and hurries to the driver seat.

Murphy rushes into the car. "You killed Phillips?"

"Not me. It's a long story, I'll tell you later." Mitchell's heart is racing and he cannot stop thinking of his son who's on the back seat with a petrified look on his face.

"I love you, Son," he tells him as he looks through the rear view mirror.

"I love you too, Dad. What's going on?"

"What happened!?" Murphy aggressively asks.

"The poison," he responds, drawing a chuckle from her.

She's thankful he didn't say they're hunting him down. Jacob had bowed his head but quickly raises it when he hears Murphy laugh.

"You can die many ways, Gregory, but the poison is not one of them."

Mitchell doesn't know what surprises him more, her assurance she'd got rid of the poison, or the fact that she called him by his real name.

Phillips and Moore rush out of the car and into the building. They run up stairs and down hallways until they reach Goodman's door.

Phillips doesn't bother to knock and barges in, making Goodman flinch.

"He got away, boss!"

Goodman's confused as to why he'd openly say it in front of Moore. That information could get them both killed, so he decides that Moore will not walk out of that office alive.

Moore senses what's going on. "Don't act like I didn't know what was occurring." He takes a step forward. "You gentlemen think I'm stupid? You two have no idea who you're dealing with."

Goodman thinks Phillips told him, so grabs the P1-Simulator and rushes to put Moore's code in.

Moore laughs. "That doesn't work with me."

Phillips knows his father is of high significance with what he said at the house but has no idea who it is.

He takes another step forward. "I quit!" he tells Goodman. He drops his badge on the desk. "This isn't even my name," he says as he points to it. "It isn't a coincidence I ended up working with you guys. I heard you were all ruthless and it intrigued me, so I asked to be transferred here. As far as I'm concerned, you're far from being the worse which is what I expected. This guy," he tells Goodman, while pointing a thumb back toward Phillips. "He just got his rocks off by killing a defenseless kid with Cerebral palsy. If that makes you feel tough," he says, this time looking at Phillips. "Then you're a pansy and not the type of guy I'd like to associate myself with." He walks toward the door, pulls it open and all they could do is watch.

"My real name is Adam Thump," he says while walking out.

Goodman's floored. He actually had the President's son working for him and screws it up. He hopes for no backlash and takes a seat.

He enters Mitchell's code in the P1-Simulator while Phillips attentively watches.

"He's dead!" He pushes the switch to complete the execution.

"I'll pay his son a visit," says Phillips...

~Chapter Sixteen~

Sophia's Journey Continues

Sophia and Felipe are kneeling on the floor huddled up and weeping. She has her face buried in his shoulder and holds him tight. This is the safest she's felt since the minute the agents knocked on her door. Seeing Felipe was a surprise, she never thought she'd see one of her relatives again. The thoughts of what happened in her house that night flash in her mind, over, and over again.

"We have to go," says Jose.

With the back of her hand, Sophia wipes her eyes. She feels a great sense of security now that her brother's around.

"This is Gabriel," she tells Felipe, while pointing at him. "And this is his friend, Jose."

Felipe turns his attention to Jose after shaking Gabriel's hand.

"You can call me Jun-jun," Jose tells him.

After shaking his hand, he turns his attention to Patrice.

"This is Patrice," she tells him.

Patrice is tired and can barely stand. She tells Sophia she can no longer walk, so they must continue without her.

"I will not leave you behind," says Sophia. "We have to go."

Patrice nags and starts crying. "I can't," she says. She sits on the floor and removes one of her shoes to show Sophia the blisters on her foot.

"She can't walk," says Felipe. "That looks like it hurts." He grabs a drop cloth that must have been left behind by painters and tells her to remove the other shoe while he spreads it on the floor.

"Get in," he tells her. Patrice doesn't know what he means, so he grabs her by the arm and instructs her to sit in the middle. Once she sits, he grabs the edges and closes her inside with only her head sticking out. He then throws it over his shoulder and declares he's ready. "I'll carry her," he says.

Sophia knows her brother is strong, but doesn't think he could make it the rest of the way with her on his back. Gabriel, and Jose agree to take turns with Felipe carrying her until they make it to the Fort. Patrice is eight years old but looks five or six. She is really small for her age so Felipe thinks he could manage. Jose peeks out the door as they prepare to leave and sees someone headed toward the house.

"We have to go out the back," he tells them. "There's someone coming."

They run across the house and reach the back door as the front one opens.

"Is there anyone in here?" they hear a lady shout.

They bolt out and head toward a septic tank for cover.

Jose knew the gun was empty all along. Even with no bullets, it's gotten him out of a lot of trouble during the years. All he has to do is pull it out and point, most people back off. He tucks it into his waistband and conceals it with his t-shirt before going to the back of the tank to look for anyone around. It'd be impossible to cross the other Communities at this time. Jose sees a man walking in their direction and warns the others. As the man walks by, they circle around the tank to avoid being seen. They're a quarter mile from Community-*four,* and can already see the fence that divides them.

Gus and Brianna arrive at his sister's house. He rushes inside and takes her upstairs to the baby. On the way up, Brianna sees a man who sits on a sofa and doesn't bother to look at them, he just stares forward at a flickering TV.

"Oh my God!" she says when she sees her child. "My baby. I missed you so much." She sits on a bed and cradles him in her arms while gently kissing his face.

Annie's on a rocking chair with an emotional grin. "God bless him," she tells Brianna. "What a cutie."

"Thank you, Ma'am," she replies. "God bless you also, and thank you for all you've done."

Annie's Gus's oldest sister but looks much younger than he does. She resides at the Community because of her husband, and like many others, doesn't agree with the laws but has no choice.

"We have to go," says Gus. "Now...!"

"Why don't you stay downstairs for a day or two? You can't go out now, they'll kill you both." Annie's referring to a hidden underground shelter her husband built before catching a stroke. It's stockpiled with food, has its own bathroom and sleeping area. Her husband was a carpenter before the war and was considered one of the best in the country. He built the shelter who's entrance is under the refrigerator just in case the Fort's residents invaded. To access, you have to move the fridge to the side, which opens a door beneath it. After entering, you slide the door closed and the refrigerator moves back into place.

"No. We have to go now!"

They hear what sounds to be cars that come to sudden halts outside. They rush down the stairs, move the refrigerator and climb down as Annie goes to answer the door.

"Good afternoon, Ma'am. I'm looking for your brother. Is he here?" Reid removes his hat and looks over her shoulder but only sees her husband staring forward. Her husband George helped in building most of the first three Communities when he suddenly collapsed one day and hasn't been the same since.

"He's not here. He came to visit me last night but left early this morning." Annie watches as two other cars pull in at high velocities.

"You gentlemen want some coffee?" She hopes they say no and go on their way, but Reid accepts.

"If you don't mind, I'm going to wait for him here," he says as he enters her home.

Reid senses something's not right and decides to search the house. He enters with eight men while Annie prances around as if nothing's going on.

"What are they doing?" she asks Reid, when he commands two of them to search the second floor of the house.

"They're making sure your brother's not here."

"But I told you he isn't here. What did he do? Is he in some kind of trouble?" she calmly asks as she passes him a cup of coffee.

Deep down inside, Reid's fuming. He really doesn't want to take it out on Annie but her calmness has him vexed. She and her husband have given too much to the Communities for him to snap. He grabs the cup of coffee, walks toward the sink and pours it out.

"Nothing upstairs," says one of his men.

Reid commands four of them to head back to Community-*three*, then commands the other four to wait for him outside.

"Why'd you pour the coffee out? You could have said you didn't want any." Annie's under no pressure, she doesn't fear Reid like most people do. They give too much to the communities and it'd be a burden to lose their generosity.

Brianna and Gus are trying to remain as quiet as possible. Gus looks over and sees the baby with a mouthful of Brianna's nipple and figures that'll keep him quiet. He passes her a jar of baby food and tells her to feed it to him if the milk isn't enough.

"He's too little for that," she whispers.

"No. It's how we kept him happy when you weren't here. He loves it," he lowly whispers back.

Annie starts to vacuum small area rugs she has throughout the house and the sound gets Reid aggravated. She figures she'll do anything she can to get him out. "Excuse me," she says, loud enough to be heard over the sound.

Reid moves to give her space and is very annoyed.

"Do me a favor," he tells her when he's had enough.

Annie turns the vacuum off to hear him.

"Tell your brother he needs to come see me. Tell him not to force me to do something I'd regret, he'll know what you mean. By the way, why did he leave his car behind?"

Annie quickly replies. "I don't know. He told me that you told him he's not allowed to drive within the Communities with a broken window."

Reid remembers telling him and walks toward the door.

As they approach the fence that divides the Communities, which is only waist high, Sophia collapses. Gabriel rushes to her. Felipe, and Jose are forced to slow down and run back. Sophia squirms on the floor with her palms on her temples.

"Ahhhh!" she screams.

"Shhh! Shhh! Shhh!" she hears them all say.

"What's wrong, Sophia?" asks Gabriel.

"My head! My head hurts!" she cries.

Patrice is on Felipe's back and is panicking. They kneel around her then all of a sudden, see she calms down.

She let's go of her head and lays on her back, staring into the murky skies. "It's gone."

They all look at each other.

"The headache, it's gone," she says as she begins to stand.

After running a quarter mile into Community-*four,* they gather on the side of a house and focus their attention on a building that's across the street, who's doors burst open and people rushed out of.

"What is that?" asks Jose. Felipe leans against the house and plops Patrice up to alleviate the weight that seems to get heavier, and heavier the further they go.

Jose peeks in a window and sees no-one's in the house. "I'll be right back," he says. "Wait for me here." He sneaks toward the back, and startles them when he sticks his head out of a window. "There's water. I'll be right out."

Gabriel's still focusing on the building. It seemed everyone had left, until he sees a man exit it and chain the doors closed behind him. Jose runs from behind the house with a bag full of bottled water and a pair of slippers in his hands.

"Look, this could help her walk," he says as he lifts them.

Patrice has a huge smile on her face and Felipe looks relieved. He slides her down the wall by bending his legs until she's secure on the ground. While sitting on the drop cloth, she grabs the slippers and puts them on her feet.

"Is that better?" Sophia asks her. With a nod and a smile, she confirms it is.

"Let's go in there," Gabriel says while pointing at the building.

They'd have to cross the street and risk being seen, but it's in the direction they have to go anyway. Felipe's been telling them they're going the wrong way since they left the house but has realized he was the one going in the wrong direction. He could have been at the Fort by now. He was trapped in Community-*two,* and followed signs saying '*Community-three,*' not knowing Community-*one* is closest to the Fort. He was caught while trying to enter the communities, knocked out, and shoved into a van. When he awoke, he was in the pit and had no idea where he was.

"Let's cross one at a time and head there," Gabriel says, while pointing to a big red barn that's by the building they intend to enter. Most of the people have dispersed, leaving only a few lingering. Jose bolts with no warning and makes it across unseen. Felipe does the same. Sophia grabs Patrice by the shoulders and tells her to run. The slippers make flapping sounds as she sprints across but no-one notices. Sophia looks down the street and sees there are only two people she has to avoid, and takes off. Gabriel's the only one left, but they see a man walking their way. As he passes the front of the house Gabriel's hiding by, he bolts toward the back and goes around it. He runs as fast as he can across the street and reaches the side of the barn. They've made it unnoticed, but have to try and get inside the building now.

When they reach it, they peek through the windows and see no-one inside. It appears to be a cafeteria with lunch tables lined up. Jose takes his t-shirt off and wraps it around his fist. He punches a window, then carefully reaches his arm inside to unlock it. When they enter, they smell the food that had just been served, so run to the kitchen like hungry vultures and start feasting on plates of leftovers. Gabriel opens a big, stainless steel door and calls them over to see the little boxes of chilled milk inside.

Gus and Brianna shuffle to make it back upstairs when Annie opens the door.

"Take this," says Annie. She passes them an old car seat.

Brianna grabs it and straps the baby in as he stares at her. She kisses him on the forehead and tells him they're almost there, then jumps in the passenger seat. Gus peels off and immediately notices a car that was parked on the corner accelerate toward them. He steps on the gas and starts fleeing.

Reid left men behind to watch but they were unable to see the front of the house and only chased them when they saw the car take off. The passenger of the car giving chase has his arm out the window and is shooting.

Brianna ducks. She tries to squirm between the seats to reach the baby, but is amazed to see him unstrapped and standing on the seat looking out of the broken back window with bullets whizzing by. She desperately tries to get to him. With bullets flying, the baby holds on to the top of the seat. Gus passes a massive tractor with tires higher than your average man, and the baby violently turns his head to the right.

The car chasing swerves in the same direction and comes to a fiery stop when it crashes into the tractor. Brianna's in shock and Gus watches in amazement through the mirror. The baby turns and sits back down with no expression on his face.

"You're meant to make it there alive. I told you," says Gus.

They zoom through the rest of the Community and reach Community-*one*. Gus's anxious. It's a straight drive through and he's certain they'll be there in no time.

"We have to keep moving," says Felipe.

They walk toward the back carrying as much as they can. Jose has his pockets stuffed with boxed milk and carries his t-shirt over his arm. They exit and encounter an old man with a sunhat on, carrying firewood toward the barn.

"What are you doing here?" he demands.

"We... we.." tries Sophia.

Felipe's ready to attack. He doesn't want to get caught again.

"You know how dangerous it is?" he loudly whispers. "My name is Luke. Come, I'll show you a way out of here."

They're stunned. They watch as the old man walks ahead and aren't sure if they should follow.

"We should keep going," says Jose.

He leads them into the barn and gives Gabriel a piece of paper. "Follow this map. It'll get you to the tunnel they've been building for years. You won't get all the way, but that tunnel will get you to the end of Community-*two*. I imagine you're trying to get to the Fort. Good luck, kids," he sincerely says. "These bastards killed my Grand children for having dark eyes."

They immediately leave, with each trying to grab the map to look at it. After a lot of running and sneaking around, they finally make it to the entrance of the tunnel.

They enter and see the tunnel's barely tall enough for an adult man, and has water at the bottom. They walk in the dark, and all they can hear besides the squishing sound their feet make, is Patrice complaining about the boggy ground. Jose stops and lets everyone pass until Patrice reaches him, then grabs her piggy back to continue the journey. It seems like a walk that will never end. Their shoes are covered in mud and there's hardly any air, but they continue in a single line.

"I think Grandpa sent us in a never ending tunnel," says Jose. He plops Patrice up and continues. They walk for hours before they see light, which makes them pick up the pace. Finally, they encounter a latter with a hole above, exposing the turbid skies. One by one, they slowly climb, and see a sign with an arrow saying '*Community-one ahead*,' when they make it to the top. They're all ecstatic and proud of themselves, even Patrice, she's on the ground acting as if she wasn't carried most of the way.

"Freeze!" they hear. They turn and see four men with shotguns.

Jose panics. "I have a gun!" he yells. "It's empty."

One of the men lowers his shotgun and makes his way toward him. "Looks like old man Luke sent us quite a few this time," he says.

Felipe doesn't want to get caught again and decides to bolt.

The man behind Jose repeatedly shoot, causing him to fall and tumble into a ditch.

"Get after him!" one of the men demand to the man that fired.

With the guns pointed at them, Sophia sobs. "That's my brother," she sadly says.

The men get behind them and demand they start walking. Jose thinks they'll get shot on the spot and is shaky. Gabriel looks calm, but deep down inside, wishes he could jump out of his skin.

"Can you shut up!?" one man says to Patrice. He pushes her forward by poking her back with the shotgun. "Stop crying already!"

"Wouldn't you be crying? I'd be shitting my pants if I were in their shoes," says another one, drawing chuckles from them all.

Felipe tumbles in the ditch but gets back up and keeps running. The jagged edges makes it difficult to keep his balance but he hears the man behind him. He's out in the open with nowhere to go, but continues when he hears another gunshot. He feels he's been hit, but his adrenaline keeps him moving. Exhausted, Felipe grabs a tree and turns behind it.

"Come out and I won't shoot you," the man says.

Felipe comes out with his hands in the air. The man moves his gun as if to tell him, *'let's go.'* Felipe obliges, but when he gets close enough to grab him, he does. He wrestles with the man and holds on to the barrel of the shotgun. The man slightly loses his balance, but Felipe's forced to release his grip when the gun goes off. He swings his fist and lands a right to the side of the man's head. The man drops the weapon and falls down. Felipe grabs it while he's down, and pins him with his back to the ground and the barrel in his face. He thinks about what happened in his house that night but it isn't in him to kill. He knocks the man out with the butt of the gun and throws it as far as he can. He looks in the direction he came from and thinks about going back to save them, but figures he's too close to the Fort to turn back. He convinces himself they didn't make it. The thought makes him feel better about his decision to continue running toward the Fort.

The men force the kids into a barn and tape them up. They kneel them on the surface full of hay, with the tape holding their ankles together and their hands tied behind their backs. They've knelt there for an hour with a guard sitting on a wooden chair, making sure they don't move. All four are terrified, they have no idea what's in store. They all look toward the entrance when they feel heavy footsteps approaching.

General Reid walks in and tells the man on the chair to get up so he could sit. He plops himself down and swings one leg over the other, while he stares at them. He digs in his shirt pocket and pulls out a partially smoked cigar. The man next to him quickly pulls out a match and strikes it. Reid takes deep puffs to make it ignite, while still staring at them. He looks toward the ceiling and blows smoke into the air.

The kids are petrified and haven't said a word. They've all heard of General Reid but have never seen him.

"You kids know who I am?"

They nod their heads, although they all kind of figure who he is now.

"I regret to inform you that I'm General Reid. I'm sure your parents have told you horrible stories about me. Just in case you were wondering, the stories are true. What are you doing in my town?" he asks. "Did you want to die? Because that's what happens here, you will all die."

Patrice starts balling. Sophia and Gabriel seem calm, and Jose has a horrified look on his face.

"What are you doing with them, Son?" Reid asks Gabriel.

He doesn't get an answer, Gabriel just stares straight ahead.

"ANSWER ME...!" he yells. Reid's getting furious.

"They're my friends," he replies as his lips tremble.

"Your friends? These aren't your friends, you traitor. You're a disgrace and will be the first to die."

Patrice wiggles around, causing another man to come over and hold her still.

"Get the ring and put him in it," Reid tells his man.

The man moves the chair under a beam overhead, then grabs a trident that's against the wall. Reid walks to the corner of the barn and grabs a rope.

The kids wonder what they're doing.

The man leans the trident against another wall, grabs the rope and tosses it over the beam. He stands on the seat and ties the end, then loosens a knot to reveal a noose.

With the trident leaning against the wall, Sophia sees it has a hoop soldered onto it, causing both pieces to form a T.

The man raises Gabriel by an armpit and stands him on the chair.

Gabriel hasn't moved or said a word.

He lifts him again, and Reid leans the trident to put his legs through the hoop.

Gabriel's now standing in a hoop that has a trident with its prongs sticking up six inches from his chin, and a noose around his neck.

Reid doesn't want him to die of strangulation, he prefers for the trident to split through his face instead. Some get lucky and miss the trident though, only to break their necks when the weight of their body drops.

"This is what happens when you betray your race," he says. He pulls out a revolver and shoots one of the chair's legs, causing it to shatter. "One more," he says and giggles.

Sophia's looking at everything and is calm. Jose, and Patrice are looking away. Reid shoots the other leg and Gabriel plunges.

Sophia witnesses her friend get impaled through the face. She watches as Gabriel wiggles around with his eyes toward them, and completely covered in blood. With each movement, his body slides lower, and lower. The prongs entered under his chin, with one of them sticking out of his mouth.

"Grab her next," Reid tells the man as he points toward Patrice. "I'm tired of the crying."

Just then, a man comes running into the barn. "We got another one, sir, another Illegal Resident," the man says.

"This must be my lucky day," Reid thinks to himself. "Put them in the pit," he tells his man, then rushes out.

The man stands each one up before cutting the tape that tie their ankles together. Each Community has a pit, some are worse than others, but Community-*two* pits are by far the worse.

They're led downstairs and shoved into a cell as they try to resist. They're nauseated when they enter, the smell is horrible. It's dark and they can't see anything. Jose starts feeling around when he kicks something, only to violently flinch and throw it back down.

"That's a hand! I just picked up a hand...!"

Sophia has to calm him down. "Shhh!" she says. "Did you hear that?"

They don't want to move around and run into any other body pieces, so all stand in the same spot. Suddenly, they hear the door to the steps open and see a light shining. They're relieved when the person approaches and see he's a priest.

"Are you children OK?" he asks. He holds a lantern close to his face. The priest has pointy features that freak Patrice out.

"Can you get us out of here?" asks Jose.

"I will not only let you out, I will also provide a safe haven for the night. They cannot enter the church."

The kids are beyond relieved, except for Jose. He wants to keep moving and doesn't want to stop again. The priest opens the door to free them and he thinks about bolting, but doesn't want to leave the girls behind.

"Follow me." The priest takes them across a dirt field and into a church. It looks like a normal building from the outside, but when they enter, they're amazed. It's lined with pews that form an aisle in the middle. There's a giant statue of Jesus Christ on a cross and the base of the podium is filled with lit candles. He leads them to the back, causing them to pass by the giant statue.

"I have a dormitory and some water back here," he tells them. He leads them to a room with four cots in it. With only three of them, it makes Sophia hope he's not planning on sleeping there.

"Shouldn't we keep moving?" Jose finally blurts out.

The priest looks at him. "Moving where, my child? It's dark out. I'll return at sunrise to wake you."

Jose feels better knowing he isn't going to sleep in there. He was thinking the same as Sophia when he saw the four cots. The priest leaves and comes back with three bottles of ice cold water, which they gulp down.

One by one, they all pass out. The effect is so quick it happens while the priest is still there.

Sophia's the first to wake back up. She's stripped to just her underwear and strapped to the cot. Her vision is blurry, but she sees a figure moving around. As her sight gets clearer, she sees Jose, and Patrice also strapped down.

The priest approaches and puts his face very close to hers. "You're awake," he loudly whispers with a grin.

She hears Jose waking and making mumbling sounds. Sophia watches the priest go to him and hears him whisper the same thing.

Patrice is awake, but hasn't made a sound and the priest notices. He walks over and stares at her with a very mean look on his face. The kids have been stripped to their underwear with no tops on, and are trapped in a tiny room with a lunatic priest. He rubs on Patrice's bare stomach with a perverted look on his face. Sophia's in the middle, but he walks around her and does the same to Jose.

The priest took advantage of the war. He's a known pedophile that was only allowed to enter the Community because he's filthy rich. To keep him under control, Reid has been known to send children of Illegal Residents to quench his thirst. He hasn't sent any in a while, which caused him to take them. He knows it might get him killed, but his desire overcame his conscience when he saw the kids being dragged into the pit.

Sophia sees a shadow in the doorway and knows Reid will be looking for them. The priest approaches a table by it to get an instrument, but is knocked unconscious by a tree log swung by someone.

"I'm back," they hear.

It's Felipe. His conscience didn't let him leave them behind. He got half way through Community-*one* and turned around. He couldn't live knowing he could have saved his sister after all they been through and didn't, he just couldn't.

"Let's get out of here!" he says. He unstraps them and throws them their clothes.

On the way out, Jose grabs a laptop the priest has on a table...

~Chapter Seventeen~

Buchanan's Fury

After the meeting with Buchanan, reality starts hitting Larry. He can think of nothing else in his mind but Krystle. Every time he tries to block her image from his mind, her face is all he sees. He thinks of how she desperately clawed at him, and cannot forget the look of fear in her eyes as he squeezed her throat with all of his might. He gets up and intends to go see Thump. He will inform him he will not take the job, and will go live with his uncle at Community-*three* instead. He cannot stick around, he's sure Thump will eventually start asking about Krystle and is afraid Buchanan might mention his wounded hands. He leaves the room and heads down the hallway as he wraps gauze bandages around them. With Buchanan's smell still lingering, he makes his way toward the elevator with nothing on his mind but Krystle.

"Good evening, sir," he says, after being let into the office by Randy. "I need to have a talk with you."

"How did the sit-down with Buchanan go?" Thump interrupts. "Where is he!?"

"It didn't go so well. I will not take the job, it is not for me."

They begin to laugh. Thump purposely did it, he considered some-one else for the job and was hoping Larry, *'who is more qualified,'* lost interest, and knew he wouldn't want it after sitting with Buchanan.

"Sir, I want to permanently resign. My time here is done."

Thump doesn't complain. He doesn't like him so much anyway. The only reason he was there was to man one of the satellites so he's worthless to him now. "I wish you the best with whatever you decide to do," he says.

Before Larry steps out, he turns to them.

"Have you seen Krystle?" he asks.

Both Randy and Thump attempt to quickly respond, but Thump takes over. "She left early today. She wasn't feeling well."

"Keep an eye on her, sir. She said something about wanting to go to the Fort."

He walks out, glances down the hallway and sees Buchanan and his men walking toward him. It sounds and feels like horses galloping as they get closer, and closer. He wants to avoid them, so walks the op-posite way.

Buchanan reaches Thump's door and loudly knocks on it. The door swings open and Randy rushes out before Buchanan could enter.

"Where is he!?" he demands. Thump sees the look in his eyes. He looks non-compos mentis and hungry.

He leads him to the third floor of the building and takes him into a dark area. Thump could feel the footsteps behind him as Buchanan and his men follow. He hits a switch and the lights start flickering, until they steadily shine.

Buchanan looks in amazement at an octagon work area built for him. They're on the outside of it looking through the glass that circles the entire structure. Thump made it just like Buchanan likes it. The in-side resembles a dark, seedy bathroom with filthy urinals and a sink. There's a huge dentist chair in the middle. Above it, swings chains that hang to the floor on its sides. The walls are tiled up to the glass and the room is illuminated by bulbs that swing from wires hanging from the ceiling. The floor is covered in tiny dull tiles and has a drain right in the middle. Buchanan loves it. He rushes inside and acts like a toddler in a candy store.

"It was specially built for you," says Thump, who's now inside with him.

"Close the door!" Buchanan loudly shouts to one of his men.

"We're in here alone now," he tells Thump with a menacing look. "I'm going to tear you up," he meanly says, and grabs a syringe off of a table.

"Sit down!" he screams.

Thump's trembling. He could feel his heart rapidly beating and doesn't know what to do.

Buchanan titters. "I'm joking," he tells him. He looks toward the door at one of his men who also chuckles. He cannot see the other two agents but can hear them laughing. The windows are only transparent from the outside. On the inside, it's a giant mirror going around the entire room. Thump has never been so horrified, and wishes he knew of an agent willing to go against Buchanan for him.

"You scared the hell out of me," he finally says. He walks toward the door. "I'll bring Weinberg. Have two of your men follow me."

Thump leads them down one flight of stairs and into a room that's pitch black. They feel their way across, until they get to a door with a small square window that dimly provides light. Thump twist the handle and tells them he's inside, so the men rush in with their guns drawn. Thump hears a scuffle as Weinberg struggles with them. One of the men swings his gun and knocks him unconscious, forcing them to have to drag him all the way back to Buchanan.

Weinberg awakes and is strapped to the chair. He hears someone, but his head is held straight by two wooden slabs placed with his face viced between them, and is positioned where he can only move his eyes. He struggles to release his arms from the straps, but the tightness prevents him from setting himself free.

"Good evening, sir," says Buchanan.

Weinberg recognizes his voice, but only because he's seen him executing terms they've televised and has seen how ruthless he could be. He hopes he's not right, until Buchanan gets in his sight. The first thing he notices are his huge ears. He's very surprised at his overall size, he seems much bigger than he looks on TV.

"My name is Buchanan. What's yours?" he sarcastically asks.

Weinberg hasn't said a word. After killing Scott he stayed local, the military wasn't required to have a chip that could be traced. He was only found because his niece's boyfriend assaulted her and happened to be the son of a top official in the N.A.A.. He was caught after beating the kid half to death for putting his hands on her.

"Weinberg," he replies. He's heard stories of things Buchanan has done but some seem to be unbelievable. Some atrocities he's accused of are things you wouldn't expect one human being to do to another.

"OK, Weinberg. Do you know why you're here?"

"I'm here because Thump's toy soldier failed him. He sent a dimwit to take me out who couldn't fight worth a crap. He had a better chance getting it done if he did it himself. What's that smell!?"

Weinberg's talking aggressively. He figures he's going to die regardless, so might as well get it over with and die with honor. "What he's done to this country is a shame!"

Buchanan walks to the table and grabs the syringe he threatened Thump with. His heavy steps could be felt as he walks across the room with Weinberg's eyes following him around. Weinberg's stuck to the chair with his legs elevated and Buchanan comes close.

"You know the dimwit you speak of? He was an agent, and agents are sacred." He pokes the needle into his skin. Buchanan didn't personally know Agent Scott but has developed an odd fascination for him due to the stories Thump has told him. The fluid injected causes paralysis, but although you can't move, you could feel everything. You can swallow and breathe, but can't make a sound. It also fills you with so much adrenaline, you cannot pass out due to pain.

He sees Buchanan loosen the straps and tries to move, but can't. Weinberg occasionally stares at the bulbs that hang and prays in his mind for a miracle. Buchanan lifts one of his arms and reaches for the chain on that side. He lifts it, and Weinberg sees it has a hook on the end. He tries to wiggle but nothing, he attempts to scream but can't. With one movement, Buchanan pushes the hook through his forearm, causing it to emerge out of the opposite side. The pain is unbearable. With tears streaming out of his eyes and rolling into his ears, he looks as Buchanan starts turning a handle in a circular motion. The hook moves upward, tearing more into his flesh, and it causes his arm to rise. The chains were built in a pulley system and Buchanan doesn't stop turning until his arm is up in the air.

Thump, Randy, and Buchanan's men are outside of the room watching it all. Randy did nothing but cringe his teeth as Weinberg's arm rose, and listened as Buchanan's men made wagers on what he'd do next.

"Don't worry," Buchanan tells him. "The shot I gave you will wear off in about an hour. I'm going to kill you the same way you killed one of our agents, only I will kill you much slower. There are going to be moments tonight, that you'll wish you were dead. Moments you'll wish I'd just grab my gun and blow your brains out, but I won't, it will not be that easy."

Weinberg stares at a hanging bulb and completely misses when Buchanan goes to the table and grabs a scalpel. Buchanan drags an oversized stool Thump had specially built and takes a seat at the side of the chair with Weinberg's arm at chest level.

All Weinberg could do is move his eyes and inhale the stench.

Buchanan grabs Weinberg's hand, and cuts straight lines from each of his knuckles to the top of his fingernails. He reaches in his back pocket, pulls out tiny tweezers covered in rust and uses them to pluck his nails off. Weinberg's screaming inside, he's running out of the strength required to handle the pain. Buchanan takes the scalpel and cuts around each finger. He sits with his tongue sticking out to the side looking very concentrated as he cuts around each of them, including his thumb. Buchanan grabs a dirty little rag out of the front pocket of his jacket and wipes the sweat off of his forehead. He then gets up, and calmly goes to his bag.

Weinberg notices Buchanan has a very bad rash on the back of his head that seems to go down his back. The bag is directly on a table in front of Weinberg. He stares as Buchanan opens it and throws the contents of it on the table. Weinberg's stunned when he sees it's body pieces that look to belong to children. Buchanan grabs a small piece and flings it into his mouth. He then grabs a finger and walks toward Weinberg.

"You hungry?" he asks with a grin. He shoves a decomposing finger into Weinberg's mouth, as he chews on his own piece which he seems to be savoring.

Weinberg tries not to swallow but it's blocking his throat.

Buchanan notices the gulp Weinberg finally takes when he's forced to consume it.

"Randy and Thump are terrified. Buchanan's men are excitedly watching and cheering him on. They stare as Buchanan goes back to the seat and starts splitting his fingers open as you would a cigar. Weinberg feels his skin cleave and is in tremendous pain. Buchanan completely peels the first finger of skin and it shines red with only the meat around the bone exposed. One by one, he peels them all. He then carefully cuts around his wrist while trying to avoid cutting a vein that might cause him to bleed to death. After cutting it, he cuts from his wrist to his knuckles, then peels the skin. Buchanan knows it's impossible for Weinberg to pass out from pain with the injection but wonders why he stares ahead and pays him no attention. He knows he has to be in pain, but Weinberg seems phlegmatic.

"He's skinning him," says Randy. "I'm out of here, I don't want to see this."

Buchanan hooks his other arm and repeats the process as he steadily stares at a light bulb. He wants to cause as much pain as possible, but it seems Weinberg is not affected and it makes him think his technique isn't working. Weinberg finally shifts his eyes. He looks at his hands and sees they're skinless.

"Nice, right?" asks Buchanan. "That takes great technique. You have to have a very steady hand to make cuts like that. I can't wait to do your face, but I'm going to get your feet out of the way."

Weinberg strains his eyes to roll them low enough to see his toes.

Buchanan drags his stool to the foot of the seat and starts cutting into them. Weinberg feels he could move his foot and kick him in the face but is physically unable to. Buchanan cuts and cuts, until both feet are skinned.

"I got the hardest parts over with," he says as he wipes the sweat off of his forehead with the dirty little rag. "I understand what you're doing you know. There's only so much pain you could take until it doesn't affect you anymore." He goes back to the table his bag is on and flings another piece into his mouth. Thump turns his face every time he does it and Buchanan's men start to chuckle.

"Do you have a wife and kids? I hope you do, and I hope they're wondering where you are right now. I bet they have no idea what predicament you're in."

Weinberg was staying with his sister and niece while on the run. When he worked for the N.A.A., he lived alone. His wife died ten years prior to him joining the force and he remained by himself, they never had any children.

Buchanan grabs another piece and squeezes it, causing thick, black, chunky fluid to seep out and drip onto the table. He scoops as much as he can up with his huge fingers, walks toward him, and puts it into his mouth. He rubs his fingers against the inside of his lips to get it all in, then licks the rest off of them.

Thump almost pukes. Buchanan's men jump around in excitement and don't notice when he leaves with his stomach turned upside down. In as much pain as Weinberg's in, he prefers the cutting over the feeding. The chunks he just swallowed reeked so much, he swallowed quickly just so he won't have to smell it. Weinberg feels one of his mangled toes move. Buchanan did a bad job on his feet and a few of them are hanging. He hopes Buchanan doesn't notice, but the drug is wearing off.

He cuts around Weinberg's knee and prepares to make the cut going down to skin his lower leg, causing it to jerk. Buchanan finishes the cut before getting up to get the syringe. When he turns, Weinberg uses all of his strength to plop himself up and swings his arms up to try and unhook them. Buchanan hurries back as Weinberg frees one arm. He thinks about stopping him but decides to let him try.

Weinberg uses the free arm to unhook the other as Buchanan watches. He slowly walks as if he's stalking his prey and lets him get on his feet.

As soon as the bare meat touches the floor, Weinberg drops. The pain is unbearable. He tries to crawl, but experiences the same pain when his bare palms touch the floor.

"Where do you think you're going?" Buchanan asks with a chuckle. "You don't leave here tonight, you die here tonight, big difference."

Weinberg looks at his hands as he's being raised by Buchanan and sees his fingers are sticking together as the blood dries. He struggles to pull them apart, then feels the pain when they peel away from each other. Buchanan lays him on his stomach, handcuffs his hands behind his back and injects him again.

Weinberg feels as his body goes limp and is ready to have another nightmare. While Handcuffed, Buchanan kneels him on the chair. He cranks the hooks higher and sticks each under Weinberg's arms. He walks back and forth, raising each little by little, until he's suspended in mid-air with the hooks buried in his armpits. Buchanan pushes the chair across the room, causing the hooks to go deeper when his dead weight drops. The hooks are forced to go so deep, they poke out of his shoulders.

"Agent Scott was a good man, and from what I've heard, he didn't deserve to die. You killed him for no reason. He was only doing his job and you should have understood. I bet you regret killing him now, don't you?"

Weinberg's paying him no attention. He's thinking of his sister and niece, which is the only family he has. He pictures his wife and re-members her exactly as she was. With the handcuffs placed over his skinless hands, he tries to move but can't. He can only watch as he dips his fingers in the jelly-like substance he squeezed out of the body part to lick them. The smell gets worse every time he touches it. Weinberg has never been in such a predicament and wishes death upon himself. With his feet hanging inches above the floor, he wishes he could at least arch them a bit to place his toes on it and alleviate the weight that's causing the hooks to rip through his skin.

Thump has gone to his office and has three agents there. Randy's still trying to get the images out of his head as he paces back and forth.

"I want you to go in, take them out, then disappear," Thump tells the men. "As soon as it's done, I'll give you an antidote that'll kill the poison."

The agents accept. They want nothing more than to leave the job alive. "Who is it?" one asks.

"It's Buchanan and his men, but don't worry," says Thump. "He's distracted, there's no way he'll see this coming. That's why it's impor-tant for you to use silencers. His men are sitting with their backs to-ward the door and will not see you enter, but you have to shoot quick and simultaneously. Buchanan's not able to see you from inside, there's a double sided mirror. Take his men out then go in and take him out of existence. There is no way you can let him live. It's imperative that you kill him," he stresses.

The agents look at each other. They don't know if they want to risk going against Buchanan, but the thought of having the poison eliminated help them come to the conclusion that it's worth the chance and they agree to do the job.

Weinberg watches as Buchanan starts walking toward him with the scalpel in his hand. He starts cutting around his other knee. After making the slit, he goes back to his other leg, which was previously cut, and struggles to peel the thick skin off of it. With sweat rolling down his forehead, he manages to get it completely off, then proceeds to peel the skin off of the other one. Weinberg's now completely skinless from the knees down. Buchanan looks like he needs a break and goes back to the table with the body pieces. He grabs what appears to be an infant's leg but struggles to squeeze rotten blood out of it.

"The best part about human meat, is that once it's decomposing, you could bite right through it like if it's bread," he says while looking at Weinberg, then takes a bite out of a thigh. He chews on it like he's really enjoying it, then swallows.

His men are outside watching his every move. "Would you do that?" one asks another, and gets a quick reply. "Hell no!"

With only Weinberg's muscles and meat covering his bones visible, Buchanan stares and looks proud of his work. "The human body is amazing," he says.

One of Buchanan's men hear a sound coming from the corridor behind them, but doesn't pay it any attention. He figures it's Thump coming back so keeps watching Buchanan work. They all turn when they hear the door open, but cannot act quick enough to grab their guns when the agents storm in firing at them with automatic rifles.

Buchanan hears the ruckus but thinks it's their reaction to what he's doing.

The agents go to the glass and are horrified to see Weinberg hanging. One of Buchanan's men manages to pull out a gun as he lays fighting for his life, and shoot an agent who's looking through the glass in the side of the head. The other agents panic and finish Buchanan's man off by filling him with bullets.

Buchanan hears the single shot from his man's gun and throws himself on Weinberg. He wraps his arms around his torso and uses his weight to pull him down. The hooks poking out of his shoulders are forced to go completely up and rip through his flesh, until Buchanan is carrying him. One of Weinberg's arms comes clean off, and is left dangling and handcuffed to the other. One agent rushes into the room and starts shooting toward Buchanan, while the other stand outside of the octagon ready to enter. Buchanan uses Weinberg as a shield and runs toward the agent, who's repeatedly firing in his direction but shooting into Weinberg's back.

With fear in his eyes, the agent watches as Buchanan gets close enough to grab the silencer, pushing it upward, making the bullets go through the ceiling.

Buchanan drops Weinberg's lifeless body and grabs the agent in a choke hold while demanding for anyone else to show themselves. He hears the agent outside drop his weapon, then watches as he appears in the doorway with his hands raised.

"Who sent you!?" demands Buchanan. None of them answer.

He puts the gun to the side of the agent's head and asks again. One thing about agents is that they never talk. They are hardened criminals who have learned long ago that you are to keep your mouth shut. Buchanan slowly leaves the room while tightly squeezing the agent's neck as the other backs up with his hands raised. Buchanan sees his men dead when he steps out. With the rifle's silencer on the man's temple, he pulls the trigger, but doesn't let him go. He holds the agent up with the sleeve of his jacket covered in cerebral matter. He kisses him on the wound before he releases his grip and quickly points the gun at the other agent.

"Who sent you!?" he shouts again.

The agent knows that no matter what happens, he's dead. He will not give Buchanan the pleasure of knowing who ordered the hit. This infuriates Buchanan, it makes him pull the trigger and keep it pressed. He empties the entire clip in the agent who's down and dead, then grabs another agent's gun and heads toward the door.

Everyone stops what they're doing when they see Buchanan rapidly walk down the hallway on the eighth floor with the rifle hanging at his side. His finger barely fits in the trigger guard, but it's ready to squeeze. He approaches Thump's door and kicks it in with so much force it breaks off of the hinges. With Randy and Thump sitting inside, he points the gun in.

"You tried to have me killed!?" Buchanan doesn't know for sure who it was, but figured he'd blame Thump. He knows deep inside that Thump knows better, but is hoping he'd give him a clue as to who it might have been.

Randy looks at Thump and gives him the *'I told you so,'* look.

"What happened?" Thump replies. "What the hell is going on?"

"Someone tried to kill me," says Buchanan. "And I'm sure it was you, or someone associated with you. So who was it!?"

Thump has no choice but to put his foot down. He cannot have people like Buchanan point guns at him. He grows bold when he sees other agents have gathered in the hallway behind Buchanan with their guns pointed at him.

"You will put that gun down now!" he shouts.

Randy's petrified.

"Do you know who I am? Don't you realize you're my best agent? Why would I want you dead?" he asks.

Buchanan lowers the gun.

"What do you mean someone tried to kill you?"

"Three agents stormed in and killed my men before attempting to take me out."

Thump wants to know if Buchanan's aware it was him. "Why didn't you demand answers before killing them? You did kill them, right?"

"Oh, they're dead. I asked but they wouldn't say who sent them. I want to know, Thump!" he aggressively says. "I need to know who did this!" Buchanan feels a warmth on his belly and lifts his shirt only to realize he's been shot.

"Go to the infirmary and get that looked at," says Thump. "I'll find out who did this to you and your men, and I will let you know."

"It's OK. It's just a scratch. You work on finding out who did this, I'll plug it with a finger," he says. Thump watches him shove an oversized finger into the bullet wound without displaying he feels any pain at all. Buchanan was hired to work for the agency when thump went into the prison he was in, and was impressed when he saw him grab another inmate by the top of the head with one hand before twisting so hard, he broke his neck. Buchanan originally wanted to stay in jail and only accepted the job when Thump agreed to give him a chip that didn't contain the poison. Thump was infatuated with his size, he knew people would fear him. Buchanan worked directly under Thump until he began collecting body pieces which made him unbearable to be around.

He decided to put him in his son's four-man team. Buchanan and Moore were ruthless, they were so horrible he was advised to split them up.

General Reid's back at the Community, and just got word that someone seen the priest take the kids. He demands them to get him, and demands them to put the Illegal Resident they've just encountered into the pit.

"They've escaped, sir," says the man that drags the priest to him.

Reid pulls out his gun as they get closer, but the priest is still dizzy from the blow to the head.

"You know something? Not one single Illegal Resident has ever been able to escape, yet five have in the last two days, thanks to you," he tells him. He raises the gun to his forehead.

"Please, sir," the priest desperately pleas. "Here, take all of my DD's and give me a pass on this one. I just had to do it, I couldn't help myself."

Reid scans the three-hundred million DD's onto his own chip and looks at him. "Let me ask you something, Father? Do you think you'll go to heaven with all the horrible things you've done to children?"

The priest doesn't know how to respond. "Yes. I guess."

"Why don't you find out," he says. He raises the gun and shoots him in the head with no warning. The blood splatters in the face of the man that brought him, forcing him to bend over to rub it off.

"Leave his body right here!" he tells the man. "I want everyone to see what happens when you double-cross me. I want a man to stay with the Illegal Resident and guard him, make sure no-one attempts to break him out. I can't believe we've let so many get away the last couple days," he says as he begins to leave. Reid's infuriated. He found out Gus was in the house all along, then received word that two of his men were killed chasing him.

The man in the pit is Dwayne Morris, Krystle's husband.

He's in the same pit Sophia was in, and also avoids moving around after picking something up only to realize it was a decomposing body part. He thinks of his wife and regrets leaving. He let his emotions get the best of him when he saw her kiss another man, and ends up in a worse situation.

~Chapter Eighteen~

The Arrival

"Where are you?" Sophia hears a voice ask as they're leaving the church. It is very dark, but they notice two men running toward it. "He took them," they hear one man tell the other as they cower behind a hearse.

"Where are you?" she hears again.

"What?" she asks Felipe. Felipe looks at her but ignores the question. He's concentrated on getting out of there and doesn't understand what she's talking about.

"Where are you? I'm almost there!" she hears.

"Shhhh," she stresses. "They'll hear us!"

Jose and Felipe look at her, then look at each other. "Let's keep moving," Felipe urges. They run across the street when the men enter the church. They're at the edge of Community-*two*, and only have to make it through the first Community before getting to the one-mile stretch that separates it from the Fort. Again, Sophia hears the voice so makes them stop.

"Who's saying that?" she asks. "Do you hear it?"

They all wonder what she's talking about.

"Hear what?" asks Patrice.

"I keep hearing a really loud voice. It keeps asking me where I am."

It is not any of their voices and it has her concerned, she fears she's going crazy.

They finally make it to Community-*one,* which is the longest, and watch as two men walk out of a house to have a conversation outside, so they hide behind a car.

"There was a really bad car wreck earlier today. Two of Reid's men were burned to death," one man tells the other. The kids patiently wait for them to go back inside so they could continue moving.

Gus and Brianna are in the middle of Community-*one.* They were forced to stop when a tire blew out and decided to cower in the car until it's dark enough for him to fix it. Brianna's in the passenger seat crouched down, staring at her son through the mirror, and wonders why he never smiles. No matter what she does, he shows no emotion at all. The only emotion he seems to express is when he cries because he's hungry, and when he does, he does so with a straight face and sheds no tears. Dr. Gus stepped out of the car and told Brianna to stay inside but is struggling to replace the tire.

The men go inside so Sophia and the rest of them run until they're by a house two blocks away. They stop so Patrice could catch her breath. They start running again, until they're stopped when they see an older man struggling to change a car tire.

"That's the man that freed me from the dungeon I was in," says Felipe.

"Let's take his car," says Jose. "We can attack him when he puts the tire on." Felipe talks him out of it, he doesn't want to risk getting caught after coming so far. Patrice accidentally kicks a tin can that's at the edge of the sidewalk, causing Gus to stand and look around.

"Who's there?" he demands. Gus doesn't want to get caught, so tightly grips the tire iron. He does a complete *three-sixty* hoping it isn't Reid's men. He runs to the front of the car and urges Brianna to get out. He tries to convince her it'd be better if they continued their journey by foot.

Sophia sees Brianna rush out of the car and open the back door. "Where are you?" she hears, this time much louder, almost as if the person's standing right next to her.

"It's an Illegal Resident," Sophia tells them, then quickly gets up. "Hi there," she shouts. Patrice, Felipe, and Jose still hide. She slowly walks toward them.

"Run!" Gus shouts at Brianna. He runs as fast as he can but barely moves.

"Who are you?" asks Brianna. She opens the door and sees her child unstrapped and standing, looking back at Sophia.

"Here you are," Sophia hears in her mind.

"My name is Sophia. My friends and I are trying to get to the Fort," she tells them. She ignores the voice and walks closer. Gus has stopped trying to run and slowly makes his way back.

"We are also," Brianna answers. She grabs the baby and cradles him in her arms. Sophia notices the child staring at her.

Jose, Felipe, and Patrice are behind Sophia now. Brianna senses relief when she sees they're all Illegal Residents, and looks at Patrice who reminds her of herself when she was a kid.

"You need help fixing that? I'll fix it if we could get a ride," Jose tells them. He asks Felipe to hold the laptop and rushes to change the tire after getting assurance from Gus. They notice the light of a house turn on, and see someone peeking through a curtain. In seconds, the lights of all the homes start illuminating and the folks start rushing out.

"Let's go," says Jose. Gus is impressed as to how fast he was able to replace the tire. They jump in the car and Gus peels off, while getting a side window broken by something someone threw. Felipe warns there are a couple of cars chasing. Gus doesn't have much further to go so steps on it. They start to scream and duck when the car speeds up and the bullets begin to fly.

"Get down," Sophia loudly hears. She ducks and hears a bullet whiz by, then looks at the back of Gus's seat and sees the bullet's penetrated it. The baby is desperately trying to pull away from his mother's grasp as he sits on her lap with her holding him tight. They could hear the bullets hitting the back of the car and are all trying to duck. Gus sees the fence that divides the Fort and guns it. He rams through it, causing both cars chasing to come to screeching halts, they will not risk entering the woods. Gus's car spins out of control before coming to a full stop and he urges everyone to get out.

"You have to put your hands up like this," he says, and shows everyone how to raise them.

The Fort's guards will not attack if you approach them with your hands up high. Sophia notices everyone's exited the car except for Patrice, so goes back and sees she's still inside. Sophia sees blood coming out of her mouth and panics.

"NOOO!" she screams.

Patrice stares at her. "Go," she says.

Everyone runs toward the car when they hear Sophia's cry. Gus immediately grabs Patrice and lays her on the ground. Sophia's being held by Felipe and is hysterically crying. A bullet's penetrated Patrice's back, but Gus sees no exit wound and it really concerns him.

"We have to get her in there, now," he stresses. He notices the puddle of blood covering the dirt she lays on slowly expand. Patrice's eyes are filled with tears. Sophia kneels by her side. She puts her forehead against Patrice's while emotionally crying. All she could think of is her short, rough life and she fears she might die.

Patrice looks toward the sky, staring into the darkness. "I see my mom," she strains to say. Felipe and Jose are teary eyed and are not trying to hide it. They have all grown very close in their journey and Sophia's reaction has them heartbroken. Tears roll down Brianna's face, and she holds the baby closely. Gus stands with his head bowed and his arms crossed, he knows Patrice will not make it.

"No," Sophia cries. "Don't you dare go to her! You have to stay here with me. Please!"

Patrice looks at her and smiles. "You're special," she tells her as she takes her final breath.

"Noooo...!" cries Sophia. "Noooo...!"

"She's in a better place now," she hears.

"Shut up!" she screams, making everyone wonder who she's talking to. "Leave me alone...!"

Brianna has a confused look on her face and Gus thinks she's lost it. Felipe comes over and grabs her in his arms.

"I can't do this anymore," she tells him as she sobs on his shoulder. "I really can't."

Jose passes Gus the laptop and bends to pick Patrice up. "We're not leaving her here," he says with a sniffle. "She will make it to the Fort with us just like she was supposed to." He grabs her upper back, shoves an arm under the joints to her knees and lifts. He begins to walk ahead of everyone with tears in his eyes as her limp limbs swing.

Mitchell, Murphy, and Jacob are approaching the entrance. They should have no trouble getting in once he shows his F.F.A. badge.

They feel the crunching caused by the tires rolling over the gravel as they come to a stop. The man steps out of the booth as Mitchell stretches his arm out of the window to show his badge.

"Step out of the car. All of you!"

Murphy and Jacob become nervous, but it doesn't seem to affect Mitchell, he knows this is procedure. The man walks around the car and demands him to open the trunk.

"I'm here to see General Reid," Mitchell tells him as he opens it.

"Are you here about the car accident? What is she doing here? I've never seen a female agent."

"What accident? This is my family," he says. "I'm here for a personal matter."

The man is skeptical of Mitchell, but doesn't want to slip up and face Reid's fury if the story holds up and he questions someone he's expecting, especially an F.F.A. agent. He grants them access by pushing a button to let them through. New faces are questioned in the Communities, so they're going straight to the Fort.

"Freeze," Gus hears.

They're approached by two men holding automatic weapons.

"What happened to her?" one asks, referring to Patrice.

"We need to make it to the Fort," says Sophia, with tears rolling down her cheeks.

"Is she dead?" the man worries. He walks toward Jose after lowering his firearm and confirms she is. "Follow me," he tells them.

They finally make it into the Fort and are greeted by Leon, who tells his men to get Patrice's body prepared for burial.

"Welcome to the Fort," he tells them. Gus doesn't want to tell him about the baby just yet.

"What are your names?"

"I'm Felipe."

"I'm Sophia," she says. She holds back tears that try to flow when she sees his men respectfully carry Patrice's body away.

Jose walks to Gus to get his laptop. "I'm Jun-Jun," he says.

"I'm Brianna, and this is my son."

"He has beautiful eyes."

"I, I'm Dr. Gus." He knew he'd recognize the name with all the work he's done with Mrs. Cryan.

"Dr. Gus?" Leon asks, getting a nod from him. "I've heard so much about you. Thank you very much for all you've done. Where's Mrs. Cryan? I haven't seen her in a while."

Dr. Gus regretfully tells him Dorothy's dead.

Leon becomes saddened. Dorothy Cryan was the best thing that's ever happened to him. If it weren't for her, the Fort would not exist. With tears welling, and making him turn his face, he asks what happened to her.

"She took her own life, sir. We have to talk in private."

Ahmed and Willie are approaching them, but Willie suddenly tells him he isn't feeling well and has to go home. The way he reacts convinces Ahmed it's an emergency.

"You OK?"

"No. I don't feel good," he says as he looks toward the group. "I'll meet them tomorrow."

"We'll talk first thing in the morning," Leon tells them. "You all look like you can use some rest."

He can't believe Dorothy's gone. The thought of her taking her own life has him convinced she's found the child, she often told him she would once she finds him.

Mitchell's stopped in his tracks. There's an angry mob in the middle of Community-*one* and they're blocking the only road available into the Fort. They've gathered since Gus took off and demand to know who Mitchell is, only to back off when he shows his badge.

"Go get those Illegal Residents!" one shouts. They make way for his car to go by.

"When we get there, we have to raise our hands all the way up," says Murphy. She looks at Jacob who's in the back seat looking excited about going to the Fort.

"I'm glad you guys decided to come along. That world back there," she says while sticking her thumb up to point backward. "It is not the world God intended us to live in."

Gus, Sophia, and the group are all placed in a house until the next day, when they'll be given different options. The baby's grown fond of Sophia, he's jumped in her arms and doesn't want to get off. He provides her with a sense of comfort. He helps her control her emotions when she thinks of Patrice. "Tell him who I am," she hears a voice say. For a second, she thinks it's the baby, but comes to the conclusion that it can't be. She tries to make him smile with a bunch of silly faces, but he only looks at her with no expression. "Tell him," she hears.

Jose's sitting on a bed with the laptop open, desperately trying to delete disturbing photos the priest has in it. Felipe has laid down and is snoring loudly. One by one, they all fall asleep until Gus is up by himself. He knows he must tell Leon about the baby and leaves the house in hopes of running into him.

After walking around for thirty minutes, Gus is confused and cannot find the house. He decides to sit on a crate that's by a trail until it's light enough to find his way back, and sees someone walking toward him.

"Hi, I'm Ahmed. Nice to meet you," he hears them say.

"I'm Doctor Gus. Nice to meet you also. Nice place you have here."

"Thank you. We try our best to provide a home to anyone willing to come in peace. We want the Fort's population to grow but it's almost impossible. I'm surprised but glad you guys made it. Leon's somehow convinced there will come a savior that'll make it possible again."

"There will," responds Gus. "He's much closer than you all think."

Ahmed doesn't really believe in a savior. He finds it hard to believe someone could predict something of such magnitude so long ago. He supports Leon one-hundred percent, but doesn't think there's any hope. They watch as a bunch of the Fort's men hurry toward the entrance.

"I have to go," says Ahmed. Gus sees there's something going on and gets up as he runs off.

He walks over a hill to get sight of the entrance and sees men walking behind Mitchell, Murphy, and Jacob with guns pointed at the back of their heads. Mitchell looks familiar but he can't recall where he's seen him.

"What do you guys want?" Leon asks.

"We come to the Fort for a better life," Mitchell responds. He's hoping no-one recognizes him. "I'm going to be honest with you, sir. I'm a former employee of the F.F.A.. I've escaped their clutches to at least bring my son here before they poison me." The statement makes Leon's men raise their guns.

"Put them down," he tells them. "I admire you risking this big a chance to provide your son with a better life. I've killed many of your agents in the past and have no problem killing another. I only hope you don't come with bad intentions, but also know it'd be impossible for you to be here if you did."

As Ahmed's approaching, he sees Willie there. "I thought you weren't feeling good," he asks as he gets close enough for him to hear.

"It was a bug. Just had to go." Ahmed grows suspicious.

Gus's flabbergasted when he sees the kid with the blue eyes there, and also just realized who Mitchell is. He turns around and wishes he had asked Ahmed for directions to the house. He must have nodded off, because he wakes up the next morning with his back against a rocky surface, and sitting on the crate. He wanders around the Fort until he finally finds the house. He walks in and is surprised to see Leon there. He has the baby in his arms, spinning him around, hoping to get a smile out of him. The baby instead extends his arms when he sees Sophia walk by.

"Tell him who I am," she hears. Sophia thinks she's going crazy. She declares she has to wash her face and passes the baby to Brianna.

"Good morning, Dr. Gus," says Leon. "Where were you?"

Gus doesn't respond to him and he finds it odd.

The baby's scanning his eyes around, looking for Sophia, and Jose is busy learning how to use the laptop.

"Does anyone know how to delete pictures off of this thing? These images are driving me nuts," he says.

Leon goes over and is surprised at the pictures. "Where did you get this? Is this yours?"

"A priest attacked us in Community-*two*, so we knocked him out and I took it." As Leon assists him with the images, the laptop makes a sound.

"There's someone messaging you," he tells him.

Jose's surprised and can't wait until he's done to see who it might be. He hopes it's the priest so he could give him a piece of his mind. Leon passes the laptop back as Sophia enters the room.

"OK, I need to speak to you all," he declares.

Everyone's attention shifts to him.

"My name is Leon Wang. I started this Fort at the behest of a lady who one day came to me after many hours of protesting, and told me I was destined to be the leader of a place that would turn this world around."

Jose becomes intrigued with what he's hearing and closes the laptop after messaging the person back.

"This lady was the nicest person you could ever meet, and she holds a special place in my heart. She was the wife of an F.F.A. agent who risked his life to save mine. He let me escape when my family was savagely murdered and paid the ultimate price for it."

Sophia feels his pain, she knows first hand what Leon must have gone through. She's cradling the baby who extended his arms when he saw her come back into the room.

"She did everything she could to get more, and more people in here. The world we live in is cruel, but she tried to make it a better place. She gave me a book and made me promise I'd read it. The book was written by a great prophet who predicted this would all take place. He says a child will arrive on this land and lead us to victory. He will be our savior."

"I've read it," Sophia interrupts. "Tell him it's me," she hears, but ignores it. Leon doesn't think it's possible for such a young child to have read the deep words of the prophet.

"We have to talk," Gus anxiously tells Leon.

"What do you mean you've read it?"

"He says the child will survive the mark of the beast. What is the mark of the beast? It can't be the chip and it can't be the vaccine, we've all survived them. I think it's all stories, I don't think there will be a savior."

"There will be a savior, my child. He will survive being injected after the thirty-minute mark. That's the indication of who it is, that's the mark he speaks of."

Brianna's shocked. This is the same thing Gus's been telling her and she didn't believe it. She looks at him but he turns his face.

"If the child survives, it's only because he's special. Mrs. Cryan also believed it. According to her beliefs, the child will end up here," he assures.

"It's children. According to his words, there will be a child born exactly twelve years before him that's supposed to join in his mission," she says. "Tell him it's me," she hears in her mind again.

This confirms to Leon that Sophia has actually read the book. Even people he knows read it, have been surprised when he mentions those details. It's as if everyone seem to miss that quote.

"You're a smart child," Leon tells her. He feels Sophia doesn't believe and figures he'd change the subject. "Here, you guys worry about nothing, we have a pantry full of food and should have steady electricity soon. Make yourselves at home. Feel free to roam the village and get accustomed to it."

"We have to talk," Gus again tells him, but again is ignored. Leon wants to speak as a group, so if it's not something that could be said in front of everyone then it has to wait.

"We practice our fighting skills twice every day, and I hope you young ones find it in you to join us. Well, it's kind of mandatory so you don't have a choice. I'll send a man to give you details of times and locations. You all have a great day."

He tells Gus to meet him outside to have the discussion he's been anxious to have.

Leon admires all that Gus has done. Mrs. Cryan has told him of the countless times she's sent him children to have the expensive procedure done for free. She's also told him of all the children she's risked trying to find the one that'll someday make it there, so he feels for Gus, and cannot imagine the stress he lives with.

"You wanted to talk to me," he tells him as they walk out.

Gus appears to be shaken. "The man that came in last night, he's not a good man."

Leon's confused as to who he's referring to. "What man?"

"The one that came in last night. He works for one of the most ruthless teams in the F.F.A. You cannot allow him in here!"

"It's OK," he tells him. He won't be around much longer. They will poison him soon if they haven't already."

"There's something else, I need to tell you something else."

Leon waits for him to speak.

"Your, your man. He works for General Reid."

Leon's stunned. "Who!? What!?"

"The kid with the blue eyes, I seen him at a meeting with Reid. He had a sit-down with all of his men and he was also there."

Leon doesn't believe what he's hearing. "What kid with blue eyes?" Immediately, he realizes he's talking about Willie, but wants confirmation. He thought the girlfriend story was out of nowhere and the thought of Willie lying has passed his mind.

"The one from last night, the one with the really blue eyes."

This infuriates Leon.

"I don't know who he is, but I'd be careful with him. I'd also be careful with the agent you let in."

The only thing on Leon's mind is Willie. He somehow felt something wasn't right with the story he came up with, and thinks of when Mrs. Kent tried to tell him something. The thought of one of his best friends backstabbing him makes him sick. He thinks of the night of the session, you'd think being a partner would guarantee him being in attendance. He remembers how his men had to fight a bunch of the Communities men and he mysteriously appeared in the battle. The thoughts are filling him with rage. He sees Ahmed and calls him over. Gus wants to tell him about the baby, but doesn't think it's the right time.

"Go and get Willie!" Leon demands.

"Is everything OK?" Ahmed has seen that look before. He knows Leon's furious.

"Go get him...!" he aggressively snaps. "Bring him to the barn!"

Ahmed's heart stops. *'Bring him to the barn,'* means he's going to kill him, and he's been his best friend for as long as he could remember.

"Whats wrong?" he tries.

"GET HIM...!" he screams.

Ahmed goes off to get Willie, but doesn't know what to say when he approaches him.

"What have you done?" he asks when he finally sees him.

Willie acts as if he doesn't know what he's talking about.

"What do you mean?" he nervously asks.

"Leon has asked me to bring you to the barn. What have you done?"

"Please, Ahmed, you must let me go. I could leave now and avoid all of this."

Ahmed's stunned. He can't believe his friend is being accused of something that might get him killed.

246

"What is it? What have you done!?"

"We been friends for years, please, help me. Just let me go. I'll leave now and you'll never see me again."

Ahmed wants to know what it is he's done.

"I've been working for Reid. Remember the other day during the session? Why do you think they thought that was the perfect time to attack?"

Ahmed's horrified. He hoped Willie had more sense than to betray them. He doesn't care who it is, it could be a sibling, he'd tear them to pieces after what he's experienced with his family. He pulls out a gun, swings it toward Willie's head and knocks him out.

Willie wakes up and is on his knees with the chains holding him up. He knows exactly what happens in these situations and hopes to talk Leon into giving him some leniency. He hears as the door to the barn opens and watches Ahmed and Leon come inside. He was about to deny everything, but knows he's already confessed to Ahmed. Leon takes his jacket off while Willie follows his every movement with his bright blue eyes.

"Let me explain," he says. He only confessed because he and Ahmed are really close and he thought he'd let it slide.

"There's nothing to explain," Leon snaps back. "You will die to-day...!" he tells him. "There's nothing worse than a traitor. I accepted you, not only as a friend but also as a brother. To know you're working for those animals kill me. I trusted you!"

"Me too," says Ahmed, with a look in his eyes that Willie has never seen...

~Chapter Nineteen~

Dwayne's Execution

Residents of all Communities gather and circle the priest's body, with many speculating it was the group of Illegal Residents they chased away that murdered him. There are people from as far away as Community-*five* who have made the trek to witness brutality at its worse. Many kneel and pray for him to reach the glories of God. They are very upset, and cannot phantom how someone could have the heart to kill a priest. There are children with their mothers, fathers with their families, and they silently stand around his body with many in tears. Suzy recites a prayer over, and over in her head. She prays for God to show mercy on him. Her husband's told her horrifying stories of things he's been accused of, so she doubts he'll be allowed into heaven. Suzy doesn't feel sorry for him, she feels sorrow for his countless victims. She worries for her husband, they had a long history and remembers all the times he's turned to him for advice. Suzy's surprised she hasn't seen him yet, and is concerned at how upset he'll be. She watches as his car approaches with two others close behind. He steps out of the car and everyone looks his way. They're expecting him to be livid, but instead, the look of surprise cover their faces when he walks to his corpse and shows no reaction.

"I found the man who did this," he exclaims. "He will pay for what he's done to our father!"

With a hand motion, he signals for his men to bring him out of the car. General Reid was ten years old when he first met the priest, and often complained to his parents that he didn't want to go to church. He showed a bit of animosity toward him but his parents were oblivious as to why. At twenty-one, the priest was considered very young to hold the position and has always had a thirst for children, especially boys. Reid remembers the feeling he felt every time his parents took him to church. Killing him gave him a bit of satisfaction, but at the same time it emotionally traumatized him.

Reid's men drag Dwayne to the body. Reid demands him to kneel, but he doesn't. He stares at the corpse and can't understand what's going on.

"I work for Thump," he says.

Reid grabs a shotgun from one of his men and smashes Dwayne in a knee, forcing him down. With his hands cuffed behind his back, he falls onto his stomach in pain.

"Lift him," Reid demands, and passes the gun back to his man. "This man here," he says to the crowd as he points toward Dwayne. "Is the man that killed our father. There's a special place in hell for you," he says as he looks at him. "We will not allow you people to enter our home and kill us!"

Dwayne's panicking, and can think of nothing other than his wife. "I didn't do this," he says with a worried tone.

"Burn it hell!" one lady shouts.

"I didn't kill him," he tries. The crowd's gone berserk and are yelling for Reid to slit his throat. They cannot stand the sight of an Illegal Resident and love to see them suffer and die. A man in the crowd rushes toward Dwayne and swings a fist, striking him in the right temple, causing him to drop on his side. Reid has a couple of men restrain the gentleman while the crowd of people cheer him on. Reid grabs him by the armpit and stands him back up.

"I didn't kill him," he repeats.

Suzy looks at Dwayne and for some reason believes him. She can see in his eyes that he says the truth.

"Look at my chip," he tells him. "It doesn't reset. I work for the government!"

Reid grabs his arm and scans it.

"I have twelve million on it. Please, you can take it all, just let me walk out of here."

Dwayne stays still as the DD's transfer and feels a sense of relief, he's sure Reid will release him.

"We have a witness who seen you commit this crime. We cannot allow for you to come in here and kill someone, especially someone of such high importance to our home. Ron!?" he calls out.

Ron steps up and admits he seen Dwayne kill the priest.

"I didn't kill him, please believe me. Why would I kill a man of the Lord!?"

The crowd becomes hostile. They have all the proof they need and are ready to see Dwayne die.

The priest lays on his back, they didn't even bother to cover his body. He lays face up with his eyes wide open and a hole the size of a fist on the side of his head.

Dwayne doesn't know how to convince them he's innocent and pleads for them to believe him.

"You deserve the stick!" says Reid.

Everyone applauds and cheer. "Take him back to the pit. The execution will take place at eight o'clock tonight."

The stick is an execution device Reid came up with. He takes a seven-foot-long metal rod, and sharpens the tip before mounting it sticking up on a five-by-five foot steel plate. With the rod pointing upward, the victim's dropped onto it, making it enter between their legs. The weight of the victim forces the rod to penetrate the rectum area. It usually exits a shoulder, but they've had instances where it e-merges out the victim's upper back. The body is left in the standing position for months at a time while it rots. Most die instantly when the rod rips through their innards, but there was one instance, when it miraculously missed most organs forcing the victim to stand there for three hours before bleeding to death.

After being knocked out and waking up to realize their son is gone, Fred and Dorothy tirelessly search. Fred was so obsessed with finding him he'd search for days at a time without eating or sleeping. Losing his son filled him with rage. Dorothy was heartbroken and of-ten thought of taking her own life. She would plead to the public for help, and approach even those she didn't know to beg them for assis-tance. Through the years, people have claimed to have found their son, only for them to be filled with false hope. People would charge them DD's claiming they knew where he was, only for them to get scam-med. Dorothy went through years of heartache. For two decades she searched, until she finally realized he was gone for good. All the while, she looked for an infant child and had no idea what he'd look like.

Fred had a friend use all of his resources to help him find his child, but they were never able to locate him. He'd listen as his wife stood up many nights weeping for their son. He became a different person when they snatched him, he was full of rage and let it out every so often. He'd cry when alone, and the thought of Gregory being kid-napped made him angry at himself for letting it happen. After twenty-four years of searching and the anger building up, he decided to join the F.F.A.. He begged his friend, Mr. Goodman, for the chance to help the government. He knew what the job entailed and figured it'd help him release some steam. Mr. Goodman was hesitant at first. He never knew Fred to be a killer as the job required, but wasn't able to say no to a good friend, especially after all he's been through.

When he took the job, Dorothy began to alienate him. She took offense to him taking it while knowing how she felt about what was being done. She'd go days without speaking to him at all. He started worrying when she went days at a time reading a really thick book she was infatuated with. He figured she didn't want to be bothered so gave her her space. She'd only talk to him when she read something so intriguing, she had to tell him about it. Dorothy loved her husband very much and was relieved when he told her he no longer kills, and instead helps people. She knew he had a good heart and worried about him every single day.

When agents came to inform her of her husband's death, she wasn't a bit surprised, she somehow knew he'd die that day.

She tried everything in her power to make him stay home, and went as far as to tell him she's very ill, but he had to go in. When they came to tell her the circumstances leading to her husband's death, she knew he died trying to save someone.

The agents told her an Illegal Resident shot him to death but got away, and promised her they'd find him. Dorothy knew she had to get to him first and was determined to. She would not fail him the way she failed her son.

Fred worked for the F.F.A. for three years before being murdered, and managed to help twenty-two people escape gruesome fates.

Dorothy begged Goodman for the name of the Illegal Resident responsible for her husband's death but he wouldn't disclose it. She made it a mission to find him, and knew the agency had the advantage because they could pinpoint him by putting his chip's code into a GPS system at any time.

While at Goodman's office the next day begging for a name, she takes a peek at the monitor he was focused on when he steps out. She sees a red dot at the location of a well known protesting spot and thinks it might be who she's looking for. She sees the name '*Leon Wang,*' and clicks on it. Leon was with a crowd of protesters that rallied against the vaccination. She saw his picture and knew she had to act quick. Most protests lasted days and it's where Illegal Residents would go for a safe haven. Agents were prohibited from arresting or scanning anyone at a protest.

Dorothy knew this and headed there before she lost him. When she first met Leon, he shewed her away. She kept telling him he was destined to be someone he knew it was unlikely for him to be, and would rant for hours about him being the chosen one. Leon would hide in the crowd when he saw her around, but no matter how much he hid, she'd always find him. She always said he had a glow only she could see which made it easy for him to be located. He started believing when he one day walked and walked, until he thought it'd be impossible to be pinpointed, but she found him with no effort at all. It was as if she could see him through the crowds of people.

Leon eventually gave in and accepted her offer.

Dorothy stressed to him that the land would be untouched by evil hands. Said that God told her he was the one, and gave him a book she made him promise he'd read. Leon became a full believer of the book, he had thought Dorothy was a crazy old lady until he read it. It was as if the book told him everything she said was true.

Leon read the book for days and couldn't put it down. Even during protests, he'd read and spread its words. Not many believed and most thought he was crazy, but he continued.

Dorothy provided the DD's required to build a fence to protect the Fort, even though she knew it'd be protected by a higher power. She paid to have houses built, and tried to persuade as many people as she could to go there. She managed to get power by hiring men to snake wires in, but after a few years, the government discovered it and cut the main line. It was the only way to attack them. They've sent countless men to the Fort but they were never able to enter, and it mystified them as to how a bunch of kids could keep it so secure.

Leon and Dorothy became very close, she had him convinced they were chosen.

Every time Dorothy went to the Fort, she'd show herself to no-one but Leon or Mrs. Kent. She didn't want recognition for anything that's been done. She also didn't want to take the chance of being seen by someone that perhaps someday would want to leave, and risk them saying they saw her there. She set everything up. She filled it with food, water, livestock and medicine. Leon always worried about the fence being easily penetrated but she'd assure him no-one would enter the land unless they're granted access. The most important thing Dorothy wanted Leon to know, is that not all people agree with what's being done in the country. She made sure he understood that the majority of people of her race didn't want it to happen. He'd respond by telling her he knows, and is aware that they want to rid the world of anyone who isn't wealthy. The majority of protesters he stood shoulder to shoulder with, were white, he'd tell her.

Leon grew so bold, one time he and Ahmed attacked a news crew only for them to televise a message he had for the American people. He dared the military to come full force, and dared them to attack with the precise satellites they're so proud of. He demanded them to bring every branch of the armed forces to his doors. He tried to provoke by telling them to fly their bomb loaded warplanes over them, and shower the Fort with fire. The broadcast was televised and had the American people buzzing for a while. The government sent teams of skilled soldiers only for most of them to be instantly killed or tortured. Many have tried to invade the Fort, but all have failed.

Leon grew very fond of Dorothy over the years, but seen her less and less often. Once the fence was up, and the food stockpiled, she could live her life in peace and hardly went. Dorothy got the idea of the land from the prophet's writings. She really believed in her heart the mark of the beast was the time limit on the injection. Fred told her all about it, he stressed the government knew of the high importance, and told her they knew it would take a special child to survive it.

After reading the book, Leon was convinced the Prophet had it right when he predicted the war would be a giant hoax, but after many years of gloomy skies, they both admitted he might have been wrong. They knew there was no way the government could make the skies remain that way for such a long period of time. He wondered how the prophet could be wrong and has almost lost hope on several occasions, but has held on to faith. He's read the book over and over, and until this day, he catches himself staring at pages hoping he missed out on some details. There was a time he thought he might be the first child born with as much faith as Dorothy had in him. She assured him it was impossible, because he wasn't injected.

Until this day, Leon waits. He knows the day will come and is determined to wait for as long as necessary. He's anxious to march across the country and make the people aware of God's intentions. The prophet says when the time comes, and the child is of age, he will take the world back untouched. He guarantees in his writings that he will not suffer a scratch. He says the child will have an army of no more than seven people who will help rid the greatest country in the world of tyranny, and they'll be worshiped worldwide when they give the great lands back to its people.

Back at the N.A.A., Buchanan is livid. He uses intimidation tactics on everyone to find out who gave the order to have him killed. He approaches everyone on Thump's floor and presses them as to why they tried to assassinate him. He's replaced the finger in his wound with the dirty rag he used to wipe the sweat off of his forehead, by twirling it up until it was slim enough to put inside. He can feel the warmth of the blood as it rolls down his leg, but is determined to find out who did this to him. He doesn't like to be interrupted when working, and the men barging in and killing Weinberg before he was finished has him furious. He's even pinned women against walls, demanding to know why they tried to slay him, bringing most to tears.

After approaching Thump, he goes back down and stuffs the body pieces back into his bag. He steps over lifeless bodies and takes one last look at his men. Buchanan is by no means a sensitive guy, so looks at their corpses but feels no empathy. Although he carries the rifle after the attempt on his life, he is not one to use a gun, and prefers to slowly cut the life out of you. He usually only carries a knife and a pair of tweezers he's had for years. He wants nothing more than for someone to tell him who ordered the hit on him, and will not leave until he finds out.

While sitting in the corridor that leads to office doors, he harasses everyone that walks past, and his looks alone are enough to creep anyone out. Buchanan sees a gentleman approaching and stands to block his way. The man looks up at him and seems very nervous. Had he seen him sitting there, he would've taken the long way around.

"Who tried to kill me!?" he angrily asks as he pushes the man, forcing him to bang so hard he leaves the implant of his body indented into the sheetrock wall.

"I don't know what you're talking about?" the man nervously says as he tries to regain his composure.

Buchanan drops the rifle, grabs the man's arm and twists until he feels the bone shatter. The man screams in pain so Thump, and Randy come rushing to see what's going on.

"Are you kidding me!?" yells Thump. "Are you out of your God damned mind!? You will go home and you will not come back until you've calmed down! I told you I'd find out who did this!"

Buchanan grunts at Thump and looks as if he's about to strike him, then looks down at the man and smirks. Randy keeps his distance and could feel his stomach turn from the smell. As Buchanan walks away, Randy and Thump cannot help but notice the trail of blood he leaves behind.

"You might want to check on that wound," says Thump, but he keeps walking. Buchanan's been wounded many times during his years with the Agency, sometimes by his own blade, but he never seeks medical attention and prefers to go home and have his wife tend to his wounds.

It is eight o'clock, and time for Dwayne Morris's execution. The leaders of the four other Communities take seats at the side of the road. Spectators fill both sidewalks that are divided by the street the execution will take place on. Not everyone came out to watch, but the majority of the residents are present.

They watch as eight men make their way out of a garage and form two lines, with the front two carrying torches as if it's some kind of sick sacrificial ritual. The pair in the back each grasp one side of the base the stick is mounted to. The rod glimmers, Reid builds a brand new one every time he uses this device. The men position the base between a wooden stage that's in the middle of the street. The tip of the rod is seven-feet high, and the top of the stage is four. General Reid arrives and climbs the little wooden steps that lead to the top of the stage, then signals for his men to bring Dwayne. With his hands cuffed behind his back, Dwayne drags his feet the entire way. The crowd starts to laugh and cheer with many pointing fingers while hysterically laughing. They loudly chortle at the woman's silky pink nightgown they've dressed him in. Dwayne's humiliated, and has no idea what's about to happen. As they reach the stage with the crowd riled up, they sit Dwayne on a wooden crate. A man comes to his feet and starts tying them together.

Dwayne tries to resist, but another man pulls his arms up, causing enough pain to make him stay still. The man places a six-inch pipe between the knot he tightly ties. They stand Dwayne up and carry him onto the stage as he desperately yells that he's innocent.

"I need to speak! Shut him up!" Reid tells a man, who puts tape over his mouth, making the people laugh as he mumbles.

"We're all here tonight to end this man's life in God's name. This man came into our home and killed one of our most precious citizens, so for that, he will pay with his own life. Our father didn't deserve to die, especially to no coward like this."

"I'd ask the Lord to forgive him but I want him to burn in hell," he says, making the crowd loudly cheer.

Suzy watches as a spectator and feels something isn't right, but cannot voice her opinion.

"Our father lived a saintly life and it was cut short by the violence of someone who shouldn't even be in this country."

Dwayne stares at the rod. He has no idea what it's used for, and thinks they're going to push him onto it.

"By God, I will avenge his death and it'll be tonight," Reid says to loud applause. "May the devil stick you in his hottest chamber," he tells Dwayne. He demands his men to grab him.

Reid's two biggest men stand at Dwayne's sides, and each grabs him under an armpit until his bare feet no longer touch the wooden stage. Dwayne tries to violently flop, but his feet being tied together makes it difficult. Another man grabs his legs and puts the pipe in the knot over the rod to keep his legs positioned straight down. Dwayne realizes what they're doing now, so tries with all of his might to wiggle away. As they slide the pipe down the rod, his life flashes before his eyes. He can't believe he left his wife to end up like this. The men hold on to him with his crotch inches over the rod. He tries to stay as still as possible. He doesn't want them to lose grip and cause him to fall on it, even though he knows it's going to happen anyway. The man who admitted seeing him commit the crime seems rattled and Suzy bows her head.

"The vengeance we give you, Lord, is for our father," Reid says with one hand in the air. He looks at the crowd as if he were a celebrity and quickly drops his arm, giving the indication that it's time to let go. The men release their grips, causing Dwayne to plunge onto the rod. In most cases, the weight of the body forces it to go completely through, but Dwayne gets stuck half way. He's impaled and coughs, causing blood to splash out of his mouth. The rod seems to have gotten stuck in his rib cage. Two men rush over to cut the rope holding his feet together, and Dwayne dies while staring down at them. They each grab a foot and start pulling down, but he's still stuck. They grab them again, and both jump, causing their bodies to hit the asphalt and his feet to hit the steel base. The crowd's enlightened and amazed. For the first time ever, the rod comes out the top of the victim's head, causing one of his eyes to fall out. It went perfectly through and they're all in awe. One man walks up to Dwayne's body and slides him up a bit, drawing a glance from Reid.

"His legs were bent," the man says.

Dwayne's deceased and in the standing position with his one eye still looking downward. The silky pink nightgown he wears is completely covered in blood.

"You see, people?" says Reid, drawing everyone's attention. "This is a sign of God."

The rod coming out the top of the head is what Reid envisioned when he invented it, but it's never occurred. The closest it's come is when the rod comes out of the victim's shoulder.

Reid declares Dwayne's body will stay there for a month.

Suzy sadly looks at him before turning around and disappearing into the crowd. The leaders of the other Communities leave with no warning, they didn't greet, nor bid farewell to Reid.

"Sir, we need to have a talk," a man tells Reid. "You might not recognize me, but I'm from Community-*one* and I come with a message from Willie. He told me to inform you that a bunch of Illegal Residents entered the Fort last night."

"Where is he?"

"He says the people that arrived can jeopardize your agreement. Told me to tell you the Doctor from the other day made it there and thinks he might recognize him..."

"Tell Willie to make his way back here!"

~Chapter Twenty~

The Beginning of the End

Leon and Ahmed are furious, and cannot believe the betrayal by Willie. Leon tells Ahmed to call off the next morning's practice and puts his jacket back on. You could see the look of relief on Willie's face. He knows they're too close for them to consider hurting him, until he hears Leon tell Ahmed he'll deal with him the next day. Leon wants Willie's screams to be heard throughout the Fort when everyone's up and about. He wants to show what happens to people that betray the Land.

"Lock him in," he tells Ahmed on his way out. "Meet me here tomorrow at noon, we'll deal with him then."

When he walks out, Ahmed tries to get answers.

"Why did you betray us!?"

Willie doesn't look at him.

"Why did you betray us?" he again asks, but gets no reply.

He grabs the gun tucked in his waistband and walks toward him.

Willie anticipates getting shot and finally looks at him. "I didn't mean to," he says. "General Reid and his men caught me in the market one day and told me they knew exactly what we were doing. They cornered me and threatened to kill me, and everyone here if I didn't give them information. They assured they'll turn a blind eye to me shopping there, but wanted to know everything."

Willie hopes Ahmed believes it.

"What information?" demands Ahmed. "What did they want to know?"

"They want to know our operation. Reid wants to know how we manage to stop them every single time with such few men. I only told them about the session because it's the only time we'd be vulnerable enough for them to attack, but they weren't able to. We couldn't even find this place, it's as if it disappeared right before my eyes. If you remember correctly, I joined in the fight and helped you kill them."

"You mean to tell me you were going to let them in!?"

"It was the only way, Ahmed! Please believe me. We've been friends for how long? You could let me walk out of here, I promise, you will never see me again."

Ahmed watches as he pulls his arms. He will not take the chance of facing Leon's wrath for letting him go but thinks about shooting his brains out just to spare the pain he's going to inflict on him. "You know I can't let you go. You brought this upon yourself. What made you think that after nine years of them not being able to even touch the fence, they'd be able to come in and hurt you? All you had to do was tell us and we would've never sent you back out. You were like a brother to us and should have known better!" Ahmed's visibly upset and Willie knows everything he says is true.

"I can't believe you did this," says Ahmed, with tears filling his eyes. "You weren't supposed to do this!"

Ahmed wants to release him. They've been friends their entire lives and there is no separating them. He remembers how Willie would hide their friendship from his family for fear of his father finding out.

He tells him he wishes there was something he could do and walks out of the barn.

"Please," he hears Willie plead.

Ahmed stands outside for a moment to think before going home. It is very late and a lot has happened. He thinks of how they've gained eight citizens only to lose one of the most important ones.

On the way home that night, Leon sees someone's dark figure and hides behind a tree. He's used to the darkness and notices the person struggle to find their way around. As the person passes by, he realizes it's Mitchell. He thinks of what he said, and what Gus has confirmed about him being an F.F.A. agent but doubts it could be true. The only way there could be a chance is if he's there undercover, but he knows it's impossible.

Mitchell's out hoping to find Brianna. The only reason he decided to go to the Fort was because they looked everywhere else and didn't find her. He's warned his son not to mention that's the reason they came though. He wants to give Leon the impression that they made it there with no other reason than to live a better life. Mitchell refuses to stay, the guilt of everyone he's killed is slowly torturing him.

The next day, Leon wakes up and there's only one thing on his mind. He sees it's only nine and realizes he has three hours to kill, so decides to visit the newcomers. As he approaches the house he put Gus and the kids in, he sees Sophia sitting on the steps, with the baby standing barefoot and clutching her fingers while bouncing his little body up and down by repeatedly bending his knees. Sophia has been trying to make him smile since she's met him, but he shows no reaction.

"There he is. Tell him it's me," she hears. She tries to ignore the voice but it's really getting to her.

"Good morning, kids," says Leon.

"Good morning," Sophia happily replies. She loves it there, for some reason it has taken a weight off of her shoulders.

"Is Gus up?" he asks.

"Yea, he's inside," She responds.

Leon enters and encounters Gus, Brianna, and Jose. They're having coffee as Jose sits with his face buried in the laptop, and a smile from ear to ear.

"Good morning," he tells them. Brianna sluggishly greets him.

"We have to talk," Leon says to Gus. "About our conversation yesterday..."

"He's an F.F.A. agent," Gus quickly interrupts. "Ask her, she'll tell you."

Brianna doesn't know what he's talking about and hopes they didn't let Phillips and his men enter, this is the first she's heard of it.

"We're settling this tonight," Leon orders. "We'll all sit down and get to the bottom of it."

"I can't let him see me!" Gus nervously stresses. "I'm sure they sent him to look for me. I just broke her out of Reid's pit and I know he sent him!"

"Don't worry, you're here now. Nothing will happen to you. I need to get this out in the open, there cannot be any friction amongst our residents. Both groups will sit and talk it out, they seem like decent people to me," Leon tells him.

"Don't be fooled," says Gus. "Why do you think he hasn't been poisoned?"

Leon's aware he has a couple of hours before dealing with Willie. He would go now but has told Ahmed to meet him at noon. The sudden silence makes it awkward, so he looks toward Jose. His curiosity screams to know what he keeps smiling about, so goes and sits next to him. He reads as Jose types and can't help but notice that he's debating with someone. The person keeps insisting they're in Japan, but Jose argues that it's impossible.

"He thinks he's in Japan," Jose tells him.

Leon asks Jose to scroll up and observes the conversation's been lengthy. He seems very interested and not only wants to read it, but also wants the chance to speak to the person himself.

"How many DD's do you want for that thing?" he asks Jose, referring to the laptop.

Jose knows it's very valuable because of the built-in technology that gives it a lifetime function without it ever having to be charged.

His father's main priority was to make sure he went to school, but Jose didn't want to bother with it. He believed school was worthless because what he wanted to learn couldn't be taught there. His interest was in cars, which his father taught him while making sure he got his education. Jose graduated with an above average grade, but it's as far as he could go. Illegal Residents aren't able to pick up a trade or advance their education by going to college, it isn't permitted.

"I don't know," he replies. "Let's see. How many markets are there here?"

The sarcasm is obvious and embarrasses Gus and Brianna, causing them to act as if they didn't hear it.

"You got me. You're right, why would you want DD's, they're worthless here."

"I'll tell you what," says Jose. "I admire how you came here as a kid to start this place. You've done a lot of good things to help a lot of good people, so I want to show you my gratitude. It's yours," he says as he passes it to him. "Thank you for providing us with a home. All I want in return, is for you to teach me everything there is to know about defending myself, and you can count on me when it's time to fight. I'm good with these..." He balls his fists and places them in front of his face as if he's prepared to box. "But I want to learn everything there is to know!"

Leon's touched. "You are welcome, and thank you very much for this. It is my pleasure to provide a home for you all. Our savior will soon arrive and hopefully you'll be by his side when it's time for him to fulfill his destiny."

Gus acts as if he didn't hear the statement and Brianna notices his reaction. She thinks about how special he keeps telling her her child is, and is concerned about what will happen if Leon finds out it's him. For some reason, Leon doesn't sit right with her.

He's noticed Brianna has given him the cold shoulder since arriving, so tries to make small talk as he prepares to leave.

"Beautiful boy you have there," he tells her. He glances out of the window and sees him on the front porch, still gripping Sophia's fingers. "He has beautiful eyes. How old is he?"

Brianna appreciates the admiration and quickly answers with Gus hoping she wouldn't.

"He's four months now."

Gus's jaw drops. He wasn't expecting for her to answer with the way she's been acting toward him.

Leon has other things on his mind so doesn't pick up on it. "Wow, he's big," he says as he turns to leave. It never occurs to him that a four-month-old shouldn't be standing yet.

"There he is. Tell him," Sophia hears. She shakes her head as if it'd help with the voice and looks as Leon walks away with the laptop under his arm. Gus hesitates to tell Brianna he eventually has to inform Leon of her son. He has seen how she's reacted every time he's brought it up, so will wait for the perfect opportunity.

Mitchell wakes up and sees Jacob and Murphy already up, dressed, and ready to go. "Give me a minute, Son, we'll go out and look for her momentarily."

"Take your time, Dad. Even if we don't find her, I love it here."

Mitchell seems confused as he grabs a mug filled with coffee Murphy passes him. It's only their second day there, and they haven't even gone out in fear of retaliation for Mitchell being an agent.

"It feels like I belong here," he tells Mitchell. He pushes a curtain aside to look out of the window and sees people starting to come out. "I didn't think there were so many people," he mumbles.

Mitchell cannot stay but doesn't let it be known. He didn't expect to wake up for the second time. He still doesn't believe Murphy was able to get rid of the poison and thought they might kill him as he slept.

"This is my new home," says Murphy, right before taking a sip of her coffee.

Mitchell realizes he's the only one that doesn't want to stay, but figures they'll go when he's ready to leave. His conscience kills him every time he looks at an Illegal Resident. He was only doing his job, which he took only because one of Goodman's men said they'll exterminate the remaining inmates when they tried to recruit him and he declined, but his conscience still kills him.

"There's no need to go anywhere else. This is a place I could grow old in," she says.

Mitchell has heard enough. He doesn't know how he'll convince them to leave once they find her, and excuses himself to go get dressed. Murphy could tell something bothers him, so decides to go find out what it is. She lightly taps on his bedroom door, which he opens wearing no shirt. He thought it was Jacob so rushes to put one on as she steps in.

"I've seen a man with no shirt on before," she says with a grin. "Are you alright?"

"Yes. Why do you ask?"

He quickly flips a t-shirt over his head.

"You seemed to be a bit bothered downstairs. Is everything OK?"

"It is. I just want to find her so bad. Can't wait to see the look on her face when she sees me and realizes I'm Jacob's father."

Murphy looks flattered. She walks toward him and straightens the neck of his t-shirt. With her fingers gripping the elastic, she looks into his eyes.

"I love how you risked it all to come here for the sake of your son, even though we both know you didn't want to," she says as her eyes sparkle. Slowly, their faces get closer until their lips lock. It's been years since Mitchell has been with a woman and it's obvious to her. She continues to kiss him, and only stops to pull the t-shirt right back over his head. Jacob's sitting downstairs with a huge smile on his face. He knows what they're up to and is happy for his dad. He decides to go for a walk and runs into Leon when he steps out.

"Good morning," says Leon.

"Hey. Good morning."

Leon and Jacob are practically the same age, but are total opposites. While Leon is a very charming but dangerous gentleman, Jacob is extremely timid and wouldn't hurt a fly.

"Is your dad up?"

Jacob takes this moment to brag for his father. "He's upstairs, you know," he says with a grin.

Leon knows exactly what he means. "Lucky guy your father is. She's hot," he says. "Do me a favor. Can you tell him to meet me in the big yellow house at the end of that trail at eight o'clock tonight?" he asks as he points.

"Will do."

"OK, thanks. See you later." Leon turns to leave.

"Can I ask you something?" Jacob asks, making him turn around. "Do you think I'm too old to join in your practices?"

"Fitness has no age boundary. You might not be as flexible as the young ones, but it's never too late to get your body into shape. Besides, you're far from old, and I would love for you to join us. Hope to see your dad in that house tonight and you on the practice field tomorrow morning," he says as he begins to walk away.

Jacob decides to walk up the trail to the yellow house so he can easily guide his father when it's time to go. He approaches it and sees Sophia, the baby, Felipe, and Jose sitting on the front porch and intends to just walk past. The baby is asleep on Sophia's lap, and Jose repeatedly throws a ball high in the air. Felipe sits on the wooden steps and just stares straight ahead. As he walks past, the ball bounces toward him. He fumbles it at first, then grabs it and throws it back.

"Thanks, man," says Jose.

Sophia looks at Jacob and notices he's very tense. "What's your name?" she shouts.

"My name is Jacob," he shyly responds. He has never been good at making friends. The only people he knows are a few former classmates that no longer associate with him, and co-workers who have no choice.

"I'm Sophia," she answers. "This is my brother Felipe, and the little fella here... his name is...!" Sophia thinks for a minute and realizes she doesn't know it. "I don't know his name, but that's Jose."

"It's Jun-Jun," Jose snaps.

Felipe stares at Jacob and makes him nervous. They're a lot alike, he has also never been good at making friends but it's his choice. Felipe is not a social person and will probably never be. He doesn't say much and gets along with very few people. He gets up to go inside and grabs the baby so he could lay him down.

"We're new here," Jose tells Jacob.

"Me too. I came a couple of nights ago. I've always wanted to come..."

"Why?" Sophia interrupts. "Why would you want to come here? You could live a normal life out there, why come here and live this way? Sometimes I wish I wasn't an Illegal Resident just to be safe," she says, causing Jose to agree.

"I don't know. I've always heard of this place and like what's being done to protect all people. I still remember the time I saw Leon on TV. Since that day, I've wanted to come. What's in the house?"

Sophia's confused. "Furniture," she sarcastically says, as she and Jose begin to laugh.

"I only ask because Leon wants my father to meet him here to-night."

"For what?" asks Jose.

"I don't know," he replies. "What nationality are you?"

"I'm American," Sophia quickly snaps. "I should have the right to live in this country just like anyone else. I was born here."

"Me too," says Jose. "My parents are from Mexico but I was also born here. That makes me American."

"I agree. Everyone should have the right to live in this country whether they were born here or not. I have to go now, I'll see you to-night." He wants to avoid the conversation and regrets starting it.

"Well, he's weird," Sophia tells Jose as they watch him walk away.

It's five minutes past noon. The people working in the fields watch as Leon rapidly walks, wearing nothing but a pair of jeans with the legs rolled up to the knees, a pair of flip flops, and a determined look on his face. He's approached by Mrs. Kent who tells him the child is near.

Leon's anxious and continues to walk toward the barn.

He enters and hears Willie moaning about his arms being numb. Leon nods his head at Ahmed before focusing his attention on Willie.

"How is the traitor doing this afternoon?" he asks.

"Please, Leon, look at me. You don't have to do this. Please!" pleads Willie.

Leon doesn't budge and walks toward the wooden table.

Ahmed sees him pick up the scoop so immediately walks forward to block his path.

"Wait! Listen to me," he tells him. "We don't have to do this. What will our people think if we kill one of our own? Let's be smart about this and use it to our advantage, he is willing to give us infor-mation about them instead."

"Get out of my way," says Leon. He doesn't even consider what

Ahmed's proposing. Ahmed will not let him do this, he will not just stand there and watch as someone close enough to be his brother gets tortured. Leon puts both hands at his side and shoves him just enough to walk past. Ahmed quickly grabs his gun and points it toward the side of his head, making him stop and stay still.

"Are you serious? This man gains our trust then betrays us, and you defend him? Your loyalty is on the wrong side, brother."

Leon can tell Ahmed isn't comfortable with the way the gun is shaking.

"We don't have to do this," he tells Leon. "I would do the exact same thing for you. Let's let him go."

Leon feels sympathy for Ahmed but wants to teach him a lesson now. "You're going to have to shoot me," he tells him, and continues toward Willie.

Leon wants him to grow bold and pull the trigger, so they can both see how real the prophecy is...

~Chapter Twenty-One~

It All Unfolds

"Don't make me do this," cries Ahmed. "I would do the same for you."

Leon sticks a finger in his right ear to avoid having his eardrum busted from the sound of the blast, and Ahmed pulls the trigger with the barrel of the gun pointed directly at the back of his head.

He's surprised he misses, and pulls again. He again misses, then repeatedly shoots into Leon's back but he isn't affected.

"Don't you realize you can't hurt me with that thing in here?"

Ahmed stares at the gun.

"Did you think I'd send you out there if I wasn't aware you couldn't be harmed?" he asks them.

Ahmed and Willie look at him in amazement.

"Tell me. Have you ever wondered why they've never invaded? They get lost in the woods, they'll never find the entrance. Yes, a couple have gotten close but they had no idea what was in front of them. This place is camouflaged to evil. No-one with wrong intentions could enter, that's why I trust everyone here, even the agent. Bullets turn to dust when they're fired, we cannot be harmed. Have you ever wondered why we never run out of ammo?" he asks, as their faces wear shocked expressions.

"You really surprised me, Ahmed. I never thought you'd raise a gun at me, let alone shoot. You really wanted me dead, huh? I'll let your friend here go, but you have to get out too." Ahmed gasps. "Yes, I want you both out of here, you have both shown where your loyalty lies. You're lucky I don't kill you both."

"Please, brother," Ahmed pleads as he drops to his knees. "I would have done the same for you. Please!"

"You would never have to do such thing for me. I am no traitor!"

Leon walks toward the table and comes back with pliers and meat scissors. He informs Willie that the only way he'll walk out of the barn alive, is with no tongue. He wants him to be unable to explain to the folks at the Communities why he's with an Illegal Resident.

Willie sticks it out, he figures it's better to lose his tongue than his life. Ahmed is down on his hands and knees, and cannot believe he must go. There is no way he'll get through the Communities without being killed. He hears Willie scream and looks up when he tries to speak with no tongue in his mouth, and blood seeping out of it, but cannot comprehend what he's saying.

"You untie him," Leon says to Ahmed. "Then you both get out!"

Ahmed tries to plead, but Leon walks past him and puts the instruments and Willie's tongue into a bucket. He walks out to a crowd that has gathered in curiosity at the gunshots. Leon approaches two men, and tells them to make sure Willie and Ahmed are escorted to Community-*one*. He demands them to make sure they leave the woods and kill them if they ever saw them again.

Mrs. Kent again approaches Leon. "The child is near," she tells him.

He grabs both her hands and looks at her. "I hope you speak the truth," he says, with Willie's blood smeared on his bare chest.

Mitchell, Murphy, and Jacob are on their way to the meet later that night with Jacob leading the way. Mitchell has no idea where he's taking him and walks hand in hand with Murphy. He would not have gone had he known it was to see Leon and would've requested to meet in their house instead. F.F.A. agents aren't looked at too kindly by Illegal Residents, and Mitchell is surprised he was even allowed to stay and not killed. They reach the final stretch of the trail and the house is now visible.

"That's where we're going," Jacob tells them as he points ahead. He could hear his father and Murphy whisper and giggle to one another like two teenagers in love. Jacob picks up his pace when he sees Sophia on the porch and leaves Mitchell and Murphy at least twenty feet behind. Mitchell sees him greet Sophia, and is surprised that his son has already made a friend, even though she seems a bit too young. He hasn't recognized her yet, and watches her stand with her back toward them as they continue to catch up.

"This is my dad," he tells her as he points over her shoulder. "His name is Bradley."

Sophia turns around and lets out a sky-piercing scream as she jumps back. It's heard by everyone inside, causing Brianna to grab the baby and run up the stairs. Leon jumps on his feet and runs toward the door, only to have Sophia run into his arms as she tries to bolt inside.

Mitchell can't believe it. He recognizes Sophia and can't believe Phillips, of all people, let her survive.

"FELIPE!" she screams, as she sees him rushing down with Jose close behind. Leon had gathered six men who stood by the house with three on each side, and they run toward the front. Mitchell thinks about running but doesn't want to look guilty. Felipe recognizes him. He jumps down the stairs but is subdued by one of Leon's men. Jose follows, but they're not swift enough to stop him. Without knowing what they're guilty of, and acting out of pure instinct, he swings his fist, striking Jacob in the side of the face so hard he knocks him out, forcing another one of Leon's men to tackle him to the ground. The other men circle Mitchell and Murphy.

"He killed my family," Sophia screams.

They struggle to hold Felipe from charging at Mitchell.

Leon commands his men to take them to the barn and tie them up.

"He killed my family!" she repeats.

Gus has built up enough courage to walk out of the house.

"I told you. He's dangerous and shouldn't be trusted," he tells Leon.

One of Leon's men pick Jacob up and throws him over a shoulder while the others escort them away.

Jose and Felipe are riled up. Gus tries to persuade them to enter the house as Leon tries to calm Sophia down.

"You have to get that man out of here," Gus turns around and says.

"I'll deal with him," Leon responds. He grabs Sophia by the shoulders while facing her.

"He killed my baby cousin. He's the partner of the monster that killed my family," she cries to him.

Jose reacted for his friends and gets a stern warning from Leon.

"This type of behavior is not tolerated here! If you have a problem with someone, you come to me! We do not fight each other!"

"He's not one of us!" shouts Felipe. "He's a killer!"

"He hung my baby cousin by the ankle and shot him in the head," Sophia tries. Just when they thought it was behind them, they're reminded of the horror by seeing Mitchell.

"I want you to take the boys inside," Leon tells Gus. "I will deal with them."

"With all due respect, Leon. You should let them deal with the agent," he says. He points toward Sophia and Felipe who are now sobbing in each others arms. Leon thinks about it, but declares only Sophia and Brianna can go. He thinks Felipe's too lit up and doesn't want to make the situation any worse. He wants them to confirm he's actually who they're accusing him of being, and he remembers Gus telling him to ask Brianna so wants her to confirm it. If it pans out, he'll happily cut the life out of them, but will not allow a child to take someone's life. He calls to another man and tells him to guide them to the barn when they're ready.

"That's my dad," Sophia hears. She doesn't want to be bothered with the voice but gets an unusual thought. She thinks it might be Jacob invading her head when she hears it say it's their father, and can't wait to get to the barn to confront him about it.

"I don't care if he's your dad. He's a killer," she shouts, louder than she wants to, causing everyone to hear her. Gus thinks she's talking to Felipe or Jose, but she wasn't looking toward them which confuses him.

After being led to the barn by Leon's man, Brianna drops a mug full of coffee, but it doesn't shatter, it bounces around until it comes to a stop on the dirt ground as she covers her mouth with both her hands. Gus and Leon watch as she runs toward Jacob. They both watch as she drops to her knees to hold him tight.

"Jacob!?" she sobs. She slaps his face to wake him. "Wake up. Wake up."

"Do you know him?" Leon asks.

"He's my son's father."

Mitchell's coming to. He was also knocked out when they shoved him into the barn. Murphy's relieved Brianna's the girl they came looking for and somehow thinks this will get them out of there. She gets sentimental when she sees Jacob wake up and lose his mind when he sees Brianna. He gets ecstatic, it brings tears to her eyes.

"He's the kid's father? Your kid?" Leon asks.

"Yes," she responds. She clutches him with tears of happiness in her eyes.

Sophia doesn't care about Jacob but wants Mitchell to pay. All she wants is for him to stop talking to her. "Why do you keep talking to me?" she yells at him.

"So this must be his grandfather," Leon tells Gus, who pays attention to Sophia.

"Your father is a killer! Stop talking to me!" she shouts.

Gus drags her outside.

Leon announces he'll spare Jacob and Murphy, and begins to untie them.

"Where's my son?" asks Jacob. "I want to meet him."

Murphy looks at Mitchell and sees he's fully alert. "Do what you want with me, just don't hurt them," she hears him say.

"I intend to do what I want with you. You're lucky he's the child's father, he would have died here with you if it weren't for this lady," Leon tells him, referring to Brianna.

"Bring me my father," Sophia hears while outside with Gus. She glances inside and sees Jacob has been untied.

"You said something earlier about someone's dad," Gus tells her. "Who were you talking about?"

"I keep hearing voices," she replies. "They're driving me crazy."

Gus panics. He doesn't want to ask the next question but knows he has to. "Is your real name Beatrice?" he hesitantly asks, and holds his breath, waiting for an answer.

"No. My name is Sophia," she says, making him exhale. "Sophia Senao!"

Gus is in disbelief. It just hits him. "Are you twelve?" he asks.

"Yes. I am...!"

Gus realizes she's the child he injected twelve years ago that he's always told Dorothy about. Her parents came to him and took the chance of injecting her after the time limit because Doctors told them they ran out of the medication and couldn't vaccinate her in time. Her parents told him her name is Beatrice. Dorothy never paid him any mind because she was born before she came to the conclusion of the time limit, and for some reason, didn't think it was possible for the child to have been born yet.

She's the child the Prophet wrote about, the one he predicted would be born twelve years before the savior. The one that will form one with him.

He turns around to hide his expression. "What do the voices tell you?" he asks with his back turned.

"Tell him it's me! Tell him it's me! I'm tired of it. Now it says that's his father. I know it's him," she says as she points inside.

Gus smiles and turns around to face her. "Tell me. When he says, *'tell him it's me,'* are you at any point next to Leon?"

"Yes. Every time he passes by," she says, with her voice dying down as she wonders how Gus would know.

"OK, kid. I need you to go back to the house and wait for us there. I will bring Leon."

"No! I want to see him die!" she says with her face scrunched up like she really means it.

"Believe me, kid. You have no idea what you'll find out tonight." Annoyed, she turns and runs off. She thinks he knows about the voices with what he asked and hopes he might be able to help her.

Leon's men and Brianna try to hold Jacob back, who's now free and frantic for his father. Brianna has not looked at Mitchell yet, she's been trying to keep Jacob under control and has gotten lost in her emotions.

"He's my dad!" he loudly screams, making her look at him.

Murphy's also frantic as she's being pulled out of the barn.

"That man saved me," Brianna tells Leon, as Jacob is dragged outside.

Leon looks at Mitchell. "What do you mean he saved you? What is going on here? Is he a killer, or a savior? You guys are full of surprises."

Brianna freezes. Leon grabs her by the arm and escorts her outside. They pass by Murphy and Jacob who are being blocked by two very big men from entering the barn.

Gus appears to have something to say but just paces back and forth. "What do you mean he saved you?" he hears Leon ask Brianna.

"Who saved you?" he anxiously asks.

"The man inside. I was at Dorothy's house and they came looking for my son."

"Cryan?" Leon tries to interrupt.

"He found me hiding and saved my baby. My child was dead in my arms but he revived him and let me go upstairs to hide. He must have known I was his son's girlfriend, but I've never met him. I thought we would die that night," she says, as her eyes glance into the barn.

"No! Didn't you see what he did in the lab? They were going to kill us, until...!"

"Until what? What about Dorothy?" asks Leon.

"One of the agents got sick," Gus quickly replies.

"I was in Mrs. Cryan's house the night she..." says Brianna, and they all bow their heads.

"I hope you understand that I have to kill him. We cannot have an agent living on these grounds."

Brianna looks toward Jacob, she sees he no longer struggles and is huddled with Murphy. Her heart breaks for him.

Leon excuses himself. He walks into the barn and closes the door behind him as Brianna tries to console Jacob who's gotten frantic again. He gets inside and faces Mitchell, who looks directly into his eyes. Leon turns and walks toward the table as he takes his shirt off.

"Tell me, Agent. How is it that your son is with an Illegal Resident, yet you go around killing them. That doesn't make sense to me."

Mitchell stays silent.

"Or maybe your son doesn't know, and you brought him here to teach him a lesson and kill her in front of him. That's what you agents do, right, kill people in front of their loved ones? I thought about carving you up in front of your family, but I'm no animal," he says. "How does it feel to know your grandson is an Illegal Resident? That must hurt!"

Mitchell's getting aggravated and begins to heavily breathe. He wants Leon to end it. He knows this is his fate and could only wish his life was with his real parents. He knows what he's done and deserves what he gets, but wants it to be over with already. He cannot stop thinking about Jacob, and hopes he doesn't hold this against Leon. He's just glad he's found the woman he loves and won't be left alone.

"As long as my son is happy, I could care less who he's with. You can criticize me for my past actions all you want. Yes, I was a killer, and you know what, I did a pretty good job at it. Heck, I killed my own mother even before I became an agent. At least the woman I thought was my mother, only to find out my real parents were probably the best people in the world," he says, hoping Leon gets it over with.

"I doubt that," says Leon, as he grabs the scoop.

"Oh, believe me. My father got killed for letting an Illegal Resident escape. Now that's paying the ultimate price."

Leon takes a step back. "What do you mean?"

"An Asian kid, just like you."

"Do you speak of Fred Cryan?"

"Yes. My name is Gregory. Gregory Cryan."

Leon is floored. "You're Dorothy's son? It can't be... That's impossible," he says.

"Ask the lady outside, she's my therapist and confirmed it. She also gave me an antidote for the poison which is why I'm not dead."

"If this is true, it's a tremendous sign," he thinks as he barges out to get Murphy.

"Who is he?" he loudly asks when he comes back with her.

Brianna, Gus, and Jacob have slowly made their way inside. The men guarding didn't hear screams or see Leon covered in blood, so allowed them to enter.

Murphy bows her head. "Tell him, honey," says Mitchell.

"His name is Gregory Cryan."

Gus takes a huge gasp. "You're...? You're...?"

Mitchell nods his head.

"It all came together on the same night, just like she said it would," Gus thinks to himself.

"Your parents were great people," Leon tells Mitchell as he begins to untie him. "I'm the Asian kid your father let escape, and for that I will always be in his debt. I hope me freeing you today begins to repay what I owe. Now we must wait on his presence," he says as he looks at Gus. He finishes untying him, then helps him onto his feet.

Brianna and Jacob hug in excitement and Murphy throws herself into Mitchell's arms.

"About that," Gus announces. "He's already arrived. It's his grandson."

"What...!?" Leon confusingly asks.

"The kid. It's him."

Brianna smiles and tells Jacob their son is very special. She thinks of Mrs. Cryan, just like she told her she would.

They arrive back at the house but the baby is asleep. Murphy provides Leon the paperwork proving Mitchell's Gregory Cryan and Gus analyzes it, confirming its authenticity.

"What is he doing here?" Sophia demands to know as she comes down the stairs and sees Mitchell. "Felipe...!" she yells.

"Calm down, honey," says Gus. "I need you down here so stay put."

Felipe comes down with Jose and they're warned to stay calm by Leon.

Brianna had gone upstairs to gently wake the baby up and they all watch as she walks down clutching him. Leon sees a mild glow around them that makes him wipe his eyes. She passes the baby to Jacob, making him get emotional.

"His name is Jacob Jr.," he says. He sniffles and kisses his forehead.

"It's him," Leon mysteriously says to himself.

"Thank you," Sophia hears.

"For what?" she snottily says to Jacob, making everyone look at her.

Jacob ignores her and focuses his attention back to his son.

Mitchell's very proud. He looks across the room and sees his son and Brianna happily hugging.

Leon looks at Gus and is as happy as can be. "You know what this means, right? We only have twelve years to wait," he tells him.

Dr. Gus pushes his glasses up with a finger. "No, we don't. She's already here," he responds as he points toward Sophia.

"Come here, sweetheart," he tells her, and motions his hand.

Leon's froze. *"There's no way this could be happening,"* he thinks.

"Ask him something," Gus tells her.

"Who?"

"The voice."

"It doesn't work like that!"

"It does. Just ask." Sophia's confused. Leon's intently looking and everyone's noticed, they're all silent .

"OK. What's your name?" she asks, and rolls her eyes up, waiting for an answer. "See, it only talks to me. I'm not crazy...!"

"Don't say it! Think it!"

Sophia concentrates. "What's your name?" she thinks.

"My name is Jacob Jr.," she hears.

"Jacob Jr.," she loudly whispers. She immediately turns around to look at him.

"Told you!" Gus tells Leon, who drops to his knees and starts wailing.

"I cannot believe this," he cries, as tears drip onto the wooden floor.

Sophia slowly walks toward Jacob.

Jose and Felipe shockingly watch.

"Is it really you?" she thinks.

"Yes. It's really me. You're the only one who will ever hear my voice."

"Jacob?" she thinks again. "Is it really you?"

"It's really me, Sophia. Can you grab me?"

She outstretches her arms when she gets close enough and he throws himself on her.

"You guys might want to look outside," Mitchell says, while peeling a curtain aside.

Leon grabs Sophia's hand as she carries Jacob and opens the door. There's a ray of moonlight cutting through a patch of missing smog that illuminates the entire house, convincing Leon they're the ones.

They walk out and see every single resident of the Fort standing outside.

It's as if Dorothy's spirit woke everyone up and guided them to the house, so they can finally meet their saviors.

~Chapter Twenty-Two~

Ten Years Later

It's been ten years since they've arrived at the Fort, and since that night, it's been nothing but peace. It took Sophia and Felipe over a year to completely forgive Mitchell, but they've all become very close. The vegetation's been growing more since then, even with little sunlight. Mitchell and Murphy have taken on the responsibility of crossing into the Communities to buy whatever is needed. They were married by the Fort's priest and now have a beautiful five-year-old daughter. Jacob's used his experience and contacts from working as an inspector to snake an electrical line to provide power.

Government agents and Community residents have tried to invade multiple times, but they can't seem to find the entrance. Leon has stopped fighting. He fought as a young man and quickly learned they couldn't be injured, so would do it for practice, until he picked up the urge to drag them inside and torture them. Since the arrival, he's focused his attention on teaching youngsters his techniques and has made them warriors. He's shown them discipline and determination, he's gotten them ready to fight. When he wasn't training, he'd spend hours at a time messaging with Moshi who's taught him all about the world a-round them. Moshi's still working on a way to activate a news feed that would alert the world of what has happened in the United States of America. He cannot expose them himself, he's wanted by various countries for espionage and has to stay off of the radar. He's been the only one able to penetrate the cyber security and the U.S. Government has been trying to track him down for years.

Moshi's proven to Leon the war never occurred. He explained the smoggy skies and convinced Leon he was telling the truth by sending him aerial photographs from around the world. He proved the so-called satellites the Government claimed to have had, have never exist-ed. He's become Leon's long distance friend and has promised he'd look for a way to deactivate the filtration systems that clog their skies.

Mr. Goodman still runs the F.F.A. and has had to poison five a-gents in the last decade. Some have grown bold and have tried to avoid executing terms, only to be killed. Goodman's up in age and frequently struggles with his health but refuses to give up his position with the agency. Moore was forced back by his father, who warned Goodman he must keep him when he showed back up at the N.A.A..

Thump has hidden his relationship with his son for years. After di-vorcing his wife, she moved away, leaving him to tend to him as a sin-gle father. He saw evil in his child long before he and his wife sepa-rated. He'd often find animal carcasses hanging in, and around the house, and it terrified his wife, causing her to leave. He sent his son to live with his grandmother, who told him she hasn't heard from her daughter since she's met him. Thump changed his son's name before sending him away, and didn't give him a poisoned chip when he ap-pointed him an agent.

Thump and Randy are still at the N.A.A..
The white house has been demolished, the damage caused by civi-

lians deemed it unsafe. The plan is to begin rebuilding it when the population's under control, and with Illegal Residents still being injected, it is rapidly dwindling down. They project to be rid of them in another fifty years. They're considering a bill that will make the law apply to all Americans, unless they have at least one-million DD's.

Randy continues to be Thump's right-hand man, but only when Buchanan is not around. He wants nothing to do with him and makes it very clear.

Leon learned Ahmed was disturbingly murdered after crossing into Community-*one* that day. The townspeople tied him to a mattress soaked in gasoline, and beat him with sticks before igniting it. Some say the fire burned the rope they tied him with, causing him to run around in flames while they laughed. Leon erected a shrine for Ahmed at the Fort's cemetery, but doesn't regret the decision to send him away. Willie has not been able to talk since getting his tongue cut out, and was the one who revealed where Ahmed was hiding. Leon was also informed that he is General Reid's youngest son, who deflected on his father to join the Fort.

General Reid's wife left with her daughter who disowned him when he had his grandson assaulted. It took her three years to convince her to leave, and after many sleepless nights, her mom has grown used to it and lives a lot less tense. Reid has sent numerous men to find and kill them but they haven't been located. When Reid's wife left, she convinced her daughter that the only place they could go and be safe is the Fort. Suzy's looked upon as a grandmotherly figure by most now, she's been there for seven years and loves it.

Word of the child arriving has spread, so he's sent countless men to the Fort, but they've been unable to find it, even though it's just a mile across the woods.

Many Illegal Residents took their chances after learning of the child's arrival to sneak in, but most didn't even make it half way. One time, a group of them armed with bats and sticks got together and were determined to make it through. They took over the booth at the entrance, only to be slaughtered when they entered Community-*five*.

Jose, Timmy, and Felipe have become best friends. They often practice together and have become fierce fighters.

Timmy's a Caucasian kid who got to the Fort almost four years after they arrived. He was a little heavy for his age, but got right into training and has become an exceptional fighter. Jose's light on his feet and very fast. Leon made good on his promise and has taught him everything he knows. Felipe's bulky and slow, but could swing combo techniques and is capable of breaking bones with his strength.

They've practiced day and night for years, and when they fight, they fight together. They often brag about being able to take on ten men in a single fight.

Felipe has had what Mitchell did to his family on the back of his mind but has learned to let it go. He's become really good friends with Jacob and looks up to Mitchell now. Jose thinks of his family a lot. He feels bad he left with no warning and thinks of how upset they must be. He practices with the intentions of becoming so good, he'd have no problem marching through the Communities to go see them. The three sometimes get bored so go to the woods to blow off steam and practice with real people, just as Leon did with Ahmed and Willie. They don't always find someone to beat on, but when they do, they tactically hunt them down and use them for practice.

Mrs. Kent died of natural causes the night it was all revealed, she was the only resident of the Fort not present in front of the house that night. She was found the next day by Leon, as she held on to Mrs. Cryan's favorite scarf which hasn't been seen in years.

Leon was amazed at the smile on her face when he found her body, and it gave him comfort knowing she passed away peacefully.

There was a beautiful ceremony for her and Patrice the following day. They were laid to rest in the Fort's cemetery, which is considered the most sacred grounds.

Until this day, Sophia goes every single day to pay respects to her little friend. She often finds herself having full blown conversations, and wishes Patrice could answer back. She misses her dearly. The thought of her short, rough life, haunts her heart. She truly wanted to get her to the Fort, and it kills her to think of how much she would have loved it.

Sophia's a fully grown young lady who's far from petite as she once was. She's blossomed into a tall, shapely woman, who's beauty and personality glow. At five-foot-nine, she's worked harder than anyone at practice through the years. She'd personally train with Leon, who has taught her very well, and it's come to the point that he cannot defeat her anymore. She's become a tremendous shot and carries a gun holstered on her right thigh, just in case. Sophia hates guns. She's always hated to practice with them, but it was mandatory and her pride prevented her from displaying her discomfort with them. The sound of gunfire reminds her of the night her family was brutally butchered. Her weapon of choice is her hands. She'd hear Jacob Jr. instructing her on what to do as she trained. He's taught her how to paralyze any part of one's body using only her fingertips. She is lightning fast and has always pictured Phillips's face every time she's struck something.

Jacob has grown and looks to be around twenty-five years old, although he's only ten. He has a really light skinned complexion with very clear hazel eyes. His brown hair is tied in a long, thick braid that hangs to his buttocks. He's developed into a six-foot-two, very muscular man, even though he's never trained a day in his life. He'd sit and watch as everyone practiced, and would mentally tell Sophia ways to change techniques to make them more effective, without even getting up.

Jacob has never cried, he has never laughed, he's never even smiled. He's expressionless.

Brianna and Jacob were wedded that night, the priest came forward and forced it upon them. It is a great sin to have a child out of wedlock, but in their case it was destined to happen and they happily married one another. Brianna resents the fact that their son is always with Sophia. Ever since they've met, they've been inseparable. Gus has explained through the years that it's how it's meant to be. He's stressed that together they form one, so she's learned to understand. She loves her son very much and cannot believe how much he's grown. She thanks Gus every single day for going to the lengths he went through to get them to the Fort.

Gus was forced to mourn his sister from afar. Word is, Reid got her and her husband murdered by Phillips and Moore. He wanted them to die painfully so told Mr. Goodman to send the most ruthless agents available.

Leon has held monthly sessions for the last ten years and everyone at the Fort attends them. With electricity flowing, they no longer have to rely on torches for light. He gives his people updates on what he's learning from the outside world, but most doubt the Government could get away with such acts. Most are convinced the war really happened but listen intently as Leon speaks. Some are ready to fight, Leon's trained more than two-hundred soldiers who are ready to die for the cause. He's told them the child will handpick his army to march across the country and give it back to its people when he's ready, and the rest of them will have to stay behind to guard the Fort. Jacob has spoken to Leon through Sophia, it's like he knows exactly what he has to do. He's informed him he's ready to march, but will only depart after they broadcast a warning on TV. He doesn't want to surprise them, he wants them to know he's coming. With electricity, most people at the Fort have TV's, so many watch terms to encourage themselves to fight.

With everyone trying to discourage him, Jacob watches them.

He breathes heavily and tightens his fists every time he sits to watch. He has no expression, but for some reason terms are able to get a reaction out of him. Not every term is televised, and with most Illegal Residents refusing to take the risk of not being injected there are fewer. Goodman's agents sometimes go months with no lists.

Phillips and Moore only take on special jobs that require a two man team, but haven't had one in over three years. They're funded by the F.F.A. to do nothing but must always be on call and available.

Phillips has changed, he no longer gets the craving to kill and has claimed he's slain over three-hundred people in his career. Moore visits him every once in a while, they've become very good friends in and out of work. Phillips has clung to him after finding out he's the President's son. He's figured he could use it to his advantage, but has no idea Moore's father wants nothing to do with him.

A term's been announced so they've decided to gather at Phillips's house. This is customary for them. Phillips's wife prepares a fine meal while they chug on poorly brewed beer and watch terms together. It usually ends up in a friendly argument with each claiming some of their past kills were worse.

"Did you bring beer?" Phillips shouts, as Moore's car pulls up.

"Of course!" he shouts back.

"This is going to be a good one," Phillips instigatingly tells him. "Guess who?" Moore doesn't know nor care, he's anxious to get inside to start drinking. "It's Buchanan," Phillips says.

Moore gets excited. It's been a while since he's seen his buddy and knows they'll get entertainment that will last a lifetime. He can't wait for Phillips to see Buchanan's ruthlessness firsthand.

Sophia and Jacob are in Brianna's house. She's cooking supper for them, Gus, Jose, Timmy and Felipe. She's ready to serve, but Jacob stands and walks toward the television. They've never figured out how Jacob knows, all they know is that when he turns the TV on, it's because a term will be televised.

Jose, Timmy and Felipe walk over to Join him. The screen flickers at first, then they see agents getting ready to knock on someone's door. They all gasp when they see the size of Buchanan.

"We could take him," says Jose, with Felipe and Timmy quickly agreeing.

"That is one big dude," Phillips tells Moore.
"I told you!" he replies.

"Come here, Sophia," she hears. Sophia doesn't want to watch but doesn't want to seem weak either. Although inseparable, they're very competitive against each other. He's the only one at the Fort she cannot beat, he toys with her every time she tries to spar. Sophia shows shock when she sees Buchanan's size. "He's huge," she says.

Buchanan plows into the door after several bangs and no answer. They barge into the house which seems to have no-one inside. He sends his agents to search upstairs, and they quickly come down with a sixteen-year-old girl and her parents who were found cowering under beds.

Jacob watches as one of the agents shove the mom, causing her to fall and smash her head into the edge of a table. He starts to breathe a little harder. He knows the love of a mom, he loves his with all of his heart. He often tries to speak through Sophia to express his feelings but Brianna rather he doesn't. She doesn't like to be told by someone else how her son feels. She tells him she knows, but wishes she could hear it out of his own mouth. Jacob feels emotions, but is unable to show expressions. To Sophia, he can sound happy, he can sound sad, he can even laugh, it's just impossible for him to show it. Sophia hates when he watches terms, because he makes her watch and tells her to remember so she'll know why he shows no mercy when they go on their journey.

"What's that smell?" the mom asks as they pick her back up.

"That's how you'll smell in three days," Buchanan answers.

The family's ancestors are from Jamaica but they're American citizens. Both parents were born in this country and don't even have accents. The dad led an early life of drugs and crime, but cleaned himself up and has been sober for over twenty years now. He thinks about going for a gun but the sight of Buchanan makes him hesitate.

An agent scans the girl and discovers she's an Escaped Illegal Resident, causing Buchanan to smile.

"Uh oh!" says Moore. He twists the cap off of another beer bottle and takes a swig.

Felipe watches and seems to be getting angry, just like Jacob.

"Oh, so you weren't injected!" Buchanan tells her.

The girl looks terrified. With no choice, her father dives forward and tries to grab a shotgun that's under a couch, causing an agent to quickly react and pull out a gun. He shoots him in the head before he could reach it. The girl and her mom begin to hysterically scream.

Sophia turns her face when she sees the man's skull splatter onto the floor.

Buchanan tells his man to pass him the gun the girl's father reached for. He grabs it, and points the double barrel toward her mother's face as he stares at her. He smiles at the girl right before pulling the trigger, making her watch as her mom's head appears to explode.

"Did you see that!?" Moore excitedly asks. Phillips refuses to admit it was gruesome and doesn't look impressed, but deep down inside, he loved it.

Jacob's rocking back and forth in his chair while heavily breathing and tightly clenching his fists. The shotgun blast was so graphic, he's the only one that didn't turn his face.

The girl drops to her knees involuntarily, she's so scared her knees give in and can't hold herself up. Buchanan sits on the couch and tells her he'll spare her life, but only if she gives him a kiss. The girl doesn't think she could do it but knows this might be her only chance. She walks toward him and they're now face to face, even though he's seated. He has his eyes closed and his lips puckered, waiting for the kiss. When she gets close enough, he grabs her with a hand on each side of her head. He locks lips with her, but doesn't want to smooch. Instead, he sucks in until her tongue's completely in his mouth. He bites down so hard he feels it crunch off, causing her to fall back screaming in pain as she covers her mouth. He chews on the piece and sticks it out for the camera to see before swallowing it.

"I want him...! He's mine!" Sophia hears Jacob angrily say. They watch as the other agents fill the girl with bullets. Jacob stands and angrily walks out of the house with a straight face.

"Did he just eat her tongue...!?" asks Phillips.
"Told you," says Moore. He guzzles the rest of the beer. "Let's eat!"

Felipe, Jose, Sophia, and Timmy are still watching. They see Buchanan break the girl's fingers, before cutting them at the inter-phalangeal joints with a pocket knife and sticking them into his pocket.
Sophia peeks out of the window and sees Jacob pacing back and forth.
"Did you see that?" she hears as she walks out to join him.
"Yes," she replies. "I've also lived through it but we must be patient."
"I know. But how...?" Jacob knows life is precious. "Let's go," she

hears.

"Go where?"

"Let's go fulfill our destiny," he tells her.

Sophia's mentally ready, but she too wants to inform the American people before setting out. She wants to assure them that it's being done for a good cause. She sees Leon running toward them. He immediately informs them he'll hold a session in an hour and they must attend.

"Tell him I'm not in the mood, please." Jacob is trapped in the body of an adult. He has the utmost respect for Leon, but the term has him in a really bad mood.

Leon notices something isn't right with him, and watches as he paces.

"He's not in the mood, Leon," Sophia tells him.

"Tell him it's imperative for him to attend. He's going to want to hear what I have to say," he says, as if he couldn't hear.

Jacob can only ask for permission to skip a session. He understands the importance of them and doesn't want to disrespect, nor disappoint Leon in any way. Sophia assures him they'll be there.

It's 8 pm, and the people of the Fort have gathered. To Leon it seems the crowd has grown even though no other Illegal Resident has entered. He feels a great sense of peacefulness as he stands looking down at the people. He sees Mitchell, Murphy, and Jacob, with Felipe, Jose and Timmy close by. Dr. Gus and Brianna are behind them. Brianna's busy making silly faces at Mitchell's five-year-old daughter to make her smile. They and a thousand other people look up, waiting to see what he has to say. Leon begins to speak when Jacob and Sophia finally arrive and join him on the makeshift podium.

"As we all know, the Fort was created by a beautiful woman I loved as if she were my own mother. She guided me to fight for what's right, and by God, that's what I'm going to do. Our creator has sent us

this man through her," he says as he points toward Jacob. *"Literally through her. I knew if there was a bloodline capable, it would be her own. Mrs. Cryan is a saint to me, and I've prayed to her every single night since he's arrived for this day to finally come. She told me I was chosen to guide the Fort, but only until he's of age. My message to-night,"* he says and takes a pause. *"My message is that I'm passing my position to its rightful owner."*

"Tell him I will not lead until the mission is over," Sophia hears.

"Excuse me, Leon," she interrupts.

The crowd is silent, no-one has made a sound or has said a word.

"His time has not arrived."

"It has, my child. He was chosen to lead us on this mission. Without him, we cannot do it."

"He will lead us when the time comes but he will not lead the Fort. Not yet, not until we return. He wants to let them know he's coming so we have to wait."

"We can leave any minute now. Meet Sherry Stein," says Leon, as he points toward her. "She will televise our message. She's a reporter."

Jacob gets anxious. He steps forward and quickly spots the news crew. "Tell her to come up here," Sophia hears.

"Can you please step up!" Sophia shouts.

Sherry climbs the steps formed by strategically stacked stones until she reaches the top. Jacob walks to her and grabs her hands. Sherry almost melts at the feeling of being held by such a muscular man as he stares into her eyes.

"Tell her, that although I'm called the savior of this land, I call her my own."

Sophia noticed how Sherry reacted and doesn't want to tell her, but feels obligated.

"I'll speak now. Ask her to record, please," Sophia hears, after giving Sherry the compliment.

Sherry rushes down and tells her man to start rolling.

"My name is Sherry Stein, and I'm here with you live at the Fort," she says as she looks into the camera. *"The residents here are somehow convinced that a savior has arrived who will change the world as we know it. I want you all to see, although this man looks grown, he was only born on December 25th, 2035, which makes him almost eleven. Yes, he's only ten and he has a message for you."*

The camera shifts to Jacob and Sophia. Through her, he begins to speak. He leans his head back with his arms outstretched and his face toward the sky, then begins to move his lips, while Sophia speaks his words.

"My name is Jacob Cryan Jr.," he says, using his great grandparents name, causing Mitchell to smile in pride.

"And I'm Sophia Senao," he says through her. *"We've been sent by our creator to save this country from the evil that's poisoned it. We will march directly to the man who somehow thinks he could take his place, by dictating who could live, and who must die. I got a message for you, Mr. Thump. We're coming for you and your men, and we're coming with as much mercy as you've shown the very people he's created. You're being frowned upon, Mr. Thump, and you should be very concerned. We are coming and there is no stopping us. Our actions will be just, and our intentions are righteous. We're going to make you absent from your body and send your soul to your creator. It's time for you to be judged."*

"I've come with a list embedded in my head, and every single person on the list is here at the Fort tonight," Sophia turns to tell the crowd, as Jacob continues to move his lips. When Jacob has much to say he takes over Sophia's vocals, but it's still her voice. He can take over anyone's vocals and make them say what he wants them to say, he can also take control of one's body, and make them do what he wants

them to do.

The camera focuses back to Sherry. *"That's right, people, you saw it here first. The man can't talk, he's speaking through her,"* she says. She quickly directs her man to focus the camera back on them.

This is live and the entire country is watching. Thump has gathered his men and they're watching it at the N.A.A. also. They shout every once in a while and dare them to come as they laugh and joke about it. "If he's so tough, why does he make his girlfriend speak?" asks Randy, causing Thump to chuckle. Phillips and Moore are too full of food and beer, they're no longer watching.

"I'll announce the names on the list now," Jacob says through Sophia. *"Before I do, I want to say this. It is up to you to accompany me on the mission our creator has assigned us, or you can stay here and guard the Fort. Just remember, you go at your own free will. You are not obligated and it will not be held against you if you decide to stay behind,"* he says.

The crowd grows confused. They can't believe they're actually going.

"Leon. Will you accompany me on the mission?"
"Absolutely!" he quickly answers. Leon's already on the podium and walks closer.
"Felipe." Felipe smiles. He wanted nothing more than for his name to be called. *"I need your strength on the battlefield. Will you join us?"*
"Yes I will," he says with a huge grin. Jose and Timmy look at each other, they hope he calls their names.
"Can you please step up," Sophia tells Felipe.

"Jose. I need your speed. Will you join?"
"Of course I will," he answers.
"Please step up."

Jose's parents are home watching. They had given up on looking for him after seven years and thought the worse. They can't believe their eyes when they see him on TV. His father's ecstatic and doesn't know which emotion fills him more, fear, or pride. They hug each other sobbing out of excitement to see him and are extremely proud. Jose climbs and looks at Felipe, he has the biggest smile he's ever seen from him.

"Timmy." Timmy knew it was coming and runs up before Sophia could say another word. He drops to one knee and looks at Jacob, who's still facing skyward. "It'll be an honor," he says.

His parents gasp. They don't want him to go and were hoping his name wasn't called. They're sure they have no chance of making it through the Communities alive.

"Last but not least. Grandpa. I need your brains and experience out there."

Mitchell's holding his daughter and doesn't know how to refuse. He doesn't want to leave his peaceful life behind until he looks at Murphy and sees the grin on her face. Murphy wants him to do it, because if he does, he might be forgiven for his past sins.

"Go save the country," she whispers to him. He passes her the child, and makes his way up while sticking a finger in his ear.

"There you go," says Sherry, as the camera focuses on her again. *"They will change the country, all seven of them,"* she sarcastically says. The camera focuses back up.

"Look...!" Jacob aggressively says through Sophia as she stares into the lens. *"These people are coming for you, so take a good look at them, because some of these will be the last faces you'll see before finding yourself kneeling in front of the man that will judge you,"* she says. They all stare with straight faces as the crowd roars.

"There it is. This is Sherry Stein reporting live from news forty-four at nine."

The broadcast is viewed all across the country and opens people's eyes. They take it as a way for them to come together, so most take to the streets in peaceful protests. By 10 pm, large crowds have gathered at all major government institutions. The F.F.A. is surrounded by pro-testers, no-one could enter or leave the building. The N.A.A. is worse, overnight the crowd's become hostile and the only thing they could do is guard the entrance. With no local law enforcement, they have no help from the outside. The crowd is biggest outside the main entrance to the Communities. The people patiently wait and hope it's true.

Everyone at the Fort is outside bright and early the next day.

Timmy's parents don't want him to go but he tells them he has to. He begs them to trust him but they persist, until Suzy steps in and tells them to let go. He hugs them, then turns to meet Jose and Felipe by the Fort's entrance. Jacob gives his parents a long hug, and tells Sophia to tell them he loves them both very much. Mitchell and Murphy hold on to each other as their daughter hugs his leg. He assures them he'll be alright as he lets go. The seven of them join at the entrance and walk away side by side. The Fort's residents can only watch as they slowly disappear into the woods.

~Chapter Twenty-Three~

The Mission Begins

They make it halfway across the woods, when they notice the people in the Communities have gathered and look to be waiting on them. There are hundreds of them, which suggest they could have come from as far away as Community-*six*. The women carry all sorts of everyday items to use as weapons, the men carry shotguns and the children have filled their pockets with stones to chuck at them.

"Ask them if they're ready," Sophia hears. She looks at them but doesn't have to, she can tell they are, it's written all over their faces.

Timmy's very anxious, they occasionally have to tell him to slow down. Reid has stayed in Community-*three* surrounded by twelve of his best men, and has stopped anyone from his Community or further from going. Many have no fight in them and have stayed indoors, but the ones that want to aren't permitted. He tells them it isn't worth the trek because the people there will kill them immediately, and promises them he'll hang their bodies for entertainment.

Sofia walks side by side with Jacob, and her head held high. She can only picture one person on her mind and hopes he's still alive.

Leon carries his signature knife that has saw-like teeth. He's also very skilled with his hands so rarely depends on it. He carries a bag on his back that contains the laptop, the journey will be very long and he wants to keep in contact with Moshi. Timmy carries a long, wooden stick strapped to his back with pointy tips, he's become a master with it and uses it wisely. Jose fights while clutching a knife in each hand. The knives were specially made by the Fort's blacksmith, the blades are razor sharp and the handles wrap around his fingers with spikes sticking out of them. Felipe depends on his strength, he's so strong, he's broken bones without using his legs for leverage. Mitchell carries his gun and can be as ruthless as anyone, he goes with the intention of getting to Goodman. He knows Phillips is dead, but has never told Sophia because she'd use getting him as motivation when training and he didn't want to discourage her. They're prepared for a long trek, there was another Community built in the past decade which makes the walk to the outside world even longer.

Buchanan walks into Thump's office at the N.A.A., making Randy rush out. "Why does he always run when he sees me?" he asks Thump. "Is he scared of me? Did you see the news last night? We have a lot of people to kill, important ones!" he tells him with a smirk.

"Please," says Thump. "They won't even make it through Community-*one*. Those kids are crazy if they think they can get to me, and even if they do, they'll die when they get here so either way, they're dead."

"Do you want me to start heading their way? I could make it there in no time and take them out, problem solved."

"No, no," says Thump. I want you close by, just in case. Besides, there are already eight agents headed toward them."

"OK. I'll be back in a couple of hours. I got something I need to do."

"I'm going to need you here so hurry back," Thump responds.

Jacob and Sophia are two steps ahead of everyone, and hear the sounds of people buzzing as they get closer. The people are impatient and with each step they take, they get louder. The folks at the Fort could hear the people at the Community getting riled up, so many kneel and pray for them to make it through.

The Communities women shout and wish death upon them, as the men, some on horses and others on nearby roofs, ready their guns. Jacob approaches the gate, closes his eyes and faces the sky. They stay silent when Sofia begins to speak on his behalf.

"I need for every woman, child, and for anyone who isn't ready to die today, to go home and stay inside, we will not invade your residence. We are here for the ones responsible for slaughtering our people. The end of this madness has arrived, we will spare no-one who decides to stay and fight," Jacob says through her.

The men look at each other and chuckle. There are at least a hundred of them with guns drawn and waiting for them to step foot on the Community.

"We will stay and fight!" one woman shouts.

Jacob walks across the fence. As soon as he does, a man on a nearby roof who has a finger on the trigger tries to squeeze while aiming at his head through a scope, but it seems to be stuck. There are as many as eight snipers laying on rooftops, and they all seem to have the same problem, none can manage to pull the trigger.

The men on horses dismount. They look back and wonder why they haven't taken a shot. The order was for them to shoot as soon as they crossed over. All the people could do is watch as the seven of them step foot on their grounds. The men desperately try to shoot, but can't. Jacob again closes his eyes and begins to speak through Sophia.

"Tell your men those things will not help them," he says, referring

to the guns. The people are confused and wondering why no-one has taken a shot yet. The last man on a horse jumps off clutching a shotgun, and shoves through the people blocking his way. Jacob is still in a trance but can see him approaching through Sophia's eyes. The man makes it to as close as a foot away from him, when they both drop to their knees, with Jacob taking control of his body. With his face skyward, he tells the man through Sophia that it's time for him to meet his maker. Jacob's controlling them all, no-one can move an inch. He shifts his arms as if he's the one holding the shotgun, with the man moving the same exact way. The crowd gasp when they see the man put the butt of the shotgun on the ground, place a finger on the trigger, and rest his chin on the barrel. Leon glances through the crowd and sees Sherry with her cameraman. Everyone wonders what the man is doing and shift their attention toward Jacob.

"I gave you all a chance to leave, just as you gave us when this all started. Difference is, unlike our people, you actually had a way out." He flicks his finger, causing the man to pull the trigger. The crowd cringes as they watch the top of the man's skull blow upward, causing his blood to rain down on the one's close enough to be showered with it. Jacob stands and the people begin to frantically run around when he releases the trance on anyone who isn't armed.

"You will have to fight by hand," he tells them through Sophia. Jacob concentrates on the men on roofs. He puts them in a trance and makes them blindly shoot at their own people until they no longer have ammunition. Everyone scatters while screaming, as the snipers take down as many as possible. Felipe, Jose, Leon, and Timmy look at each other in disbelief. Mitchell's glad he made it to the Fort, he'd hate to be on the opposite side of this attack. It's as if Jacob's turned them against each other. Mitchell was always weary of things Moshi told Leon and his son, seeing this only assures him anything's possible. They begin walking, and the few people who didn't flee cowardly hide behind cars. As they continue, they look up and see the eight snipers standing

on the ledges of different buildings with the guns by their sides. With his mind, Jacob makes them dive head first in sync onto the concrete grounds below. The men that had gotten off of the horses and weren't victims of the snipers cannot move, he's released the trance on everyone but them. His intention is to fight people that fight back. Not one single victim of the sniper attack was a woman or child.

They step over bodies and approach the men that still carry guns. The men try hard to lift their weapons but it seems impossible to them.

"Tell them to have fun," Sophia hears.

"You can have your fun," she tells Felipe, Jose, Timmy, Mitchell, and Leon.

With that being said, they start to attack. Mitchell pulls out his gun and starts shooting as many of them in their heads as possible with tremendous accuracy, while Felipe, Jose, Leon, and Timmy team up and use their skills to take down the one's closest. The men are able to fight back but can't use their weapons so they're no match and are easily defeated. With tactical fighting skills, they take them all down without Jacob's help.

Sherry panics when she sees Jacob and Sophia walking in her direction. Her cameraman quickly puts the lens down and expects to be slain. "Spare us, please!" she pleads. "General Reid demanded me to catch the footage of you all being killed. I'm so sorry!" she desperately says.

"Tell her we don't harm people that don't fight us," Sophia hears.

She explains to Sherry it's alright to record, but warns it can only be aired after the mission has concluded. Sherry's man lifts the camera and catches Jose cut the last man's throat with a swing of his knife. Everyone has dispersed, a few have jumped into cars to hurry and tell Reid what's happened.

They unite again and begin to walk. They could see people cowardly peeking out of windows as they pass through.

A little kid comes running out of a house and toward them. "Can I join you?" he asks as he stops in front of Jacob.

Jacob closes his eyes. *"When your time comes, you are welcomed to join us, as long as you fight for a just cause."* The kid is confused as to why Sophia answered while Jacob moved his lips.

His mom is in front of the house he ran out of, begging for him to come back. She fears for his life.

"We will not hurt your child," Sophia says, as Jacob's mouth moves. Sophia looks at the kid. "Take your mom to the Fort," she tells him as he runs off. Jacob snaps out of the trance and watches as the boy's mom grabs him by the arm and shoves him into the house. Community-*one* is awkwardly quiet at this point, they had expected a much bigger fight. They're not aware that Reid has prohibited anyone from his Community or beyond from going there. As they walk through Community-*two,* they're met with no resistance. It's empty, the residents had all went to Community-*one* and have been killed or forced to flee when the attack took place.

Jose, Felipe, and Timmy are gloating to one another about what they've just done, each one claims their kills were better than the other.

Sherry got in her van and drove ahead. She enters Community-*three,* and sees a much larger crowd but doesn't spot Reid. She stops the vehicle after passing the majority of the people and positions her man to film. She patiently waits with the crowd, then sees Reid come out of a house surrounded by a dozen men.

"Kill them all!" he shouts to them, as he pumps a fist in the air. Reid didn't watch the broadcast the night before, so doesn't know who's coming. He was on the road when it was televised and is going by what he was told. He's aware there are only seven of them, and was guaranteed they'd be taken down easily. Being knowledgeable about how many people they've taken out in Community-*one* has him skeptical. His intention is to stay indoors and let them pass, then attack from behind.

The people outside the gates at the end of Community-*six* stare inside and wonder why it's so empty. They've gathered there all night and are getting impatient, but don't want to enter for fear of it being a setup.

As they get to the end of Community-*two,* they begin to hear the large crowd that have gathered. Timmy's heart rapidly beats from the excitement of facing another fight. He walks with a voracious appetite and has to be warned again.

"Tell him to slow down," Sophia hears. They have no clue why he rushes. Sophia again admonishes him about walking so fast.

Timmy has a really bad temper and is a fierce fighter. For as long as they've known him, he's always been very impatient. As they enter the Community, they're approached by a man in blue jeans. He has a gun holstered on his side and allows them to walk passed him. He doesn't say a word at first, but begins to follow them.

"Are you ready to die?" he asks as he keeps pace. He won't attack because Reid's instructed to let them enter. Sophia looks back at the man, but hears Jacob tell her not to worry about him. He instructs her to continue looking forward and focus ahead. Jose, Felipe, and Timmy are ready to take him down but are warned not to.

The crowd is standing behind a line of men with guns pointed at the seven of them in the middle of Community-*three.* Jacob feels Reid and his men join the man walking behind them but ignores it. He doesn't seem concerned about them at all. They reach the men pointing guns and are surrounded, so Jacob closes his eyes.

"I'm going to give each and every one of you the chance to drop your arms and leave," he says through Sophia. *"You must face the fact that the world you're used to no longer exist."*

The men try to pull their triggers but can't.

"Shoot them, damn it!" Reid shouts. The men attempt it but cannot move their fingers.

Leon, Jose, Felipe, Mitchell, and Timmy immediately turn around at the sound of Reid's voice, but he's fixated on Jacob. He steadily stares from behind at his long, woolen, dark brown braid. Timmy steps forward and gets Reid's attention, stunning him when he finally looks.

"Timmy...!?" he confusingly asks.

"Hi, Grandpa...!" Jose and Felipe look at each other, they now know why Timmy's always said he was training to kick his grandpa's butt. Sherry hurries her man closer.

"What are you doing with these hooligans? You will only die with them, and after I kill you I'm going to kill your mother for taking my wife away. I now know where she is and for that I thank you," he says, referring to his daughter.

Jacob and Sophia turn around. The men are tired of trying to pull their triggers, so try to rush forward as they turn their attention toward Reid, but are unable to move. The crowd of ordinary people can only move their arms at this point, they cannot move their legs to get a step closer. The one's closest to the men try pushing them forward to fight as Timmy steps toward Reid.

"These are not hooligans. These are the people that will stop you. You've gotten away with this for far too long. I'm going to give you a chance, grandpa. I'm going to let you pick your toughest man, and if he beats me, I'll try and convince him to let you live," he says, while pointing toward Jacob and knowing damn well Reid will die no matter what happens.

Reid's sure this is a wager he'll win. Not that he's worried, he knows Jacob and his friends have no chance of getting out of there a-live. He hand picks his biggest man Hugo, who happens to be the bully he paid to beat Timmy up. Timmy doesn't look like he'll be able to take him on. Hugo's bigger than Jacob, and with him being only five-foot-seven, Jacob asks through Sophia if he wants him to take care of it. Timmy remembers that day in his childhood, and wants payback, so tells Jacob to release Hugo's trance.

"I remember you," says Hugo, as he rushes toward Timmy and swings a punch with all of his might. Timmy steps aside and calmly avoids the hit, then lands a right hook to Hugo's ribs that makes him back up. Hugo again rushes, but this time tries to grab him. Timmy avoids the grip by spinning, and with one movement, grabs the stick off his back and lands in his fighting stance. He rapidly swings the stick, connecting it to Hugo's face, causing teeth and saliva to spray out of his mouth as his head viciously turns to the side. Reid's men try hard to intervene, but can't move. Timmy runs toward Hugo and jumps as high as he can with his knees bent. They collide with his chest, causing Hugo to fall back as he lands on top of him holding the stick. Hugo screams as Timmy stabs the tip of it into his mouth with so much force, it impales his throat and exits the back of his neck before making contact with the ground. Reid's shocked, but still can't move. He didn't think Timmy could beat him, much less so easily. Timmy pulls the stick out of Hugo's mouth by stepping on his face and pulling it upward. Hugo squirms on the floor, holding his neck and choking on blood.

"He gets you guys," Timmy tells Felipe, Leon, and Jose, referring to Reid, then all of a sudden, they see Larry and Willie quickly approaching. They're not in the trance Jacob has everyone else in because they just came out of a house. With no warning, Leon runs toward them and swings at Willie. Willie ducks, he's also very skilled at fighting but hasn't practiced in years and it's evident.

Felipe rushes toward Larry when he sees him try to interfere and grabs him in a chokehold from behind. He grabs his head and effortlessly twists, causing his neck to snap. Sherry motions for her cameraman to focus on Hugo who's on the ground and has stopped moving. Reid watches Willie and Leon go to blows. Leon overcomes, and gets on top of Willie. He repeatedly stabs him in his chest until he's too tired to continue, and unable to see, due to the blood that splatters onto his face and into his eyes.

Reid's furious, he's forced to stand there and watch as Leon kills his son. Reid is old in age but looks better than ever. He hasn't slowed down a bit and claims he's healthier now than he was ten years ago. "You will not get away with this," he tells Timmy. He drops his gun and gets into a fighting stance as soon as Jacob releases him from the trance. Felipe grabs him in a chokehold and Jose swings his knives at his abdomen once with each hand. Felipe releases his grip as Reid grabs his stomach. He struggles to hold his innards in and falls on his knees with his guts hanging out.

"I want his head!" Timmy states. Leon gets behind him and cuts his throat, then viciously saws on his neck. Reid raises his bloodsoaked hands to try and grab the knife only to get three fingers cut off. The residents watch in horror as his intestines hit the asphalt as soon as he raises his arms. Leon decapitates Reid and lifts his head by its hair. Jacob accelerates the hearts of all armed enemies. The people watch as everyone carrying a gun drops to the ground, holding their chest. He stops their hearts by accelerating them to rates they can't sustain, causing instant death. Jacob once again closes his eyes to take over Sophia. She turns to the residents, who are no longer in a trance but looking down at the men.

"Let this be a lesson to you all. This has ended. Our people will no longer die!" he says.

Timmy grabs Reid's head and pokes the stick through the opening of the neck and raises it. The townspeople stare up at it, and move aside to form an aisle for them to pass through. As they walk by, the residents stare at them. They feel powerless and have lost all hope. The leaders of the other Communities are among the people and want to leave. They don't think it's worth staying and want to avoid having to face them again. Sherry has her man focus the camera on them, with

Timmy holding the stick that carries Reid's head high in the air.

They continue through the next Communities and the few residents that stood behind stare as they walk by. They look in horror when they see Reid's head bobbing with each step Timmy takes. They make it to the middle of Community-*six,* which is the furthest but closest to the outside world, and notice the hundreds of people who have gathered outside of the entrance. The people see the seven walking toward them side by side and erupt into loud cheers.

"Jacob! Jacob! Jacob!" they hear them chant, followed by louder cheers. Leon, Felipe, Jose, and Timmy have delightful smiles on their faces. They are very proud of themselves and each other, and are determined to finish the mission. It means so much to Leon, he's dedicated his life to this but gives the credit to Dorothy, and wishes she was around to see.

Jacob senses there's no-one that'll try to harm them there, so walks toward the gate that moves from the pressure of the people on the other side. He stops fifty feet away from it and stands still, with the cheers getting louder. The crowd's been growing since the minute the message was broadcasted the night before and it took them all day to walk the communities, but the people have waited the entire time. Some come from as far as sixty miles away, knowing they'd most likely have to pass them on their journey but their curiosity wouldn't let them stay home to wait and get a glimpse of them. With all races and religions cheering them on, the seven of them stand side by side. Jacob swings his hand and grabs Sophia's, who seems surprised and looks at him with a huge grin on her face. Sophia treats Jacob as if he were her little brother, and he loves her like a big sister. Together they all begin to walk, until they reach the gate. Timmy got rid of Reid's head when he heard cheers, he would not have rolled it away if it were another fight. The crowd roars as Jacob closes his eyes.

"I'm glad to see so many of you come out to support us," Sophia

says, as Jacob moves his lips. The crowd goes silent. *"We will continue our journey and show the world that there's a higher being that is disappointed in what is happening to his children. We will together continue in our quest to put a stop to the despicable acts being committed. Unfortunately, I was sent to send them to be judged, and judged they will be. Don't be discouraged or allow your heart to feel fear, because your creator wins battle after battle and will always be with you. He looks down and is proud of his creation, all he wants is for us to love each other. He will refresh your life and soul with his blessings, so always keep him in your hearts."*

The crowd goes crazy. The weight on the gate seems to be lifted as they all take a step back. The people move onto both sides of the street, leaving enough space for them to walk shoulder to shoulder while praising them, with many having looks of amazement on their faces as they cheer. A lady runs out of the crowd but comes to a sudden halt when Jacob penetrates her brain with his mind. He senses she has no ill intentions so quickly releases her.

"Mom!" Jose shockingly shouts. "That's my mom!" he happily tells the rest of them. He runs toward her and into her arms. Jose looks toward the crowd and sees his father walking toward them as he tries to hold back tears. Mitchell stares at them and can only wish he had such a moment with his real parents. Jacob and Sophia still hold hands, and although he can't smile, he's filled with happiness. Felipe bows his head with a tear rolling down his cheek. The moment reminds him of how much he wishes his mom was still around.

"I must continue, Mom," he tells her. Leon stares with a huge grin on his face. Although he's ruthless, he has a loving heart. Mrs. Cryan made sure she taught him to be empathetic when he showed violent aggression as a child. Jose's mom struggles to let go, and wishes she could take him home. He regretfully pulls his hand away as her husband convinces her to let go. They watch as their son walks off with

311

the six of them and doesn't even look back, as the crowd closes behind them. Sophia's ears ring from the loud sound of the crowds roar culminating, as they walk off with her, Mitchell, and Leon, to Jacob's right, and Felipe, Timmy, and Jose to his left.

Twenty miles into their eighty-mile journey they're approached by eight of Thump's agents who come to screeching stops in three different cars.

The people on the streets witness them come out of the vehicles and line up across from them, so cower behind anything big enough to shield them. Jacob and Sophia look at one another. The agents hold guns at their sides.

"It's time for you all to give up!" one shouts.

Jacob closes his eyes and begins to speak through Sophia. *"You're the one's that need to give up,"* he says. Leon's ready to attack, the image of his little brother being smashed through a table by an agent plays over and over in his mind. He breathes heavily and can no longer take it, so lunges forward gripping his knife as Felipe, Timmy, and Jose follow. The agents lift their guns and are surprised they're able to pull the trigger. They've been in contact with the department and were informed they wouldn't be able to squeeze. As they pull, the guns just click as if they're empty. Mitchell recognizes one of the agents as the one Phillips punched in the face ten years prior and pulls his gun. With flawless aim, he shoots him right between the eyes, causing chunks of brain to land on the hood of one of the cars, as Leon sticks his knife through another one's throat. One of the agents run toward Sophia, but she steps aside to avoid the tackle. As he passes her, she slightly grabs the back of his neck with her fingers. Jacob watches as the man's body goes stiff and immediately drops to the ground, then hears him scream that he can't move. Jacob has yet to show any fighting skills. He's only shown mind control, but has warned them that Buchanan is his.

Leon elbows an agent in his face, causing him to hit the ground. He pins him down and savagely barrels his fists down onto his face repeatedly, until he could no longer continue. He pauses for a moment to catch his breath, then starts again, until his knuckles are covered in wounds.

Felipe, Jose, and Timmy attack the remaining agents and gruesomely kill them as the crowd watch in terror. Jacob looks down at the man Sophia paralyzed, as Mitchell walks closer. He closes his eyes and begins to speak.

"Go and be judged before being sent to a fiery pit," he says.

Mitchell points his gun downward and puts a bullet into the side of the agent's head with no hesitation.

"Violence will be met with violence," Jacob tells the crowd through Sophia. *"We will rid the world of them all!"* he says to loud cheers. They continue to walk and people line the streets just to get a glimpse. Kids laugh and dance around them, but they utter not a single word. Through the walk, crowds of supporters follow, until they are too tired to continue, with new people joining along the way. People offer them food and water but they decline, the only thing on their minds is to get to the F.F.A..

Sophia grows more and more anxious with each step, she desperately wants to make it there already. People stand on roofs and stick their heads out of windows just to take a look at them, and wildly cheer as they pass by. Parishioners of all religions kneel on streets and pray, as they march shoulder to shoulder with Jacob holding Sophia's hand.

The only other interruption they encounter is three-quarters into their journey, when they're forced to pass through an upscale neighborhood. It is very late and the crowd following stops. They refuse to enter for fear of getting killed, so stay at the entrance and watch as the seven of them disappear at a distance. Jacob's the first to spot two men who walk side by side in the middle of the road toward them. They notice that little by little, the houses start to light up and can see people peeking through curtains. As the two groups approach each other, the men pull out pistols.

"What are you doing here!?" one demandingly asks.

"You're not welcome, so turn around and get out!" says the other.

"We're getting through!" Sophia angrily says without the help of Jacob. She wants to make it to the F.F.A. and feels they're very close.

One of the men points his gun at her. "Over our dead bodies," he says.

"Make him shoot his partner," she hears.

She turns to look at him, and sees he points the gun at her but struggles to pull the trigger. "I can't," she thinks back.

"Yes you can. Just think it. Act as if you're him."

Sophia gets a determined look and feverishly tries. Her face scrunches up but she just can't do it. Jacob has the men frozen and unable to move, then takes over when he sees she isn't focused enough. He lifts his arm and turns to the side, until the man has the gun aimed at his partner's face. The man looks to be desperately trying to drop the weapon but is unable to. Jacob moves his finger, causing the man to shoot the other under his right eye. Jacob then motions his hand under his own chin and flicks his finger again, forcing the man to drop from a self-inflicted gunshot wound. It surprised Sophia for Jacob to tell her to do it knowing she isn't capable.

"You can do it," he tells her. "I will teach you."

They lock hands again to continue their journey. Many more people have gathered on the other side of the neighborhood, hoping to just see them, and all go wild when they finally do.

Twenty-four hours after leaving the Communities they finally make it to the F.F.A..

~Chapter Twenty-Four~

Jacob Meets Buchanan

They approach the agency, but come to a sudden stop, due to the massive amount of people in front of the building who have been protesting since the message aired. They carry signs condemning the government and jeer non-stop, they haven't realized they've arrived. The crowd blocks the entrance to the building, letting no-one in or out. They start to hear shouts from the people that's followed them there, and slowly start looking back, causing the jeers to turn to cheers when they finally see them. Sophia's very anxious being in front of the building the men responsible for killing her family work in, her heart rapidly beats. The crowd splits to allow them a path to walk to the entrance as they cheer and applaud uncontrollably. They no longer walk shoulder to shoulder, the crowd is too huge to provide such a wide space. They approach and see the glass doors are bolted shut, and observe at least fifty agents inside who carry sub-machine guns and look to be expecting the crowd to rush in so they can spray them with bullets. Jacob turns around with his back toward the entrance to look at the people, and closes his eyes. Felipe, Timmy, and Jose focus their attention on the entrance and notice agents with their hands cupped against the glass, looking out.

"The madness will soon end in the name of our Father," Sophia says, as he moves his lips. *"For I know the plan he has for you. He plans to fill your lives with joy and enlightenment, and plans to restore your faith in him by showing you he does indeed exist. Tonight, there is only one religion, and we must put our differences aside to get through this victoriously. With him guiding us, we can do the impossible. Our creator gave his one and only son for us. Whoever believes shall be filled with his love and blessed with his holiness for eternal life."*

The crowd grows so intense Leon covers his ears. Jacob opens his eyes and turns around. He scans the men inside, then hears the shouts of the crowd behind him when the agents turn the guns on themselves. They shoot at each other as if they're enemies for two minutes straight, until each lay dead. Many in the crowd stampede away when they hear the shots, but the majority watch in amazement. Felipe walks toward a door and punches the glass, making it shatter to pieces, and Timmy uses his stick to collapse the remaining fragments that cling on to the frame. One by one, they step inside, with Mitchell leading the way.

Timmy stabs an agent who squirms on the floor through his heart with the tip of his stick as he begs to be spared. The crowd outside silently stare into the building in awe, they don't make a sound.

"They've penetrated the entrance!" an agent shouts as he barges into Goodman's office. Goodman doesn't budge, he figures the building is way too big to be found and believes he can talk sense into them anyway. The sounds of the agents on his floor can be heard in his office, so he demands the one who notified him to stay put. They panic when they hear multiple gunshots by many different weapons go off in the hallways, as Jacob makes them attack each other. Goodman's sure his men handled them, but wonders how they made it to him so quickly.

Jacob kicks his office's door open and Sophia barges in. Leon sits on the carpeted floor to check the laptop. Jose, Timmy, and Felipe take cover and guard the ends of the hallway. Mitchell stays outside of the office with his back against the wall. Jacob follows Sofia inside and immediately makes the armed agent incapable of moving.

"Phillips and Moore! Where are they?" Sophia demands.

Mr. Goodman stares at Jacob. "I can't disclose their whereabouts, young lady," he tells her.

"Make him tell me," Jacob hears Sophia say. He concentrates on Goodman and makes him grab a pen to write the addresses.

Goodman involuntarily passes Sophia the paper with the information on it. "Let me ask you something," he says, then lights a cigarette. "Let's say you do find them. What are you supposed to do?"

"The same exact thing they did to my family," she quickly responds.

"Your family?"

"The Senao's," Sophia says. "That's right, your men didn't kill me and that was a big mistake on their part."

Goodman doesn't believe her, especially since she only asked for two of them. "They are really vicious men. You'd be a fool to face them. Besides, I think it takes four agents," he sarcastically says.

Jacob's just listening and lets Sophia deal with it while maintaining the trance on the agent behind Goodman.

Mitchell hopes Sophia brings him up, he wants to hear what Mr. Goodman has to say before he enters.

"You killed Agent Brown, which takes him out of the picture," she answers.

Goodman's taken aback. *"How could she possibly know,"* he wonders. "What are you talking about?"

"I can prove it. All we have to do is ask Agent Mitchell. You remember him, don't you?"

"Mitchell's dead, young lady. I had the pleasure of putting his code in myself. He turned out just like his father, and their bleeding hearts got them both killed."

Mitchell walks in and shocks Goodman. He was certain he was dead and thinks he's looking at a ghost. He shakes his head to help convince himself he's actually looking at him.

Jacob closes his eyes and Sophia begins to speak. *"You, Mr. Goodman, are on your way to the heavens to be judged before being denied entry into our Lord's kingdom..."*

"Wait wait wait!" he interrupts. "This wasn't me. I was only doing my job. I didn't want this, I've been against it all along. These men are animals!" He grabs the P1-Simulator and enters a four digit code. "They shall all die!" he shouts before pressing the button.

They watch as the agent behind him drops the gun. His body contorts from the spasms caused by the poison and falls to the floor shaking, then goes motionless.

Jacob looks at Goodman. He doesn't appreciate being interrupted or having his trance broken but figures he'll leave him to Mitchell.

"You'll never change," Mitchell tells Goodman. Jacob and Sophia leave the office.

"Where's Phillips? Why isn't he here? I hoped he was dead!"

Goodman lights another cigarette.

"Phillips doesn't live here anymore. He moved to the N.A.A. soldiers residence camp with his family to be closer to his friend Moore, and is as alive as you are."

Mitchell laughs. "Friend? Phillips couldn't find a friend if he went out and bought one."

"Well, when you're around the President's son, things could turn out really well for you."

"The President's son?"

"Yes. Jack Moore's real name is Adam Thump, also known as the body piece serial killer."

Mitchell cannot believe Moore's Thump's son, and can't wait to tell Murphy. "I guess it's true that the apple doesn't fall far from the tree after all," he says.

"In your case neither," Goodman sarcastically responds. He's hoping Mitchell shows leniency for the information he's given him. "How did you do it, Bradley?" he asks. "How did you get rid of the poison? It was Murphy, wasn't it? She must have given you the antidote."

"That doesn't matter. If I were you I'd be praying to God for forgiveness instead of concerning myself with how someone got rid of a poison."

"Please, Mitchell, you don't have to kill me. An old man like me will die any day now. The least you could do is allow me to go home to my family one last time," he says, as he puts out the cigarette.

"Did you think of other people's families for the last twenty-three years? You reap what you sow, Mr. Goodman. It's time for you to be judged." He raises the gun to Goodman's head and sees a single tear roll down his cheek.

"Can I at least smoke one more cigarette?"

Mitchell grants his wish, but as soon as the flame hits the paper he pulls the trigger, putting a bullet through his head and watching his blood splatter onto framed family portraits that lean against books on a cluttered shelf behind him. He didn't even give him the pleasure of inhaling the smoke into his lungs for the last time.

Thump's at his office, he's been staring at the TV for the last few hours. The footage that was caught of the journey through the Communities has been televising all day, and his men claim they're capable of taking them down. They wage bets against each other, with each being concerned but none willing to admit it. Knowing they're unable to use firearms have them jittery.

Buchanan roams around the building frightening everyone he comes in contact with. He has a huge grin on his face and paces back and forth in anxiousness. He's the only one who really wants to face them, and cannot wait until they arrive.

Sherry's contacted by Thump, who scolds her for televising it and demands her to report to the N.A.A. immediately. He wants her to pay for it and intends to feed her to Buchanan.

Mitchell walks out of Goodman's office and hears Leon informing them that Moshi was able to open a line and it is now possible to televise footage to the rest of the world, but they need a camera. He's also instructed him on what to do when they arrive at the N.A.A. to deactivate the filtration systems that clog their skies.

"Where's that newswoman when you need her," Sophia says.

They prepare to make the final stretch of their journey. On the way out, they're forced to step over countless bodies, every single employee of the agency was killed by a fellow agent. They're met with a huge roar as they exit, and are provided an opening to walk through.

It takes them another twenty-four hours before finally reaching the N.A.A..

Leon tells Jose, Felipe, and Timmy what to do to deactivate the systems when they arrive. The switch to power them off is on the third floor, but unbeknownst to them, Buchanan's room was intentionally built around it.

"There's a hole in the floor that has a switch inside," Leon tells them. "It releases a magnetic lock on a door securing another switch that powers the systems off. You guys go ahead, we'll wait an hour before moving forward."

With the crowd behind them, it's difficult to go unnoticed.

Mitchell escorts them toward a nearby alley as Jacob puts the crowd of followers in a trance and makes them roam away. Sophia questions Jacob as to why they don't go in and get it over with, before hitting the switch. Jacob could continue, and easily force Thump himself to personally turn the systems off, but wants everyone to have a part in completing the mission they were all destined to achieve. He tells her they'll take a break, so everyone could clear their minds before continuing.

Timmy, Felipe, and Jose enter the building through a grate on its side that gives them access to the agency's parking garage. They duck behind pillars that hold the structure up when they hear someone coming. When all is clear, they enter the stairway and make their way up. They reach the third level, and end up in a long, dark hallway that has a door shining light through the bottom. They slowly walk toward it, with Jose gripping his knives and Timmy holding his stick. Felipe leads them through, slowly opens the door, and the first thing he notices is Buchanan's octagon. The lights flicker and make buzzing sounds as they enter. The hole they're looking for is the drain in the octagon, but they don't know it yet. They search around before opening the door leading into the octagon, and are hit with a horrible odor that makes them pinch their noses as they step inside. There's a decomposing arm on a table that's gray in color and seem to have bite sized pieces missing.

"There it is," says Jose. Felipe immediately grabs a metal instrument and kneels down to pry the drain cover open. The switch is around a foot deep and he sticks his hand in. It gets completely covered in partially dried up blood that seems to have the drain clogged. They hear the lock disengage as he hits the switch, and are forced to gag at the smell when he pulls his hand back out. They're ready to leave, but feel very heavy steps walking down the hallway. They duck low enough to avoid the glass and hope the person doesn't enter the octagon. They think about fleeing, but can't see who it is. They can only see their reflection when they look out, so remain low enough to avoid being seen through the glass from the outside.

Buchanan enters and stares at the octagon. "Who's in here?" he shouts. "Come out, I can smell you!" Buchanan hasn't seen them but somehow knows there's someone inside. He slowly walks toward it and reaches for the knob.

"You two are going to have to fight him while I run and hit the switch," Timmy whispers.

At this point, they have no choice, they're going to have to fight him. As soon as he steps foot in the octagon, Timmy runs toward a window and extends his stick to crash through the glass, while Felipe and Jose pop up to get his attention.

"You boys smell good," Buchanan tells them with a huge grin, then rushes toward Felipe.

Jose throws himself on the floor after taking a few steps and rolls, to try and stop Buchanan's forward progress by tripping him with his body. Buchanan jumps over him and continues at Felipe, who rushes forward and squats down, only to rapidly stand back up with one movement and all of his might. He goes airborne and connects the top of his head to the bottom of Buchanan's chin, making him take two steps back. Jose jumps out of the window Timmy broke when he sees him signal that he hit the switch. Buchanan regroups and again rushes toward Felipe, but he avoids his grasp before jumping out of the window to flee. Felipe wishes he could stay and fight but knows Jacob wants him. They rush out of the room and down the hallway. The three exit the building and join the rest of them in the alley across the street. They find it weird that the hum they've heard their entire lives is gone, it's eerily quiet without the sounds the filtration systems make.

"We will see God's blue sky tomorrow," Leon says, while focusing upward.

Mitchell spots Sherry's van park across the street and watches as she steps out of it. He walks across and approaches her. She's scared to death, and tells him she's there to see Thump but doesn't know how she'll get in with the amount of people at the entrance. She confirms her cameraman's with her, and decides to enter with them when he guarantees her safety if she records. She's seen first hand what they're capable of and doesn't doubt she'd be safe, so agrees.

They start making their way toward the entrance. The people start noticing them and slowly begin to holler and shout, until everyone wildly cheers when they finally see them. The crowd opens up to let them through. Sherry gets a strong sense of importance walking with them. The agents have barricaded themselves in the lobby of the building, just as they did at the F.F.A..

"They're here!" Buchanan happily says as he barges into Thump's office.

"OK! So what are you waiting for!? Go get them!" Thump angrily demands.

Sherry's recording this live. Thump's tuned in from his office so will witness it. Jacob instructs Felipe to break through the door, and puts the agents in a trance to make them stay still.

"You, you, you, you, and you," Jacob says through Sophia.

She points toward five agents and snaps them out of the trance. They immediately raise their guns before realizing they're useless.

"They're yours, Leon," Jacob says through her, as he stands with his eyes closed.

Leon doesn't wait and immediately attacks with his blade, slaying all five very easily. He cuts each of their throats in less than a minute with slick movements and fine swinging.

Sophia points toward ten more agents and Jacob releases them from the trance. They also try to rely on weapons before being taken down by Felipe, Jose, and Timmy, who quickly slay them with a stick, knives, and fists. The other agents stare while stuck in the trance, each secretly hope she doesn't point toward them. All they could hear besides the grunts of their men as they're beaten, is the crowd outside who cheer every move, and seem to enjoy seeing blood splatter with the way they roar after every swing of a blade. The agents relax when they realize who's barreling down the stairs. Buchanan reaches the ground level and walks toward Jacob with a mean mug, while swinging his arms wildly. Jacob senses him, but hasn't seen him yet. With his back turned, he lets him get close enough before he stops him with his mind. Buchanan displays a strain on his face as he tries to desperately move. Jacob turns around to face him, closes his eyes, and Sophia begins to speak.

"I know you! I've seen you on TV, and I must say, I'm very disappointed. You are the complete opposite of what our Lord intended when he created us. I'm going to release you from this trance, and you will fight me. I am going to forcefully send you off to be judged."

Buchanan wants nothing more than to be released so he can kill them all. He finds it awkward how Sophia speaks while Jacob moves his lips. Being over a foot taller than Jacob convinces him he has the advantage, while taking into consideration that he's never been beaten in a fight.

Sherry's man is recording this live, the entire country is watching. Phillips and Moore gawk at the TV over at Phillips's house. They were called in by Goodman, but on the way there they found out the F.F.A. was overtaken so decided to turn back and have remained together since.

Sophia moves aside as Jacob releases the trance he has Buchanan in. As soon as it's released, Buchanan swings his right arm with all of his might and his hand balled up. Jacob lifts his arm and calmly catches Buchanan's fist, surprising him. He swings his other arm to try and connect, but Jacob calmly catches that one also. They stand face to face, with Jacob having to look up to stare into his eyes. He clutches both his fists so tight, Buchanan can't pull away. While holding on to them, he jumps and plants both feet on Buchanan's chest. He uses it to push away and does a back somersault onto the floor. Jacob's never trained a day in his life, he's learned by observing. Everyone's impressed with his skills, with the crowd outside confirming they are with each move he makes. Buchanan takes a few steps back and appears to be losing his balance. Jacob runs toward him and jumps, connecting three quick individual kicks to his chest, making him fall back onto his butt. Looking a bit confused and embarrassed, he quickly stands and wildly runs toward Jacob, who crouches down and lands a right punch to the underneath of his stomach, making his gut jiggle and forcing him down to one knee.

Thump and Randy watch in dread.

Phillips and Moore cannot believe he's being beaten. They'd discussed going to the N.A.A., but stood behind at the behest of Moore. He refuses to go although they're only a five-minute car ride away. His father is in the N.A.A. and will most likely be killed, and with Reid being dead, it's highly likely he'll be chosen to succeed Thump once he discloses their relationship.

Buchanan is down on one knee. Jacob punches him in the face with so much force he shatters his jaw. He isn't only beating him, he's manhandling him. He's shattered his jaw and he can't keep the bottom section closed. His mandible hangs open when he stands, making everyone close enough to notice it gasp. There is no quit in Buchanan, he rushes at him again. Jacob makes him miss and shoves him into the glass, causing him to crash through it and land on the sidewalk outside.

The crowd cheers as Buchanan falls face down. Jacob tells Jose through Sophia to pass him his knives and he quickly obliges. He steps outside and stands behind Buchanan as he rises to his feet. As soon as he turns, Jacob squats down and quickly starts cutting him. He cuts at Buchanan's lower body, swinging the blades back and forth through all major arteries while slowly standing, and blood flings everywhere. He quickly swipes the blade with tremendous speed before jumping up to give the final blow with a swipe through his jugular. Blood sprays onto

Jacob as he spins and lands on his feet in front of him. The crowd watch in amazement as Buchanan stays on his feet. He wobbles around in shock, then takes two steps forward and falls face down. The crowd watch and cheer. The ones close enough could see the puddle of blood expand around him.

"We have to get out of here!" Randy stresses to Thump.

"And go where!?" he snottily snaps. "The men out there will not let them make it in here," he says. He's not aware Jacob has stopped their hearts. He hasn't realized they're all dead.

"Are you kidding me!? Did you not see that!? We don't stand a chance, I'm out of here!" He rushes out of the office, leaving Thump alone.

Jacob tells Sophia to have Sherry guide them to Thump's office and she gladly directs them. Thump's inside staring at the door. He sits behind his finely crafted desk with two American flags behind him. He doesn't like the silence, but then hears rapid footsteps and is sure it's his agents. They barge into his office and his heart drops. He finds himself speechless, and thinks of his inevitable death.

"Are you ready for your speech?" Jacob asks him through Sophia.

"What?" he asks, with the expression of a deer caught in the headlights.

~Chapter Twenty-Five~

Sophia's Revenge

Leon tells Sherry to put the camera on channel sixty-six, so the entire world can see the footage live. Thump immediately stands when he hears that, but Jacob forces him to sit back down with his mind. Jacob stands by the cameraman, closes his eyes and faces the ceiling. His lips begin to move as Thump begins to speak.

"To the people of the United States of America, and the people of all nations. Good and evil have faced off the last few days, but evil is no match to the glorious graces that bless the good. Our never-ending search for freedom will prove to be worth the wait, that I promise you. I have a confession to make. Forty-seven years ago, a bomb was detonated on our soil which was bigger than any man has ever seen. I regret to inform you that I was the one who gave the order."

People across the country and around the world gasps in disbelief. The international committee suspected something was amiss, because when it occurred, several nations were immediately accused.

The United States, under international law, chose to close its borders and didn't allow anyone in to investigate and prove their innocence.

"I didn't think it was logical to change leadership every four to eight years, so took inflicting such tragedy to the greatest nation on God's green earth upon myself. I was selfish and intended to remain in power for the long haul. This nation, was once dedicated to guaranteeing our freedom, and assuring us that everyone is created equal. The cries for help, and the hymns of protest by our people weren't heard. We turned a deaf ear when they sounded, and for that, I deeply and sincerely apologize. The future of this nation looks promising, and by God, it will become what it once was, the greatest. No matter how long it takes, we will overcome this. Our unbounded determination will not allow us to fail, we will be persistent and move in the right direction," he says, with a straight face while looking into the lens, as Jacob moves his lips.

Leaders of other nations call each other requesting a world meeting. Everyone's watching. It's being displayed worldwide on giant monitors on city streets, and heard on small radios by the less fortunate as others huddle around to listen to him.

"I lied to our people. I convinced them the world around us was in ruins. The fog that surrounds our country was intended to make the rest of the world think it was so they wouldn't look in, but it was actually intended for our people to believe the lies were true. The system has been shut off by a special group of people who brought this all to light. They are trying to pull us into the future and we will not resist, we will follow them. This nation, under God, will experience a resurrection and bloom into a superpower once again. As a matter of love

for life, I want everyone to stand by one another. I want our citizens to cherish each other without regards to one's difference or nationality. Hold hands and consider yourselves equal."

People all over the United States and the entire world take this moment and grabs the nearest person's hand. Strangers on city streets, children in schools, people at home, everyone takes this chance to connect with the person beside them.

"I've slaughtered many people that for many generations have called this country home, and I will have to answer to God for that. There's no cause to deny what I've done, and can only hope I'm shown mercy when I cross into the next life. I know this country can, and will again become the greatest country on earth, but we need assistance. If you can find it in your heart to send humanitarian aid it would be greatly appreciated, if not, a simple prayer will do. I now step down as leader of this wonderful nation and God willing it gets back to its full potential. God bless you all, and as always, God Bless America."

Jacob releases the trance.

Thump quickly opens a drawer in his desk, pulls out a gun and shoots himself in the head before the camera was turned off. He didn't give them the pleasure of killing him themselves, although Jacob was going to spare him and let the justice system throw the book at him instead. The entire world watch in horror as the President of this country commits suicide on a live feed. Sherry's man rushes to turn it off, but it's too late, everyone saw.

They exit the N.A.A. and Sherry convinces them to do a live interview.

"My name is Sherry Stein, and I'm here tonight with the group responsible for stopping Mr. Thump and his men from turning this

country into a dictatorship. They hail from a village far away called the Fort, which they consider home."

The camera focuses on them, but it's as if nothing happened. They are full of pride after honorably defending the country as they set out to, but don't show it. They feel the effects of their long journey. It's as if the energy that was in them to endure the mission has left their bodies now that it's over. Sophia and Jacob are fine, they do not feel a bit fatigued.

The crowd has tripled and is extremely loud. Jacob closes his eyes and Sophia begins to speak.

"I want to thank my people," he says through her. *"Without them, I would not have made it as far as I have. Jose, Felipe, Timmy. I could not have done it without you, you should all be very proud. This most certainly gives you direct passage into our Lord's heaven."*

The crowd is silent. Sherry televises it worldwide.

"Leon. What can I say? This was all possible because of you. Without you, it would not have happened. I thank you now and always will from the bottom of my heart for all you've done."

Leon bows his head after nodding.

"Grandpa. You're the greatest, and I thank the lord every day that I come from your bloodline. Thank you for being there when called upon."

Mitchell also nods after getting recognition.

Jacob can't give Sophia his thanks through her in front of everyone so breaks the trance and puts Mitchell into one.

"Sophia," he says through him. *"You are part of me. When the sky opens up and our Lord looks down, he will see you in the same light he sees me. You were created to help me lead this conquest and did a tremendous job. You were chosen as I was, and together we made it possible. Believe me when I say, I could not have done it without you."*

"God works for the good of those who love him," Jacob says through Mitchell as he turns to the crowd that begins to hectically cheer.

Sophia's full of pride, but wears a face as straight as Jacob's.
He grabs her hand and announces it's time to go back home.
"I have two more stops to make," she tells him.
Mitchell doesn't think Goodman was being truthful when he told her where to find Phillips, so decides not to go. He was present when the suicidal agent shot at him so is sure he's dead. Sherry volunteers to take them back to the Fort in her van. Although Leon and Felipe really want to get Phillips, they're physically unable to continue. Jacob and Sophia watch as Mitchell, Felipe, Jose, Timmy, and Leon pile into the van looking exhausted.

They arrive at the first address which happens to be Moore's residence, and walk through the waist high fence surrounding the house that's freshly painted white. The house is completely dark, with only one window on the second floor toward the back illuminating. They head toward the rear and easily enter the house through the back door. Sophia walks behind Jacob. They slowly climb the stairs and are hit with an awful odor when they reach the top. They see the door with light shining onto the floor from the crack at the bottom of it down the hallway. The closer they get to it, the more potent the smell becomes.

Jacob twists the knob and pushes the door open. Sophia jumps back when she takes a look inside and covers her face. There's a chair in the middle of the room facing the door. On it, sits a body that's sloppily sewn together at each joint. Jacob walks closer. He sees the limbs have different shades, suggesting they're from different victims. Some parts have rotted more than others and have holes of decomposing skin that reveal the bone. The head is poorly sewn on, and looks to be in an awkward position. Jacob takes a finger and rubs it against one of the body parts.

"He uses some kind of fluid to delay decomposition," Sophia hears.

Unable to find him, they set off to Phillips's house. Sophia hopes they weren't killed in an attack, although Jacob's assured her neither Moore, nor Phillips were victims. They arrive and notice the house shining brightly. They smash through the back door, causing them to quickly grab their guns. None want part of Jacob and neither recognize Sophia. The sound of the door being kicked in causes Phillips's wife and youngest daughter to wake up and bolt down the stairs, so Jacob immediately puts them in a trance.

"Wow. I never thought I'd see you two again," Sophia says.

Both men try to pull the triggers. Moore stares at Sophia. She looks familiar to him but he can't recall where he's seen her. Jacob has the four of them in a trance. He makes them drop their weapons and lower their arms, and forces the women to sit on the couch across the one they're on.

"Who are you!?" Phillips shouts. "What do you want with me? Leave my family out of it!"

Sophia walks closer. "I'm Sophia Senao! You remember me now? You didn't leave my family out of it, did you!?"

Phillips and Moore are shocked. Moore thinks back to that day and remembers thinking he might've left her alive. Phillips knows exactly who she is but acts as if he has no idea. He looks at her eyes and is convinced it's her when he sees the dotty scars below her eyebrows.

"Remember back then? You only let me live because you wanted to do it again! Guess what? I get the pleasure this time." She walks to the middle of the room and looks at his wife and daughter. "Do you know what these animals did to my family?"

All any of them could do is move their eyes and talk. Phillips is in his wife's sight and she steadily stares at him.

"He killed my entire family. My mom. My dad." She turns to face him. "My brothers and sister, aunt and nephew. You know I could do the same to you now, right?"

"Leave my family out of this," he tells her. "They have nothing to do with it." Moore sits quietly, he's sure this will not end well.

"Why should I spare your family? You didn't spare mine!" she emotionally says. "I wish I was an animal like you! I wish I had the heart to kill them!"

She again shifts her attention to Phillips's daughter. "What's your name?" she asks her.

"Cathy," the girl softly responds.

"How old are you, Cathy?"

"I'm fifteen."

"Do you know what your father does for a living?" Sophia gets no response. "Do you know his job is to go around killing babies and their entire families? Did he tell you he sewed my eyelids open because I wouldn't look as he murdered mine?"

Phillips's daughter looks at him and can't believe he'd be capable.

"This animal was with him!" she says, as she points a thumb back at Moore. She looks back at him. "You're a sick one! I will deal with you also!"

"Your father will be judged for his sins tonight," she tells his daughter, making the girl sadly sniffle. Phillips's wife gets teary eyed. They've been getting along more than ever, and she loves how much quality time he's been spending with them as a family. She'd always worry this day might come. He proudly told her what he'd done to the Senao's one night after having a bit too much to drink.

Phillips's and Moore's eyes follow Sophia as she navigates around the room. Jacob steadily holds them in the trance and closely monitors. Sophia walks toward them, crouches down, and grabs the guns they were forced to drop. She aims one at each of their heads as she stands between them. All they could do is roll their eyes to the side to focus on her. "It will not be this easy," she says. She lowers the guns, turns around and puts them on a glass coffee table in the middle of the room.

Phillips doesn't think Sophia has what it takes to kill him, so starts provoking her. "Tell me," he says. "What took you so long? I want you to always remember, you're only alive because I've allowed you to live. I should have killed you just like I did your family." His wife tries to give him eye contact but he doesn't look at her.

Sophia walks toward a table with a sewing machine on it. She grabs the biggest needle she could find that pokes out of a cloth ball and is already threaded. They can't see what she's doing but Phillips has an idea.

"I remember your brothers and sister scream and run around when I killed Oscar. That was good aim, wasn't it?"

His wife tightly closes her eyes and a tear rolls down the side of her face. She hopes he says this because he's intoxicated and not because he literally means it.

Sophia approaches them with the needle pinched between two fingers. "Ten years ago, you sewed my eyes open because I refused to watch. Today, I will sew your mouth closed because you refuse to shut the hell up." She sits on him as he did to her, and begins poking the needle through his face. She has to push with a lot of pressure for it to penetrate his skin. He screeches with each poke, but his pride will not let him scream.

"That man is full of evil," Sophia hears.

"He won't shut up," she thinks back.

"I speak of the one next to him. I've never felt such negative energy from anyone. He's done some horrible things and must be judged immediately." Sophia stops sewing and grabs the gun on her thigh. She rapidly points it to the side of Moore's head and pulls the trigger unexpectedly. Phillips struggles to move his eyes far enough to see Moore but can't manage. His wife and daughter closed theirs while he was being sewn, but the sound of the blast caused them to flinch and open them. They see Moore has fallen sideways on the couch with his head leaking a massive amount of blood, so quickly close their eyes again. Sophia grabs the needle and proceeds to sew until his mouth is completely shut. Phillips's wife opens her eyes when she hears him mumble, then cringes, and closes them again when she looks at his stitched face.

Sophia grabs scissors off the same table she got the needle and cuts off his right earlobe. Phillips's pale skin turns red. He wants to loudly scream but doesn't want to give her the pleasure. Piece by tiny piece, she continues to cut at both ears until there's nothing left but holes. His daughter's kept her eyes closed through the entire ordeal. All Sophia can hear is his wife pleading for her to show mercy, but the assault takes hours as she patiently cuts.

"We have to go home now," she hears. She's lost in time and doesn't realize it's daylight. She apologizes to his wife and daughter, and just when they thought it was over, she grabs both guns off the table and walks toward him. She puts the barrels on his shoulders and begins to speak as he rolls his eyes up to stare at her.

"You're on your way to a place you'll call home for the rest of eternity. I hope that's ample time for you to think about the people you've harmed. May your skin melt off continuously," she tells him.

With the guns resting on his shoulders, she lifts and digs the barrels downward into them. She pulls both triggers simultaneously, causing the bullets to ricochet inside his body with no way out. His wife and daughter sob as he closes his eyes and perishes.

Sophia stands over him. She leans her head back and deeply inhales, just as he did when he killed Angie. She's dreamt of sucking in his soul for many years and finally gets the pleasure.

"I will leave them in the trance for an hour," Sophia hears.

"You can release them. They're harmless," she thinks.

He snaps them out of it as she walks toward him. He watches them rush to Phillips, and hears them wail as they hold his lifeless body.

Sophia immediately looks skyward when they step out. She sees how blue the sky is, and how bright the sun shines. "Oh my God," she says in wonderment.

"That's God's blue heaven," she hears. "Let's go home."

It takes two and a half days to reach the Fort, which is one-hundred-sixty miles away. They tirelessly walk around the clock without a second's rest. They receive the same treatment on the way back, as crowds gather along the way at every turn just to get a glimpse of them. With everyone cheering and applauding, they hold hands and look straight ahead as they continue moving forward. They walk through the Communities that are desolate, seems the residents have packed up and left after the attack.

They arrive at the Fort and are greeted by thousands of people on both sides of the fence. Mitchell, Leon, Felipe, Jose, and Timmy welcome their arrival with huge grins on their faces. Brianna runs toward Jacob and holds him tight as he enters. Everyone from the Fort, including many that have flocked there for the last few days loudly cheer as he grabs Sophia's hand. He closes his eyes to speak through her, and everyone goes silent.

"Our creator sent me to go on a mission with a specific group of people he's chosen," he says.

The seven of them come together and huddle as everyone listens.

"With his guidance, we accomplished it. He can again be proud of his creation and smile down upon us. I've called this place home for the last ten years, and will continue to do so until the day he calls me back. This will be the home and sanctuary for anyone who enters, it'll be a place of peace as it was intended to be."

The crowd roars as Sherry records it for the world to see.

It's been five years and the United States of America have come a long way in rebuilding the country. Tons of aid poured in from all nations across the globe. Workers from around the planet flocked in, just for a chance to be part of knocking the walls down. Businesses flourished, people are back to work. The people elected President Gerald Tooney into office, he's already in his second term. He's vigorously worked with world leaders to restore civilization to this country. The people have united, with the most fortunate still keeping themselves barricaded in certain parts of the country, they want nothing to do with the hoi-polloi.

The Communities built to keep people out of the Fort are used for shelter now, the fancy houses and buildings are occupied by your average American Citizen.

The Fort has become a tourist destination for people all over the world. The current residents of the former Communities are required to provide the one's waiting to get in with anything they may need for free. There are no longer markets, nothing is sold. There's been a line for the last five years of people waiting to get in, just so they could say they've walked the grounds. It's considered the most sacred place on earth, with the waiting period at the end of the line being at least two weeks.

Jacob, Sophia, Leon, Mitchell, Jose, Timmy, and Felipe are worshiped worldwide. They're often invited overseas to pray for the people and get the same frenzied reaction from crowds everywhere. Always being somewhere different, people that enter the Fort when they are present consider themselves very blessed.

Doctor Robert Gustoff won the Nobel Peace Prize in 2049, after singlehandedly coming up with the solution to reverse the effects of the injection. The most prominent scientists from around the world desperately tried for three years, but none were able to hit the milestone. Many say it can't be a coincidence that a resident of the Fort was able to accomplish it. Illegal Residents flocked to locations that would cure them for free and the population is slowly beginning to grow.

Dollars are being used again and have already become the most valuable currency in the world. Church goers have quadrupled, most masses have to be performed outdoors with the number of people that attend. Many more believe in a higher being now. The military' has strengthened the once most powerful armed forces in the world, with young men and women joining every single day.

It's March 22nd, 2051. Leon walks toward the fence to inform the people that no-one else will be allowed to enter for the night. He sees the next one's on line is a small Asian family. The mom begs to be allowed in after waiting fifteen days. He plops the fence open and lets them enter, the joy on the kids faces was worth granting them access.

"This is a beautiful place," says the dad as his kids run ahead, with their mom close behind. He looks around in amazement. "Can my family and I stay?" he asks with a smirk.

Leon explains it's full to its capacity, but might be able to get them a place in one of the former Communities.

The man shows dissatisfaction.

Leon apologizes and introduces himself. "My name is Leon," he tells him, and extends his hand.

The man grabs it and holds on.

"I know," he tells him. "Mine is Moshi. Moshi Kazui. Nice to finally meet you, my friend."

Leon stands in shock...